Before Pornography

Studies in the History of Sexuality
Guido Ruggiero, *General Editor*

IMMODEST ACTS
The Life of a Lesbian Nun in Renaissance Italy
Judith Brown

THE EVOLUTION OF WOMEN'S ASYLUMS SINCE 1500
From Refuges for Ex-Prostitutes to Shelters for Battered Women
Sherrill Cohen

AUTHORITY AND SEXUALITY IN EARLY MODERN
BURGUNDY (1500–1730)
James R. Farr

SEXUALITY IN THE CONFESSIONAL
A Sacrament Profaned
Stephen Haliczer

COMMON WOMEN
Prostitution and Sexuality in Medieval England
Ruth Mazo Karras

HOMOSEXUALITY IN MODERN FRANCE
edited by Jeffrey Merrick and Bryant T. Ragan, Jr.

THE IMAGE OF MAN
The Creation of Modern Masculinity
George L. Mosse

BEFORE PORNOGRAPHY
Erotic Writing in Early Modern England
Ian Frederick Moulton

MASCULINITY AND MALE CODES OF HONOR IN MODERN FRANCE
Robert A. Nye

FORBIDDEN FRIENDSHIPS
Homosexuality and Male Culture in Renaissance Florence
Michael Rocke

THE BOUNDARIES OF EROS
Sex Crime and Sexuality in Renaissance Venice
Guido Ruggiero

THE MYSTERIOUS DEATH OF MARY ROGERS
Sex and Culture in Nineteenth-Century New York
Amy Gilman Srebnick

Further volumes are in preparation

Before Pornography

Erotic Writing in
Early Modern England

Ian Frederick Moulton

OXFORD

UNIVERSITY PRESS

2000

OXFORD

UNIVERSITY PRESS

Oxford   New York

Auckland   Bangkok   Buenos Aires   Cape Town   Chennai
Dar es Salaam   Delhi   Hong Kong   Istanbul   Karachi   Kolkata
Kuala Lumpur   Madrid   Melbourne   Mexico City   Mumbai   Nairobi
São Paulo   Shanghai   Taipei   Tokyo   Toronto

Copyright © 2000 by Ian Frederick Moulton

Published by Oxford University Press, Inc.
198 Madison Avenue, New York, New York 10016

Oxford is a registered trademark of Oxford University Press

Library of Congress Cataloging-in-Publication Data
Moulton, Ian Frederick, 1964–
Before pornography : erotic writing in early modern England / Ian Frederick Moulton.
p. cm.—(Studies in the history of sexuality)
Includes bibliographical references (p.) and index.
ISBN 0-19-513709-4; 0-19-517982-X (pbk.)
1. English literature—Early modern, 1500–1700—History and criticism.
2. Sex in literature.   3. Erotic literature, English—History and criticism
4. Sex customs—England—History—16th century.   5. Sex customs—England—
History—17th century.   6. Sex customs in literature.   I. Title.   II. Series.

PR428.S48 M68 2001
820.9'3538'09031—dc21   99-044061

1   3   5   7   9   8   6   4   2

Printed in the United States of America
on acid-free paper

To Alice and Edward Moulton

Acknowledgments

This book was written over a period of almost ten years, in a bewildering variety of places, from condos in Phoenix to flats in London; from a studio in Venice Beach to an apartment in Park Slope; from a hotel room in downtown Chicago to a Folger guest room on Capitol Hill; from a student apartment at Columbia overlooking Harlem to a room overlooking Sherlock Court at St. Catharine's College, Cambridge. It was begun on a computer that didn't even have a hard drive, and is being finished on an IMac G3.

In all this time, and all these places, I have received an inordinate amount of encouragement and incurred a predictable number of debts—academic, intellectual, and otherwise. Sitting down to enumerate them is a surprisingly pleasant experience; it's nice to have a chance to thank and remember the people who have helped to shape this project in so many ways—and of course anyone who doesn't want to read this bit can just skip it, unlike those interminable speeches at the Academy Awards.

The project began as a dissertation at Columbia University, directed by Jean E. Howard and David Kastan. I could not have wished for better advisors. Any scrap of professionalism I have acquired I owe to Jean in particular. Scruffy first drafts of many sections of the book were beaten into shape at meetings of the Columbia dissertation seminar. I owe a debt to all the members of that seminar, faculty and students alike, but especially to Mario DiGangi, Heidi Brayman-Hackel, Jim Berg, Jill Smith, and Douglas Brooks.

Many people, including James Mirollo, Margaret Ferguson, Peter Stallybrass, and Anne Lake Prescott have read the manuscript in whole or in part at various stages over the years, and offered countless suggestions on how it could be improved. As goes without saying in such situations, their advice was all wonderful—and if I didn't always follow it, it's my own fault. The book has also profited immeasurably from the from the frank and detailed comments by four anonymous readers at Oxford University Press, and from the assistance of my Oxford editors, Guido Ruggiero, Thomas LeBien, and Susan Ferber.

I have presented portions of the manuscript at several academic meetings, including the Modern Language Association and the Shakespeare Association of America. Among the many people with whom I've shared panels and exchanged ideas, I'd especially like to thank Mary Gallucci and Margaret Gallucci, Lynda Boose, and Bruce Smith.

Portions of the book have been previously published. An earlier version of chapter 4's discussion of Nashe's "Choice of Valentines" appeared in *English Literary Renaissance* 27(1) (Winter 1997); and chapter 2's analysis of Marlowe's Ovid appeared in *Marlowe, History, and Sexuality: New Critical Essays on Christopher Marlowe*, edited by Paul White (New York: AMS Press, 1998). The passage on Antonio Vignali's *La Cazzaria* in chapter 3 provides the basis for a chapter in Peter Herman's collection *Opening the Borders: Inclusivity and Early Modern Studies, Essays in Honor of James V. Mirollo*. (Newark: University of Delaware Press, 1999). And chapter 3's analysis of *The Crafty Whore* appears in more detail in a special issue of *Critical Survey* edited by Sasha Roberts (vol. 12[2] [Spring 2000]).

Arizona State University was generous enough to give me two consecutive summer research grants, which were crucial to the project's success. At an early stage of the project I also received a summer grant from the Mellon Foundation, as well as a dissertation support grant from the Social Sciences and Humanities Research Council of Canada.

I would also like to thank the staffs of the following libraries, who gave invaluable information and assistance: the Bodleian Library, Oxford; the British Library, especially the old North Library and the Department of Western Manuscripts; the Inner Temple Library, London, which kindly gave permission to examine the Petyt manuscript of Nashe's "Choice of Valentines"; the National Art Library at the Victoria and Albert Museum; the Rosenbach Foundation, Philadelphia; the Library of Corpus Christi College, Oxford, especially Christine Butler; the New York Public Library; the Newberry Library, Chicago; the Folger Shakespeare Library; the Huntington Library, San Marino, California; Butler Library at Columbia University; and last but by no means least, the superlative staff of Fletcher Library, Arizona State University (ASU) West, especially Dennis Isbell.

I thank Vic Cowie and George Toles for inspiring me to be a scholar and for teaching me how to be a teacher. I thank Elizabeth Harvey for encouraging me to apply to the best schools in the world. I thank Joseph Dane for the use of his apartment in Venice Beach—and for always knowing where to find the best Chinese food. I thank Larry and Susan Green for their hospitality. I thank Peter Blayney—as everyone does—for taking the time to talk to me. I thank both William Sherman and Marty Craig for their companionship and conversation when far from home. I thank Susan O'Malley for her bluff integrity (and for employing me to do some editing when I was a starving student living in a basement in Brooklyn).

At Arizona State University, it has been my good fortune to be part of two stimulating and energetic academic communities: first the College of Arts and Sciences at ASU West, where I have taught since 1995, and second the Arizona Center for Medieval and Renaissance Studies. At ASU West I have been particularly fortunate to work with both Dottie Broaddus and Eric Wertheimer, good friends and even better colleagues, who have made the task of building an English program in the deserts of West Phoenix a pleasure rather than an ordeal. Besides Dottie and Eric, I would especially like to thank Cat Nilan for her friendship and enthusiasm, for her wry, critical intelligence, for sharing innumerable cups of coffee—and most of all, for the conversations we had walking across the desert to get to the coffee shop. At ASU West I must also thank Amy Davis, who spent months transcribing my scribbled notes and learned more than she ever wanted to about Elizabethan spelling.

The best friends are the ones you can talk to seriously for days on end without ever getting bored. I thank Christine Hutchins for all those breakfast meetings at Henny's Diner in Brooklyn, in the course of which this project slowly began to take shape. I thank Pam Brown for her passionate intellect and her sharp wit. I thank Goran Stanivukovic for the walks we've shared from Washington, D.C., to Oak Creek Canyon, Arizona. I thank Sasha Roberts, dearest and most generous of friends, for her unfailing good humor and clear, straightforward intelligence. I thank all four for their honesty and friendship over a period of many years.

Most of all, I thank my parents, Ed and Alice Moulton, for their love and support; my sister Celia for being her wonderful self; and Wendy Williams for being a constant source of joy and inspiration and for being the only person I've ever met who is more fascinated with Aretino than I am.

Contents

A Note on Manuscript Transcriptions

In my quotations from previously unpublished early modern manuscript sources, I have generally not modernized spelling, but in order to make the texts easier on nonspecialist eyes, I have modernized common early modern abbreviations and peculiarities, such as the use of thorn ("y") for "th," "i" for "j," the tilde ("~") for "m" or "n," and other superscript characters. Passages in square brackets indicate my own additions of elided or abbreviated material.

Before Pornography

Fountain of Youth, *block 3, Hans Sebald Beham, woodcut (1 of 4 blocks) c. 1536
(Pauli 1120; Rosenwald Collection 1943.3.9328-9329886). National Gallery of Art,
Washington, D.C.*

Introduction

The Prehistory of Pornography

*A*ny attempt at constructing a history of sexuality must include a history of erotic representation—that is, a history of the representation of sexual acts. The history of erotic representation is largely unwritten, partly because such a project tends to be conceived as a history of pornography—and pornography is a discourse that seems to have obvious, self-evident meanings and to promulgate predictable misogynist and patriarchal ideologies of power and gender. Yet subsuming the history of erotic representation to the history of pornography is limiting because not all explicit representation of sexual activity can be meaningfully defined as pornographic. In particular, "pornography" is too historically and generically specific a term to be much use in a discussion of the early modern period, for the erotic writing of the sixteenth and early seventeenth centuries—whatever its explicitness—is different in both form and content from the genres of pornography as they developed in later periods. Rather than say, as some recent studies have done,[1] that pornography is worthy of study and so "Renaissance pornography" is worthy of study too, I wish to study early modern erotic writing in its specificity, without assimilating it to later forms, without automatically assuming that since erotic writing and the representation of sexual acts occupies a certain place in the cultures of the late twentieth century it must have occupied an analogous place in the culture of sixteenth-century Europe. In what follows I shall concentrate first on what distinguishes early modern erotic writing from modern forms of pornography, and then on the socially engaged nature of much erotic writing in the early modern period, in particular its role in discourses of national and gender identity.

"Pornography" is a word notoriously difficult to define, and it is in part its amorphous nature that makes it problematic as an analytical term. In its widest application, pornography may be said to refer to cultural productions that depict human sexual activity in a relatively explicit manner, and that are seen by some observers as being offensive or morally reprehensible. As this formulation suggests, the fundamental problem with definitions of pornography is that the term is applied simultaneously to the content of a given product, to the manner in which that content is represented, and to the attitude of the observer toward the product. Add to this the fact that pornography is a term that carries a strong moral valence and that discussion about it may involve some degree of hypocrisy (one is not supposed to "like" pornography—though many people obviously do), and the issue becomes more complicated still.

There is no question that pornography exists. That is, there are some representations of sexually explicit material that are offensive to some viewers. But in this form the concept is almost entirely subjective. And—in part—because modern and postmodern cultures tend to see sexuality not only as private but also as fundamental to personal identity, subjective opinions about pornography are often strongly held and not open to refutation by reasoned argument. If I find a book or a picture or a video offensive or arousing, my reasons for feeling this way may be so personal that I may feel strongly that no one has the right to contradict me on the subject. It is arousing or offensive to me, and that is enough for me. In this context "pornography" must be seen as a relative term referring to a subjective category. It is relative because there is often little consensus on whether or not a particular cultural product is pornographic. It is subjective because the ultimate arbiter is the personal response of the individual. Thus, while "pornography" is no doubt a useful term to describe personal opinion and experience, it is not much more rigorous as an analytical category than the term "fun." Everybody knows when they're having fun, but who would try to establish its universal laws?

"Pornography" is a more complex term than "fun" because besides referring to intimate and subjective impressions, it is also used to refer to a literary genre and related modes of visual representation. While these genres can, to a certain extent, be described and defined, there is no necessary connection between the genre of pornography and the subjective experience of the pornographic. That is, materials such as certain late eighteenth-century French novels or engravings, for example, though referred to as pornography by scholars, do not necessarily arouse in all viewers the emotions—either of sexual arousal or disgust—associated with "pornography" as a term used to describe subjective experience. Material seen as scandalously titillating in one cultural context often seems innocuous in another.

One might think that the sexual explicitness of a given work would provide a simple way of measuring pornographic content. But although it would, I suppose, be possible to create an absolute scale of explicitness, such an index would always remain an abstraction, for the relative explicitness of an image or text is to a large degree culturally determined. In 1945, the famous scene in Howard Hawks's film *To Have and Have Not* in which the young Lauren Bacall instructs Humphrey Bogart on how to whistle was considered extremely sexually explicit—especially within the context of the Hays code restrictions on film content. The same scene raises few eyebrows today. Conversely, a film like Stanley Kubrick's *Spartacus*, whose gay subtext seems painfully obvious to many 1990s viewers, did not seem quite so explicit to most audiences when the film was released in 1960. Are sepia-toned postcards of couples having sex from the turn of the century as explicit as the hardcore Internet images of the same acts at the turn of the millennium? Or have age and changing technology made them seem quaint and distant, oral sex and all?

Until recently, the various genres of pornography have been excluded from mainstream academic analysis, partly because of the explicit nature of their erotic subject matter, but also because they have been understood to be self-explanatory. Since everyone feels they understand pornography subjectively (they know it when they see it), the *genres* of pornography have been understood to be transparent in their significance and self-evident in their meaning. But however ambiguously defined, these genres have specific histories that can be studied.[2]

As Lynn Hunt and others have suggested, pornography is not an essential category but rather a historical one—it did not always exist, but at a certain cultural moment came to be invented. While it is possible (but by no means certain) that the subjective feelings one associates with the pornographic have always existed, the genre has not, and the term itself is a relatively new one. In the nineteenth century, the Greek "pornographoi" ("porno" and "graphoi": "whore-painters") was coined to describe ancient erotic frescos.[3] As the genesis and etymology of the word suggests, "pornography" has always referred primarily to visual rather than literary artifacts, and at present it is most commonly used to describe developments in the relatively novel media of video recording and the Internet.[4] Whatever modern definition of pornography one chooses (and in both critical and legal discourse the term has proved notoriously difficult to define) it carries with it a wide range of value judgments and assumptions about the modern sex industry—assumptions that are often irrelevant or misleading when applied to a preindustrial society that had comparatively primitive technologies of reproduction.

Calling pornography a genre is not to say it is simple or that its meanings are self-evident—quite the opposite. As various studies have shown,[5] pornography is not the monolithic, transhistorical mode of discourse it is often assumed to be; it has a history and, I believe, a prehistory. The forms of erotic representation that we think of as pornographic did not simply appear, fully formed, in eighteenth-century Europe. They developed from earlier, pre-Enlightenment, preindustrial forms of erotic representation, whose modes of production and whose social function have been little examined.

Problems of definition do not stop with the term "pornography"; defining what is erotic is a proverbially difficult task. In recent decades, respectable or socially acceptable erotic writing has often been called erotica in order to distinguish it from pornography, which is presumed to be sleazy or socially unacceptable.[6] But this distinction is often contentious, arbitrary, and highly subjective. Though many people feel they know the difference for themselves, there is no real consensus on where these boundaries lie. One person's "erotica" is another person's filth, while to a third reader it barely seems erotic at all.

If the term "pornography" is meaningless in the context of early modern Europe, the more recent "erotica" is even more so. To study early modern erotic writing is not to study early modern "erotica." For the purposes of this study, the term "erotic writing" refers to any text, regardless of genre or literary quality, that deals in a fundamental way with human physical sexual activity. Sex and love often go together—and often they don't; thus not all "love" poetry is necessarily erotic, and not all "erotic" writing deals with love. Some of the works I address are explicit in their language, some are elliptical or metaphoric, but all are concerned with physical sexual actions—from vaginal intercourse between men and women to genital play and anal eroticism, sex between members of the same sex, and masturbation. Although these texts are about sex, they are not necessarily "sexy." While some were clearly intended to be arousing when they were written, others probably were not, and in any case, what is and isn't arousing is—as I've already suggested—a highly subjective and personal distinction. As Roland Barthes reminds us in *The Pleasure of the Text* (New York, 1975), almost any writing *can* be erotic— to some reader, in some circumstance. By focusing on so-called erotic writing I by no means wish to deny the erotic potential that circulates throughout writing in general. Nor am I suggesting that a theoretical division of texts into "erotic" and "nonerotic" existed in any systematic, conscious way in the period itself.

Although "erotic writing" (like "pornography") was not a term used in early modern England, it has the advantage of being a descriptive, not a generic, term, and it is relatively free of moral judgment. I use the term "erotic writing" primarily as an analytical device to bring together widely divergent texts; I am not particularly interested in establishing a canon of erotic texts or of debating whether or not individual texts should or should not be included. I am interested in gathering together certain texts that share certain concerns, not in policing generic boundaries. Most of the texts I discuss fall comfortably into the category as I have defined it, but "early modern erotic writing" is not a genre—like the elegy or the epic, or like pornography.

Why bring together such disparate texts? What does Shakespeare's *Venus and Adonis* have in common with Thomas Nashe's "Choice of Valentines"? (They are both Ovidian poems dedicated to fashionable young aristocrats). What does *The Faerie Queene* have to do with crude jokes on the word "prick"? (It begins with one). Once one puts aside the social and moral assumptions that go with the notion of "pornography," one is in a much better position to understand the place of sexuality in early modern English culture. Erotic writing is not confined to low genres, unsophisticated readers, or marginal texts. Sexual representation of all kinds permeated literary culture in ways that were often profoundly different from what our own cultural experience of pornography might lead us to expect. This book represents an attempt to follow some of the implications of this fact.

If erotic writing in the early modern period was not pornography, what was it? The question is impossible to answer completely or definitively, for such writing was not one thing but many. In England it included ironic Ovidian narratives such as Shakespeare's *Venus and Adonis*, obscene satire by railing writers such as Marston, and Petrarchan sonnets by courtly poets like Sidney and Spenser; it took the form of bawdy epigrams and lewd ballads, both often anonymous. It circulated in manuscript as well as print, in foreign and ancient languages as well as in English. It was read by men, and—sometimes—by women. Rather than being limited to one genre, mode of circulation, or gender ideology, it circulated throughout literate culture. It expressed—along with many other things—male aggression and masculine anxiety, female frustration and social discontent. It was by turns funny and joyful, cruel, leering, and sly.

Given this diversity of content, genre, and tone, a history of erotic representation must be far more than a history of pornography. Over the last fifteen years, various theoretical developments have made possible a reevaluation of erotic writing in the early modern period. Feminist works have both examined the social place of women in the period and stressed the socially constructed nature of gender.[7] In addition, works by queer scholars have for the first time devoted serious and sympathetic scholarly attention to "sodomitical" and nonprocreative sexual practices.[8] If feminist criticism has made gender studies possible by nsisting on the fact that subjects are always gendered—one can no longer ignore gender by merely assuming a neutral, normative masculinity—then queer studies has opened the field even further by allowing one to speak of a multiplicity of genders. Both developments have had the effect of moving discussions of gender away from biology. The mere possession of a penis or vagina does not by itself determine gender within a given culture; the question is what one does—and what is one permitted to do—with what one has.

The recent emphasis within academic discourse on the constructed nature of gender identity facilitates the historicization of both gender and sexuality. If gender is to some extent socially constructed as well as biologically determined, then both gender and sexuality will be differently constructed at different times and places. One may object to the constant use of the term "construction" in these formulations, especially as it implies a conscious volition that is often absent from the production of social structures of gender, but the term is useful in that it also implies agency—gender roles within a given society are determined by innumerable social interactions, not by some abstract social force or spirit of the age.

Work on the history of pornography has demonstrated a linkage between pornography and political discourse in the eighteenth century,[9] and in some cases a similar linkage exists between erotic and political discourses in the sixteenth century. But beyond its status as a weapon for political satire, in early modern Europe erotic writing was also intimately involved in the politics of gender; in a period when modern notions of marriage and of sexual identity in general were in the process of formation, erotic writing played a major role in the construction of gender identity.[10] In a patriarchal culture with a relatively rigid gender hierarchy, the formulation of gender identity and the representation of sexual acts in erotic writing could easily become issues of national politics: in late sixteenth-century England, literary writing played an important role in the construction of English national identity.[11] Poets like Philip Sidney and Edmund Spenser wrote enormously ambitious works, in part to prove that English—the language of the southern half of an island on the periphery of Europe—was the literary equal of ancient Latin and Greek (to say nothing of contemporary French and Italian). The writing they produced was marked both by a concern to "fashion a gentleman" and by a fascination with the erotic. Such fascination did not pass without comment, for other writers and cultural authorities saw the development of English erotic writing as socially and politically dangerous. There was, for example, widespread concern that "womanish" poetry would weaken England's martial resolve in its conflict with Spain: erotic writing was perceived as emasculating and effeminizing and was accused of sapping the nation's military might. Erotic writing was seen on the one hand as manly and English and on the other as effeminate and foreign. These categories were not immutable—there were plenty of texts seen as English and effeminate, for example—but the debate between these two opposing views of erotic writing is to a large extent the subject of my study.

Pornography Historicized

As I have already suggested, the term "pornography" is an anachronism when applied to the early modern period. The word *pornographoi* appears only once in classical Greek writing, in the *Deipnosophistae* of the second-century compiler Athenaeus. Speaking of an author who had written books dealing with prostitutes, Athenaeus says, "One would make no mistake in calling you a pornographer also, like the painters Aristeides and Pausias and . . . Nicophanes" (8.567b). While little is known of Aristeides or Nicophanes, Pausias was a genre painter of the fourth century B.C. who came from the town of Sikyon near Corinth. Two of his paintings, one of Love, the other of Drunkenness, decorated the Tholos, or Round House, at the grove of Asclepius, the god of healing, near Epidaurus.[12] If Athenaeus is indeed referring to Pausias of Sikyon, then the term *pornographoi* would seem to refer to artists who painted pictures of whores or courtesans. Its application to describe a writer is a coinage by Athenaeus, and in any case the word does not seem to have been repeated in written discourse for more than fifteen hundred years. To all intents and purposes, "pornography" is a word coined in the nineteenth century; the earliest modern use of the term dates from 1850 (*OED*), and it was originally used to describe the erotic wall paintings found in the ruins of Pompeii. After its initial appearance it was appropriated by medical writers to describe works that dealt with the threat of prostitution to public hygiene and morals. Only by the late nineteenth century had it come to assume the range of meanings it connotes today.

Although, as I have suggested, "pornography" is often a useful term to describe one's own subjective reaction to certain materials, as an "objective," descriptive term, "pornography" is notoriously difficult to define, and useful or meaningful definitions are even more difficult when one is discussing cultures distant in time or space from one's own.[13] Often, pornography is taken as a transhistorical category and is used to describe a wide range of cultural material—including texts and artifacts, rituals or performances—in which, generally speaking, women are represented as objects of sexual desire or as objects of violent aggression by men. Such a wide application of the term—useful as it may be as a means of focusing attention on the ubiquity of misogyny and violence against women—weakens the effectiveness of "pornography" as a term for specific analysis. The unspecificity of "pornography" as a category in cultural history can be seen in a 1992 collection of essays on "pornography and representation" in classical Greece and Rome:[14] the book includes essays on topics ranging from the representation of rape in Ovid's *Metamorphoses* to discussions of mute, nude female characters in the plays of Aristophanes, visual depictions of sex acts on Attic pottery, the murder of female characters in Greek tragedy, and the violent nature of gladiatorial scenes in

Roman mosaics. Despite the high quality of many of the individual essays, taken as a group they provide a definition of pornography so broad that almost any form of representation that portrays sexual acts, nudity, or violence—even violence against animals—must be considered pornographic.

As a literary genre "pornography" is associated with a set of characteristics that are worth briefly reviewing: pornography is writing aimed primarily at sexually arousing its reader;[15] its structure is one of infinite enumeration (of positions, of partners) within a field that is always and only sexual[16] (although generic conventions may exclude certain forms of sexual activity);[17] it is written by men for men and is circulated primarily among men;[18] it objectifies women[19] and denies female autonomy and subjectivity—so much so that some critics see it as a form of violence *in itself.* In Robin Morgan's memorable formulation, "Pornography is the theory, and rape the practice."[20] Pornography is also, of course, a term defined by its opposite—it is not-art, not-literature, not-feminist, not-liberating, not-acceptable. And despite its frequent claims to be "adult," it is often seen as a discourse not of complex maturity but of immature fixation.[21] I am not interested here in evaluating the aptness of any of these descriptions, short of pointing out that the debate over pornography becomes enormously complicated when one considers the recent publishing phenomenon of "erotica" written by and for women,[22] the popularity of pornography aimed at heterosexual couples, and the role of various forms of "pornography" in the expression of gay and lesbian sexualities.[23]

While one can compile lists of characteristics of pornographic texts, generalizing about pornography is difficult to do with any confidence. One of the enduring fictions about pornography is that it is static—offering the same sexual material and attitudes over and over. This is, on one level, an astonishingly reductive and condescending way to look at sexuality, but more important, such generalizations ignore the element of subjective response that is crucial to discourses surrounding contemporary pornography. Even if a pornographic text is simple, repetitive, and obvious, its effect on its readers can range from powerful sexual arousal to bemused curiosity to indifference to disgust. Those who oppose pornography often see uniformity of content as an indication of uniformity of response: that is, they assume that since pornography is always only about one thing, there can only be one response to it—or rather, two responses, each strongly morally coded: "good" people will be disgusted; "bad" people will be sexually aroused. Both responses are generally seen as automatic: that is, pornography serves as a moral litmus test that confirms preexisting dispositions. This formulation becomes the ultimate justification for censorship: those who are disgusted have a moral duty both to protect the innocent from corruption and to deny illicit pleasure to the corrupted. All arguments for censorship ultimately depend on this morally coded distinction between subjective responses of readers rather than some objective evaluation of content. Censors always assume the materials they ban are dangerous to others or to society at large, but they seldom question their own ability to read the texts they condemn. Because they hate the texts, they can read them safely; it is always others who will be tempted. Such a view of reader response not only is authoritarian, it is reductive in its assumption that the only responses to pornography are attraction or repulsion. Such common notions about the way pornography is read deny the possibility of more complex or disinterested reactions. No one would dream of judging "literature" in this fashion.

A few decades ago, it would have been obvious to most commentators that the audience for pornography was male. Generally speaking, this was true: pornography was (and is) overwhelmingly aimed at men. But by making the assumption that only men will be attracted to pornography, one perpetuates one of the most enduring essentialist sexual stereotypes: that physical sex itself is uninteresting to women (they want "love" instead) and that women take no pleasure from viewing the naked bodies of either sex—let alone the sight of those bodies aroused and engaged in sexual activity. This is patently ridiculous. Another similar assumption is that women are naturally sexually gentle and that they prefer soft fuzzy cozy images and texts to explicit images and fiercely passionate, even violent narratives.[24] Beginning in the 1970s, feminist theorists tried to separate violent male pornography from gentle female erotica. While this distinction served some purpose, it is in many ways a false dichotomy. Many people of both sexes who are gentle and caring to their loved ones are turned on by rough sex—or by its representations. Human sexual emotions are not so simple that they can be neatly categorized and easily labeled—though our society devotes an enormous amount of energy to such categorizations.

The moral significance of pornography becomes even more confused because of a widespread social tendency to conflate sex and violence. Clearly sadomasochistic pornography exists, and there is no doubt that many who come into contact with it find it disturbing, distasteful, and disgusting. And yet, violence in S/M culture itself is often a controlled and regimented consensual activity, which in many cases has little to do with spouse abuse or rape.[25] Conflating sexual violence against unwilling victims with willing participation in a fetishistic sexual subculture only confuses the issues at stake. In any case, most pornography is not sadomasochistic. Unless one believes that graphic depiction of naked bodies and sexual activity constitutes violence *in itself,* a lot of pornography is not particularly violent. Most pornographic images on the Internet are simply pictures of naked people (mostly women) or of people engaged in various sexual activities: masturbation, oral sex, vaginal or anal intercourse. The cultural tendency to link "sex and violence" leads to frequent blurring of the boundaries between the two. It is a cliché among advocates of pornography that hard core pornographic films are not violent—blockbuster action movies are. And while one may doubt the sincerity of pornographers' concerns about the negative social impact of violent films, their argument remains valid.

I should be clear about my own position. It seems obvious to me that most pornography is produced for a male audience—and that the producers' notions of what that audience wants are often calcified, repetitive, and dull. But that is no reason to argue that sexual explicitness is only attractive to men or that men tend to be turned on by violence whereas women are naturally nurturing. There are men who are deeply offended by pornography; there are women who enjoy it. Some people find it comical, others pathetic. Some, like Beth Mansfield, the Tacoma,

Washington, housewife who set up "Persian Kitty's Adult Links"—one of the primary erotic Internet sites—see it as a way to make money.[26] One's reactions are also bound to change with age; there are few adolescents of either sex who are not curious about nudity, sex, and pornography. As new technologies of cultural reproduction develop, as women gain more social control over their sexual lives, and as alternative sexualities come out of their closets, the nature and social place of "pornography" is likely to undergo enormous changes.[27] Erotic representation is not static—it is potentially as fluid as desire itself.

In thinking about debates over what pornography is or is not, I have often thought that it might make more sense to see pornography as a way of reading rather than as a mode of representation. As a way of reading, pornography would be characterized by an obsessive interest in the material read, an abstraction of the self and an abdication of critical faculties, and a sense of voyeurism—of observing without being observed in return. Pornographic reading would often be followed by a lingering sense of disgust, guilt, or sheepishness which nonetheless would not preclude an urge to repeat the experience. There is no doubt that many people read pornography in this manner. Others have a similar experience with mainstream television shows—especially "live action" cop shows, coverage of high-profile murder trials, and disaster reporting. It may be that to understand pornography as a way of reading it will be necessary to desexualize the concept. Sexual pleasures are not the only ones that can be enjoyed vicariously and at a distance. Pornography in this sense may have more to do with conditions in which normal sensory experience is transcended: violence, death, dismemberment, physical ecstasy, trance states, than it does with sexuality as such. It may be that only certain societies and cultures see sexuality in pornographic ways.

Is pornography a way of reading? An expression of misogyny? A symptom of immature fixation? A form of sexual violence? A sexual safety valve? An emblem (or distressing consequence) of freedom of the press? Whatever definition of pornography one chooses, the term carries with it a wide array of contemporary value judgments and assumptions about the modern sex industry, assumptions that are often irrelevant or misleading when applied to a preindustrial society with relatively limited technologies of reproduction. Pornography is arguably a product of the industrial and technological revolutions, and in present-day Western society it is primarily a cinematic and photographic rather than a literary phenomenon.[28] Contemporary debates over Internet transmission of pornography make almost no reference to text—people are concerned about pictures. Many of the social and moral issues surrounding pornography are fundamentally linked to the medium of photography. Unlike text, or paintings, or engravings, photographs provide specific and detailed (though not always strictly accurate) representations of actual individual bodies. And thus antipornography activists argue that pornographic photos are degrading not just as representations, but to the specific individuals depicted in them. Whatever one's position on this issue, there is no doubt that— unlike textual pornography—pornographic photographs make actual peoples' bodies visible to a wide audience, perhaps in ways or contexts that their subjects would find objectionable. Because it is an industry that profits from the display and exploitation (in an economic sense, at the very least) of its workers' bodies, many of the moral concerns about contemporary pornography are in fact issues of fair labor practice. Are models' rights adequately protected? Are people participating freely or are they coerced? Are workplace conditions safe and clean? Is pay equitable?[29] None of these important concerns arise in anything like the same configuration when one deals with pornographic texts.

It has long been recognized that sexual representation frequently functions as a driving force behind new technologies of representation.[30] Even before the rise of cyberporn, some theorists had gone so far as to suggest that pornography as we know it was brought into being by modern technologies of mass production and could not exist without them. In her comprehensive study of hard core pornographic film, for example, Linda Williams argues that cinematic pornography (and indeed cinematic pleasures in general) owe their emergence not to earlier traditions of erotic representation but to what Michel Foucault has termed "*scientia sexualis* and its construction of new forms of bodily knowledge." Indeed, Williams goes so far as to suggest that the "transfer point" of power, knowledge, and pleasure that constitutes *scientia sexualis* is itself specifically cinematic in nature, for both cinema and contemporary discourses of sexuality have their genesis in a late-nineteenth-century desire "to see and know more about the human body" (36). Although Williams may overstate her case (the Renaissance was also characterized by a strong desire to see and know more about the human body),[31] it is obvious that the aesthetic dynamics of film and video cannot easily be equated with those of written text. And while Foucault's problematic distinction between a demonized *scientia sexualis* and an idealized *ars erotica* is in many ways an oversimplification not necessarily borne out by historical evidence, there are nonetheless fundamental differences between modern and early modern notions of sexual activity and sexual identity.

Many of the most striking differences between pre- and post-Enlightenment attitudes to sexuality have to do with the relation of sexuality to privacy. Although some of the most influential definitions of pornography see it as a genre that focuses on the arousal of its readers to the exclusion of all else,[32] the erotic writing of the early modern period is not so single-minded. It often addresses social or political issues as well as erotic ones. In early modern culture sexuality does not seem to have constituted a separate sphere of identity formation; instead, it informed a broad range of social domains, including networks of friendship and patronage and relations of service and commerce.[33] Erotic texts often warn of venereal disease or describe male impotence and incapacity—subjects studiously avoided in most pornographic texts. Whereas modern pornography tends to construct a fantasy of male potency and female passivity, early modern erotic writing often acknowledges female sexual desire and agency—as a source of male anxiety if not necessarily as a site of female empowerment. Indeed, this gender dynamic reflects early modern theories of physiology that saw women as more sexually avid than men and less capable of rational control of their desires.

As recent debates over pornography on the Internet suggest, one of the fundamental assumptions of pornography as a genre is that it ought not to be part of "mainstream" culture but should be cordoned off from other forms of discourse. If in modern culture sexuality is seen as essentially private, then it follows logically that erotic representation ought also to be private. Of course in many ways—one could argue—pornography is not at all private: its aesthetic and assumptions are pervasive in visual advertising, for example, and the generic lines separating pornography and art or fashion photography are increasingly porous. Corporations that produce and disseminate pornography are not segregated from the rest of the business community. The publishers of *Penthouse* also produce *Omni*, a popular science magazine, and *Spin*, a magazine dealing with popular music. Tashen, a prominent German firm, publishes collections of pornographic prints and photography as part of its extensive line of respectable art books. Whatever its moral valence, pornography is good business: in 1996, sales of pornography and sex toys were an estimated $8 billion in the United States alone.[34]

Obviously the social role of pornography extends far beyond the world of detached and narcissistic sexual fantasy it pretends to inhabit. The links between pornography and male aggression have been the subject of several studies, and pornography is often seen as constructing and disseminating a vicious misogynist ideology whose effects can be seen far beyond the sexual sphere.[35] These arguments have also been strongly resisted, not least by feminist theorists.[36] That modern pornography has as its ultimate aim the arousal of its readers does not limit its role in promoting certain sexual hierarchies and power relations. Pornography is intimately caught up in discourses surrounding war and nationalism; it comes as no shock to hear, for example, that in the Bosnian war of the 1990s, Serbian troops besieging Sarajevo spent much of their spare time perusing pornographic magazines. More ominously—though equally predictably—pornographic photographs were found pinned on the walls of burned-out houses in sacked Bosnian villages.[37] It would be foolish to claim that the circulation of such materials is utterly unrelated to the systematic rape of civilian women that was a commonplace horror throughout the conflict. However, while pornography is enlisted in such brutality, even complicit in it, to see pornography as its prime cause is to oversimplify the situation. Rape of civilians has always been a common feature of military conquest. If pornography was the cause, its removal would presumably remove the problem, which in this context is clearly not the case.

Despite the manifest connections between pornographic discourse and social attitudes, pornography nevertheless tends to present itself as something private and set apart from mainstream social discourse. On many American newsstands, pornographic magazines are sealed in plastic and kept on special shelves. In video stores too, "adult" videos are given their own section—often their own room. While these segregations are designed to limit accessibility of pornography to minors or to shield pornographic images from those who find them offensive, one of the effects of such common merchandising practices is to strengthen the notion that sexuality and erotic representation are somehow "secret" or hidden—private rather than public. These attitudes are hard to escape. Even those who enjoy pornography may be disturbed or startled to see someone reading or perusing such material in a public place, at the beach, or on a bus. The proper place for pornography—if not the incinerator—is behind closed doors.

Such a division of sexuality from so-called mainstream public life is not necessarily pernicious. But it is not a division that existed in anything like the same form in the sixteenth and seventeenth centuries. For one thing, in contemporary culture there is a theoretical and structural division between the public and private spheres that did not exist in a similar form in early modern Europe. Contemporary pornography is not detached from political and social concerns; but the perception that it is, the notion that sexuality itself is private and set apart from—even irrelevant to—broader social concerns, is one of the enabling fictions of pornography as a discourse.

Erotic writing in the early modern period does not tend to construct a similar fiction of privacy. There has been a good deal of debate in recent years on the origins of the modern notion of privacy and the bourgeois private sphere. While in both classical and medieval culture a theoretical distinction existed between the public realm associated with the state and the private realm associated with the family, privacy in the modern sense seems to have come into existence only with the rise of the modern bureaucratic state and with the development of Enlightenment and post-Enlightenment notions of individual subjective truth.[38] Francis Barker and others, drawing on Foucault, have speculated that until the mid–seventeenth century "the public and private as strong, mutually defining, mutually exclusive categories, each describing separate terrains with distinct contents, practices and discourses are not yet extant."[39] Both Foucault and Barker have been much criticized for suggesting that before the Enlightenment people had no "individuality" at all—that is, they understood themselves primarily as parts of communal units, or through their socially established roles in cultural hierarchies of rank and status. In its most reductive form, this proposition is clearly untrue—even ridiculous. Certainly there is ample evidence from the medieval period of intense self-examination by devout Christians. The pilgrims journeying to Chaucer's Canterbury are not merely representative of social types; they are marked by detailed individual characterization, as is the figure of Dante in the *Commedia*. Obviously people living outside of Western culture have had, and continue to have, widely varied notions of individual identity that have little or nothing to do with Enlightenment thought, industrial modes of production, or postindustrial technology. Nonetheless, whatever the interior sense of "self" of people in earlier periods and other cultures, the Enlightenment and industrial technology transformed and gave rise to new concepts of individuality and possibilities of self-consciousness.

Leaving aside changes in notions of subjectivity, in the material social world of the seventeenth and eighteenth centuries there were enormous transformations in the possibilities for private or secluded existence. Bedchambers—and beds themselves—slowly shifted from being common living areas (in lower-class homes) or sites for social gatherings (in upper-class ones) to being what they are today—private space for the single person or couple who sleep in them. Reading became predominately private and silent rather than spoken and communal.

Given the massive social and cultural changes that took place between the seventeenth and nineteenth centuries, it is clear that not only erotic representation but the place of sexuality itself must be vastly different in pre- and postindustrial societies. This difference constitutes the primary reason to reject "pornography" as a useful term to describe the representation of sexuality in pre-Enlightenment culture. Even if one puts aside the fact that the term is primarily used in reference to subjective impressions and that it often carries a strong moral valence, as a descriptive term "pornography" refers both to a historically specific genre of writing and to a range of generically specific visual representations. It seems to me pointless to apply it to a culture in which these technologies of visual reproduction did not exist, in which the moral and social ideas surrounding erotic representation were fundamentally different, and in which the literary genre in question had not yet developed. It makes no more sense to speak of sixteenth-century English pornography than it does to speak of sixteenth-century English haiku. Neither of these genres existed in that culture, though that did not stop people from writing about sex or writing short striking poems. But just as epigrams are not haiku, so early modern erotic writing is not pornography. In the context of the early modern period, the use of the term "pornography" obscures more than it reveals.

Erotic Representation and
Early Modern Gender Identity

One of the primary differences between early modern erotic writing and later forms of pornography is the way in which they represent and construct gender. Although the development of pornography is a complex phenomenon whose precise social valence and impact is as yet unclear, it seems to have been generally accompanied by a denial of female desire and sexual agency.[40] Much erotic verse of the late sixteenth and early seventeenth century, on the other hand, acknowledges—even obsesses over—autonomous female sexuality.

Take, for example, the following riddle, found in an early modern collection of manuscript poetry:[41]

> Thus my riddle doth beginne
> A mayde would have a thinge put in
> And with hir hand she brought it to
> It was so meeke it would not doe
> And at the length she used it soe
> That to the hole she made it goe
> When it had done as she could wishe
> Ah ha quoth she, I'm glad of this.

The riddle's answer: "A Mayde wente to thridd a nedle."

In this poem women are represented as sexually active and sexually avid. The maid is in control of the sexual encounter throughout, and part of the playful humor of the riddle is that the mysterious "thing" she wants to "put in" could as well be a dildo as a penis. The riddle's deflating answer stresses the ways in which everyday activities could be (and were) perceived as sexual by both women and men.

As scholars such as Thomas Laqueur and Gail Kern Paster have demonstrated, early modern understanding of gender was influenced by commonly held theories of humoral physiology.[42] While it is by no means clear that the galenic model that understood women as imperfect men rather than a biologically distinct gender was as widespread as Laqueur suggests, it is nonetheless clear that notions of humoral balance were crucial to the way that gender and sexuality were understood in the period. Commonly accepted humoral theory posited that men were "hotter" and "drier" than women, whose bodies were relatively "cold" and "moist." It is not surprising, given the patriarchal nature of early modern society, that men's hot, dry bodies were seen as superior to women's.[43]

Women's sexual desire was, in this model, understood as a natural urge to raise themselves on the Great Chain of Being by joining themselves to masculine heat. The energies of this conjunction would provide the vital force for the engendering of children. Thus, healthy women would naturally desire sexual intercourse with men, not merely because it was pleasurable but because it supplied them with the heat they lacked. This "natural" craving, however, could not simply be left to run unchecked, for it would lead to widespread social disorder. Since women were often understood to be the property of their male relatives—especially their husbands and fathers—and their sexual productivity was a valuable and necessary resource of the patriarchal family, they could not simply be left to run wild. Their desires needed to be channeled in socially productive and orderly directions. Since—according to prevailing patriarchal theory—hot, dry bodies were also more rational, men were believed to be more capable than women of regulating sexual passion—their own and others.

But, of course, men also desired sex. While in many circumstances and situations such desires were seen as natural and unavoidable, even proper, humoral theory could be used to argue that by having sex with women, men were going against nature—or at any rate, against their higher nature. They were seeking to debase themselves by entering into a physical union with a colder, moister body. The consequences could be dire—weakness, loss of physical strength, loss of rational control. And if a man engaged in such practices often enough, his humoral balance could be permanently altered—he could become moist and cold himself: he would be effeminate.

As I will show, effeminacy was often understood literally. An effeminate man's body would be physically womanly: he would lose body hair, his muscles would soften, and he might become impotent. In such a state, he would have lost not just his gender identity but also his social identity, for in the patriarchal world of early modern England, social authority and status were largely, though not exclusively, tied to gender. Thus, while sexual activity is at all times and places a potential source of anxiety as well as pleasure, the social configuration of that anxiety for many early modern English men was quite different than it would be in later periods or other cultures that did not tie sexual activity to gender and social identity in the same ways.

While sexually weak men and sexually demanding women are not conspicu-ous features of most pornography, many early modern erotic texts focus on male anxiety about effeminacy and impotence or present women as sexual predators. The notion that women were woe-to-men is a cliché of the period, and for an ex-ample of this attitude one need look no further than a set of verses attributed to Benjamin Stone, an early-seventeenth-century student at New College, Oxford. Stone's "verses on womens tempting" are found in several Oxford manuscripts[44] and provide an excellent compendium of the sort of misogyny to be found at the all-male universities. The poem begins by blaming Eve, not Satan, for the fall of mankind, and throughout women are seen as a source of specifically sexual weak-ness and corruption:

> In halfe an houre they will tempt a man
> & make him subject to th[e] falling sicknesse
>   yet in the fall least they should hurt a limme
>   theyle interpose themselves twixt harme & him
>
> They have a power beyond our power commaunding
> Mans strength is feeble now w[hat] ere it was
> we sweate & strive, they conquer not w[ith]standing
> And make us vaile our bonnet ere wee passe
>   In these short seas whither so e're wee fare
>   they take us prisoners and enjoy our ware

It is men's genitals, not women's, that are here objectified as commodities, as "ware." Men, not women, are sexually conquered and forced to "vail their bonnet"—a phrase that describes both the customary submissive gesture of doffing one's hat and a flaccid, postcoital penis; sexual submission is represented through a gesture of social submission.

Women's dominion, Stone suggests, is universal:

> It is too truee there is noe man alive
> English or Scottish, Spanish, welshe or dutch
> that doth his line from Adam old derive
> but will acknowledge & confesse thus much
>   That they sometimes doe even melt like waxe
>   At the temptation of the femall sexe

Stone warns that such temptations will lead an innocent young man to the "losse of his mayden-head," an incongruous phrase that clearly demonstrates the extent to which seduction in this context is seen as effeminating. He goes on to describe the "slender shankes & hollowe eyes" characteristic of the effeminated lover and to suggest that women are so sexually insatiable that they keep their victims in a con-tinual state of sleep deprivation. Stone's poem ends with a metaphoric shrug of the shoulders, admitting that "though [women] are bad: some men are ten times worse." But despite this retreat from the harsher judgments of the rest of the poem, the attitudes and fears Stone expresses were widespread.

Another poem found in manuscript, entitled "The variablenes of a Womans mind or a Constant Lovers conceit," puts the matter in a more humorous light: [45]

> Within my Mistresse Garter
>   The Raine-bow representinge
> Is figur'd forth her chaingeginge thoughts
>   Most subject to repentinge:
> For all within the Rainebow
>   One coulor's mixt with many
> Even so I find my Mistresse mind
>   She Loves not one but any
>
> One for his wealth she loveth
>   Another for his favour,
> A third for witt and qualitie
>   Lives in fayn hope to have hir
> She loves Marke in the morninge,
>   At noone Paul passed many,
> At night comes Nicke, and chants the Pricke
>   She loves not one but any
>
> .   .   .   .
>
> For every sundry fashion
>   She hath a fancy fittinge,
> Fro[m] fayre to blacke, fro[m] blacke to Browne
>   Her mind is allwayes flittinge,
> The longe, the short, the middle
>   Hir love is linkt to many,
> The grosse, the small, she likes 'um all
>   She loves not one but any.

The poem continues in this vein for some time, comparing the mistress to monsters of sexual avidity such as the legendary Athenian courtesan Thais, and concluding:

> Thus have I brightly gathered
>   Out of my Mistresse Garter:
> If deeper secrets you would know
> Search in her higher quarter.
>   She singes much like [that] Poet
> That loves noe Lasse but many
>   Her love extends to all her freinds
> She loves not one but any.

The Objectification of Women: Two Early Modern Examples

Texts such as these clearly offer a gender dynamic different from that typical of pornography. But even those early modern texts that present women as passive objects of male desire and power differ in crucial ways from later pornographic texts, as the two following examples will suggest. The first, a poem circulated in manuscript, reveals the links between eroticism and male discourses of power and property. The second, a poem published and circulated through the book market, suggests the ambivalent social space of erotic writing in early modern England. Both texts represent women as sexual objects; and neither can be properly understood if one approaches them armed with the set of assumptions associated with pornography.

The first poem is found in a poetic miscellany compiled in the early seventeenth century (Folger MS V.a. 399). The identity of the original compiler is not known, but the volume was later owned by a Mr. Charles Shuttleworth, who signed it (fol. 94v) in 1695. An eighteenth-century hand, perhaps Shuttleworth's, marks each bawdy poem in the manuscript with the letters "Ob"—a designation of obscenity not made by the original compiler, who made no noticeable distinction in the volume between erotic material and other texts. Among the many poems in the manuscript is an anonymous piece entitled "A Perfect president of a deede of Intayle" (fols. 14r–14v), which far from being the legal document its title would suggest is in fact a bawdy ballad. It begins:

To all true Christian people which
   this deed shall reade or see
I Richard Ambler greetinge sende
   from harte unfainedly
Knowe ye that I for five pence paid
   to me in my distresse
By Edwarde Loyde of Wattlesburighe
   a gentleman doubtlesse
Have given, granted, bargained
   confirmed, sett & soulde
Unto the foresaide Edwarde Loyde
   a plott more worth than goulde

This plot turns out to be not land as such, but the body of Ambler's mistress Elinor, described in appropriate topographical metaphor:

A meadowe grounde that lies belowe
   cauled Elnors close cunnerighe [that is, a "cunnerye" or rabbit warren]
Which boundeth upon buttockes dale
   adjoyninge to the thighe

. . . .

Upon the fourest side thereof
   two little hillockes are
Which for my pleasure manie times
   I have uncovered bare
Within the countie of Cuntington
   neare to the Navill downe

> In midst whereof ther springes a well
>> that cost me many a crowne

In a parody of the entailment of a landed estate, in which the owner of a property establishes a legally binding line of inheritance, Ambler entails Elinor to his friend Edward Loyde:

> To have & houlde to him & his
>> whiles that the winde doth blowe
> Whiles Sonne doth shine & trees doe growe
>> her water runnes beloue
> With all appurtenances due
>> In tayle & not in fee

But as is the case with most entailments, there is a catch. Ambler stipulates:

> For the reversion of the haunch
>> I still reserve in me
> Yeldinge & paying quarterly
>
> .   .   .   .
>
> And if the rent should chance to be
>> by him unpayd behinde
> Whereby my Nell for want of right
>> with him a fault shall finde
> Then by this deede I doe provide
>> that it shall lawfull be
> For me to enter into her
>> & straigne her secretlye
> And the distresse with him to keepe
>> until the rent be payde

Terms such as "straigne" and "distress" (both relating to the legal seizure of a chattel) continue the legal parody. After promising to otherwise defend Loyde's rights in Elinor, Ambler has the document witnessed:

> I witnesse call to this my deede
>> Sir William Clearke devine
> Whose stalion ofte hath fed within
>> that meadowe plott of myne
> He was a ready neighboure sure
>> & headed well the ground
> And used still to stop the gap
>> when he it open founde
> He hath a pasture of his owne
>> which is both faire and sounde
> Yet he delightes as manie doe
>> to grase his neighboures grounde

The poem—and the legal jests—conclude with a rider:

> This deed is seald & delivered
> yet all not worth a figge
> Untill there be possession had
> by turfe upon his twigge

The expression "by turf and twig" refers to the late-sixteenth-century practice of taking a sod cut from the turf of an estate as a token of legal possession. But it is also a bawdy pun: the term "twigging" was used in contemporary manuals of husbandry as a synonym for "breeding."[46]

Like later forms of pornography, "A Perfect president of a deede of Intayle" represents a male fantasy of sexual possession of a willing and available woman, and the poem treats the female solely as a passive object of desire. But although the text may at first glance seem to function like much modern pornography, closer inspection reveals many differences. Certainly the joking suggestion in the final lines that in taking possession of Elinor Edward and Sir William may also acquire the pox (in the form of scurf or turf upon their twigs) moves the text beyond the generic conventions that structure most twentieth-century writing aimed at arousing its male readers. Furthermore the manner in which Elinor is objectified is extremely specific: she is not the cliché "pet" or "bunny" of mid-twentieth-century "men's magazines"—she is landed property. Her body is construed as a landscape— a topological space to be surveyed, explored, cultivated, and dwelt in.

The metaphorical equivalence of the female body and landscape is a common trope in early modern English poetry, but it is important to distinguish exactly what sort of landscape Elinor represents. Whereas John Donne in Elegies 18 and 19, for example, describes the body of his mistress as an exotic New World to be explored and seized, the "Deede of Intayle" sees Elinor as a territory whose ownership depends on ancient traditions of land tenure and English common law. She is a domestic English landscape rather than the wild country of America and Newfoundland. Donne's masculine explorer faces strange dangers and perils in his conquest; in Elegy 18, "Love's Progress," he must pass "a forest of ambushes" (l. 41), risk shipwreck (44, 70), and negotiate "the Sestos and Abydos of [his mistress'] breasts" (62), and even then his safe arrival is far from assured. Elinor, on the other hand, presents no such threat—her gentle meadows, little hillocks, and flowing springs may cost "many a crowne" to possess, but once purchased, she is tame and may be enjoyed in comfort.

Elinor's pastoral passivity serves to accentuate her status as property to be passed between men. The poem is arguably as interested in the relationship between the three men—Richard Ambler, Edwarde Loyde, and Sir William Clearke—as it is in their desire for Elinor. While Elinor is as powerless and unthreatening as a grassy lawn on a summer's day, the relationship between the men is fraught with peril. Their rivalry is stressed throughout the text; even when regulated by law, it seems, they are constantly encroaching on each other's turf. In the "Deed of Intayle," the sharing of Elinor relates sexual possession not only to the possession of land but to the transmission of the text itself. Like the manuscript volume in which her topographied body is described, Elinor is the property of a coterie—passed from one friend to another.

The legal terminology of the poem marks its semantic space as a masculine one, and the poem is as much a student's parody of the law as it is a sexual jest. The legal jests in the "Deede of Intayle" are similar to those found in more familiar poems by John Donne, such as "The Will" or "The Legacy," and this similarity is not surprising. Many surviving manuscript collections of poetry have associations with the Inns of Court.[47] Another copy of the text, also at the Folger, makes this masculine context even clearer. This copy, entitled "A deed in Tayle" is found in a miscellany compiled by George Turner between 1624 and 1636 (MS Folger V.a.275, p. 124). Turner's copy of the "deed" is preceded by "Charles the kinge in his speech at Whitehall the 24th of January 1628" (pp. 128–9) and followed by "Duke of Buckinghame his Speech at the Councell table on ffrydaye the 4th of Aprill 1628" (pp. 131–3). Indeed Turner's volume is almost entirely made up of political prose texts, not verse. It includes the confession of the Duke of Norfolk (1572); the arraignment of Essex and Southampton (1601); the letter to Lord Mounteagle revealing the gunpowder plot (1605); and lists of the King's ships for the years 1627, 1635, and 1636.

My second example of an early modern poem objectifying women is more complex than the "Deed of Intayle." In the past, some critics have seen the satiric writing of early modern England as a form of pornography—a discourse of sex that is void of affection and filled with loathing of its object.[48] If one were tempted to apply the term "pornography" to any text of the English Renaissance, it would be to John Marston's "Metamorphoses of Pigmalion's Image"—not because it is the most explicit in its sexual description but because it combines explicitly sexual language with a blatant objectification of the female and a deep concern with the power of the male gaze. Marston's "Pigmalion" encapsulates just those aspects of early modern erotic writing that seem most pornographic, while at the same time demonstrating a range of qualities that differentiate such writing from later forms of pornography.

To understand the erotic dynamics of Marston's "Pigmalion," one must place it within its social context—that is, one must examine how it was produced and circulated and also how it was shaped by specific generic conventions. Important as manuscript circulation was in the transmission of erotic discourse in early modern England, erotic works of various kinds were also bought and sold in the printed book market centered around St. Paul's Churchyard.[49] Printed erotic texts included collections of sonnets by authors such as Sidney, Spenser, and Shakespeare, verse miscellanies that attempted to duplicate in print the coterie manuscript collections kept by the social elite,[50] and translations of classical texts such as Ovid's *Amores* and *Ars Amatoria*. Arguably the most popular genre of printed erotic writing was the Ovidian narrative poem or epyllion,[51] the most important and influential of which were Marlowe's *Hero and Leander* and Shakespeare's *Venus and Adonis*. Partly because of their length, these texts circulated far more widely in print than in manuscript and were in fact among the most popular poetic texts of any genre in the period. Perhaps because they were suited to a youthful sensibility, epyllia proved effective vehicles for writers attempting to establish themselves as serious poets. Marston, Thomas Lodge, and William Shakespeare all chose to make Ovidian erotic narratives their first printed works.

Beginning with Lodge's *Scylla's Metamorphosis* (1589), which concludes with an extended description of the aggressive wooing of the sea-god Glaucis by the lovesick nymph Scylla, Ovidian narrative poems tend to feature characters whose sexual passions and actions transgress traditional gender roles. Such poems explore issues of gender identity and sexual desire in a fundamentally playful manner. While they were often criticized as being slight or immature forms of verse, they were broadly popular—and it is not unreasonable to suggest that their light, ironic portrayal of gender expectations was part of their seductive appeal to the literate, book-buying public. Although they were frequently dismissed as "foolish" or juvenile, no one tried to have them suppressed.

Hero and Leander and *Venus and Adonis* were the most popular Ovidian poems of the period, but the text that best reveals the strengths and weaknesses of the genre is Marston's lesser known "Pigmalion" (1598). This poem and the volume in which it appeared explore the relation between Ovidian irony and savage Juvenalian satire. In doing so, Marston's text breaks with the conventions that made Ovidian narrative poems such a popular erotic form. Instead of presenting eroticism as a sophisticated, ironic game, Marston's poem sees erotic writing as a deeply conflicted and ambivalent activity—seductive but shameful, pleasing but vile.

Marston's poem reworks the Ovidian tale of Pygmalion, a young male sculptor seized with sexual desire for the beautiful statue of a woman that he has created. He prays to Venus, asking that he be allowed to consummate his passion, and his prayers are answered: as he embraces the statue it becomes a living, breathing, and sexually willing woman under the touch of his fingers (*Metamorphoses* 10.243–97). From Ovid to Bernard Shaw the story of Pygmalion is one of the most resonant mythic accounts in Western culture of the objectification of the female by the male. Marston uses this narrative of the construction of the ultimate female object of desire by a male artist as the occasion for a strange, contradictory debate on the moral status of erotic representation, a debate that reveals a deep uncertainty about the manner in which erotic activity ought to be represented and that may serve to demonstrate the conflicted status of erotic writing in late sixteenth century.

Throughout Marston's poem, the male construction of female perfection is deeply misogynist. This misogyny is already present in Ovid, whose Pygmalion rejects marriage and is moved to sculpt his statue by his loathing for prostitutes (*Metamorphoses* 10.243–56). Although the misogynist dynamics of Marston's poem clearly derive his Ovidian model, in his reworking of Ovid, Marston casts the objectification of the female in specifically Petrarchan forms. He provides a lengthy Petrarchan catalogue of the statue's attractions, detailing her bright eyes, her hair shining like the sun, the mixture of red and white in her cheeks, her perfumed breath, her breasts (ironically described as being "*like* Ivory"), and finally her genitalia, "Loves pavillion: / Where *Cupid* doth enjoy his onely crowne, / And *Venus* hath her chiefest mantion," (l. 9). Faced with the inability of consummating his passion, Pigmalion feels the "pleasing smart" of Petrarchan frustration

(12). His marble beloved, "which no plaints coulde move" (13) is, of course, the ultimate cold lady of the Petrarchan imagination, and Pigmalion's heartfelt lament at the height of his frustration both restates the questions of gender power and reinscribes the dynamic of dominance and submission that are at the heart of Petrarchism:

> why were these women made
> O sacred Gods, and with such beauties graced?
> Have they not power as well to coole and shade,
> As for to heat mens harts? or is there none
> Or are they all like mine? relentlesse stone.
>
> (21)

In Marston's retelling of the Pygmalion story, the Petrarchan conceit of the unobtainable stony lady is utterly literalized. This literalization allows Marston to subject Petrarchan discourse to a satirical critique; the stock figure of the Petrarchan courtly lover is revealed to be a ridiculous obsessed idolater, who like "peevish Papists" worships "some dum Idoll with [his] offering" (14). He prays not only to Venus but to the very sheets on his bed, which "his nimble limbes do kisse" with almost as much ardor as his lips kiss his statue (26–7). Indeed, Marston's "Pigmalion" suggests that the ultimate consummation of Petrarchan desire is not sexual union with the beloved but rather a form of transcendent masturbation, in which the frustrated lover "finds how he is graced / By his owne worke" (29). Stripped "naked quite, / That in the bedde he might have more delight" (25), Pigmalion rubs himself madly against his statue, an image that—as the ambiguous genitive of the title suggests—may in fact be that of Pigmalion himself. In its literalization of Petrarchan tropes and in its reduction of sexuality to autoeroticism, Marston's "Pigmalion" would thus seem to conform to Steven Marcus's characterization of nineteenth-century pornography as a discourse in which "persons . . . are transformed into literal objects; these objects finally coalesce into one object—oneself" (277).

The "pornographic" quality of "Pigmalion" is clearly related to Petrarchism; it is, paradoxically, the Petrarchan discourse "Pigmalion" mocks that most closely approximates the objectifying and voyeuristic dynamics characteristic of much modern pornography. Yet few would suggest that Petrarchan poetry, for all its misogyny and obsessiveness, is *itself* a form of pornography; while both misogynist and erotic, Petrarchan verse has traditionally been seen as too high and refined to be easily assimilated to the low genre of pornography. Marston's poem seems pornographic because it brings to Petrarchan discourses of voyeurism and misogyny an unaccustomed literal-mindedness and explicitness: here the stony lady *really is* made of stone and we see the lover rubbing against his sheets with frustration.

Although Marston ridicules Petrarchan conceit in "Pigmalion," his poem nonetheless reaffirms a misogynist Petrarchan construction of sexuality in which cold women must be conquered by aggressive men. Although Pygmalion is ridiculed for his obsessive idolatry, he is also presented as a model for the reader—a lover who can effectively petition the goddess of love and end by getting what he wants. Indeed the narrator compares his own seductive prowess to Pigmalion's, bragging that

> Had I my Love in such a wished state
> As was afforded to *Pigmalion*,
> Though flinty hard, of her you soone should see
> As strange a transformation wrought by mee.
>
> (32)

Marston's "Pigmalion" shares with later pornography a certain self-consciousness of its own erotic effects. The text's acknowledgment of an autoerotic element in Pigmalion's desire is paralleled by its awareness of the arousing effect its narrative of self-seduction will have on its readers, whose

> wanton itching eare
> With lustful thoughts, and ill attention,
> Lists to my Muse, expecting for to heare
> The amorous discription of that action
> Which *Venus* seekes.
>
> (33)

But Marston's text differs crucially from later forms of pornography in its contradictory and conflicted attitudes toward the arousing material it represents. Having provided Pygmalion with a living image of a woman with which to satisfy his desire, the text promptly refuses to satisfy the desires it has attempted to provoke in its reader. After asking the (male) reader to "conceit what he himself would doe" (34) if graced with a "woman" as willing as Pigmalion's Image, and meditating on how "arms, eyes, hands, tong, lips, & wanton thigh, / Were willing agents in Loves luxurie" (37), the text refuses to give "the amorous discription of that action" (33):

> Who knows not what ensues? O pardon me
> Yee gaping eares that swallow up my lines
> Expect no more. Peace idle Poesie,
> Be not obsceane though wanton in thy rhimes.
>
> (38)

After this refusal to give the reader the image of the erotic satisfaction Pigmalion enjoys with *his* Image, the poem abruptly ends.

The reader's status as voyeur is thus clearly alluded to—and disapproved of. Flirting with (and laughing at) its reader, the poem withholds the titillating details it promises; it teases and provokes, and ends by disclaiming its own obvious intent to arouse. While the narrator expresses the heartfelt wish "that [his] Mistres were an Image too, / That [he] might blameles her perfections view," the conclusion of the poem argues that looking at lascivious pictures, or reading erotic verse, is *not* blameless but shameful. Whereas pornography never admits to its frustrations and insists on the seriousness of its fictions, Marston's text makes Petrarchan eroticism literal in order to make it ridiculous. The poem's Ovidian awareness of the mechanics of seduction offers a sharp satiric contrast to Petrarchan idealism. "Pigmalion" critiques its own form and function in a way no pornographic text does.

As we have seen, Marston ends his poem by saying "Be not obsceane though wanton in thy rhimes," and at first glance this distinction between "obscene" and "wanton" seems to offer a way to categorize the poem. While wanton verse is permissible, a poem must not become obscene. But how are these categories to be understood? In the late sixteenth century, "wanton" carried a range of meaning from lewd and lascivious to reckless and irresponsible—it was not an exclusively sexual term but it often had a primarily sexual meaning. Thus in affirming that its verse may be wanton, the text seems to suggest that lewd or teasing verse (like "Pigmalion" itself) is permissible.

The primary meaning of "obscene" in the 1590s was not necessarily sexual: "obscene" derives from the Latin "obscenus" (ominous), and in the sixteenth century its primary range of meaning was "disgusting," "repulsive," "filthy," or "offensive." In Shakespeare's *Richard II*, for example, the deposition of King Richard is described as a "heinous, black, obscene" deed (4.1.132). Now of course the word has a broader, sexualized, range of meaning and is often used in reference to things that are deemed impure or sexually indecent. The Latin "obscenus" also carried a secondary meaning of "immodest," "impure," and "lewd" (Lewis and Short), but those connotations of the word "obscene" were just coming to prominence at the time Marston was writing; the *OED*'s first instance in which the English word carried a sexual connotation is this very line from Marston's "Pigmalion." Adding to the ambiguity surrounding Marston's use of the term is the possibility that he was thinking not of "obscenus" but "ob scaena" (not to be staged). Thus while the distinction between wanton and obscene in "Pigmalion" is difficult to define precisely, it would seem to be that between the lewd and the repulsive. Lewd verse is acceptable, offensive verse must be avoided. That Marston here and elsewhere sees lewdness *as* repulsive results in the contradictory language of "Pigmalion," which alternately encourages and condemns sexual pleasure.

Stranger still, the volume in which "Pigmalion" first appeared largely rejects the lewd and flirtatious mode of "Pigmalion" in favor of offensive, repulsive, and harsh Juvenalian railing satire. "Pigmalion" was the centerpiece of Marston's first published collection of poems, *The Metamorphosis of Pigmalions Image and Certaine Satyres* (1598). This short volume was published anonymously, and the text is divided into two sections. The first contains the poem "Pigmalion," which is preceded by several prefatory pieces. The second section is entitled "Satires" and contains six poems—five numbered satires preceded by the poem entitled "The Authour in prayse of his precedent poem." In this text Marston violently attacks his own "Pigmalion" for its reckless licentiousness, asking ironically,

> Hath not my Muse deserv'd a worthy place?
> Come come Luxurio, crowne my head with Bayes,
> Which like a Paphian, wantonly displayes
> The Salaminian titillations,
> Which tickle up our leud Priapians.

(ll. 2–6)

In these lines, the implication that "Pigmalion" does *not* deserve a worthy place is clear, yet the poem clearly occupies just such a place in the volume itself. Not only does "Pigmalion" give the volume its title, it also has pride of place, appearing before the sequence of satires, and is accompanied by elaborate prefatory material. The organization of Marston's volume is thus clearly at odds with the rejection of "Pigmalion" in the "praise of the precedent poem."[52]

The "Prayse," in fact, serves as a fulcrum on which the volume turns. With this text, the volume switches abruptly from Ovidian titillation to Juvenalian railing, from wantonness to obscenity, from erotic fantasy to harsh moralizing:

> I see
> My lines are froth, my stanzaes saplesse be.
> Thus having rail'd against my selfe a while,
> Ile snarle at those, which doe the world beguile
> With masked showes. Ye changing *Proteans* list,
> And tremble at a barking Satyrist.
>
> (ll. 41–46)

Such a shift in tone is all but unknown in later forms of pornography, marked as they are by the exclusion of any details that might deconstruct the fantasies they create. The contradictions of Marston's *Pigmalion* volume demonstrate the extent to which erotic discourse was marked by uncertainty in early modern England— uncertainty about the moral status of poetry as a discourse, about the appropriate modes of erotic representation within the conventions of particular genres, about whether condemnation or praise of eroticism was a more effective stance to adopt in launching a poetic career. (The 1598 *Pigmalion* volume, though published anonymously, was Marston's first work to see print, and it may represent an attempt to replicate the success of Shakespeare's *Venus and Adonis*).[53] Marston's volume attempts to both praise and condemn its sexual subject matter, and as a result his authorial persona is contradictory, even incoherent.

The contradictions and uncertainties in Marston's "Pigmalion" point to larger social uncertainties about erotic writing in early modern England. Is there an appropriate ethical or moral stance to take toward erotic writing? Is it shameful to write? Is it harmful to read? Is one destined—like Pigmalion—to be corrupted by one's own erotic creations? The society that took such pleasure in *Venus and Adonis* and *Hero and Leander* was obsessed with these questions.

Erotic Writing, Effeminacy, and National Identity

To understand the social position and function of erotic writing in early modern English culture one must look at the whole range of that writing, the reactions it provoked, the attitudes it supported, the ideologies it promoted, the desires it aroused. What sorts of erotic writing were circulating? Which texts or genres were publicly condemned? Which went unremarked? To begin with, there were classical erotic texts—including poems by Catullus, some of Martial's epigrams, and Ovid's *Ars Amatoria* and *Amores*. As long as such texts circulated only in their Latin originals, among an educated male elite, they do not seem to have provoked a high level of social anxiety. Erotic works in English, however—whether translations of ancient erotic works or original compositions—were a different matter. In the late sixteenth and early seventeenth centuries erotic poetry in English circulated either in manuscript among a select coterie of readers or in print through the London book market. The latter form of circulation was especially disturbing to contemporary moralists. Printed materials, of course, reached a larger and socially broader audience than texts circulated (however widely) in manuscript. And as the market grew in importance in the latter years of the century the regulation of erotic writing in print became a matter of increasing official concern. It seems the Bishops' Order of 1599 was designed in part to curtail the circulation of works perceived as erotically disorderly by the ecclesiastical and civil authorities. Manuscript texts, circulated primarily in elite male social circles, were not subject to regulatory legislation, although some explicitly erotic manuscript texts were violently condemned in printed polemic.

The early modern period was a time in which gender roles, family structure, and notions of masculinity were undergoing significant changes,[54] and erotic writing was one of the arenas in which such changes were negotiated and contested. In England erotic writing played a crucial role in the construction both of gender identity and of authorial power. Given the powerful and pervasive hierarchy of gender in early modern society, the construction (and deconstruction) of masculinity was highly politicized. For with a few prominent exceptions—notably the queens Mary and Elizabeth—ability to rule or to be master was theoretically predicated on masculinity.

Erotic writing and indeed poetry in general in early modern England were often linked to the notion of effeminacy—that is, to the various processes by which a man could show himself womanly, thus losing his claim to the powers and prerogatives granted him as a male by the established hierarchy of gender. To modern ways of thinking that divide sexual activity and identity into the homo- and the heterosexual and associate effeminacy with male homosexuality, the notion of effeminacy in early modern England seems both complex and in fundamental ways contradictory. A man could become effeminate by spending too much time with women and by acting too much like women in speech, dress, and deportment. But a man could also be considered effeminate if he took the passive (i.e., feminine) role in intercourse with men. In many ways, the concept of effeminacy put early modern men in a double bind: sexual relations between men and women were conceived of as a "natural" site for the demonstration of masculine mastery, and the assumption that a man should naturally take the active role in sexual encounters was fundamental to early modern constructions of masculinity. Yet to take erotic possession of a woman was to weaken oneself as a man, spiritually, through a moral surrender to effeminate pleasure, and physically, through the spending of valuable seed. To escape such weakening, men could leave the company of women for that of men—literally or metaphorically abandoning a "thrice-driven bed of down" for "the flinty and steel couch of war" (*Othello* 1.3.233–4). But the exclusively homosocial company of men was no guarantee against effeminacy, for to be a passive or subordinate partner in a sexual relationship with another man was also conceived of as "womanly."

The specter of effeminate weakness not only threatened to undermine the basis of domestic mastery of a husband over his wife and children; it also had the potential to destabilize national structures of mastery by putting in question the authority of England's male, aristocratic ruling class. Contemporary moralistic pamphlets by Stephen Gosson, Philip Stubbes, and others explicitly connect lascivious poetry, effeminacy, and military weakness.[55] Individual effeminacy thus has dire national consequences; if the prime of English manhood become effeminized, how will they defend the country against its foreign enemies?

While it is anachronistic to refer to nationalism in the sixteenth and seventeenth century, there is little doubt that a lot of cultural energy was devoted in the period to constructing and promoting various notions of national identity and Englishness. The fact that after the 1550s England was an island kingdom with its own national church certainly encouraged the idea that England was unique and set apart from other nations. Often, as is the case with Spenser's avowed desire to "fashion a gentleman" by writing *The Faerie Queene*, notions of Englishness were class-specific rather than socially inclusive. But other texts, most famously Shakespeare's *Henry V*, were beginning to gesture toward the idea of a brotherhood of Englishmen, irrespective of status differences. What Spenser's "gentleman" and Henry's "band of brothers" have in common is their gender; national identity in the period was often tied to masculinity. Despite the many representations of Queen Elizabeth as the feminine embodiment of the nation, women were often excluded from appeals to Englishness. England's military strength was largely measured by the manliness of its men. And it is this partial and contentious formulation of national strength that proves itself so vulnerable to fears about effeminacy.

Partly because of the connection between effeminacy and poetry, the construction of authorship in early modern England was highly politicized and deeply marked by concerns about gender identity. As Wendy Wall has argued, to be an author was to assert one's masculinity, to show oneself "a man in print."[56] To claim authorship was to claim authority—broadly speaking a male prerogative. But erotic writing complicated this formulation, for what sort of authority was possible if the writer was unmanned by his production of effeminate verse? The discourses that figured poetry as effeminizing were not monolithic; they were countered by defenses of poetry such as Sidney's that argued that the ability to write erotic verse was a useful and virtuous attribute of the humanist courtier. The issues involved in the debates over erotic representation and effeminacy were in no sense merely "literary" nor were they confined to the field of printed or manuscript writing—the theater too was figured as a site of effeminacy for both players and spectators.

This study follows attempts to make connections between various discourses and areas of knowledge—English and Italian literary and cultural history, the history of textual transmission and of manuscript culture, theories of gender and of the representation of gender. As is inevitable in any such work, some of what I have to say in each of these fields will sound familiar to scholars versed in that particular area. But just as on a long journey it is refreshing to stop for a while in a familiar place before setting out into the wilds again, I hope that readers will encounter familiar ideas and texts here more as a comfort than a bore. One of the joys of travel, after all, is to see home through foreign eyes.

The book is divided into two parts, "English Erotic Writing" and "The Aretine and the Italianate." Part I gives an overview of erotic writing in early modern England and explores the relationship of erotic representation to the formation of English national identity in the late sixteenth and early seventeenth centuries. The first chapter provides a detailed discussion of manuscript transmission of erotic poetry in verse miscellanies kept mostly by young men at the universities and the Inns of Court. Though erotic texts are very common in such manuscripts, they are almost invariably mixed with other sorts of texts—devotional, satirical, courtly, or panegyric. I argue that the mixing of erotic and nonerotic texts in commonplace books provides compelling evidence of the way in which the sexual was integrated with other social spheres in early modern England.

The second chapter deals with the relation between erotic writing and effeminacy, and the effect of these relations on notions of English national identity. It begins with a discussion of John Fletcher's play *The Custom of the Country* (c. 1619). Though it is now all but forgotten, Fletcher's play was notorious in the seventeenth century as one of the bawdiest plays ever staged in England. Besides providing a powerful example of the eroticism of the London theaters, *The Custom of the Country* also demonstrates the ways in which, for men, erotic activity could be perceived as debilitating and effeminizing. I then turn to an exploration of moralistic writings, including antitheatrical pamphlets by Stephen Gosson, Philip Stubbes, and others that explicitly connect lascivious poetry, effeminacy, and military weakness.

The fear that lascivious poetry would effeminize its readers was fiercely countered by the aristocratic and eroticized nationalism of writers such as Sir Philip Sidney and Edmund Spenser. Both Sidney and Spenser were engaged in an attempt to write English poetry that would equal or surpass the literatures of classical antiquity and of contemporary Italy. And both saw courtly erotic poetry as central to this avowedly nationalist enterprise. Insofar as he argues that poetry's superiority is based on its capacity to please and seduce its readers, Sidney's *Defense of Poesy* is also a defense of eroticism. And Spenser's *Faerie Queene* incorporates discourses of eroticism to a far greater extent than Virgil's *Aeneid*, its classical model.

Although Sidney and Spenser both gained prestige from their writings, cultural authorities such as the bishop of London were outspoken in their concern about the corrupting effects of erotic texts. I contend that concern about eroticism and effeminacy partially motivated the Bishops' Order of 1599, which decreed that several specific volumes be burnt—an overt attempt to control the printing trade. One of the goals of the Bishops' Order was the suppression of erotically charged satires, and I examine the case of a banned volume that included ten of Marlowe's translations of Ovid's *Amores*. I argue that the selection of Marlowe's elegies was especially offensive because it portrays sexual love as a pleasing surrender to weakness and servitude.

While both Sidney and Spenser attempted to portray the court as a source of national virtue, ambivalence about the moral status of life at court led the humanist scholar Roger Ascham to posit a foreign origin for aristocratic corruption. Ascham's *Schoolmaster* (1570)—one of the most popular manuals of education in Elizabethan England and a key text in the formulation of English nationalism[57]—contains a sustained attack on the vices of Italy and warns aristocratic Englishmen not to send their sons there. As Ascham's concerns make clear, the specter of effeminate weakness not only threatened to undermine the basis of the domestic mastery of a husband over his wife and children, it also had the potential to destabilize national structures of mastery by putting in question the authority of England's male, aristocratic ruling class.

Taking English denunciations of the Italianate as its starting point, part II examines the significance of "Aretine" erotic writing in early modern England. Pietro Aretino, whose reputation and writings I discuss in detail, was the most notorious figure of italianate eroticism in Tudor-Stuart London; he was emblematic of erotic corruption just as Machiavelli was of political corruption. In the third chapter I discuss Aretino's place in sixteenth-century Italian and English culture, exploring the relation between his erotic writing, his scandalous reputation, and his political and social power. In England many of Aretino's texts were known only by reputation, but his cultural importance extended far beyond the small group of men and women who had actually read his works. Besides being seen as the quintessential erotic writer, Aretino was also seen as a significant political figure, a "Scourge of Princes," who represented authorial independence and power freed from the strictures of patronage. Born the son of a craftsman, he also served as an indication of how—under the right conditions—authorship could be a source of great social power and authority. Most scandalously, Aretino was also marked as a sodomite and an atheist. In the word "Aretine" the Elizabethans coined an adjective that powerfully linked troubling notions of foreignness, authorial power, social mobility, and erotic disorder. An examination of how the figure of Aretino was constructed and deployed elucidates some of the crucial ways erotic representation functioned in England prior to the rise of pornography.

The fourth chapter focuses on the works of Thomas Nashe, the English writer who responded most positively to the mix of political authority and disorderly eroticism represented by Aretino. I explore the anxieties about effeminacy and the italianate that surface in the highly charged polemic between Thomas Nashe and Gabriel Harvey. In deliberate contrast to Harvey, Nashe saw Aretino as an enormously attractive model of authorial practice and gleefully accepted the title "the English Aretine." Unlike many English writers in the 1590s, Nashe saw Aretino primarily in political terms, as a satirist whose railing eloquence could serve as a model for Nashe's own writing. Nashe's most concerted attempt to employ "Aretine" writing in his quest for authorial and social power is his erotic narrative poem "Choice of Valentines" (c. 1592). I concentrate on the way Nashe's poem—which portrays male sexual dysfunction and female use of a dildo—sheds light on anxieties about masculine gender identity, sexual power, and social control. The chapter concludes with a discussion of the manuscript transmission of the poem, which exists in six widely divergent texts.

In the fifth and final chapter I discuss Aretine eroticism in the works of Ben Jonson. Many of Jonson's writings can be read as a sustained attempt to appropriate the subversive energies of "Aretine" writing and yet to distance himself from social and erotic disorderliness. I address in particular Jonson's staging of sodomitical, italianate characters such as Carlo Buffone in *Every Man Out* and *Volpone*, as well as his radical reworking in *Epicoene* (1609) of material from Aretino's 1533 play *Il marescalco* (*The Stablemaster*) (1533). In all these plays, Jonson dramatizes the conflict between contemporary practices of erotic authorship and classical models of detachment and propriety. I argue that by rejecting both the flexibility of Aretino's representation of gender and the explicitness of his erotic writing, Jonson succeeded in effectively appropriating the legacy of Aretino while at the same time erasing the sensual delight, the love of disorder, the celebration of the low-born, and the crossgender identification with the feminine that were fundamental to Aretino's erotic and political vision. Jonson's work thus offers an excellent example of the ways in which troubling yet exciting "foreign" eroticism was safely assimilated into domestic English culture.

Part One

ENGLISH
EROTIC
WRITING

Erotic Writing in
Manuscript Culture

for opening line

*E*rotic writing pervaded early modern English literary culture. It c̶ coterie manuscripts; it was bought and sold in printed books claimed on the public stage and embodied in private entertainments. A great deal of scholarly attention has been paid to certain manifestations of erotic writing, especially the eroticism of the public theater—an area this study addresses in later chapters. And there is no denying the eroticism of the great genres of Renaissance poetry—the Ovidian, the Petrarchan, the metaphysical.[1] Although studies of Renaissance drama have not only examined the playtexts themselves but also recognized the importance of the theater as a social space, much analysis of poetic texts has paid insufficient attention to the social *place* of poetry in early modern culture. If one wishes to explore the nature of erotic poetry one must focus not only on texts but on the ways they circulated.

Most erotic poetry in early modern England—including such now canonical texts as Donne's elegies or Shakespeare's sonnets—circulated primarily in manuscript, not print. Such texts were thus the product of a specific literary and cultural environment that remains unfamiliar to many modern readers who encounter these poems in anthologies of canonical texts or in carefully assembled editions of a given author's oeuvre. An examination of surviving manuscript collections quickly reveals that in range of tone and subject matter erotic writing goes far beyond the Petrarchan discourses of Sidney's *Astrophil and Stella* and the metaphysical wit of Donne's "The Ecstasy." As I will show, manuscript collections are enormously varied in their content, and their promiscuous mixing of texts creates fascinating juxtapositions—of tone, of genre, of subject matter, of poetic sophistication. An examination of the place of erotic poetry in manuscript culture not only clarifies the fundamental differences between early modern erotic writing and later forms but also leads to a better understanding of the larger social functions of erotic poetry in the early modern period. Two aspects of manuscript culture are particularly important in this context: the communal nature of manuscript production, and the role of literate women in manuscript circulation.

The Conditions of Manuscript Circulation

In what has become one of the better known passages from his diary, Samuel Pepys described his purchase and consumption of the lewd French book *L'école des filles*, an "idle and roguish" volume he bought on February 8, 1668, from his bookseller in the Strand.[2] The following night, after an afternoon spent singing with friends, Pepys finally had time to devote his attention to his recent acquisition:

> We sang till almost night, and drank my good store of wine; and then they parted, and I to my chamber, where I did read through *L'escholle des filles*, a lewd book, but what doth me no wrong to read for informa-tion sake (but it did hazer my prick para stand all the while, and una vez to decharger); and after I had done it I burned it, that it might not be among my books to my shame. (February 9, 1668)[3]

Pepys's experience with *L'école des filles* fits easily into conventional notions of the nature and function of pornography.[4] The book is read privately, ostensibly to provide "information" about the ways of the world, but actually for sexual stimulation, as an aid to self-arousal and masturbation—an activity recorded by Pepys in the macaronic code he frequently used for the description of sex. De-spite his insistence that such use of the book is legitimate and "doth . . . no wrong," Pepys is clearly ashamed of his actions and destroys the book so that no one will know of his interest in it, and perhaps so that he himself will not later be re-minded of it. The book, purchased in the marketplace, is literally a product to be consumed—when it has been used up, it is destroyed.

I focus on Pepys because of the familiar modernity of his account of the con-sumption of explicitly erotic literature. Searching for a single figure, a single mo-ment to emblematically represent the inward-turning subjectivity of the enlight-enment, Francis Barker chose Pepys reading *L'école des filles*, "alone in his chamber with his discourse and his sex; raging, solitary, productive" (69). But in fact, in that he recorded his purchase, employment, and destruction of an erotic text, Pepys is anything but emblematic; comparable testimony from the seventeenth century is extremely rare.[5] What gives resonance to Pepys's encounter with *L'école des filles* is not that it is necessarily representative of seventeenth-century practice but that it prefigures later, modern practices. In the dynamic of public purchase and private, pleasurable, and shameful consumption, a late-twentieth-century reader may detect a recognizable situation, a narrative of erotic activity familiar as cultural practice, if not perhaps as personal experience.

Whether or not Pepys's consumption of *L'école des filles* was typical, Barker is right to stress the link between modes of erotic experience (including the con-sumption of erotic texts) and modes of subjectivity. The seventeenth century is often thought of as a time when modern or "bourgeois" notions of privacy, selfhood, and individuality were in the process of formation.[6] The rise of the Enlightenment subject, whose subjectivity is founded on his or her individual-ity, and for whom that which is most private is also that which is most true and authentic, is accompanied by a shift in the social dynamics of eroticism.

It would be fascinating to study the subjective responses of early modern readers to the erotic texts they read, but there is so little record of such responses that such a project would be impossible. What is possible is to examine the artifacts that remain, to trace their production and circulation, and to examine the range of social attitudes (as opposed to individual responses) that these texts provoked. Let me concentrate for a moment on the environments in which erotic texts were circulated and the ways in which they were produced: Pepys buys an erotic text in the public marketplace and consumes it at home, in private—he does not share the text with his friends but waits till they are gone before he examines it. Fifty years earlier, erotic texts in England were, in general, produced and consumed quite differently. In early seventeenth century England most explicitly erotic writing consisted not of French prose but of English lyric poetry, and it was not published and sold by booksellers but circulated instead in manuscript miscellanies compiled mostly by well-to-do young men at the universities or the Inns of Court. Unlike Pepys's copy of *L'école des filles*, these texts were not for sale in the marketplace, nor were they disposable commodities. Collections of manuscript poetry were frequently passed on somewhat in the manner of landed property, bequeathed to descendants or given as gifts to friends. In the course of the seventeenth and eighteenth centuries a movement may be observed from the communal sharing of poems that characterized the transmission of coterie verse in the early modern period to solitary figures like Pepys, alone in his room with *L'école des filles*. This movement is not only marked by an increasing separation of sexuality from other realms of social life, but also by the growing importance of the private sphere as a space for the establishment of identity.

Pepys not only consumed *L'école des filles* in private, he also kept a private record of that consumption, in which he attempted to explain to himself why he took pleasure from the text and why he subsequently destroyed it. Although for the modern reader manuscript miscellanies and similar materials might seem analogous to private journals, such volumes were in fact often exchanged and the texts inscribed in them shared with others. In such a context, the erotic texts frequently found in manuscript collections should be considered cultural property shared in common (albeit among a select group) rather than evidence of individual private fantasy. Manuscript miscellanies constituted the site not of private and intimate individual personal confession or sentiment but of a social exchange—a circulation of texts that were rarely principally "authored" by the person who had written them down.[7] In the sixteenth and early seventeenth centuries, when private diaries of the sort written by Pepys in the late seventeenth century were rare,[8] one might well question the extent to which any writing can be considered private. Certainly in the early modern period books were *read* privately, in silence, but they were also often read aloud in groups, in families and at gatherings of friends,[9] and the practice of writing for one's own private consumption, as Pepys did, had not developed to any great extent.[10] Such journals as did exist tended to be more records of accounts or devotions than secular narratives of the writer's inner life.[11]

The mixing of erotic and political texts in manuscript commonplace books offers convincing evidence of the embeddedness of sexuality in other social spheres in early modern England. And the fact that manuscripts were produced and frequently exchanged in coteries challenges present-day notions that the erotic is a fundamentally private rather than public domain. In these volumes one finds no separation, common in later periods, between explicitly erotic "low" material and more mythologized, symbolic, and allusive Ovidian or Petrarchan writing. There is no parallel here to the division our own society constructs between "romantic fiction," "erotica," and "pornography."

As several recent studies of manuscript circulation have suggested, erotic texts were central to manuscript culture; erotic writing played a larger role in manuscript culture than it did in print culture. In *Manuscript, Print and the English Renaissance Lyric*, Arthur Marotti demonstrates that erotic and political verse, in particular, were primarily circulated in manuscript rather than in print in early-seventeenth-century England.[12] This is significant because, as Marotti points out, if one ignores manuscript materials in favor of print, one will have a fundamentally false sense of the literary landscape of early modern England. More important, the coming together of erotic and political texts in manuscript miscellanies is in itself a significant characteristic of that landscape. In manuscript collections such as George Turner's,[13] which juxtaposes speeches by Charles I and Buckingham with the bawdy verses of "A deed in Tayle," one can detect an early form of the eroticized political space that would develop fully only after the Restoration and _____ st enduring monument is the poetry of Rochester. Another striking _____ the mixing of erotic and political texts may be found in a collection _____ sh Library compiled in 1603.[14] This volume includes many political _____ petitions—among them a copy of Walter Ralegh's 1603 letter to King _____ wing his arraignment (fols. 17v–18r) and a series of mottoes addressed _____ lizabeth and her ladies (fol. 49)—as well as a good deal of amorous _____ verse, including one piece with the lengthy title "A proper new Bal- _____ Countess [who] would be a notorious woman out of Italy and of a _____ promoter of Love amonge the Augustine Nunnes. Translated out of _____ Devonshire into true Suffolk. And is to the tune of Lighte of Love, or _____ s you can decide" (fols. 43v–48v). While the particular mix of sexual _____ nd politicized invective that characterizes much Restoration satire had not yet developed in the early seventeenth century, in manuscript miscellanies a social space was being created that was both erotic and political.

In recent years many theorists, following Michel Foucault's fascinating and idiosyncratic *History of Sexuality*, have speculated that in the early modern period sexuality did not constitute a separate sphere of identity formation but rather informed a broad range of social domains, including networks of friendship and patronage and relations of service and commerce.[15] In this view, in pre-Enlightenment, preindustrial Europe sexuality was not a private and privileged area of one's life, in which one's deepest tendencies and desires were revealed; it was not the naked truth of the self, free of encumbering masks and facades. Instead, sexual activity was integrated into other social activities.

Of course, sexual activity is always integrated into other social activities to some extent. The question is not whether sexuality is completely cut off from other areas of life, but rather how it relates to other areas within a given culture. Much recent debate about the relationship of sexuality to identity has arisen out of an attempt to write the history of homosexual relations and practices and to study the differing valences of same-sex relations in various societies and cultures. Searching for a history of gayness or gay identity, queer scholars have uncovered instead a complex historical integration of same-sex erotic relationships with other social bonds—bonds of friendship as well as servitude, power as well as pleasure. Important as this work has been for queer studies, its relevance is by no means confined to this area. Work done on the history of same-sex desire has revealed structures of desire that characterize early modern culture as a whole, whether or not certain forms of sexual relations between men were a central part of "mainstream" sexual culture—as was in many ways the case in fifteenth-century Florence, for example.[16]

As I have suggested already, the tendency for early modern European culture to see sexual activity as a series of actions rather than as an indication of an essential identity can partly be accounted for by premodern notions of privacy and individual identity. While it is ridiculous to say that early modern people had no sense of their own identity beyond their status as members of various social hierarchies, it nonetheless seems clear that formulations of individuality and notions of privacy were different in the early modern period than they have been in later centuries. Certainly, the conditions of production and circulation of erotic texts in early modern England would seem to corroborate arguments that in the early modern period sexuality was not—as it is today—singled out for special attention and given a unique ontological status but rather was more or less integrated with other spheres of life: the political, the social, the religious, the philosophic.

Support for this hypothesis can be found by examining the circulation of erotic verse in manuscript miscellanies. Poems were written on loose sheets and circulated among the author's circle of acquaintance. Some recipients of the poems would then copy the texts into bound books. As poems circulated more widely, they became detached from the original social circumstances in which they were created. Compilers would often rewrite texts to suit their own needs and tastes. Establishing and recording the authorship of poems was not necessarily a high priority in networks of manuscript circulation; texts were often unattributed, or misattributed.[17]

Early modern manuscript volumes mingle an enormous variety of poetic texts—joking epigrams, sober elegies, flattering presentation verses, courtly sonnets, bawdy ballads, devotional lyrics, and epitaphs both serious and satirical. Nor are their contents limited to poetry; copies of letters, recipes for wine and ale, cures for common ailments, school exercises, inventories, and financial reckonings are all found in "poetic" manuscripts. In a collection kept by the theologian Anthony Scattergood (1611–1687) when he was a student at Trinity College, Cambridge, in the 1630s, Thomas Randolph's erotic poem "On 6 Cambridge

Maids bathing themselves by Queen's Coll[ege]: Jun 15 1629" is followed immediately by the following recipe:

> For the eyes: Take snailes & pricke them through the shells with a great
> pin, & there will issue out a fatt water, droppe the same into the eyes
> evening & morning[.][18]

Besides such medical advice, Scattergood's book contains English poems by Ben Jonson and others, as well as verse in Latin and Greek, the text of a contemporary Latin play, and various academic exercises.

In their heterogeneous mixture of poems, volumes such as Scattergood's give little comfort to those who would defend the notion of a canon of self-evidently great texts. While a few such collections are organized by genre,[19] most are not; indeed they mix poems (and prose texts) so as to defeat any organizational scheme, whether based on form, genre, or subject matter.[20] As a result, most English manuscript volumes containing erotic writing do not set it apart from other sorts of texts in the way that pornography is set apart from other texts in our own culture. Instead, they mingle explicitly erotic texts with devotional poems, copies of political speeches, school exercises, Petrarchan sonnets, verse satires, and epitaphs on illustrious persons; a lewd sonnet may share the page with a reverential epitaph, a devotional poem, or a political satire.

The manuscript in the Inner Temple library that contains the most complete extant version of Thomas Nashe's erotic narrative poem "Choice of Valentines" (fols. 295v–298v) is exemplary in this regard.[21] The section of twenty odd pages (fols. 284–303v) in the same hand as "Choice of Valentines" also contains the countess of Pembroke's translations of the Psalms (fols. 284–6), Latin verses to King James by Alexander Seton, the lord chancellor of Scotland (fol. 292v), the political satire "Bastards Libell of Oxford" (fols. 301–3), a "foolish song upon Tobacco" (fols. 293v), a poem addressed to the Earl of Essex (fols. 291–2), an abstract of a play (fols. 293–293v), several epigrams by Sir John Harington (fols. 289v–290), including "Of the Cause of Death" and "Of Reading Scripture," and a letter from Harington to Lucy, countess of Bedford. "Choice of Valentines" is immediately preceded by three model prose "speeches of a Prince requiring the Opinion of some of his Counsellors touching the scope of governement" (fols. 294–5), and directly following Nashe's poem is a prose "Dialogue between Constancie and Inconstancie spoken before the Queen's Majestie at Woodstock," attributed to one Doctor Edes (fols. 299–300), whose poem "The melancholie knights complaint in the wood" is also included (fol. 300v). In its mixture of texts, this manuscript is typical of most other collections of the period: a commonplace book kept by an Oxford man in the first half of the seventeenth century (Bodleian MS Rawl. poet. 142) includes directions concerning fighting cocks (fol. 6v) as well as poems by Francis Bacon, Robert Herrick, and Ben Jonson. A manuscript volume in the Huntington Library compiled in the 1630s contains both a collection of poems—including works by Donne, Jonson, and Carew—and a treatise on justices of the peace and criminal law; the legal treatise is written on the same pages as the poetry, at right angles to the poetic texts.[22]

While the few examples presented thus far may serve to suggest some of the more significant features of manuscript circulation of poetry in the period, to fully understand the place of erotic writing in manuscript collections, one must grasp the broad outlines of early seventeenth-century manuscript culture as a whole. Approximately 230 poetic collections are extant from the period 1580–1640.[23] Most of these are located in the collections of the British and Bodleian libraries, though the Folger Shakespeare Library also has a good number, and others are found in manuscript collections throughout England and the United States. Many of these manuscripts contain erotic verse of various kinds—from elegies by John Donne or lyrics by Ben Jonson to bawdy ballads and salacious epigrams. The overwhelming majority of surviving manuscripts containing erotic verse can be linked either to the Inns of Court or to the universities (especially Oxford), and thus it is hard to avoid the conclusion that in early modern England such poetry—as indeed poetry in general—was largely the purview of aristocratic or otherwise well-off young men. Yet the chance that such material would survive outside the libraries associated either with the universities or with aristocratic families is fairly small—especially given the "disposable" nature of much obscene material and the vagaries of censorship both public and private.[24] Given the paucity of surviving manuscripts associated with the Royal Court[25]—in all probability a locus of much poetic activity—one must be cautious about overgeneralizing about overall social practice from the narrow sample of texts that have survived.

For obvious reasons, very few of the loose sheets on which poems first circulated have survived,[26] though some are preserved in "composite volumes"—collections of loose pages gathered together by collectors or librarians. Some composite manuscripts were bound by collectors in the period,[27] but most were put together at a later date. More common are manuscript miscellanies that consist of poems copied by one or more persons into blank books.[28]

Bound books containing manuscript poetry are now often referred to as commonplace books, though they are also known as table books or, more accurately, miscellanies. Properly speaking, of course, commonplace books need to be distinguished from poetic miscellanies: a "commonplace book" is a collection of useful quotations, usually in Latin, gathered from authoritative texts. In her study of the influence of Renaissance commonplace books on patterns of humanist thought and argument, Ann Moss contends that "the feature which distinguished the common-place book from any random collection of quotations was the fact that the selected extracts were gathered together under heads." While "commonplace books were the principal support system of humanist pedagogy," manuscript poetic miscellanies were social rather than pedagogical documents.[29] Most were not organized according to any recognizable principle, and most contained texts by contemporary writers, not classical or humanist authorities. These miscellanies were primarily in the vernacular, not Latin.

While one may generalize about these documents, calling them poetic manuscripts or manuscript miscellanies, even these generic terms blur significant distinctions between individual volumes; each surviving poetic manuscript is a distinct and individual object. Some "miscellanies" are elaborate, elegantly written presentation volumes; others are small notebooks covered with messy scrawls. Some are exclusively poetic collections; others contain all manner of prose texts. Some were the property of one person; others passed from hand to hand—even from generation to generation—and were used for different purposes by different compilers at different times.

As already suggested, the conditions under which coterie texts were produced do not conform to modern notions of individual creativity and intellectual property.[30] Authorship seems not to have been particularly important to many compilers. Poems in manuscript miscellanies are seldom grouped according to author; they are often unattributed, or misattributed, even when their authors were relatively well known.[31] In surviving manuscript commonplace books, poems by John Donne appear more frequently than those of any other known author,[32] but by far the bulk of the poems in these volumes were circulated anonymously, and remain anonymous today.

Some volumes clearly bear witness to the networks of friendship that produced them: a book of Latin and English verse at the Huntington Library (MS HM 8) was collected by three friends: "Ro.[bert] Talbot, Thomas Buttes, and Frances Aunger." On July 2, 1581, as an inscription on the title page indicates, the book was given to Aunger as a gift from Buttes. There is a mixture of hands throughout the volume, and the devotional and gnomic verses it contains were gathered over a period of several years between 1550 and 1585.[33] A slim volume of English ballads and songs at the Bodleian Library (MS Rawl. poet. 185), compiled in the late sixteenth century, is written in two hands, which may be those of Thomas and William Wagstaffe, who owned the book around 1600 (fols. 25, 9). Other manuscripts focused on the writings of members of a particular college at one of the universities (for example, Bodleian MS Rawl. poet. 206). Still other manuscripts were kept in families: a volume at the Huntington Library (MS HM 904) has two hundred leaves mostly in the hand of Constantia (Aston) Fowler and contains many poems by the Aston family as well as texts by Ben Jonson and others.[34]

Some volumes are made up primarily of poems composed by their compiler: one (Bodleian MS Rawl. poet. 166), for example, is made up mostly of courtly romantic poems attributed to "Alphonso Mervall," which may be an assumed name—the outer cover claims the volume contains "English versse by J. Cobbes." (To complicate the issue further, many of the poems are signed "Tettix.") Whatever the compiler's name, this seems to be an autograph collection. Other volumes are devoted to the texts of a single author who is not the collection's compiler.[35] Disappointingly for literary historians, autograph manuscripts by "major" poets such as Donne, Spenser, and Shakespeare have almost all been lost.

Most surviving miscellanies were transcribed by their owners, but some, like that belonging to Chaloner Chute, a successful lawyer, were produced by professional scribes. This volume, transcribed by a "playhouse scribe" in the 1630s, contains poems by Jonson, Beaumont, Herrick, and other courtly poets.[36]

In contrast to the haphazard appearance of many collections, Chute's volume, like most professionally produced texts of the period, is neatly written on pages clearly laid out with ruled margins. The poem's title and author (where the scribe knew them) are included within ruled boxes at the head of each piece. Most pages have catchwords at the foot that helped the scribe keep his place as he copied. And at the end of the volume is "An Index of ye Pieces in this Booke" (fols. 97r–97v). Much more lavish is the "Bridgewater Manuscript" of Donne, a gorgeously written scribal volume now in the Huntington Library.[37] This volume, one of the most complete manuscript collections of Donne's poetry, was transcribed in the early 1620s for Donne's friend John Egerton, later earl of Bridgewater (1579–1649). The cover is vellum, with gold trim—both front and back covers still show remnants of painted crests, flanked by the Earl's initials in gold. Not all well-ordered or elegant collections are scribal, however. In the 1640s, Peter Calfe, the son of a Dutch merchant, compiled two neatly written companion volumes of poetry, now in the British Library. In both, the poems are separately numbered, and the first volume has an alphabetical first line index.[38]

While Peter Calfe clearly took some pride in his collection of poems, other owners were not so careful with the precious cultural artifacts in their possession. One of the most striking examples of this is a manuscript in the British Library (MS Egerton 2711) that contains many autograph poems of Sir Thomas Wyatt the elder (fols. 54v, 66–101), as well as a copy of the penitential Psalms in six-line English stanzas in the hand of Sir John Harington (fols. 104–7). Wyatt wrote his poems in the volume in the mid-sixteenth century; Harington added his some years later; in the seventeenth century, however, the volume was used as a commonplace book by members of the Harington family, especially by John Harington, M.P., justice of the peace and chairman of the sessions in Somersetshire from1635 to 1653. As a result, in the words of the British Library catalogue, "some of the leaves have been torn out; and the pages originally left blank, together with the margins of the rest and even the spaces between the poems, are more or less covered with miscellaneous matters." These miscellaneous texts, which are at times written on top of Wyatt's poems, include "abstracts of sermons, mathematical problems, business and literary memoranda, recipes"—including one on how to boil an egg (fol. 116r). John Harington, M.P., clearly saw this unique autograph manuscript by one of the greatest sixteenth-century English poets not as a priceless cultural artifact but as a useful source of writing paper.[39]

Although manuscripts were sometimes treated casually or even carelessly by their owners, one must not assume that handwritten texts were seen as inferior to print or as a marginal form of literary discourse in the period. In fact, as students of period marginalia will readily attest, the two systems—print and manuscript—were often intermingled in the same volume. Beyond those texts in which readers recorded their reactions to the printed text in handwritten marginalia, some manuscripts were actually written in the margins and on blank pages in printed books.[40]

As Harold Love stresses throughout his important study *Scribal Publication in Seventeenth-Century England* (Oxford, 1993), manuscript culture was not simply replaced by the new technology of print; the two modes of textual production coexisted in England until the early eighteenth century. While print offered some obvious advantages over manuscript in its ability to cheaply and accurately make available multiple identical copies of a given text, manuscript was prized for its personal quality and its ability to limit circulation to a small, specialized group. While the "stigma of print"[41] has probably been overstressed in accounts of the period, there were clear advantages to having one's works circulate in manuscript.

Manuscript Circulation of Erotic Texts

A bound collection of printed texts in the British Library (catalogued as C.39.a.37), most of them erotic, includes Ovid's *Art of Love*, translated by T. Heywood (1630?); Shakespeare's *Rape of Lucrece* (1624); *The Scourge of Venus*, by H. A. (1614); a volume containing John Marston's "Pigmalion" (1619); and Ovid's *Remedy of Love*, translated by Thomas Overbury (1620). These texts are followed by several pages of manuscript poetry, much of it on erotic themes.[42] In its gathering of disparate erotic materials under one cover, this volume is atypical. Of all the manuscript miscellanies and commonplace books containing erotic verse from early modern England only a few are clearly organized as collections of erotic writing.[43] The few such collections that do exist differ widely in content and form: a manuscript compiled by Henry Price (1566–1600), an Oxford graduate, noted preacher, and elegant Latin poet, combines an English translation of a classical erotic text—Ovid's *Ars Amatoria*—with contemporary antifeminist poems, bawdy riddles, and Nashe's "Choice of Valentines." Almost all 349 poems in an early seventeenth-century manuscript now in the Rosenbach Collection, Philadelphia, are erotic or satirical or both.[44] In this case the owner is unknown, but there are four separate hands, suggesting either that the manuscript was communally compiled or that it was passed from one friend to another; based on content there is an obvious connection to both Oxford and the Inns of Court. A miscellany in the Bodleian,[45] compiled around 1640, opens with an English translation of the Song of Solomon, which is then followed by a collection of popular verse, including several bawdy texts. Did the unknown compiler consider the Song of Solomon primarily as an erotic text? Whatever he may have thought of it, it is intriguing that he included it in a volume with contemporary erotic and political verse, rather than with other sacred or devotional texts.

As this example suggests, it is difficult to generalize about the erotic texts found in manuscript; while most are relatively short lyric poems, they encompass a wide range of attitudes toward sexual activity—from childish humor to leering celebration to witty observation. While most deal with sexual relations between men and women, some—most famously the sonnets of Shakespeare and of Barnfield—deal with erotic relations between men. Few copies of these poems survive in manuscript, though presumably manuscript copies, especially of Shakespeare's sonnets, did circulate. Poems dealing explicitly with sex between women are even rarer. Erotic lyrics are at times eloquent in their praise of female beauty, at times brutally misogynist. Although manuscript erotic poetry is multivocal and multivalent, taken as a whole it not only provides an excellent record of early modern attitudes toward sexual activity and gender identity, it also played an important role in shaping those attitudes.

The juxtapositions of tone and subject matter in manuscript miscellanies are frequently shocking to readers used to finding their seventeenth-century lyrics in Norton anthologies. For example, in a thin, vellum-bound quarto now at Corpus Christi College, Oxford, transcribed around 1630 and probably connected with the Inns of Court,[46] Donne's sardonic poem "The Will" is immediately preceded by the following lines:

> Epitaph
> Here lyes one enclosed under this Bricke
> Who in her life time Lov'd a P[rick]
> You that passe by pray doe hir your honoure
> To pull out the P[rick]. and pisse uppon hir.

> (f . 5v)

Besides "The Will," the volume contains thirteen other poems by Donne, including his anti-Puritan devotional poem "The Cross" (fols. 6v–7).

While the "epitaph" just quoted is a particularly crude example, the poetic quality of much manuscript erotic verse is low: many poems are not far removed in diction, tone, and subject matter from the graffiti found on the bathroom walls of the research libraries in which they are now housed. But this does not mean these texts should simply be dismissed as irrelevant or inconsequential. The men and women who copied them into their books clearly valued them enough to expend ink, paper, and the time to write them down. In an age of ball point pens and cheap, plentiful stationery (to say nothing of printers and word processors) it is easy to forget that writing in the early modern period involved a fair bit of work.[47] How many scholars or students today, one wonders, would own copies of Donne's poems if they could only acquire them by copying each one by hand with a quill pen?

Of course, Donne's poems seem much more valuable to most of us than this crude mock "Epitaph." But the compiler of the Corpus Christi manuscript thought both the "Epitaph" and "The Will" worth preserving. Traditionally, the task of literary scholars and historians has been precisely to deny and undo the mix of sublime and ridiculous texts characteristic of many surviving miscellanies, establishing "accurate" texts of canonical poems by "great" writers and consigning the rest to oblivion. From a purely literary point of view, such a task is not without value, but from the point of view of cultural history its consequences can be disastrous. The efforts of literary historians to establish definitive canons of manuscript poetic texts create the fiction that texts were read primarily in this way in the past: that truly discriminating early modern readers would have kept only a kernel of great texts by brilliant writers, casting aside as worthless the chaff of texts that were crude, unsophisticated, or dull.

If surviving manuscript collections are any indication, such discriminating readers were few and far between. On the contrary, it is thanks to readers who valued texts such as the "Epitaph" that some of the greatest erotic poetry in the language—by Donne, Jonson, Carew, and others—was preserved. When trying to place early modern erotic texts within their social context, one must remember that the same readers who preserved copies of "A Valediction: Forbidding Mourning" and "The Rapture" also set aside space in their collections for such masterpieces of wit as the following lament on the untimely death of an Oxford scholar with an unfortunate name. This little poem is one of those most widely found in surviving poetic manuscripts:[48]

> "On the death of Master Pricke, late of Christ Church College"
> The thirtieth of the month December
> Christ Church lost a privy member
> And treacherous earth did spread her womb
> Decayed Pricke for to intombe
> Maydens lament, and widdowes spend your moanes
> For now the Pricke doth ly beneath the stones
>
> (MS Egerton 2421, fol. 20v)

"Stones," of course, was a slang term for testicles in the period. This particular double-entendre found its way into many bawdy epitaphs. For example, in a manuscript at Corpus Christi College, Oxford, one finds the following verses "Uppon th[e] Lady [Penelope] Rich"—who was, it will be remembered, Sidney's "Stella":

> Here lyes Penelope or the Lady Rich
> or the countesse of devonsh[ire]: choose you which
> One stone suffices (for what death canne doe)
> Her that in life was not content with two.[49]
>
> (MS CCC 328, fol. 43)

Clearly, the author of these lines had a very different opinion of Stella's sexuality than Sidney did. Salacious mock epitaphs such as this are quite common in manuscripts—and at times appear in close proximity to serious epitaphs on respected persons.

Bawdy epigrams are also very common. Brief, comic, and easily memorized, they were ideal for filling in small blank spaces at the end of pages or in margins. The following verse, with its topical reference both to the burning of the steeple of St. Paul's and to the prevalence of venereal disease, was quite popular.

> "In Brennum"
> Brennus his Pr[ick] was like Pauls Steeple turnd,
> It was a goodly one before twas burnd,
> Pauls Steeple still is highest in the towne
> If Brennus Pr[ick] be such, twas well burnt down[50]
>
> (MS Rosenbach 1083/15, p. 120)

Just as many doggerel epitaphs play with the pun on "stones," so too many epigrams rehearsed quibbles on the term "prick." A common epigram addressed "To woeman" states:

> Ye that have beautie & withall no pittie
> Are like a pricke songe lesson without dittie

(MS Dyce (44) 25 F 39, fol. 81v)

Prick-song—a phrase begging to be put to use as a double-entendre—was a term for written music.

Bawdy wordplay also took the form of acrostics. The following popular riddle offers a predictable cure for "green-sickness"—an anemic condition in maidens believed to be caused by physical longing for sexual intercourse.

> A maiden faire of the greene sicknesse late
> P itty to see perplexed was full sore
> R esolving how to mend her bad estate
> I n this distress Apollo doth implore
> C ure for her ill. The oracle assignes
> K eepe the first letters of these several lines

(MS Egerton 2421, fol. 46 reversed)[51]

While verses such as these may seem so puerile and slight as to preclude serious analysis, they nonetheless were characteristic features of manuscript circulation of verse, and their bawdy vocabulary and wordplay is echoed throughout early modern literary culture. In *Romeo and Juliet* Mercutio calls Tybalt "a very good whore" who "fights as you sing prick-song" (2.4.20–30), and Capulet, furious with Juliet's refusal to marry the County Paris, calls her a "green-sickness carrion" (3.5.157). Similarly, Polonius dismisses Ophelia's naive response to Hamlet's affection by calling her a "green girl" (1.3.101).

A poem (in Rosenbach MS 1083/15, fol. 15) entitled "A medicine for the greene sicknes" provides much more detail. The cure is found in a special plant, punningly called a "Vir tree":

> His grothe must bee some twenty yeares at least
> his barke mixt white and red like milke & bloud
> his roote black mossy is wch shewes him best
> some white & yellow ar but not so good
> Out of whose cave well warmed by your heat
> such tickling droppes do issue
>
> . . . .
>
> the oftner that you use this pretious oyle
> by so much shorter time you gaine your helth

As this excerpt demonstrates, whatever their quality as verse, bawdy manuscript poems reveal a good deal about attitudes to gender and sexuality. In this poem, men under twenty years of age are seen as immature or inadequate sexual partners for women; men whose pubic hair is black are seen as more virile than those with blond or whitish hair; and genital organs are described in terms that suggest their opposite—the penis is briefly seen as a "cave." Such formulations suggest the ways in which gender in the period was often conceived of as a continuum, rather than a binary opposition.[52] In the right circumstances and context, a penis could seem like a vagina, and vice versa.

A riddle describing a penis in a series of elaborate metaphors survives in several manuscripts.[53] Entitled "Riddle me Rachell whats this / that a man handles when he does pisse," this comic poem provides an excellent synopsis of the contrasting and paradoxical notions about both the penis and masculinity in early modern culture:

> It is a kind of pleasing sting
> a pricking & peircinge thing
> Its a stiff short fleshy pole
>   thats fitt to stopp a maydes mous hole
> Tis Venus wanton-playing wand
>   that neare had feet & yet can stand
> It is the pen fayre Helen tooke
>   to wright within her two leavd booke
> It is the strong familiar spright
>   that wenches cunger [conjure] in the night
> Its the Shooinghorne Mars did use
>   when he pluckt on black Vulcans shoes
> Tis cald a grafthorne for the head
>   a staff to make a cuckoldes bedd
> It is a thing thats deaff & blind
>   Yet narrow holes in dark can find
> It is a dwarff in hight & lenght
>   & yet a giant for his strenght
> Tis a Bachalours button ripe
>   the kindest true Tobacco pipe
> ffor mooneshine bank it is a provision
>   an instrument for maydes incision
> Tis a prick shaft of Cupides cutt
>   yet men do shoote it at a Butt
> and every wench by her good will
>   would keept it in her quiver still
> The fayrest shee that ere tooke life
>   for love of it became a wife

Incapable of being rationally controlled, the penis is monstrous and deformed—a paradoxical creature "that neare had feet & yet can stand." It is "deaff & blind"—"a dwarff in hight & lenght / & yet a giant for his strenght." A "strong familiar spright," it is not under the control of the man it is attached to; it has an independent spirit of its own. It is a weapon of aggression, "an instrument for maydes

incision"; yet it is also the plaything of the gods: "Venus wanton-playing wand"—
"a prick-shaft of Cupides cutt." It is both a focus for male bonding, "the kindest
true Tobacco pipe"; and an instrument whereby one man can gain leverage over
another: "the Shooinghorne Mars did use / when he pluckt on black Vulcans
shoes."

In a fascinating reworking of one of the traditional tropes of masculine authorship, the poem sees the penis as pen and vagina as book—but here the masculine implement is in the hand of that most infamous of women, Helen of Troy:
the penis "is the penn fayre Helen tooke / to wright wthin her two leavd' booke."
Genital penetration here is seen not as an act of male domination, but as an activity
controlled and directed by the female, who takes her male partner in hand. Helen,
the passive motive of the Trojan war, is seen here as sexually dominant. She
controls the masculine energies by which the war is fought; she is the author of
her own tale, as it were.

The image of a penis held firmly in hand reappears at the end of the poem:
in a parody of the printing information given at the end of broadside ballads the
text is said to be:

> Imprinted at Poule Barr
> at the signe of the hand and ye star
> if you put ye S after ye R

That is, at the sign of the hand and the "tars"—or "tarse"—a slang term for penis.
Whose hand holds this symbol of writing and authorship?

While this phallic riddle is fairly common, a manuscript in the Rosenbach
collection[54] includes a rarer companion poem on the facing page, entitled "Now
riddle me Robin & tell me thus much / Quid significat a Cut in Dutch." This
poem is in different hand and was probably added by a different compiler. Structural similarities make it clear that this riddle was written as a companion poem
to the previous piece; the images of Cupid's quiver, Venus and Mars, and Helen
of Troy all recur. And, if anything, this poem is even more comprehensive than
its companion in its enumeration of early modern attitudes toward and images
of its subject. It concludes, unsurprisingly, that "in English blunt / A Dutch cut
is an English [cunt]."

> It is a wound that nature gives
> the cause few weomen chastly lives
> it is a marker the mother lendes
> Its all (maydes say) that god them sendes
> a faryry circle whear inherrittes
> nought but Hobgoblins Elves and spirrittes
> a holy water bottle for the nonce
> to charme raw head and bloody bones
> a black that shooters levell at
> that lacks a pin to measure at
> tis Doctor Dildoes dauncinge schoole

and many a bare bald frieres coole
two letteres tis in criss crosse row
stante fit I sedente O
tis Priapus his windinge sheet
so oft as he his death doth meet
tis Cupides quiver where ar borne
nought but prick shaftes headed with horne
a two leaved booke whear thou mayst read
the massacre of a maydenhead.
Tis Joves Tiburne whear be hangd
such as in their offences stand.
tis the bell that Hellen to to toald
when Menelaus died of catchinge co co coald.
the alter whear Mares his incense spread
offringe to great god Vulcanes head.
A sculler in the Ocean plac't
transporting thinges to the land of wast
it is a tarses quaffinge can
a spectacle for an one eyd man
and yet tis naught for the eye
for t'will make it weepe pitteously.
right she-ffeild sheath for Tunn-brick knives
houlds two and a bodkin yet never rives.
the womans best part call it I dare
whearin no man comes but must stand bare
and let him be never so stout
t'will take him downe before he goes out
it is a gash a slash a wound
a bogg a cliff a gulf sans ground
a watery fire a scaldinge well
a torturing pleasure and a pleasing hell
well what it is I cannot guess
but well I wott some thinge it is
Ile therefore conclude in English blunt
a Dutch cut is an English [ ]

Like the penis, the vagina is a paradox—it cannot be defined because it is fundamentally illogical: "A watery fire a scaldinge well / a torturinge pleasure and a pleasing hell." These are, of course, the familiar Petrarchan tropes of love itself in the early modern period. Just as love represents an ambivalent victory of passion over reason, so the genital organs of both sexes are paradoxical in their makeup and multiple and contradictory in their significance. A similar view is put forth by Montaigne in his essay "On some verses of Virgil" (3.5):

The gods, says Plato, have furnished us with a disobedient and tyran-
nical member which like a furious animal undertakes by the violence

of its appetite to subject everything to itself. To women likewise they have given a gluttonous and voracious animal, which if denied its food in due season, goes mad.[55]

The "cut in Dutch" riddle represents the vagina as "a wound" that makes female chastity almost impossible—a point on which Montaigne emphatically agrees: "It is madness to assay restraining so blazing a desire, so natural to women" (292). In the riddle, the vagina also has a range of associations with magic and witchcraft: it is "a fayry circle" inhabited by "nought but Hobgoblins Elves and spirrittes." It is a "marker" passed from mother to daughter, "a holy water bottle" with the power "to charme raw head and bloody bones." If men in the period referred to orgasm as "dying," it is the vagina that kills: "tis Priapus his windinge sheet / so oft as he his death doth meet"; "Tis Joves Tiburne whear be hangd / such as in their offences stand." It is a cliché that the penis is represented as a weapon throughout Western culture; it is less often recognized that in the early modern period the vagina is—at least symbolically—equally threatening. Female genitalia are powerful—so much more powerful than the male genitals that they compel a gesture of respect we have already encountered in the verses of Benjamin Stone (standing uncovered, with all the expected double meanings):

> ye womans best part call it I dare
> wherin no man comes but must stand bare
> and let him be never so stout
> t'will take him downe before he goes out

Although the vagina is seen as a threatening, engulfing wound, the poem explicitly rejects the notion, fashionable in many circles in more recent periods, that it is an absence, a lack—mere emptiness: "well what it is I cannot guess / but well I wott some thinge it is." For one thing, it is a locus of pleasure—possibly of autonomous pleasure that has no need for men. In a wonderfully alliterative phrase, the vagina is described as "Doctor Dildoes dauncinge schoole."

As in the riddle on the penis, female genitals are imagined as a textual site. The connection between female genitalia and writing or inscription is emphasized by the following couplet, which plays in a sophomoric way on a perceived difference in the shape of the vulva when a woman is sitting or standing: "two letteres tis in criss crosse row / stante fit I sedente O." [standing it makes an "I", sitting, an "O"] The Nurse in Shakespeare's *Romeo and Juliet* makes the same pun when she asks Romeo "Why should you fall into so deep an O?" (3.3.90).

But whereas in the penis riddle the vulva is seen as a space for the inscription of pleasure—where Helen takes pen[is] in hand to write the text of her desire—here the significance is quite different and pleasure has little place in the system of representation. The vulva is "a two leaved booke whear thou mayst read / ye massacre of a maydenshead." Here the only text the vulva can display is that of its own violation—seen here as a painful "massacre."

This, of course, is a more habitual way to see the relation between women and writing in the period. Texts are female, authors male.[56] As an epigram found in two different manuscripts in Corpus Christi College, Oxford, puts it, "Women are Epigrams, Epigrams doe goe / Once prest common to all, don't women soe?[57] John Taylor, the Water Poet, in his poem entitled "A Comparison betwixt a Whore and a Booke," asserts:

> To give a Booke the Title of a Whore:
> . . . sure I think no Name befits it more.
> For like a Whore by day-light, or by Candle,
> 'Tis ever free for every knave to handle:
> And as a new whore is belov'd and sought,
> So is a new Booke in request and bought.
> When whores wax old and stale, they're out of date,
> Old Pamphlets are most subject to such fate.

While a text such as Taylor's is a good reminder of the way in which sexual metaphors were broadly applied throughout early modern literary culture, it also, of course, serves to indicate the ways in which erotic writing was often an expression of misogyny. Erotic writing in early modern England was primarily—though not exclusively—a male discourse, and it was as frequently used to express disdain for women and their bodies as it was to celebrate them.

In a British Library manuscript compiled in the mid–seventeenth century by a man named Thomas Crosse, one finds a ballad, with the simple title "A Songe," that offers a humoral classification of women based on the color of their pubic hair.[58] A woman with "a redd haire" has a "moist and dry" nature; women with "yellowe haire / resemblinge golden wire" are insatiable lovers who "will never tire"; "Shee that hath a flaxen haire" and a fair complection runs the risk of being "spoiled" by "the greene sicknes"; a woman with "a browne haire" is threatening: "her natures moist and thicke / oh shee hath haire uppone her geere / longer than yor pricke"; a black haired woman "all men count the best," for "her cunny for the most parte / is allwaies moist and could"—a humoral balance traditionally seen as feminine. The ballad ends with a warning against venereal disease:

> But shee whose haire itt molteth
> and cunny waxeth bald
> her nature is like boylinge lead
> itt will both burne and scald
> therefore I wish all younge men
> for to take heed of such
> for flies that dally with the flame
> are scorched when they touch.

The classifications offered in this song are neither serious nor logical, but the text nonetheless points toward larger social structures of eroticism by which an individual woman's erotic behavior is seen as biologically determined by identifiable, classifiable signs. Ridiculous as such classifications may seem, they nonetheless carry cultural weight: the notion that "blondes have more fun" and the allegedly "feisty" nature of "redheads" are mid-twentieth-century examples of the same phenomenon. While the song's classifications by color of pubic hair in some sense foreshadow the structure of many pornographic Internet pages, in which pictures of women are divided into "blondes," "redheads," and the ubiquitous (and utterly confused) category of "Asians," the song's concluding warning about venereal disease marks its difference from the pornographic forms of the late twentieth century, which almost never mention such issues overtly. In addition, in early modern culture, such classifications, however fanciful, are part of a larger system of humoral physiognomy, which applies to men as well as women. As we have seen in the poem "A medicine for the greene sicknes,"[59] men's sexual prowess is also indicated by the color of pubic hair. Interestingly, in both these poems, black hair is seen as most sexually promising, although in the "song" it is also seen as humorally cold and wet—that is, feminine.[60]

As well as disseminating sexual lore, manuscript erotic verse also gave voice to persistent cultural erotic fantasies. One common subject is a young girl's erotically arousing dream. The most common poem on this topic is entitled simply "A mayde's dream":

> As I lay slumbringe in my bed
> noe creture with me but my Mayden head,
> lying alone as maydens use
> me thought I dreamt as we can hardly choose
> & in my drame me thought I was too much wronge
> being a pretty maide to live alone soe longe
> At last a gallant comes & courts me at once
> twas vertue to say nay, but to be nice
> agreed not with my humor, he was soe long a wooing
> I rather could have wishd he had been doeing
> some other businesse, but at last we agreed
> I[t] weare strange if earnest sutors could not speed
> Me thought we married were & went to bed
> he kisd me sweetly, & bad me be kindhearted
> he turned unto me & so my legs he parted
> And then got up with that for feare I quaked
> I screecht cried out & soe a waked
> It wold vext a saint my blood did burne
> To be soe neare, & misse soe good a turne

(MS Egerton 923, fols. 59r–59v)[61]

Though most poems in manuscript that describe wet dreams attribute such dreams to women—as did Ovid's *Heroides* 15, perhaps the most prominent classical model—two texts printed in *Wit and Drollery*, a 1661 anthology of early-seventeenth-century manuscript poetry, describe men's dreams of women (sigs. E4v–E6).

Another common fantasy, perhaps unsurprisingly, is the voyeuristic one in which a male narrator comes upon a naked woman in an appropriately bucolic landscape. One of the most representative of these poems is Thomas Randolph's "Upon 6 maides bathinge themselves in Cambridge river."[62] In Randolph's poem "a scholler" going for a meditative morning stroll comes upon "Six Venuses at once"—local girls bathing naked in the River Cam. Like many poems of this type, Randolph's poem is coy about whether or not the scholar has sex with any of the maidens. A similar poem, entitled "A fayre Ladye washing herselfe in a River" ends with a shepherd leaping upon the naked bather:

> [He] threw his hooke and scripp asyde and naked leapt unto her
> She shreiking div'd to hyde her selfe, but it was all in vayne
> The waters to preserve her life did beare her upp agayne
> The shepheard tooke her by the hand and ledd her to the brinke
> whear what he did I may not tell; I knowe and you may thinke

(MS Ashmole 38, p. 153)

Texts such as these, insisting as they do on a male narrative voice, on masculine sexual desire for women, and a male community of readers ("I knowe and you may thinke") create the impression that early modern erotic writing was an all-male discourse—a masculine preserve. As I will show, this was not entirely true.

Female Readers of Erotic Manuscript Poetry

While most surviving commonplace books were kept by men, the coteries in which such volumes were written and exchanged could nonetheless include women. We have already encountered the example of the Aston family manuscript now in the Huntington Library that is primarily in the hand of Constantia Fowler. Though far more men than women participated in the manuscript production of poetry, it is certain that women played a greater and more active role in manuscript culture than they did in print culture. Besides the obvious educational biases that assured that in early modern England men were more likely to be literate than women, even literate, educated women were strongly discouraged from having their writing appear in print. As Wendy Wall and others have demonstrated, the emerging figure of the print author was consistently gendered male in contemporary discourses.[63] Thus, as seventeenth-century female writers themselves often pointed out, the stigma attached to print was especially strong in the case of women.[64] While some women did indeed have works printed under their names, it was more common for women to confine their writings to manuscript. In some rare cases, poems in miscellanies are explicitly ascribed to female authors: A verse miscellany of around 1640 contains an amorous poem, entitled "Mrs. Elizabeth Linseys songe," that begins "why should you be so full of spight" and protests the speaker's constancy to her lover (Bodleian MS Rawl. poet. 153 (A), fol. 26v). Indeed, many of the greatest female poets of the seventeenth century, such as Lady Mary Wroth, Mary Sidney, countess of Pembroke, and Katherine Philips ("Orinda"), circulated their works primarily in manuscript.[65] While coteries established in the all-male environment of the universities and the Inns of Court would generally have excluded women, women played an active role in other social settings in which manuscript poetry circulated—in particular at court and in the houses of provincial nobility and gentry.[66] Some women, such as the prolific calligrapher Ester Inglis, even trained as scribes.[67]

Women authors were far more likely to circulate their works in manuscript than in print, and erotic writing was pervasive in manuscript culture. But what is the relation between these two observations? What role did women play in the production and transmission of erotic texts? Although it is impossible to determine the extent of women's readership of erotic texts with any certainty, there is no reason to assume that erotic texts were kept from women readers. Most manuscript miscellanies containing erotic texts mingle them with other types of poetry; if women had access to one of these books they would have been able to read the erotic texts as well as the political, satirical, devotional, and funerary verse (figure 1.1). While many coteries, especially at the universities and the Inns, were doubtless made up entirely of men, manuscripts owned by women often look just like those owned by men.

Very rarely, bawdy poems in manuscript are explicitly ascribed to women authors. A good example of this occurs in the second part of the commonplace book of Sir Stephen Powle, clerk of the crown. Most of Powle's book contains prose copies of letters and state documents, often in the hands of his secretaries. But he frequently uses short poems to fill empty spaces. Thus, in Powle's own hand, one finds a Latin version of a popular English bawdy jest:

> Vespertina Venus an matutina salubris
> Sit magi dum medium bella puella rogat:
> Is contra, fiat si mane salubrior, atque
> Nocte sit Avenus, dulcior esser solet.
> Applaudens maribus respondet Nympha, voluptas
> Sit mihi nocte Venus; site mihi mane salus.

> (Bodleian MS Tanner 169, fol. 68v)

A clumsy translation follows—Sir Stephen presumably did not know the commonly circulated English version:

> A ladie late that now was fullie sped
> Of all the pleasures of a marriage bed
> Askt a physition whether were more fit
> For Venus sports the morning or the night.
> The good olde man made answer as twas meet:
> "The morne more wholesome, but the night more sweet."
> "Nay then, i'fayth," quoth she, "since we have leasure,
> Let's to't each morne for health, each night for pleasure."[68]

The Latin verses are preceded by a note explaining how Sir Stephen found them: "Owld Mr Ked: gave me these verses followinge which he sayd weare made by a learned wooman"—and then, immediately following, in the same hand but differ-

Figure 1.1. *The literate woman in a world of men. Though women were encouraged to read sacred texts, their actual reading went far beyond devotional material. Engraving from John Foxe's* Actes and Monuments *(1563) STC 11222. Henry E. Huntington Library. Shelfmark 59840.*

ent ink—"in Latin: but Dr Franke my tenant sayed he made at the request of a fine Lady."

What can one say of evidence such as this? Whether or not the bawdy Latin verses were actually written by an educated woman, Sir Stephen seems to have found it plausible that they could have been. That is to say, despite the claims of "Dr Franke," that it was believable that women might write bawdy verse, and write it in Latin, at that. In any case, Dr. Franke's remark makes it clear that women were seen as a potential audience for bawdy verse: whether or not she was an author herself, a "fine Lady" might well request a male acquaintance to provide her with copies of erotic texts.

Further indirect evidence for women's familiarity with erotic manuscript texts can be found in a letter written around 1626 from Lady Anne Southwell to Lady

Ridgway, a copy of which is preserved in Southwell's own poetic miscellany.[69] Lady Anne suggests that Lady Ridgway may have come to disdain poetry because "some wanton venus or Adonis hath bene cast before[her] chast eares" (fol. 3v). Though it seems neither Lady Anne nor Lady Ridgway were fond of scurrilous verse it appears they both came in contact with it. Lady Anne's miscellany includes a list of her books (c. 1635) that suggests that her reading was broad and certainly not limited to polite texts (fols. 64v–66). She owned copies of *Orlando Furioso* and "Dr. Donnes Poems" as well as Suetonius's scandalous history *The Twelve Caesars* and Montaigne's *Essays*—in which she could have found his remarkably frank essay on sexual relations, "On Some Verses of Virgil." The fact that Lady Anne's library also contained numerous books on warfare and military strategy, including Machiavelli's *Art of War*, serves as a useful reminder that texts are not only read or owned by those for whom they are primarily intended.

More direct evidence for women's familiarity with erotic texts is found in another Folger manuscript (MS X. d.177), this one a mere scrap of paper containing only eight leaves, several of which are blank. The first sheet is signed four times by "Elizabeth Clarke" whose name also appears on the final sheet, following a short poem that she may have written herself. While some pages are torn or missing, what remains of Elizabeth Clarke's manuscript includes several bawdy jests, such as the following: "a gentlewoman one a time seeing one want a knife she sayd cut my finger he replyed you would say finger my cut" (fol. 3v). Although the jests are childish, there is no doubt Elizabeth was familiar with them. In fact, most are in abbreviated form, as if they were written as mnemonic devises to help their compiler remember their salient points, rather than as full transcriptions.[70]

Elizabeth Clarke's manuscript is just a scrap of paper. Beyond the fact that a woman signed her name on a paper containing lewd jests it cannot tell us much. Questions of women's role in the manuscript system—as compilers, as authors, as readers—can be explored much further by a detailed examination of a duodecimo commonplace book of 155 leaves, believed to have been transcribed around 1630, in the British Library (Add. 10309). Like Anne Southwell's manuscript, this volume is one of the few surviving manuscript verse miscellanies that seems to have been owned by a woman: the final page of the volume bears the signature "Margret Bellasys." There were five different Margarets in the Bellasis family in the early seventeenth century, and the identity of the owner of the volume is unclear, but as Sasha Roberts argues, it is more than likely that the Margaret who signed and presumably read the volume was the eldest daughter of Sir George Selby of Whitehouse, who married Sir William Bellasis of Morton House (County Durham) in 1610–11.[71]

One book cannot tell us what women in general read or wrote or how they felt about it. Nor can it tell us what Margaret Bellasys thought or felt as an individual. But it can teach us something about what one woman (probably) read, and under what conditions she (probably) read it. The three-hundred-page volume is almost entirely devoted to poetic texts, though it opens with a collection of short essays in prose entitled "The Characterismes of vices"—a collection of nineteen thumbnail portraits of the reprobate, from the Flatterer and the Prodigal to the Lustful and the Busy-body. The manuscript is written in one neat italic hand throughout. Though every page has a ruled margin on all four edges, there are no marginalia. Catchwords appear at the bottom of almost every page, even when the next page begins with a new poem. Short poems, especially two-line epigrams, are often used to fill space at the end of pages. The evenness of the hand, the tidiness of the layout, and the presence of catchwords all suggest that the hand is not Margaret's own but rather that of a professional scribe, paid to copy out the book.[72] This raises additional questions. Was the scribe working for Margaret, to copy out poems of her choosing, or was he working for someone else, who then gave the finished book to Margaret?[73] Did Margaret oversee the work? How closely?

One's curiosity about Margaret's collection becomes more acute after examining the following poem, entitled simply "An Elegie."

> where is that hottest fire, which verse is sayd
> To have: is that inchanting fire decay'd
> Venus that drawes natures worke for natures law
> The (her best worke) to her worke cannot draw.
> Hath my love-tears, quencht my poetique fire?
> why quench they not as well my hot desire?
> Though my thoughts creatures, often are with the,
> yet I their forger want that libertie
> Onely thy Image in my hart doth sit
> But it is wax, & fires there surround it
> My fires have drawne, & thine hath drawne that hence
> And I am rob'd of picture, hart, and sense.
> with me still dwells my irkesome memorie,
> which both to keepe and loose, greeves equallie.
> That tells me how faire thou art, even soe faire,
> As Goddesses which I to the compare
> Are grac'd by the, & to make blind men see
> what things good are, I sweare they are like the.
> ffor if we justly call each sillie man
> A Microcosme, what shall we call the then?
> Thou art not soft, & cleare ; but straight, & faire,
> As downe & stars, Cedars to lillies are.
> But thy faire hand, & checke, & eye trulie
> Are like thy other hand, & cheeke, & eye.
> Such was my fancy once but shall be never
> As thou wast, art, & maist you be so ever.
> Heare Lovers sweare in their Idolatry
> That I am none, but griefe discovers me.
> And yet I grieve the lesse, least griefe remove
> My beauty & make me unworthy of thy love.
> Me in a glasse I call the, but the a lasse

wher I would kisse, tears dims my eies & glasse.
(Deere) cure this loving madnesse and restore
My self to me, my hart, my all, and more,
So may thy cheekes out-weare the scarlet dye,
Thy face out-lustre the most glorious skye.
So may thy much amazing beautie move
In women envie; and in all men love
And change & sicknesse be as far from the
As thou by coming neere keepe them from me.

(fols. 95r–95v)

If this poem seems oddly familiar, that is because it is a version of the verses now known commonly by the title "Sappho to Philaenus" and usually attributed to John Donne. There is nothing remotely sapphic, however, about Margaret's version. A section of twenty-four lines has been excised from the middle of the poem, removing all explicit and implicit description of lesbian love, and leaving in its place a seamless, if somewhat flat poem dealing with more conventional passions between man and woman. Gone are the lines "Likeness begets such strange self flattery, / That touching myself, all seems done to thee," which give resonance to the poem's image of the looking-glass and also suggest autoeroticism. Gone as well is the complete poem's witty critique of the love of men:

> why shouldst thou then
> Admit the tillage of a harsh rough man?
> Men leave behind them that which their sin shows,
> And are as thieves traced, which rob when it snows.

And gone is the poem's celebration of the nonprocreative delights of sex between women:

> But of our dalliance no more signs there are,
> Than fishes leave in streams, or birds in air.
> And between us all sweetness may be had;
> All, all that Nature yields, or Art can add.

Of these familiar passages, no more signs there are than fishes leave in streams, or birds in air.

Since many compilers changed poems in the process of transcription—adding verses, deleting lines, or even recasting poems written in one verse form into another,[74] on one level, there is nothing very remarkable in this reworking of "Sappho to Philaenus." Yet the fact that this manuscript was proabably owned by a woman tempts one to ask questions about principles of inclusion and to examine the collection for signs of a feminine viewpoint or a woman's voice, especially—given the elisions in Margaret's Sappho—of a female perspective on eroticism and sexuality. But tempting as such inquiry is, it is doomed to failure. Why were the lines describing lesbian sex excised from Margaret Bellasys's copy of "Sappho to Philaenus"? Did she choose to omit them? Was she unaware of their existence? Would she have added them had she been aware? Did she care at all? At this remove, we cannot know. Miscellanies are not homogenous documents. They are not analogous to diaries, and they do not pretend to reveal the truth of the self. Instead, they collect texts brought together by their compilers from a wide range of sources for a variety of reasons. One should not automatically assume that the fact a text is copied in a manuscript suggests that the compiler agreed with the sentiments the verse expresses.

One might think lines are missing from Margaret's "Sappho" because of their sexual explicitness. Another poem in the manuscript, entitled "In praise of his mistresse parts" (fols. 104–106v), offers a model for this sort of decorous silence. The poet describes each part of the mistress' body in detail, until he reaches her genitals, at which point "[his] pen halts"; "For my Muse stops me, & sayes to me No / Leave that, describe the rest, then on I goe" (fol. 105v). An epigram found elsewhere in the volume praises abstinence from sensual delights: "He that in youth is not to pleasures given / May smile in death, & dying sing in heaven" (fol. 53). And in the moralistic prose condemnation of vices that opens the manuscript, lust is seen as an exclusively male failing. The "Character of the Lustful" (fols. 7–8v) attacks male promiscuity in no uncertain terms. "The lustful man," it begins, "is a monster . . . carelesse of his owne name, of his owne soule," who is characterized by his perversion of female virtue.

From the evidence assembled thus far, one might be led to assume Margaret Bellasys felt (or was encouraged to believe) that lustfulness was an exclusively masculine trait. While it is unlikely that Margaret Bellasys authored "The Characterisms of the Vices," whatever she thought of "The Character of the Lustful," of lustful men, or of her own lusts, her miscellany does not heed the text's warning about lascivious language. Far from avoiding erotic subject matter, her book is filled with lustful, flirtatious, and lascivious texts that deal with sexual relations from a wide variety of perspectives. And in these texts, lustful desires are by no means confined to men. As another epigram in the collection admits, although social conventions may cause women to conceal their desires, they exist all the same: "women are nice when simple men doe crave it / And will say No, when the[y] fain'st would have it" (fol. 84v).

Scholars studying manuscript miscellanies have often dismissed the erotic works found in them by appealing to the notion that many of the collections were written by adolescent boys.[75] But this hypothesis is inadequate to explain the erotic verse in Margaret's volume, a collection belonging to an aristocratic woman living on a country estate. For example, three short poems on erotic subjects, differing widely in tone and attitude, are included (fols. 45–46). The first is courtly and refined:

> The fragrant flowers the Lillie and the Rose
> ffor smell and show, all other flowers exceed,
> The rose for smell, the Lilly next we chose
> ffor colour fayre to be the princely head.
> I love a Rose, but Lilly holds my hart,
> The rose for smell, the Lillie for desart.

The second is a bawdy jest:

> A Gallant lasse from out her window saw
> A Gentleman whose nose in lenth exceeded
> her boundlesse will, not limited by Law
> Imagin'd he had that which she most needed;
> To speake with him she kindly doth intreat
> And him desir'd to solve her darke suppose.
> She deeming every thing was made compleat,
> And correspondent equall to his nose,
>   But finding short where she expected long,
> She sigh'd & sayd, O nose thou'st done me wrong.

The third is simple and personal:

> Sweet I cannot be from you:
> ffor all my sense are on you:
> And what I thinke it is of you:
> That which I seeke it is in you:
> All that I doe shall be for you:
> Thus all that I am it is you:

Erotic texts are found throughout the manuscript: a satire on the lust of puritan women (fols. 60v–62); anatomical blazons of female beauty (fols. 71v–73r, fols. 104r–106v); Donne's ironic praise of polygamy in his elegy "Variety" (fol. 54r); a poem celebrating Venus's victory over Mars (fol. 88v); a poem mocking a young man too dense to realize when a woman is flirting with him (fol. 59v). As is often the case in early modern manuscript miscellanies of poetry, erotic poems are not set apart from other types of text in Margaret's volume.[76] On two consecutive pages (fols. 62v–63r), for example, a witty poem critical of Protestantism is followed by a bawdy jest, which is followed in turn by a solemn epitaph.[77]

How did Margaret come by these poems—did someone give her the book? Is it a copy—or, as the elisions in "Sappho to Philaenus" might suggest, an expurgated copy—of an inns or University manuscript compiled by some male friend or relative?[78] If so, the copy text has not survived. In terms of its contents, Margaret's manuscript is as varied as any volume associated with the young male wits of the universities and the Inns of Court. It contains some texts to my knowledge found nowhere else, as well as many that were quite popular. Besides the truncated "Sappho to Philaenus," there are other poems by Donne, including "Break of Day" (fol. 48v), "The Will" (fols. 50v–51), "Variety" (fols. 53v–54v), "A Valediction, Forbidding Mourning" (fols. 126r–127r); "The Broken Heart" (fols. 127r–127v); "The Message" (fols. 132–32v), and "The Indifferent" (fol. 141v). The manuscript contains poems by Jonson and Carew, by Richard Corbett and Thomas Randolph, Walton Poole's "If Shadows be a Picture's Excellence" (fols. 47v–48r), and William Basse's epitaph on Shakespeare (fol. 119v) as well as a copy of Shakespeare's second sonnet (fol. 148r). It also includes two of the most popular scurrilous poems of the period—the ubiquitous epitaph on Mr. Prick of

Christ's College quoted earlier (fol. 145r) and that staple of university manuscripts "The Parliament Fart"—a lengthy satire on Henry Ludlow's famous gastric accident during the parliamentary debate on Union in 1607 (fols. 123r–124v).[79] In fact, like the collections kept by young men, Margaret's volume has much political verse, including several poems satirizing the Duke of Buckingham (fols. 39v, 40r–41r, 42r–44r, etc.)—one of which accuses the Duke of effeminacy; a poem on social mobility that begins "a beggar got a beadle" (fol. 83r); a satire against Louis XIII of France by Thomas Goodwyn (fols. 101r–103r); two epigrams on the fall of the earl of Essex (fols. 103v, 142v); a poem protesting the impeachment of Sir Francis Bacon (fols. 128v–132r); and a series of poems critical of yearly memorials to Prince Henry (fol. 150v–151r). As far as religious matters go, there are several pro-Catholic pieces (fols. 62v–63r, 148v–149v, 152v), as well as some anti-Puritan satire (fols. 142r, 148r).

Texts in Margaret's manuscript display a wide variety of attitudes toward women. Jonson's antifeminist song from *Epicoene* "Still to be neat" is found in the volume (fol. 100v), as is Sir John Roe's elegy to Jonson's nemesis, the female poet, wit, and courtier Cecelia Bulstrode (fols. 66v–67r). There is a poem critical of pampered women (fol. 58r) and another praising country women over city women, which warns of the dangers of urban life (fols. 78r–79r). Another, by Joshuah Sylvester, warns young women against seducers (fols. 133v–134r). Texts praising and blaming women are often found in close proximity. One finds the popular epigram "We men have many faults, women but two/No good can they speake, no good can they doe" (fol. 103), followed immediately by William Browne's "Epitaph on the Death of the Countesse of Pembroke" (fol. 103v), which praises "Sidney's sister, Pembroke's mother" and declares that her greatest monument shall be "Some kinde woman borne as she."[80] A poem entitled "Erat Quidem homo" (fol. 108v), which jokingly argues there has never been such a thing as certainty in women, is followed by another called "Erat quidam mulier," which forcefully contends "That no man yet could in the Scripture finde/A Certaine woman, argues men are blinde" (fols. 108v–109r). The poem goes on to list several biblical examples of female virtue, including the Virgin Mary. The first of these texts is usually found alone, without the rebuttal. Perhaps here we have an example of Margaret responding as a reader to the texts she encountered. On the other hand, it is a common feature of miscellanies to pair poems presenting arguments for and against women[81]—a habit that would come naturally to men trained to argue *pro* and *contra* in university debates. While, as Arthur Marotti suggests, it is possible that many anonymous texts found in miscellanies were composed by women,[82] poems such as John Donne's "Break of Day," in which male authors "ventriloquise" women's voices, are also quite common. One must be wary when attempting to judge the sex of an author on the basis of subject matter and point of view. If one came upon the catalogue of Lady Anne Southwell's books without knowing to whom it belonged, one might immediately assume a male owner based on the preponderance of historical and military texts.

The poems in Margaret's manuscript contain a wide range of attitudes toward female sexuality. Some poems are outspoken in their praise of women's desires (fols. 54v, 57v); others are harshly critical (fol. 145r). Perhaps the elisions in "Sappho" can best be explained by the other glaring omission in Margaret's manuscript. Among its erotic verse, Margaret's book contains one of the six surviving manuscript versions of Thomas Nashe's "Choice of Valentines," a poem that in other manuscripts is entitled "Nashe's Dildo."[83] Margaret's version, while including much explicit description of sexual intercourse, omits the poem's most scandalous feature—the dildo that Francis, the poem's female protagonist, uses to satisfy herself after her lover Tomalin has failed her. Margaret's text of the poem, entitled "Gnash his valentine," follows complete versions closely, but ends at line 232—concluding with Francis's complaint of the transience of sexual pleasure and her frustration with Tomalin's inadequacy. The Bellasys text leaves its readers with the eloquent voicing of a woman's dissatisfaction without offering the solution of the dildo; it thus becomes a narrative that stresses female sexual frustration rather than focusing—as more complete versions of the poem do—on male anxiety about sexual performance. As I will show in a later chapter, "Choice of Valentines" was frequently altered in transmission—sometimes drastically so, and the radical differences between surviving texts reveal much about debates over sexuality and gender identity in the period.

When one considers the elisions in "Sappho to Philaenus" and "Choice of Valentines" in light of the contents of the volume as a whole, it seems that what Margaret was missing was not accounts of sexual relations but accounts of autonomous female pleasure—sex between women and masturbation. When it comes to women engaging in sexual activity without men, it seems, the "pen halts" (fol. 105v). One might be tempted to go on from this observation to posit a theory of what sexual knowledge was and was not acceptable for transmission to daughters of the gentry in the early seventeenth century. But one would be wrong to do so: miscellanies are not homogenous documents. The dildo erased in one place pops up in another. A poem against male jealousy on folio 49 of the volume, beginning "When you sit musing Ladie all alone," describes female sexual desire in terms that insist on its power—including its power to use an "instrument" in the place of a male partner:

> Debar her Lord, she to supply his rome
> will take a serving-man or stable groome
> Suspect her faith with all & all distrust
> She'le have a monkey to supply her lust.
> Locke her from man & beastes from all content
> She'le make him cuckold with an instrument
> ffor women are like angry mastives chain'd
> They bite at all, when they're from all restrain'd
> You may set lockes & keies to [ ] their fires
> But have no means to quench their hot desires
> Man may as well with running goe about
> To stop the Sunne.

"Where is the hottest fire which verse is said to have?" In Margaret's manuscript the enchanting fire is not so much decayed as masked. The fiery sun of female sexuality may shine through clouds of antifeminist polemic, but it shines all the same. As another poem in her collection, anonymous but speaking in a woman's voice, puts it:

> Shall savage things more fredome have
> Then Nature unto woman gave?
> The Swan, the Turtle, & the Sparrow
> Doe bill & kisse: then take thy marrow
> They bill & kisse, what else they doe
> Come bill & kisse and I'le shew you.
>
> (fol. 54v)

Manuscript Exchange and Erotic Friendship

To judge by her manuscript miscellany, erotic writing played a fundamental role in Margaret's reading. This is not to insist on the primacy of erotic texts in the volume—one could also focus on the political or devotional texts in the collection. But as two poems in Margaret's book suggest, eroticism was not only an element within collections: the exchange of texts could itself be eroticized. The first of these poems (fols. 83v–84r) is entitled "upon his sending his M[istress] a booke." In this text, the lover sending a book to his mistress sees his book as an emblem that "boldly may my true love signifie," and he speculates that

> she may please some-while
> In sporting moodes to use the for her mate.
> Then shalt thou swim in seas of heavenly blise,
> Injoying oft her deerest companie

He imagines the "high advancement" and "height of Joyes" the book will enjoy when "on her lap [it] sitts." Here the book is imagined as taking the place of the lover himself, representing him, standing in for him, an extension of his body. A few pages later is a similar poem: "upon Sydneis Aracadia sent to his M[istress]" (fols. 86v–87v). Once it is held by the narrator's mistress, the Arcadia—"the most delicious booke that is"—will "swim in seas of blessednesse / in sweetest sweets, & heavens delightfulnesse," held "in sweetest bands," "happie" to feel her "tender touch." In turn, her eyes will "boyle with fresh desires" as she reads the Arcadia's "layes" of "strange passion" done "in the aptest fashion."

Whether or not Margaret's book was itself presented to her by a man with access to the Inns and university coteries in which many of its texts circulated, in both of her poems on the erotic exchange of texts the gift is given to a woman by a male lover. But women could send bawdy texts to men too. One such text, consisting of a collection of worn papers covered with verses and scraps of poetry in an extravagant hand,[84] dating probably from the mid–seventeenth century, has survived buried in the midst of a large composite quarto manuscript in the British Library (MS Harley 7332, fols. 40–51v). Some of the pages are damaged, and some texts only partly legible. Besides John Harington's epigram 404, "Of a Lady that Left Open her Cabinet"—not here ascribed—the authors of the poems are unknown.

On the first of the twelve leaves, the following appears:

> ffeargod Barbon of Daventry in the County of Northampton being at
> many times Idle and wanting employment beestod the time with his
> penne & inke writing these sonnets songes and epigrames that it weare
> better so to do for the mendinge of his hand in wrighting than worse to
> bestow the time. (fol. 40r)

Almost every page is signed, in letters sometimes an inch high, "FEARGOD BARBON" or sometimes "FEAREGOD HONOR THE RIGHT." The identity of this oddly named compiler is unclear—it may be a parodic reference to Praisegod Barbon (1598–1679), a Puritan preacher and radical M.P. But besides the well-known (and often mocked) Praisegod Barbon, there was "another prominent puritan" by the name of Barbon, living in Northamptonshire, in the period.[85] And so, while this ragged collection of obscene verse may constitute a parody or a prank, it is nevertheless possible that a radical Puritan politician named Feargod Barbon did exercise himself in the transcription of these poems (figure 1.2).

The poems with which Feargod Barbon occupied his idle hands are well represented by the following dialogue:

> [SHE:] Come drinke old ale with mee Ile call
>   Come drinke old ale with mee
>   And I will brooche a new vessall
>   A foote above my knee
> [HE:]   And can you not singe nig noge
>   And will you not nig nog mee
>   And sell thy petticoate smocke and all
>   And pawne this c[un]t ffor mee
> [SHE:] And I can singe nig nog
>   And well I would nig nog thee
>   And sell my petticoate smocke & all
>   And pawne my c[un]t ffor thee
>   And pawne my c[un]t for thee
>
>   (fol. 50v)

While this poem gives a good indication of the subject matter of most of the texts in the volume, the tone and form of Feargod's songs, sonnets, and epigrams are widely varied. Some, like this poem, are very likely to have been songs whose transmission was more often oral than written. Other poems include a narrative of an erotic dream, pastoral lyrics and laments for lost love, a bawdy ballad on maying, and Harington's lewd epigram. All that unites these texts is their focus on sex between men and women: some poems are crude, some are tender; some

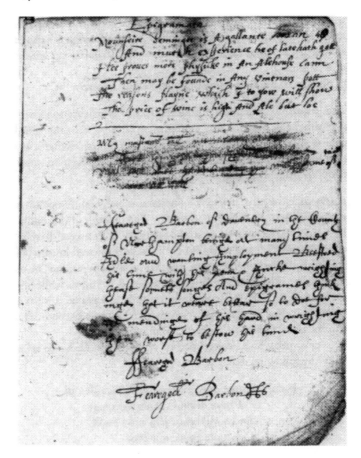

Figure 1.2. *A page from Feargod Barbon's manuscript—whose bawdy poems were given to him, he claims, by a female friend. (MS Harl. 7332, fol. 48r) By Permission of the British Library.*

serious, some comic; some are misogynist, some are not; some follow sophisticated literary conventions, others are scraps of street verse.

Perhaps—given its coy references to idle hands—Feargod Barbon's manuscript was designed to fulfill the function of arousing the autoerotic imagination that is now commonly seen as characteristic of pornography. If so, as the following poem, which begins the manuscript, suggests, this imagination was not seen as being exclusively masculine.

> This Booke wast given me by A frende
> To Reade And overlooke
> Because she often Did Commende
> The pleasure that shee tooke

By readinge it I needes would Crave
This gistore At her hande
Which shee Did grante I straighte should have
To be At my Commande
I tooke it then being ofte Desired
To read it for her sake
I have performed what she required
And Did sutch pleasure take
That twice or thrice I red it over
And plainely there Did ffinde
I received good that did before
Commend the same in minde
Wherefore to show my thankefulnes
Unto my frend so kinde
I wish that shee all happynes
for evar more may Fynd.
                              Finis

                    per me Fearegod Barbon
                              (fol. 40r)

According to this verse, the bawdy poems in Barbon's manuscript are the gift of a female friend, who herself has taken (possibly autoerotic) pleasure in reading them. Barbon reads it "for her sake" and in taking pleasure himself, acts as "she required." Erotic discourse is not conceived of here as the exclusively male one characteristic of literary pornography in later centuries but as a provocative, exciting exchange between male and female "friends." That Barbon, contrary to common practice, produced a manuscript in which almost all the poems were erotic does *not* indicate that in doing so he was constructing a realm of exclusively male fantasy, from which female sexual agency and desire were excluded. In fact, two poems from the manuscript deal comically with male impotence and sexual failure.[86]

In addition, such texts provide useful evidence on the larger question of eroticized "friendship" in the early modern period. As has long been recognized, the concept of friendship in the early modern period is a complex one.[87] Friendship was often idealized as a relationship between equals, and it was often argued that such relationships were only possible between people of the same sex, since men were thought superior to women. Some scholars have seen early modern friendship as being ideally a fundamentally pure and therefore asexual relationship; others, noting that the emotional passions associated with friendship are often described in the language of eroticism, have argued that such relationships could well have been erotic. Erotic texts found in manuscripts demonstrate that the word "friend"—whatever its general cultural valence—could also refer to a lover of either gender, especially to a sexual partner with whom one was particularly intimate. In a court manuscript dating from the first years of the seventeenth century (British Library MS Add. 22601), these lines appear in an erotic poem that begins "More sweet contentment have I had wth thee": "The pleasure wth a naked freind is sweete / where 2 kinde freinds in kindly friendship meete" (fol. 84–85). This erotic pleasure with a naked friend (of indeterminate gender) is contrasted to the brutish sexual pleasures of the unlearned:

> The vulgar people know not what it is
> to act th[e] furious sport is all their bliss
> They know not what to daliance pertaineth
> Nor feele th[ei] what th[e] hand of kindnes gaineth
> Embracements full of pleasure, full of secreat joy
> w[ch] kills all sorrow & ill griefs destroy
> It makes th[e] spirits quick w[th]in th[e] flesh
> & every member stirringe light & fresshe

Another poem (in Bodleian MS Rawl. poet 172) makes graphically clear that while the vocabulary of friendship was often eroticized, so too erotic relations between men and women could be described in the terminology of friendship:

> Two freinds affecting one each other
> Did putt there bellies the one against the other
> and did when they were so disposed
> the thinge they would not have disclosed
> the work was sure they did so grinne
> The one sate up the other did put in
> The thinge was harde & stiffe did stand
> wch shee vouchsaft to take in hand
> ffor length twas a handfull longe and more
> wch stopt where was a hole before
> there labour lasted late at night
> they felt it cominge wth delight
> there buttockes moved toe & froe
> and from the hole a rich juyce did flowe

(fols. 3v)[88]

Another poem (MS Folger V. a. 345, p. 289) refers to an unmarried man's female lover as "his effeminate friend." Such usage makes it difficult to see friendship in the early modern period as a purely platonic relationship of spiritual companionship, opposed to eroticism by its very nature. In commonplace books, eroticism is everywhere.

By this point it should be clear that a survey of erotic manuscript poetry such as I have provided can do little more than scratch the surface of the vast amount of extant material. There are over one hundred surviving manuscript collections containing substantial quantities of erotic verse, almost all of which would repay the sort of detailed study that I have given to only one or two collections here. For now, I hope that certain large points are clear: much erotic writing circulated primarily in manuscript, rather than print, and erotic writing played a significant, even crucial role in manuscript culture. Manuscript collections are inherently heterogeneous documents, presenting a variety of ideologies and points of view, few of which can straightforwardly be identified with the personal sentiments of either an identifiable author or of a compiler. Not only do collections contain a generically wide range of texts, they also present a wide range of gender ideologies and responses to sexual activities, passions, and practices. Manuscript erotic texts, while primarily male-authored and overwhelmingly representing a masculine view of sexual activity, were not limited to an exclusively male readership. And coterie circulation of texts—a social activity that embodied and established networks of friendship and patronage—was also, at times, conceived of as a flirtatious, erotic activity.

While manuscript erotic texts do not all deal with the issues of effeminacy and national identity that are the focus of the rest of this study, it is literally impossible to discuss early modern erotic writing without acknowledging the important role of erotic texts in manuscript culture. Manuscript miscellanies provided a forum for the formulation, articulation, and transmission of social attitudes and debates on a wide range of subjects, from political policy to gender identity. While they were not necessarily private documents in the sense that diaries and journals would later be, they did circulate in a social space relatively free from censorship. Ideas that could not safely be printed could be expressed, shared, and debated in manuscript. Although the chapters that follow deal not only with manuscript texts but also with those printed and sold in the book market and those staged in the public theaters, the attitudes expressed in all these texts—about masculinity, about Englishness—were formed and debated in a literary culture in which manuscript circulation and the habits of thinking and reading that that culture encouraged were of crucial importance.

The integration of erotic writing with other forms of poetry in commonplace books could only encourage the view, frequently expressed in the period, that *all* poetry was effeminizing and corrupting and that it undermined traditional notions of appropriate masculine behavior. Men ought to spend their time learning martial skills like riding or archery rather than writing sonnets, reading epigrams, or singing ballads. The sense that poetry, and erotic poetry in particular, posed a serious threat to society was intensified by the fact that poetry was a social rather than purely private activity in the period. In addition, poems produced in the relatively limited environment of a gentlemen's coterie tended to circulate more widely than the original producers intended. As we have seen, women read erotic poetry, and so did commoners. Furthermore, the burgeoning book market at Paul's Cross ensured that poems like *Astrophil and Stella*, Marlowe's translations of Ovid, and Shakespeare's sonnets were accessible to an audience far more socially heterogeneous than the private friends for whom such works were originally written. The conditions of manuscript circulation—its integration of eroticism into other social spheres, its social, collaborative nature, and the fact that it was very difficult to limit circulation of manuscript texts—all helped insure that erotic writing and its social effects would be a particular source of anxiety, concern, and fascination in early modern England.

Erotic Writing, Effeminacy,
and National Identity

Erotic Texts on Stage: "The Custom of the Country"

Metamorphiz'd Mick: where's thy Target man?
What chaung'd into a lisping Ladies fann?
Is dubb a dubb Bellonas warlike noates,
Chaunged to fa la la, streind through shrill Eunukes throates?
Art turn'd from grimm-fac't Mars his valiaunce,
To smiling Venus hir tempting daliaunce?
Me thinkes those leggs oft harnest with bright steele,
To twind with Nimphes weake limmes no sweet should feele,
Hast learn'd to skipp, smyle, kisse, & looke demure?
I'th steede of charge or raise a counter mure.
    For shame reechaunge, thou maiden-chaunged Mick
    Come use thy pyke; tha'st use'd too long thy—

This poem, satire 62 in William Goddard's collection *A Mastiff Whelp* (sig. E4r)—published in 1598, probably at Dort in the Netherlands—sets out in admirably clear and detailed terms one of the structural principles of English notions of gender identity in the early modern period: the opposition between aggressive, martial, active masculinity and enervated, sensuous, passive femininity. Mick, the poem's subject, has been "metamorphiz'd"—his shape has been changed from male to female. The change is expressed in a wide variety of registers. Mick serves not Mars, god of War, but Venus, goddess of love (figure 2.1). His "target," or shield, has been changed into a "Ladies fan." The martial trumpet's deep "war-like notes" have changed to the delicate high-pitched tones of a castrato. The masculine skills required for a martial charge have been replaced by womanly skills of seduction: skipping, smiling, kissing, and looking demure. Mick now seduces his foes instead of storming them.

Mick has clearly abandoned his natural gender role. But why? Why do Mick's manly legs prefer the feel of a nymph's soft skin to a harness of steel armor? As the poem's last couplet suggests, Mick's metamorphosis has been brought on by

Figure 2.1. *Adulterous sex and its effeminizing punishment: Mars and Venus make love as Vulcan forges the chains to bind them.* Mars and Venus Embracing with Vulcan at His Forge, *Enea Vico, after Parmigianino, engraving, dated 1543 (Bartsch 27 1/3; Ailsa Mellon Bruce Fund 1972.34.5). National Gallery of Art, Washington, D.C.*

inappropriate activity: he has used his prick instead of his pike. His engagement in erotic activity—even in an appropriately masculine capacity—has resulted in effeminate weakness. Two aspects of Mick's effeminacy are particularly noteworthy: first, his masculinity is *not* seen primarily in biological terms—he is a man not because he has a prick but because he knows how to use a pike. Rather than being an emblem of his masculinity, Mick's prick is the agent of his effeminacy. Second, Mick's effeminacy is not simply a private, personal problem—it is a public, social one. If Mick has forgotten how to use his pike, England is the weaker for it.

Unremarkable as poetry, the verses in Goddard's volume are nonetheless typical examples of the satiric writing of early modern England. They are aimed at a wide range of "abuses": he attacks flamboyant gallants, impoverished students, criminal youth, fraudulent doctors, foppish courtiers, foolish gulls, shrewd con men, mannish women, and effeminate men. What most of his targets have in common is their failure to maintain their proper social status. They are not what they seem; they dress beyond their station, pretend to authority beyond their wealth, and fail to fulfill their proper social or familial or gender roles. All these figures are set against Goddard himself. In an introductory verse "To the Reader," Goddard identifies himself as a "Souldyer" and apologizes for the harshness of his satiric style by admitting that soldiers "the bluntest are of men" (sig. A2). In marked contrast to the figures he ridicules, Goddard presents himself as straightforward and honest. What you see is what you get. Goddard's bluff openness is itself an emblem of his gender identity. The roughness of his verse, as of his manner, is a sign of his manliness; the volume he has brought forth is figured as a fierce masculine beast—a "Mastif whelpe which bites." It is no pretty creature, he says "to please a ladyes sight."[1]

While effeminacy is only one of the many social transgressions attacked by Goddard, it was nonetheless a focus of concern throughout Elizabethan and Jacobean culture. Though it is misleading to suggest that anxieties over gender identity were the paramount social concern of the time, such issues are surprisingly prevalent in the surviving writing of the period. While as Laura Levine, Steven Orgel, and others have demonstrated, concerns about effeminacy often focused on the public stage with its tradition of crossdressed men playing female roles, fears and fantasies about the erosion of English manhood were by no means limited to the discourses in and around the theater. Most important, as Goddard's Mick suggests, concerns about effeminacy were seen as having public as well as private consequences. In the patriarchal ideology of the period, the English nation was in many ways identical with English manhood. And as I will show, notions of manhood and effeminacy were frequently bound up with the opposition between the native and the foreign.

In the mid–1650s a man by the name of John Evans set about compiling a collection of memorable excerpts from the English texts of the preceding seventy-five years. It was to be entitled *Hesperides, or the Muses Garden,* and gathered texts from a wide range of authors, including Shakespeare, Jonson, Beaumont and Fletcher, Francis Bacon, Robert Burton, Chapman, Crashaw, Milton, and Sidney. In the manner of scholars' commonplace books that collected important passages from classical texts, Evans grouped his quotations under subject headings. Though his massive compendium was entered in the Stationer's Register by the eminent printer Humphrey Moseley in 1655, it was never published. It does, however, survive in manuscript,[2] and the entries under the heading "Effeminacy" (p. 251) provide an excellent compendium of early modern attitudes toward the subject.

Evans's first selection demonstrates the wide range of disorder associated with effeminacy. Effeminacy entails a surrender not only to the pleasures of sex with women but to almost any kind of sensual pleasure—from eating fine food to playing games of dice or tennis. It is the rejection of manly reason, an indulgence in sensation:

> What can one imagine more weake & childish, then to have received a courage from god, capable to conquer heaven & to employ it in petty fopperies, wherein thoughts better part & the dayes actions, are wasted, to court a Ladie, to gormandize a banquet, nicely to quarrell upon interpretation of a word, to buy plumes of feathers, to confuse mens apparel, to dress himself up for danceing, to play at dice, to hold a racket in a Tennis Court, to play the Buffon in a Jeast, to divulge a secret, to forge a calumny, to envy one greater then himself, to despise equals, to baffle inferiours, & a 1000 suchlike other practises.[3]

A surrender to pleasure results in a loss of masculinity, which manifests itself as specifically social disorder. The man who indulges in dancing, tasty food, witty wordplay, sumptuous clothes, tennis-playing, and buffoonery will end up making a mockery of the social order—envying his superiors instead of deferring to them, being contemptuous of the social equals with whom he should bond in masculine friendship, and mistreating those beneath him. The effeminacy of one man will lead to a thousand abuses.

And, as in the case of Goddard's Metamorphiz'd Mick, these abuses have national consequences, as the longest of Evans's excerpts makes clear. As a cautionary tale of the dangers of effeminacy, he puts forward the case of

> [t]he Sybarites, an effeminat kind of people, who live so intoxicated and addicted to dances & balls that not so much as the horses but learned to dance. In the meane time their enemies awakened them—they were forced to take arms for the defence of their lives. They drew into the field a brave squadron of Cavalry, the flower & strength of the Citie, but a fidler hearing the approach mounted on those dauncing horses, promised their Adversaries to deliver them into their hands—He began to strike up his Violin, & the horses to bestir themselves in dancing, to break all their ranks, & put the army into disorder, which shamefully made them become a prey to their enemies.

This tale of the Sybarites, clearly too fanciful to be taken literally, has a serious and obvious symbolic significance: an effeminated, intoxicated nation will not be able to defend itself militarily. The Sybarites fall because the "flower and strength of the city"—the mounted nobility—are too effeminate to control their horses.

Goddard's Mick is clearly not an aristocrat—he is a pikeman, a footsoldier. Anxieties about effeminacy, though generally preserved for us in texts written by middle or upper-class men, did not focus exclusively on a particular social class. On the one hand, there was a concern about the habits of common men, who could easily be seduced from proper masculine behavior by such corrupting elements of urban life as prostitutes, pamphlets, and plays. On the other, it was feared that luxurious habits and soft living would effeminate the aristocracy. Concerns about effeminacy in early modern England can thus be seen as responses to two contemporary shifts in social and cultural conditions. First, urban growth—and the development of urban institutions like public playhouses and the book market—was creating new and disturbing sites and possibilities for sensual corruption. Second, the process of what historians have called courtization—by which a warrior aristocracy was slowly transformed into an educated, cultivated nobility that valued eloquence and grace more than physical force—was changing the notion of what noble manly virtue should entail.

As is clear from Evans's excerpts, effeminacy resulted in a wide range of inappropriate behavior. Such behavior could be provoked in a huge number of ways. In fact, effeminacy as a concept is extraordinarily multivalent. Short of living a ferociously Spartan life engaged in military service—like Shakespeare's young

Mark Anthony, who was said to have drunk "the stale of horses" and eaten "the roughest berry, on the rudest hedge" (*Anthony and Cleopatra* 1.4.62–4)—there was little a man might do that could not, in some context or other, be labeled effeminate. And, as the example of Anthony suggests, masculinity was a condition that had to be continuously monitored and upheld. Anthony's vigorous youth did not stop him from succumbing to Egyptian sensuality in middle age.

As Goddard's Mick demonstrates, the contradictions in early modern notions of masculinity were revealed most starkly in notions about masculine sexuality. On the one hand, the penis served as a potent marker of difference between men and women. And male dominance was seen to be proven by the act of physical sexual penetration of the bodies of women—and also of boys. Yet the very sexual act that set active masculinity off from passive femininity was itself seen as debilitating. We don't know exactly what "maiden-changed Mick" has been doing with his prick, though it seems from context that he has been having sex with "Nimphes." But, as we have seen already, his presumed potency in sexual encounters with women does not make him masculine. Instead it is the cause of his effeminacy (figure 2.2).

Sexual activity is seen as effeminizing in the period in part because women were perceived to be more sexually active and avid than men. One of the texts that sets out most clearly the perceived incompatibility between male and female capacities for sexual pleasure is Fletcher and Massinger's play *The Custom of the Country*, entered in the Stationers' Register on February 22, 1619, and first performed by the King's Men around 1619–20. Though virtually unknown to modern scholarship, the play was quite popular in its day—it was still being performed in 1628 and was acted at court before Charles I in 1630 and 1638.

After the Restoration, it was twice revived—on January 2 and August 1, 1667. Samuel Pepys, an avid theater-goer, saw both of these productions though he liked neither of them. Although the play does not seem to have pleased Restoration audiences, it was certainly not because it was dull. After the second performance, Richard Legh remarked that the play was "so damn'd bawdy that the Ladyes flung their peares and fruites at the actors."[4] And in his preface to *Fables Ancient and Modern* (1700), John Dryden—defending his own writing from charges of immorality—wrote "There is more Baudry in one play of Fletcher's, called *The Custom of the Country*, than in all ours together."[5]

Although it is filled with bawdy episodes, ideologically Fletcher's play is a conservative defense of marriage. It condemns the odd custom that dictates

> That when a maid is contracted
> And ready for the tye o' the Church, the Governour
> He that commands in chiefe, must have her maiden-head
> Or ransom it for mony at his pleasure.

> (1.1.29–32)

It also celebrates the wedded chastity of its central characters, Arnoldo and Zenocia, whose virtue is threatened by the evil governor Count Clodio.

Figure 2.2. *Effeminate exhaustion; Mars sleeps in Venus's bower as cupids play with his armor. Sandro Botticelli's panel painting* Venus and Mars, *c. 1485 (69.2 x 173.4 cm, NG 915). National Gallery, London.*

It is likely that the pears and fruits of the female spectators were directed not at the ideal couple whose story forms the play's main plot but at the scandalous subplot, in which Rutillio, a hot-blooded rake, is made a slave in a male brothel—a brothel whose customers are all female (3.3). Randy as he is, Rutillio is soon reduced to a walking corpse by his exertions on behalf of his female clients (4.5). He is eventually rescued, renounces whoring forever (5.1), and ends the play safely betrothed, like his virtuous friends. The play stresses throughout the importance of personal repentance and reformation. The wedded love of Arnoldo and Zenocia shows itself invincible—not only do the lovers overcome temptation, their example leads to the repentance of their enemies.

In contrast to the socially orderly and beneficial sexual relationship represented by Arnoldo and Zenocia, Rutillio's service in the male brothel reveals both the destructiveness of masculine promiscuity and the need to limit and constrain women's desires in order to safeguard men's health and well-being. That the passages dealing with the male brothel (ss. 3.3 and 4.5) were given the title "The Stallion" and printed separately from the rest of the play in the collection *The Wits, or Sport upon Sport* (1662), offers some indication that Restoration readers were fascinated as well as repulsed by this aspect of the play. One could argue, in fact, that the very aspects of the scenes found to be repulsive or unpleasing when presented on the public stage were the same elements that were appealing in a book read privately.

While some of the most intriguing evidence on the reception of *The Custom of the Country* comes from the Restoration and late seventeenth century, the play's depiction of promiscuous sexuality as a threat to masculinity is very much a part of the cultural environment of the early years of the century when the play was first staged. Because the play is so blatant and straightforward in its representation of masculine weakness, these scenes are worth examining in some detail—especially since they are representative of the broad cultural trends linking sexuality and national identity in early modern England.

First of all, as *The Custom of the Country* makes clear, no matter how strongly a man may be moved by sexual desire, women's sexual desires are seen as immeasurably greater (figure 2.3). Though Rutillio is a confirmed rakehell, "the lustiest fellow" in the play, he is no match for his female clients. Men are seen as being incapable of performing the sexual labor required for that most notorious of female professions: prostitution. In the following exchange, Jacques, a serving man, argues with his mistress, Sulpitia, the owner of the brothel, that "a man is but a man" and cannot long survive the conditions Rutillio labors under.

> *Sulpitia:* How many had he yesterday?
> *Jacques:*   About fourteene, and they paid bravely too:
> But still I cry give breath, spare him and have him.
> *Sulpitia:* Five Dames today; this was a small stage,
> He may endure five more.
>
> . . . .
>
> *Jacques:*   He cannot last, I pitty the poor man,
> I suffer for him; two coaches of young City dames,
> Are now ready to enter; and behind these
> An old dead-palsied Lady in a litter,
> And she makes all the haste she can: the man's lost,
> You may gather up his dry bones to make nine-pins.

(4.4.1–10, 25–30)

As in other contemporary plays, such as Jonson's *Epicoene* (1609), the women seen as most lustful are those who live in the City. Here as in Jonson's play, the City women's social and sexual mobility is emblematized by their means of transport—they own coaches, a new and much criticized addition to London street traffic.[6] The appearance of the old Lady, clearly past childbearing, presents female sexual desire as a pursuit of physical pleasure, not limited by the biological need to bear children. Forced to service this desire, Rutillio will melt—that is, expend too much of his seed—and be left dried up—weak and prematurely aged. Promiscuity is not only morally wrong, it is physically harmful.

In a later scene Rutillio himself complains of his weakened state:

> Now I do look as if I were Crow-trodden
> Fy how my hams shrinke under me; ô me,
> I am broken-winded too; Is this a life?
> Is this the recreation I have aimd at?
> I had a body once, a handsome body,
> And wholesome too. Now I appeare like a rascall
> That had been hung a yeare or two in gibbets.

Reduced to the state of a dried-up corpse, Rutillio would prefer even battle or torture to the "pleasure" of serving in the brothel.

> Fye how I faint; Women? keep me from women;
> Place me before a Cannon, 'tis a pleasure;
> Stretch me upon a rack, a recreation;

Figure 2.3. *The sexually voracious woman and the terrified man: Joseph flees Potiphar's wife.* Joseph and Potiphar's Wife. *Marcantonio Raimondi, after Raphael, engraving, c. 1517 (Bartsch 9; Rosenwald Collection 19433.7349). National Gallery of Art, Washington, D.C.*

> But women? women? ô the Divell! women?
> *Curtius* gulfe was never halfe so dangerous.

(4.5.1–12)

In an image that reveals much about larger social attitudes toward female sexuality in the period, Rutillio refers to the Roman myth of Marcus Curtius. It was said that in 362 B.C. a gaping gulf opened in the heart of the Roman forum, literally and figuratively undermining the heart of the state. Oracles announced that the chasm would close only if the Romans would throw their most valuable possession into it. Declaring that a republic's most valuable possession was its brave citizens, Marcus Curtius, a noble general, manfully leaped into the pit, whereupon the gulf closed shut behind him, leaving behind a firm foundation for the Roman state. Rutillio's comparison of women's sexual desire to Curtius's gulf makes the gender dynamics of this political myth clear. As in the manuscript riddle on female genitalia quoted earlier, women are figured as a devouring "gulf sans ground" that feeds on manhood. The noble soldier, brave and battle-hardened, is no match for the withering power of female desire. Women suck up men's strength. As Rutillio puts it a few lines further on,

> I feare nothing now, no earthly thing
> But these unsatisfied Men-leeches, women.
> How divellishly my bones ake: ô the old Lady!

(4.5.17–9)

In *The Custom of the Country*, the remedy for such aches and stings is clear. Marriage is the cure for promiscuity. Poor worn-out Rutillio definitively rejects his former loose living and exclaims:

> Would I were honestly married,
> To anything that had but halfe a face,
> And not a groate to keep her, nor a smocke,
> That I might be civilly merry when I pleased,
> Rather than labouring in these fulling mills.

(4.5.51–5)

In *The Custom of the Country*, sexuality, despite its perils, is not rejected outright. But a man should not exhaust himself pounding away harder than a mill-worker fulling cloth; he should limit himself to one sexual partner, be she never so unattractive. The ideal is to be "civilly merry" in the bonds of monogamous wedlock. As I will show, this was by no means universally considered to be an adequate solution.

In early modern England, individual masculine weakness was seen as a national concern. If, as Marcus Curtius claimed, a state's most valuable commodity is its male citizen-soldiers, personal weakness will necessarily affect national strength. In an era of growing national consciousness, there was much speculation about England's strength relative to its European neighbors, and this comparison was often made in erotic or sexual terms, as the following discussion between Sulpitia and Jacques suggests.

> *Sulpitia:*   Where's the French-man?
> *Jacques:*   Alas, he's all to fitters,
>   And lyes, taking the height of his fortune with a Sirreng.
>   Hee's chin'd, he's chin'd good man, he is a mourner.

The French man has been torn to pieces (fitters) by his service in the brothel and is cleaning his wounds with a syringe of water (a Sirreng). "Chin'd" is a term which referred both to kissing and to pressing, thus suggesting at once the erotic nature of the Frenchman's disease and the pressure to which he has been subjected. The conversation continues:

> *Sulpitia:*   What's become of the Dane?
> *Jacques:*   Who? goldy-locks?
>   Hee's foule i'th touch-hole; and recoiles againe,
>   The main Spring's weakned that holds up his cock,
>   He lies at the signe of the *Sun*, to be new breech'd.

The military puns here, all relating to cannons, are clear enough. But they point once again to the notion that erotic weakness is a military matter. The next foreigner discussed is a "rutter"—that is, a "ritter" or German cavalry soldier (with a pun on "rutting"):

> *Sulpitia:* The Rutter too, is gone.
> *Jacques:* O that was a brave rascall,
> He would labour like a thresher: but alas
> What thing can ever last? he has been ill mewd,
> And drawne too soon; I have seen him in the Hospitall.

Finally, after having run through these descriptions of various foreigners, we come to that of the native Englishman:

> *Sulpitia:* There was an English-man.
> *Jacques:* I there was an English-man;
> You'le scant finde any now, to make that name good.
> There was those English that were men indeed,
> And would performe like men, but now they are vanisht:
> They are so taken up in their own Countrey,
> And so beaten off their speed, by their own women,
> When they come here, they draw their legs like hackneys:

> (3.3.1–22)

Englishmen, Jacques claims, are no longer men at all—they have been destroyed "by their own women." While overindulgence in alcohol is also offered as a possible excuse for the corruption of English manhood, the primary cause of male weakness, throughout this passage and throughout the play, is erotic.

Stephen Orgel has argued that "the deepest fear in antitheatrical tracts, far deeper than the fear that women in the audience will become whores, is the fear of a universal effeminization."[7] More precisely, what was feared was specifically English effeminization—a weakness of English manhood that would leave the nation defenseless against foreign foes.

Poetry and Effeminacy: Gosson, Stubbes, and Beyond

If erotic activity was seen as a major cause of effeminization, what about erotic representation—what about erotic writing? As I showed in the preceding chapter, early modern literary culture—which was largely, though not exclusively a male culture—was suffused with erotic texts. Not only was erotic writing ubiquitous in coterie manuscripts produced and circulated among the social elite, eroticism was also a prominent feature of books sold in the public market and plays performed on the public stage. Not surprisingly, the reading and writing of erotic texts was an important focus of the debates around effeminacy in the period. Since early modern concerns about effeminacy on the public stage have been well documented in several recent critical studies, I focus here instead on debates over the status of poetry (that is, fictional writing broadly defined) and the attempt to regulate erotic texts in the public book market.

It is well known that the public theater of Elizabethan and Jacobean England was perceived as a locus of erotic performance. Although erotic acts themselves were not staged—even on-stage kisses were rare, to judge from the surviving play-scripts—the theater was nonetheless continuously attacked by polemicists and moralists as a place of erotic display and temptation. From John Northbrooke's *A Treatise wherein Dicing, Dauncing, Vaine Plays or Enterludes . . . are reproved* in 1577 to William Prynne's *Histrio-Mastix* in 1633, a series of tracts by preachers and moralist such as Stephen Gosson, John Rainoldes, and Philip Stubbes decried the moral corruption of the public stage—a corruption frequently figured as erotic.

Despite their canonical status in the nineteenth and twentieth centuries as artifacts of high culture, it has always been admitted that the plays of Shakespeare are filled with scenes of bawdry—and indeed a vast literature has sprung up to explain, excuse, and explicate the erotic language, situations, and characters in Shakespeare.[8] In the 1980s and 1990s, the early modern English theatrical practice of having female parts played by crossdressed "boys" has been at the center of a wide-ranging scholarly debate over the precise nature of theatrical eroticism—were the "boys" pre- or postpubescent; was their attraction to male spectators primarily homoerotic; to what extent was their performance of femininity parodic and misogynist; what was their appeal—erotic or otherwise—to female spectators; was their crossdressing seen as a transgression of social hierarchy or of gender boundaries; were they remarked upon at all or merely accepted as an invisible convention of performance? Literary critics and cultural historians have explored the notion of eroticism among spectators as well as the social and cultural significance of erotic situations enacted on stage.[9]

Given these debates, the works of antitheatrical polemicists such as Stephen Gosson, John Northbrooke, John Rainoldes, and Philip Stubbes are now fairly well known to students of early modern culture.[10] It is worth reviewing them here, however, for the light they shed on the relation between erotic *writing* and effeminacy. While all these writers attacked crossdressing on stage and decried the opportunities for immoral behavior offered by the spectacle of the public theater, their attacks were not limited to theatrical performance and practice. Gosson in particular sees not only the theater but poetry itself as effeminizing; he attacks not only actors but poets and scholars.

Our convenient modern label "antitheatrical" does not adequately describe many of the moralistic texts traditionally grouped together under that heading. Although they all attack the theater, they are often equally incensed at other social abuses such as gambling and drunkenness. While texts such as Gosson's *Plays confuted in five actions* (1582) and William Prynne's mammoth *Histriomastix* (1633) are obsessive in their focus on the theater, other texts, like Gosson's earlier *Schoole of Abuse* (1579) and Stubbes's *Anatomy of Abuses* (1584), have many other concerns. Despite their many similarities these are not merely interchangeable texts. Gosson attacks poetry far more than most others. Northbrooke focuses on the dangers of idleness, Prynne on acting and crossdressing; the eminent divine John Rainolds was primarily involved in a scholarly debate over academic plays performed at Oxford and Cambridge. Like Philip Stubbes, many "antitheatrical" writers fixate on the notion that theatrical performance constituted a profanation of the Sabbath and were incensed that many people seemed to prefer to spend their time watching plays instead of listening to sermons.[11] The variety of focus and nuance found in "antitheatrical" pamphlets suggests how widespread and multivalent the attack on eroticism and effeminacy was.

Early modern moralists tend to see all sinful or unlawful activity—from Catholicism, to murder, to acting—as fundamentally interrelated. Linkage of what modern readers would tend to see as separate areas of disorder—some sexual, some not—is typical of all these texts. Here, for example, is John Northbrooke on "ydlenesse":

> [idleness is]the fountayne and well spring whereout is drawne a thousand mischiefes; for it is the onely nourisher and mayntainer of all filthinesse, as whoredome, theft, murder, breaking of wedlocke, perjurie, idolatrie, poperie &c. vaine playes, filthy pastimes, and drunkenness.[12]

Within the broad continuum of sinful behavior, what precisely was the matter with the public theater? Beyond the question of Sabbath-breaking or the sinfulness and hypocrisy involved in the business of acting, there is no question that for most antitheatrical writers, the theater was perceived to be a social space that encouraged disorderly erotic behavior. Here is a representative passage from *A second and third blast of retreat from plays and theatres* (1580):

> The Theater I found to be an appointed place of Bauderie; mine owne eares have heard honest women allured with abhominable speeches. Sometime I have seene two knaves at once importunate upon one light huswife, whereby much quarel hath growen to the disquieting of manie. (sig. E2v)

The author of this tract is unknown, but more important than the author's identity is the pseudonym he used: "Anglo-phile Eutheo" ("inspired with the love of England")—a name that clearly reveals the national concerns at stake in antitheatrical polemic. "Anglo-phile Eutheo" is certain that effeminization brought on by erotic representation will lead, unless stemmed, to the destruction of the English nation, and he parallels the impending collapse of England to the fall of Rome (sigs. A3–A4).

As many commentators have pointed out, brothels and playhouses shared the same urban space in the suburban "liberties" on the edge of the cities, and the two forms of "entertainment" were frequently equated, as they are in poem 64 of William Goddard's 1615 collection *A Neaste of Waspes*:

> Goe to your plaie house, you shall actors have
> Your baude, your gull, your whore, your pandar knave,
> Goe to your bawdie howse, y'ave actors too
> As bawdes, and whores, and gulls: pandars also.
> Besides in eyther house (yf you enquire)

> A place there is for men themselves to tire ["attire,"
>   but also exhaust themselves]
> Since th'are soe like, to choose there's not a pinn
> Whether bawdye-howse or plaie-howse you goe in.
>
> (sigs. F1r–F1v)[13]

While most writers attack actual practices that occurred at public theaters—
flirting, assignations, and so on—Stephen Gosson's argument in the *Schoole of
Abuse* is more subtle and wide-ranging. Not only do theaters provide a social space
for adulterous and promiscuous flirtation, theatrical performances themselves are
designed to seduce their audiences. The beautiful music, gorgeous costumes,
bawdy gestures and lewd speech constitute a systematic assault on the audiences'
senses (B6v). But Gosson goes further—whereas cooks and painters abuse the
senses by providing empty pleasures for taste and sight, theater is far more dangerous: for through its poetic texts, it attacks not only the senses but "the minde,
where reason and vertue should rule the roste" (B7).

This is a fundamentally different order of critique. While other moralists
attacked the theater largely on the grounds of its performative practices, Gosson
sees theatrical corruption as having its origin in poetry. He argues that poetic
texts themselves are erotically disorderly and that they are more, not less, dangerous than physical actions such as rude gestures. Effeminacy need not come
from seeing men onstage in women's clothing. It can come from reading.

Philip Stubbes makes a similar point in his *Anatomy of Abuses* (1584).

> As for the reading of wicked Bookes, they are utterly unlawfull, not onely
> to bee read, but once to be named . . . [for they] tende to the dishonour
> of God, depravation of good manners, and corruption of christian
> soules. For as corrupt meates doo annoy the stomack, and infect the
> body, so the reading of wicked and ungodly Bookes (which are to the
> minde, as meat is to the body) infect the soule, & corrupt the minde,
> hailing it to distruction. (sigs. P7r–P7v)

Whereas Gosson is engaged in a full-scale attack on poetry as a discourse, Stubbes
is specifically concerned with the availability of corrupting materials in the public book market. Stubbes asserts that, contrary to established law, the state
refuses to effectively regulate the sale of books. No matter "how unhonest" or
"unseemly of christian eares" a book may be, it is "freendly licensed, and gladly
imprinted, without any prohibition or contradiction at all." The result, Stubbes
claims, is "that bookes & pamphlets of scurrilitie and baudrie are better esteemed,
and more vendible, then the godlyest and sagest bookes that be" (sig. P7v). He
goes so far as to suggest that the Bible and Foxe's *Booke of Martyrs* are now "little
to be accepted" (P7v).

One should not be too quick to take Stubbes at his word here; he makes his
argument about the book market and licensing in the context of a discussion of
Sabbath-breaking, and his claim that scurrilous texts are supplanting devotional
ones is carefully paralleled with the notion that common folk would rather lis-

ten to a play than a sermon and other examples of a misguided populace favoring the secular over the sacred. And yet, while he may be exaggerating for effect, there is no doubting his virulence.

> These prophane schedules, sacraligious libels, and hethnical pamphlets of toyes & bableries . . . corrupt mens mindes, pervert good wits, allure to baudries, induce to whordome, suppresse vertue & erect vice: which thing, how should it be otherwise? for are they not invented & excogitat by Belzebub, written by Lucifer, licensed by Pluto, printed by Cerberus, & set a-broche to sale by the infernal furies themselves, to the poysoning of the whole world? But let the Inventors, the licensors, the printers, & the sellers of these vaine toyes, and more than Hethnicall impieties, take heed; for the blood of all those which perish, or take hurt thorow these wicked bookes, shalbe powred upon their heads at the day of judgement. (sigs. P7v–P8)

What books, precisely, is Stubbes talking about? We can't know for sure. Like Northbrooke railing against idleness, he takes arms against a thousand mischiefs at once: sacrilegious texts, foreign texts, frivolous texts, erotic texts. His diatribe is aimed at Catholic prayer books as well as Ovidian poetry, jest-books and political satire as well as almanacs. Given an understanding of sin and disorder where one corruption leads inevitably to another, it is at times difficult to separate them all.

What is clear though, is that these texts—whatever their precise content may be—are described throughout in erotic language: they "pervert" and "allure"; they lead to "whoredom" and "erect vice." On one level, this use of the language of sexuality is not surprising. By analogy with the whore of Babylon in Revelation the term "whoredom" had long been used to refer not just to prostitution or promiscuity but to idolatry or unfaithfulness to God. But while this usage demonstrates once again the way that early modern thought linked a variety of sins in a continuum of perversion, one should not infer that the connotations of the term "whoredom" ever ceased to be erotic. Indeed, erotic disorder was often seen as the fundamental sin underlying the rest. Thus, although Northbrooke sees idleness as the wellspring of a thousand undifferentiated mischiefs, he nonetheless declares that "she nourisheth nothing more easie then sensualitie and unlawful luste (of whoredome)" (p. 59).

Northbrooke's casual gendering of idleness as feminine is unsurprising (figure 2.4). Easy sensuality and unlawful lust are nothing if not effeminizing. In Gosson's *School of Abuse*, poets are attacked with the same register of terms employed against women in contemporary antifeminist tracts and sermons. Like vain women adorning their bodies with jewels, poets use "good sentences . . . as ornamentes to beautifye their woorkes, and sete theyre trumperie to sale without suspect" (sigs. A2r–2v). Gosson's analogy between the poet and the prostitute— implicit here—is soon openly formulated:

> pull off the visard that Poets maske in, you shall disclose their reproch, bewray their vanitie, loth their wantonnesse, lament their follie, and per-

Figure 2.4. *Idleness leads to erotic temptation; Venus whispers in the ear of a dozing scholar.* The Dream of the Doctor (The Temptation of the Idler), *Albrecht Dürer, engraving, 1498/1499 (Meder/Hollstein 70; Rosenwald Collection 1943.3.3481). National Gallery of Art, Washington, D.C.*

ceive their sharpe sayings to be placed as Pearles in Dunghils, fresh pictures on rotton walles, chaste Matrons apparel on common Curtesans. These are the Cuppes of Circes, that turne reasonable Creatures into brute Beasts. . . . No marveyle though Plato shut them out of his Schoole, and banished them quite from his common wealth, as effeminate writers, unprofitable members, and utter enemies to virtue. (sigs. A2v–A3r)

Gosson goes on to trace the effeminacy of poets to their having had a female precursor: Sappho, most renowned of the Greek lyric poets. "Sappho," he writes, "was skilful in Poetrie and sung wel, but she was whorish" (sig. A5).

Philip Stubbes is similarly explicit about the effeminate corruption of ballad makers.

Who be more bawdie than they? Who uncleaner than they, who more licentious and loose minded: who more incontinent than they? And briefly, who more inclyned to all kind of insolencie and lewdness than they: wherefore, if you wold have your sone softe, womanish, uncleane, smooth mouthed, affected to bawdrie, scurrilitie, filthie rimes and unsemely talking; briefly if you would have him, as it were transnatured into a woman or worse, and inclyned to all kind of whordome and abhomination, set him to dauncing school, and to learn musicke, and then you shall not faile in your purpose. (sig. O5)

For Stubbes, ballads actually have the power to "transnature" their male listeners, turning them into "women or worse." While Stubbes is concerned here primarily with the corrupting effects of singing and dancing, the rhetoric of effeminacy addressed itself to all poetic forms, from street verse and ballads to vernacular translations of classical texts and aristocratic coterie verse.

Indeed, for Gosson, all poetry is effeminizing, unless its content is explicitly martial or devotional. He is quite clear about what social role poetry should play.

The right use of aunciient Poetrie was to have the notable exploytes of woorthy Captaines, the holesome councels of good fathers, and vertuous lives of predecessors set downe in numbers, and song to the Instrument at solemne feastes, that the sound of the one might draw the hearers from kissing the cupp too often; the sense of the other put them in minde of things past, and chaulk out the way to do the like. . . . To this end are instruments used in battaile, not to tickle the eare, but too teach every souldier when to strike and when to stay, when to flye, and when to followe. (sig. A7v)

Poetry should reinforce the patriarchal, martial basis of society in a straightforward, practical way. It should transmit paternal wisdom and example and thus make young men more manly. It will stop them from "kissing the cup"—a beautifully concise phrase that conflates erotic dalliance with intoxication and drunkenness. It will even—like trumpet calls—provide soldiers with useful tactical information.

Gosson reserves his highest praise for soldiers, whom he sees as the guardians of patriarchal order. He calls soldiers "the Sonnes of Jupiter, the Images of GOD, and the very sheepeheards of the people" (sig. D6v). It is patriarchal order, not masculine aggression, that Gosson finds attractive; he condemns fencing (sigs. D4v–D6r), for fencers fight in private quarrels rather than for the public good. At his most extreme, Gosson tends to see any masculine activity that is not devoted either to the physical or spiritual defense of the realm as being effeminate and wasteful. He has a particularly chilling description of the uselessness of scholars in wartime.

> If the enemy beseege us, cut off our victuals, prevent forrain aide, girt in the city, & bring the Ramme to ye walles, it is not Ciceroes tongue that can peerce their armour to wound the body, nor Archimedes prickes, & lines, & circles, & triangles, & Rhombus, & rifferaffe, that hath any force to drive them backe. (sigs. D8r–D8v)

Rather than strengthening the nation, in Gosson's eyes poets are weakening it by their morbid concentration on effeminate sensuality. In his *Apologie of the Schoole of Abuse* (1579) Gosson links the eroticism of poetry to an erosion of civil order in his attack on poets' pagan subject matter: "Al these whome the Poetes have called gods and goddesses, for the most part, were bastardes begotten in adulterie, or very lewde livers" (sig. L3). The two most outrageous examples Gosson gives are Jupiter, a usurping parricide, and Venus, a common whore (sig. L3). Poets' refusal to act responsibly, their fascination with usurpers, their eroticism and sensuality, their praise of classical gods over the Christian God all make them dangerous to the patriarchal order: "monsters of nature [rather] then men of learning" (sig. L4).

The Defense of Eroticism: Sir Philip Sidney

While few writers openly and profoundly questioned the patriarchal hierarchy of gender in early modern England, Gosson and Stubbes's attack on the immorality of erotic verse was nonetheless contested within literary culture. The most articulate defenders of poetry were those like Sir Philip Sidney and Edmund Spenser who were actively committed to the establishment of a national poetics. Both Sidney and Spenser saw poetry as essentially English, associated with the native virtue of both the English landscape and the English language. Both saw poetry as a moral force, a weapon to strengthen the national character by inculcating virtuous behavior. As Spenser indicated in his letter to Ralegh, the purpose of his great national epic *The Faerie Queene* was "to fashion a gentleman or noble person in virtuous and gentle discipline" (737).[14] The term "discipline" is worth noting: for Spenser, poetry is a discipline—a means of creating order, not a source of disorder and chaos.

Sidney and Spenser's role in constructing both English Poetry and English national identity has often been remarked. But at the same time that they stressed the socially and morally beneficial aspects of poetry, both poets insisted on writing erotic verse—and in fact their most renowned and ambitious texts are erotic ones. If, as Richard Helgerson has suggested,[15] Sidney and Spenser are the two most influential figures in the establishment of English national literature, they achieved that status by writing poetry that is fundamentally erotic. Sidney defended the writing of martial poetry while producing *Astrophil and Stella*, the first great Petrarchan sonnet sequence in English. Spenser wrote a national epic—the saga of the great English hero King Arthur—whose endlessly elaborating plot has its genesis in Arthur's dream vision of sexual union with the Faerie Queene, Gloriana. In *The Faerie Queene*, Saint George, the patron saint of England, is introduced with a bawdy pun on "pricking"; Artegall, the poem's embodiment of English justice, is the object of an erotic quest; and the English national adventure begins with Prince Arthur's wet dream. Spenser's persistent eroticism is all the more astonishing in a poem that purports to base itself on Virgil's *Aeneid*, a national epic whose hero manfully rejects sexual passion at the outset in order to devote himself to the serious business of nation-building.

Both Sidney and Spenser see eroticism as positive, within certain limits. First, especially for Spenser, virtuous erotic pleasure is monogamous, not promiscuous. Like Fletcher's *Custom of the Country*, Spenser's *Faerie Queene* is a defense of monogamy. But rather than looking forward as Fletcher does to middle-class notions of companionate marriage, both *The Faerie Queene* and Sidney's *Astrophil and Stella* look nostalgically backward to medieval conventions of aristocratic erotic "service" and devotion outside marital bonds. Furthermore, virtuous eroticism is presented as the preserve of the "gentle" aristocracy. For both Sidney and Spenser, erotic poetry is an elite, courtly discourse, set off at some distance from vulgar, savage passions and crude, unlearned writing. Sidney insists that "poets have in England flourished . . . even in those times when the trumpet of Mars did sound loudest" but decries verse written by "base men with servile wits" (p. 241). On this point, he agrees with Gosson, who argues forcefully that only the learned and well-born should be permitted to write books (Schoole, sig. E4).

But while Gosson sees erotic writing as a threat to national patriarchal order, Sidney and Spenser see it as a fundamental attribute of the aristocratic warrior class on which—all three agree—that order depends. Simply because antitheatrical writers are all profoundly conservative, one should not make the mistake of associating their adversaries with liberal public opinion or with free speech. Sidney and Spenser were as ardent supporters of the patriarchal state as can be found.

Gosson's *Schoole of Abuse* is best remembered today because of the part it may have played in provoking Sir Philip Sidney to write his *Defense of Poesy*—one of the most eloquent pieces of literary theory in English. Gosson dedicated his pamphlet to Sidney, and scholars have often speculated that Sidney wrote the *Defense* as a private response to Gosson's public attack on poetry and plays.[16] Whether or not Sidney was responding specifically to Gosson, the *Defense* is clearly at pains to refute the notion that poetry is debilitating and effeminizing. And while Sidney often equivocates about precisely what sort of poetry he is defending—sometimes "poetry" refers to the Psalms, sometimes Homeric epic, sometimes amorous sonnets—the charges against which he defends poetry are those articulated in Gosson's pamphlet. Poetry is accused of being "the nurse of abuse, infecting us with many pestilent desires; with a siren's sweetness drawing the mind to the serpent's tail of sinful fancies." It is said that "before poets did soften us, we were full of courage, given to martial exercises, the pillars of manlike liberty, and not lulled asleep in the shady idleness with poets' passtimes" (234). Sidney sets out to prove precisely the opposite: that poetry is not "an Art of lyes, but of true doctrine; not of effoeminatenesse, but of notable stirring of courage; not of abusing mans wit; but of strengthening mans wit" (p. 240).

To an extent largely unremarked, Sidney's *Defense of Poesy* is also a defense of erotic writing. Although Sidney's greatest praise is for heroic verse that will inculcate martial values, poetry proves its superiority as a discourse by its capacity for seduction. Poetry is the most pleasurable writing to read, and it achieves its socially useful effects by delighting its readers.

> Now therein of all Sciences . . . is our Poet the Monarch. For hee doth not onely shew the way, but giveth so sweete a prospect into the way, as will entice anie man to enter into it: Nay he doth as if your journey should lye through a faire vineyard, at the verie first, give you a cluster of grapes, that full of the taste, you may long to passe further. (226)

Sidney's Poet, who can "entice any man" with his succulent cluster of grapes, bears a striking similarity to Spenser's personification of Excess in the Bowre of Blisse in book 2 of *The Faerie Queene*, a "comely dame" who crushes grapes for travelers to eat.

> In her left hand a Cup of gold she held,
>   And with her right the riper fruit did reach,
>   Whose sappy liquor, that with fulnesse sweld,
>   Into her cup she scruzd, with daintie breach
>   Of her fine fingers, without fowle empeach,
>   That so faire wine-presse made the wine more sweet:
>   Thereof she vsd to giue to drinke to each,
>   Whom passing by she happened to meet:
> It was her guise, all Straungers goodly so to greet.
>
> (2.12.55–6)

There are, of course, many differences between Sidney's Poet and Spenser's Excesse: the Poet is masculine, Excesse feminine, and in *The Faerie Queene*, Excesse is immediately overthrown. Guyon, Spenser's embodiment of Temperance, quickly dashes her cup to the ground, virtuously rejecting the proffered wine. Clearly Sidney does not wish readers to respond to poetry in the same fashion, but it is worth noting that the images he uses to describe the Poet are highly morally ambiguous and—as in *The Faerie Queene*—were often associated not with masculine virtue but effeminate corruption. For Sidney, to accept the pleasures of Poetry is to transcend the mediating virtue of Temperance in a flight of ecstasy. Poetry initiates its readers to the highest form of learning, "a purifying of wit" whose "final end is to lead and draw us to as high a perfection as our degenerate souls . . . can be capable of" (p. 219). Avoiding both the cold abstractions of philosophy and the morally ambivalent detail of history, poetry instructs by pleasing. It is delightful; it moves its readers emotionally. In defending poetry, Sidney is, on one level, defending the sensuous pleasure of the text and seduction of gorgeous language—the very aspects of poetry that Gosson and others attacked. If Gosson sees the poet as an effeminizing Circe, who turns strong men into beasts, for Sidney the process is exactly the opposite: "The poet is indeed the right popular philosopher . . . whose pretty allegories . . . make many more beastly than beasts, begin to hear the sound of virtue" (223). For Sidney, the seductiveness of poetry is what makes it the most powerful of the discourses of human knowledge. It is only because poetry is so erotically powerful that its abuse is seen as such a threat.[17]

Unlike the *Schoole of Abuse*, Sidney's *Defense* is a complex and sophisticated essay; its arguments are multivalent and sometimes contradictory. Despite his praise of poetry's seductive power, Sidney is eager from the very first to establish poetry's martial credentials. Far from being an effeminizing discourse of weakness, Sidney maintains, poetry is noble and virtuous—a necessary feature of the culture of any civilized nation. In addition, for Sidney poetic eloquence is specifically and intrinsically English: "certain it is, that in our plainest homelines, yet never was the Albion Nation without Poetrie" (237).

Sidney opens the *Defense* by speaking not of poetry but of the quintessential attribute of the masculine aristocrat and soldier: horsemanship. (Evans's Sybarites, we remember, were unable to control their dancing horses.) Sidney tells of his visit to the court of the Holy Roman Emperor Maximillian II and of his conversations with Maximillian's esquire of the stable, John Pietro Pugliano, a man outspoken in his enthusiasm for his office. Sidney is taken with Pugliano's enthusiasm, and like a "scholer . . . that followeth in the steps of his master" he feels that he too ought to speak in praise of his own vocation—that of the poet (212). Sidney thus elegantly sets up a parallel between the masculine and warlike art of horsemanship and the more ambiguous skills associated with poetic eloquence. Horsemanship is not merely martial, it is also aristocratic. And it is a skill associated in Western culture since the time of Plato not merely with rulership but also with rational restraint of the passions. A mounted man emblematizes not only his own superiority over men on foot but also the mastery of animal passion by human reason. By subtly paralleling poetry with horsemanship, Sidney implies that poetry is noble, not base; rational, not passionate; empowering, not debilitating.

What is more, Sidney the poet, whose skill is the ambivalent one of eloquence, has—he claims—learned his skills of (verbal) defense not from a philosopher or balladeer but from Pugliano, a soldier. The martial pedigree of Sidney's project is only accentuated by his calling it a "defense"—and the use of military terminology continues throughout the essay. Poetry is a powerful "army of words" (236), and the attack on it will lead to "civil war among the Muses"

(212). Sidney thus appropriates the martial vocabulary characteristic of Gosson's essay and asserts that warlike nations have always valued poetry.

> In Hungarie I have seene it the manner at all Feastes and other such like meetings, to have songs of their ancestors valure, which that right souldierlike nation, think one of the chiefest kindlers of brave courage. The incomparable Lacedemonians, did not onelie carrie that kinde of Musicke ever with them to the field, but even at home, as such songs were made, so were they all content to be singers of them. (231)

"Poetrie is the Companion of Camps." Indeed, even the most popular sixteenth-century romances are fit reading for warriors: "Orlando Furioso, or honest king Arthure, will never displease a souldier" (237).[18]

Despite his idealistic claims for the superiority of poetry over other forms of humanist discourse, Sidney still feels compelled to address Gosson's accusations head on: he lists four objections to poetry. The first two, that poetry has no practical value and that its fictions are nothing but lies, Sidney deals with in short order. The fourth, that Plato cast poets out of his republic, is also quickly refuted. But the third objection is more weighty.

> Their third is, how much [poetry] abuseth mens wit, training it to wanton sinfulnesse, and lustfull love. For indeed that is the principall if not onely abuse, I can heare alleadged. They say the Comedies rather teach then reprehend amorous conceits. They say the Lirick is larded with passionat Sonets, the Elegiack weeps the want of his mistresse, and that even to the Heroical, Cupid hath ambitiously climed. (236)

Even martial, heroic poetry has become eroticized—which is certainly the case with *Orlando Furioso*, whose very first line announces it will be a tale "Of ladies and cavaliers, of love and war." As John Harington was compelled to admit in the preface to his 1591 translation of the *Furioso*, "if anything may be [truly objected against poetry], sure it is this lasciviousnesse" (p. 8).

Less conciliatory than Harington, Sidney defends the eroticism of poetry by eliding sexual with spiritual love: "lustful love" is quickly redefined as "love of beauty."

> Alas Love, I would thou couldest as wel defend thy selfe, as thou canst offend others. . . . But grant love of bewtie to be a beastly fault, although it be verie hard, since onely man and no beast hath that gift to discerne bewtie, graunt that lovely name of love to deserve all hatefull reproches, although even some of my maisters the Philosophers spent a good deale of their Lampoyle in setting foorth the excellencie of it. (236)

And if love is understood as reprehensible lust, this is a criticism of lust itself, not of poetry:

> graunt I say, what they will have graunted, that not onelie love, but lust, but vanitie, but if they will list scurrilitie, possesse manie leaves of

the Poets bookes, yet thinke I, when this is graunted, they will finde
their sentence may with good manners put the last words foremost; and
not say, that Poetrie abuseth mans wit, but that mans wit abuseth
Poetrie. (236)

Here Sidney comes close to conceding the entire argument. If poetry is lewd,
then of course it ought to be condemned, but because lewdness is bad, not because poetry is. The unanswered question—as always in such debates—is what
constitutes lewdness. Is it *Astrophil and Stella? The Custom of the Country? The
Faerie Queene?* Ovid's *Amores?* an English translation of Ovid's *Amores?* Then as
now, different readers would be bound to provide different answers.

Sidney himself refuses to discuss particular texts in this context, though he
does suggest that he would draw the line at writing depicting homoeroticism and
polygamy. Those who criticize lewd poetry, he suggests, ought to compare it to
respected works of philosophy:

one [should] read Phaedrus or Simposium in Plato, or the discourse
of love in Plutarch, and see whether any Poet do authorise abhomin-
able filthinesse as they doo. Againe, a man might aske, out of what
Common-wealth Plato doth banish them, in sooth, thence where
himselfe alloweth communitie of women. So as belike this banish-
ment grew not for effeminate wantonnesse, since little should Poetical
Sonnets be hurtfull, when a man might have what woman he listed. (239)

While an elegant tactical move, this argument is—on one level—beside the point.
None of the antitheatrical writers would have praised sodomy or polygamy because they are found in Plato. But Sidney's larger point is clear—serious, foun-
dational texts of Western culture are filled with depictions of erotic "corruption"
and this is no reason to reject them. Certainly Sidney's own *Arcadia* devotes a
good deal of space to gender ambiguity and "perverse" eroticism.

While Sidney's *Defense*, like the poetry it praises, often makes its points more
through convincing rhetoric than coherent logic, it nonetheless represents a
powerful counter to notions that poetry in general and erotic writing in particular constitute a threat to English manhood. And although the *Defense* was not
written for mass consumption, the fact that it appeared in print after Sidney's
heroic martyrdom fighting for England in the Netherlands gave weight to its
argument that one could be both a warrior and a poet.

The National Erotic Epic: Edmund Spenser

The work that most profoundly links eroticism to English national identity in
the sixteenth century is Edmund Spenser's epic *The Faerie Queene*. Spenser's poem
is a consciously ambitious attempt to write the English national epic—a poem
that would define the English nation and establish the seriousness of English letters
in the way that Virgil's *Aeneid* glorified imperial Rome and proved the Latin
language to be the literary equal to Greek. But although it has clear Virgilian

antecedents and invokes a Virgilian tradition of epic writing, *The Faerie Queene* is a very different poem from the *Aeneid* in form, style, and content. It draws its subject matter from medieval as well as classical legend, and its episodic form and proliferation of incident owe more to medieval romances and sixteenth-century epics such as *Orlando Furioso* than to any classical model.

It is a commonplace of Elizabethan history that in the last decades of her reign, the queen encouraged a culture of politicized Petrarchan wooing at court— courtiers such as Philip Sidney and Walter Ralegh are still identified, in the popular imagination, with their role as political "suitors" to the Virgin Queen..The situation at court was, of course, more complex than this idealized model would suggest.[19] One of the consequences of the widespread notion of the "courtship" of Elizabeth has been to blind readers to the strangeness of the eroticism of Spenser's *Faerie Queene.* Seen within a context in which idealized wooing of the monarch as a lovely virgin was a customary court strategy, it seems only natural that an ambitious young man like Spenser, who aspired to a court appointment, would write an epic poem that presented the queen as an object of erotic desire. But Spenser's eroticization of national epic seems far more radical when seen in other—equally valid—contemporary contexts: why, in a culture that valued masculine authority and had a horror of effeminate weakness, did Spenser write an epic that presents national heroes such as King Arthur and Saint George as lovers on erotic quests? And why, in a humanist literary culture that reserved a special disdain for popular romances such as *Amadis of Gaul,* did he write an epic that draws strongly on medieval romance?

Spenser's poetic models provided him with various examples of how to handle erotic desire and gender relations within an epic context. Ariosto's *Orlando Furioso*, enormously popular throughout sixteenth-century Europe, took an ironic and playful attitude toward gender roles and sexual activity not unlike that found in English Ovidian poems such as *Venus and Adonis* or *Hero and Leander.* Though Ariosto's poem was ostensibly written in praise of the Este family of Ferrara, at whose court the author served as a diplomat, it is a work touched only occasionally by high seriousness. It delights in amorous misadventures and the vagaries of desire—women are mistaken for men, princesses find romantic and sexual bliss with low-born shepherds, and in the central event of the poem the primary hero, Orlando, is driven mad by sexual jealousy and can only be cured by his comrade Astolfo's fanciful trip to the moon. Ariosto begins his poem by announcing he will write of "Of Dames, of Knights, of armes, of loves delight"[20]—thus mixing the heroic and masculine with the erotic and feminine, the public affairs of war with the private affairs of love. This mixture is accentuated by the poem's choice of subject matter. Following Boiardo, Ariosto chooses to write of the masculine warrior heroes of the Charlemagne legends in a manner more appropriate for courtly Arthurian legend. Orlando, or Roland, the great military hero of Roncevalles, is made to fall in love as if he were Sir Launcelot.

By making lovers of his heroes Ariosto set himself firmly against Virgilian precedent. In the *Aeneid,* manly Aeneas must leave his beloved Dido behind to kill herself in Carthage before he can get on with the serious business of settling

Latium and thus make possible the Roman imperial future. Virgil not only has Aeneas reject womanly pleasure early in the poem, he also separates the "private" wanderings of Aeneas and his household in the first half of the poem from the "public" warfare of the second half—a division Spenser remarks on in the famous letter to Ralegh published along with *The Faerie Queene*. Popular as Ariosto was in the sixteenth century, Virgil remained the most powerful epic precedent, and the opening of *The Faerie Queene* closely follows lines believed in the period to open Virgil's poem. As a political statement too, Virgil's praise of Augustus in the *Aeneid* was a far more powerful and auspicious example than Ariosto's almost ironic championing of what in late-sixteenth-century England must have seemed a decidedly minor Italian noble house.

Moreover, the great Italian epic of the late sixteenth century, Tasso's *Gerusalemme Liberata* (1581) restored to a great extent the division between manly warriors and effeminate lovers that characterizes Virgil's epic. Godfredo, the central hero of the poem, is a purely martial figure, with no erotic interests or temptations whatsoever. One of the poem's secondary heroes, Rinaldo, is ensnared by the lust of the enchantress Armida, but he is rescued by masculine companions (canto 16) in an episode that parallels both Guyon's destruction of the Bowre of Blisse in Spenser's poem and Aeneas's rejection of Dido in Virgil. Only once he is free of Armida can Rinaldo perform heroic deeds, and he is one of the leaders of the assault on the pagan stronghold of Jerusalem in the final books of the poem. Armida finally submits to him and begs forgiveness—he accepts her, but as his handmaid (20.136). Female sensuality is firmly subordinated to masculine force. The treatment of gender identity and sexuality in Tasso's poem is much more complex than this brief summary can suggest. But for all its complexity, it is a much sterner and more hierarchical treatment of gender than that of Ariosto.

Given that both current practice and epic precedent argued for a definition of masculine heroism that entailed a rejection of sexual desire, Spenser's attitude toward eroticism is especially remarkable. One may argue that a poem praising Queen Elizabeth could not simply reject the feminine in favor of a purely masculine heroic ethos, and there is some truth to this. But the necessity of praising a female monarch does not, in itself, account for the prevalent and privileged place of eroticism in Spenser's epic. It is not necessary when praising a virgin who is past the age of childbearing to idealize wedded chastity or to see masculine heroism as bound up with sexual desire.

Amid its Virgilian echoes, the proem to *The Faerie Queene* also appropriates the opening of *Orlando Furioso* in declaring that its subject will be not "Arms and the man" but "Knights and Ladies gentle deeds . . . Fierce warres and faithfull loves" (proem.1). The proem invokes not only the epic muse (and Queen Elizabeth) but also Cupid—this last a source of inspiration firmly rejected by both Tasso and Virgil. Cupid, significantly, is invoked not only as "Venus sonne" but also as the "most dreaded impe of highest Jove"—a formulation that stresses that erotic love is not incompatible with masculine rulership and patriarchal authority (Proem.2). Cupid and Venus in turn summon Mars, god of war. Spenser thus—paradoxically—uses the adulterous relationship of Venus and Mars to legitimize the compatibility of fierce war with *faithful* love. Mars makes his appearance "In loues and gentle jollities arrayd"—a formulation that would not have encouraged Stephen Gosson, William Goddard, or Philip Stubbes.

Cupid is invoked by Spenser because it is he who has provoked in Prince Arthur, nominally the poem's central figure, a passion for Gloriana, the Faerie Queene. Far from being denigrated as unmanly, Arthur's passion is a "glorious fire"—a formulation that suggests Arthur's sexual desire is not only valued *as* sexual desire but that it also constitutes an honorable lust for glory.

Like so much in *The Faerie Queene,* Arthur's quest is never fulfilled. In the poem as it exists, the Faerie Queene never appears, and apart from the dream vision he describes in book 1, Arthur never has sex with her. But if we are to take seriously the structural principle that Spenser outlines in the letter to Ralegh—that Arthur is the central character in the poem and that his virtues comprise those of all the titular knights whose adventures are chronicled in the various books—then Arthur's erotic desire for Gloriana is the motive force of the whole poem. It is the force of desire out of which all the epic's many stories are generated.

In canto 8 of the first book, Arthur tells Redcrosse, the Knight of Holiness, and Una, the personification of Truth, of his love for Gloriana, the Faerie Queene. His story begins predictably enough. As a youth, Arthur feels the usual stirrings of sexual desire:

> It was in freshest flowre of youthly yeares,
>> When courage first does creepe in manly chest,
>> Then first the coale of kindly heat appeares
>> To kindle loue in euery liuing brest;

(1.9.9)

But Arthur has received a proper humanist education, and has been warned not to succumb to sexual feeling; he knows he ought subdue "those creeping flames by reason / Before their rage grew to so great vnrest." And so he rejects love and mocks those who foolishly succumb to their desires. In doing so, he is acting as any Elizabethan moralist would have him act. But eventually—as is always the case in such stories—his reason proves incapable of controlling his passion:

> But all in vaine: no fort can be so strong,
>> Ne fleshly brest can armed be so sound,
>> But will at last be wonne with battrie long,
>> Or vnawares at disauantage found;
>> Nothing is sure, that growes on earthly ground:
>> And who most trustes in arme of fleshly might,
>> And boasts, in beauties chaine not to be bound,
>> Doth soonest fall in disauentrous fight
> And yeeldes his caytiue neck to victours most despight.

(1.9.11)

The martial metaphors here replicate language Stephen Gosson used to warn of national military weakness: "There never was fort so strong," Gosson warned, "but it might be battered" (Schoole 50). Arthur's youthful acceptance of sexual desire is figured as a military defeat. He surrenders the fortress entrusted to him[21] and is made a helpless captive in the victor's public triumph. Such a defeat is clearly effeminizing: not only was the sack of captured fortresses referred to metaphorically as a "rape," but many actual rapes often occured when towns and fortresses were stormed. One recalls Shakespeare's Henry V before Harfleur, threatening that if he is compelled to take the town by force, the enemy's "pure maidens [will] fall into the hand / Of hot and forcing violation" (3.3.20–1).

Arthur's own fall happens when he is—like Shakespeare's Adonis—out hunting. Engagement in properly masculine activity is no defense against effeminate pleasures. Arthur rides out "prickt forth with iollitie / Of looser life." Eventually, he is overcome with fatigue, and needs to rest:

> For-wearied with my sports, I did alight
> From loftie steed, and downe to sleepe me layd;
> The verdant gras my couch did goodly dight,
> And pillow was my helmet faire displayd:

> (1.9.13)

The metaphorical transformation of steely helmet into soft pillow offers an indication of how Arthur's fatigue is seen as a surrender to feminine weakness. Of course, he has no choice—even the most hardy warrior needs to sleep. But it is precisely this natural inability of the body to remain perpetually hard and vigilant that Spenser is referring to when he says " no fort can be so strong" and that it is futile to trust in "fleshly might." In his *Treatise against Dicing, Dancing, Plays, and Interludes* (1577) John Northbrooke cautions against too much sleep because "it maketh heavie the spirites and sences, the partie also becommeth slouthfull, weake, and effeminate, with overmuch ydlenesse." He sees sleep as a loss of natural [masculine] heat and claims it "ingendreth much [feminine] humiditie and rawe humours."[22]

Once Arthur falls asleep he is defenseless—and he immediately succumbs to an erotic vision:

> Whiles euery sence the humour sweet embayd,
> And slombring soft my hart did steale away,
> Me seemed, by my side a royall Mayd
> Her daintie limbes full softly down did lay:
> So faire a creature yet saw neuer sunny day.

> Most goodly glee and louely blandishment
> She to me made, and bad me loue her deare,
> For dearely sure her loue was to me bent

> (1.9.13–4)

As we have seen, sexual dreams were a recurrent topic of erotic poetry circulated in manuscript. Significantly, however, almost all the poems describing sexually arousing dreams in the period describe women's dreams.[23] While twentieth-century culture has tended to see "wet dreams" as a primarily male phenomenon, in the early modern period it seems they were associated with women—especially with young girls who had not yet experienced sexual intercourse.[24] Thus Arthur is effeminized not only by the eruption of sensuous erotic fantasies but also by the fact that such an eruption is itself characteristic of virginal femininity. Describing the experience to Redcrosse and Una, Arthur says that he has been "ravisht with delight" and concedes that his experience has been shared by "ne living man."

After telling Arthur many things (which he does not share with us) and revealing that she is the Faerie Queen, Gloriana departs and Arthur wakes to find himself alone, though the "pressed grass" next to him suggests his erotic encounter was not entirely imaginary. He is profoundly moved by his dream, and his emotion reveals itself in not particularly manly fashion—he cries like a baby: "I sorrowed all so much, as earst I ioyd, / And washed all her place with watry eyen" (1.9.15). His emotion remains even as he speaks to Una and Redcrosse:

> his visage wexed pale,
> And chaunge of hew great passion did bewray;
> Yet still he stroue to cloke his inward bale,
> And hide the smoke, that did his fire display
>
> (1.9.16)

It is as if he had the green sickness.[25]

This is a crucial moment in Spenser's poem, and Arthur's vision is treated with the highest moral seriousness. For many readers this passage is one of the most moving in all of Spenser, and speaks profoundly to the unattainable human desire for perfect companionship and to the transitory, dreamlike nature of deep affection. Yet the episode need not be read so sympathetically. One remembers that in Ben Jonson's play *The Alchemist*, Dapper, the foolish clerk, is gulled with promises that he will be favored by the Queen of Faeries and is punished for his stupid credulousness by being locked in a shit-filled privy (Act 5. Scene 3–4). In this episode Jonson is clearly ridiculing what he perceives as the effeminate preciousness of Spenser's narrative.[26]

Given the hostility within early modern literate culture for just the sort of effeminate weakness Arthur displays in his dream of Gloriana, it is perhaps surprising to see the vehemence with which Spenser affirms his hero's experience. After hearing his tale, Una (i.e., Truth personified) turns to Arthur and says:

> O happy Queene of Faeries, that hast found
> Mongst many, one that with his prowesse may
> Defend thine honour, and thy foes confound:
> True Loues are often sown, but seldom grow on ground.
>
> (1.9.16)

There is no question, within the context of *The Faerie Queene*, that Arthur's erotic dream of Gloriana is seen as a divine visitation rather than an effeminate failing.

Once again, Spenser is taking Virgilian material and eroticizing it. At the outset of the Aeneid, Aeneas is visited by the goddess Venus, who is his divine patron (1.327–8). But she is his mother, not an erotic object, and though she is goddess of love, her appearance is characterized by its awe-inspiring divinity, not by its seductiveness.

The centrality of Arthur's erotic vision to *The Faerie Queene* is seen most powerfully in the way in which it is echoed in the Legend of Redcrosse, the Knight of Holiness—the subject of the poem's first book. After Judith Anderson's insightful reading of the poem's opening line,[27] there is no doubt that the phrase "A Gentle Knight was pricking on the plaine"—which perennially evokes giggles among the uninitiated—contained the same bawdy pun for Spenser's first readers as it does for us today. Gosson plays on the same pun in *The Schoole of Abuse* when he writes that tunes played in theaters are "comforts" which "rather effeminate the minde, as pricks unto vice, then procure amendement of manners, as spurres to vertue" (sig. B3).

Redcrosse's "pricking" is ironic, for like many of Spenser's knights, he has a fear of sexual arousal and avoids erotic situations wherever possible. Though he seems a "full jolly knight," he in fact is melancholy: he "of his cheere did seeme too solemne sad." Despite his "pricking" he does not share in the "jollity" that characterizes both Arthur dreaming of Gloriana and Mars accompanied by Cupid and Venus in the proem.

Like Prince Arthur, Redcrosse's quest is marked at its outset by an erotic dream—but it is a dream with a completely different valence than Arthur's. After Redcrosse has won his initial battle with the Dragon of Error, Redcrosse and Una are deceived by the enchanter Archimago, who appears to them as a humble hermit and offers to give them shelter in his rustic hut. That night, while Redcrosse sleeps, Archimago attempts to seduce him with a false dream. He fashions a sprite in the form of Una, who appears to Redcrosse and attempts to seduce him (1.1.45)

Redcrosse's "weaker sence" is assaulted by lustful dreams:

> And comming where the knight in slomber lay,
> The one vpon his hardy head him plast,
> And made him dreame of loues and lustfull play,
> That nigh his manly hart did melt away,
> Bathed in wanton blis and wicked ioy:
> Then seemed him his Lady by him lay,
> And to him playnd, how that false winged boy,
> Her chast hart had subdewd, to learne Dame pleasures toy.
>
> And she her selfe of beautie soueraigne Queene,
> Faire Venus seemde vnto his bed to bring

(1.1.47–8)

Redcrosse manfully resists these temptations, and on a certain level he is right to do so. Yet in doing so he is rejecting two of the very figures Spenser has invoked to inspire his epic: Cupid and Venus. If Cupid and Venus are appropriate inspiration for epic poetry, why are they wrong for Redcrosse? Where Arthur eagerly embraces his erotic vision of Gloriana, confronted with a seductive Una, Redcrosse is filled with violent ambivalence. While he is clearly physically attracted to her, he is horrified by her metamorphosis from "the chastest flowre, that ay did spring / On earthly braunch" to "a loose Leman to vile service bound." He is so terrified by his vision that he almost kills her in a fit of rage and frustration:

> All cleane dismayd to see so vncouth sight,
> And halfe enraged at her shamelesse guise,
> He thought haue slaine her in his fierce despight:
>
> (1.1.50)

He restrains himself with difficulty but still struggles with his "great passion of vnwonted lust." Not only does Redcrosse's murderous impulse seem an overreaction to the unsolicited appearance of a half-naked woman in a man's bedchamber, it is also quite different from Arthur's reaction to a similar situation.

Clearly in the two cases—Redcrosse's vision of Una, and Arthur's of Gloriana—we are dealing with two different conceptions of masculine virtue within Spenser's text. How is that difference defined? In resisting sex with Una, what is Redcrosse resisting? On one level, he is resisting falsehood—the Una he sees is not Una, she is a false vision created by an evil enchanter. Clearly Redcrosse is right to resist such hypocrisy and deception. Specifically, Redcrosse's rejection of Archimago's seductive visions can be read as warfaring Christianity's resistance to popish sensuality. No problems there for a Protestant poet writing an English epic.

But Redcrosse's erotic vision needs to be situated in the larger context of his quest. He is tormented by Archimago's vision immediately following his defeat of the Dragon of Error. At first, Redcrosse's slaying of Error seems allegorically straightforward: Holiness begins his quest by eliminating Error; masculine heroism destroys feminine monstrosity. But, like everything else in *The Faerie Queene*, Redcrosse's triumph over Error is not as simple as it seems. The struggle of Holiness with Error is a constant one, which will not end until the day of Judgment. If Redcrosse's defeat of Error were definitive, how could he fall into Archimago's trap?

There is no question that in his encounter with Archimago, Redcrosse falls immediately into error. But the precise nature of his error is ambiguous. Clearly he is deceived by Archimago's disguise as a holy man. But does Redcrosse's reaction to the erotic vision of Una constitute a valiant defense against temptation or a fall into greater error? Redcrosse's quest is to kill a dragon who is ravaging the land of Una's parents. His companion on his quest is Una (Truth) and though he may not realize it at the outset, his destiny is to marry her. Again, allegorically this seems straightforward enough: Holiness should defeat Evil and marry Truth. But what is marriage without sexual relations? Should Holiness be sexually attracted to Truth? Why shouldn't he be, if his destiny is to marry her? The brilliance of Spenser's allegorical technique is that his allegorical figures are represented as fallible human beings with human needs and desires. It is one thing to say Holiness should love Truth. But when Holiness wants to fuck Truth the allegory becomes much stickier.

Part of what Redcrosse resists when he resists the false Una is a vision of his own destined marriage with the true Una:

> And eke the Graces seemed all to sing,
>> Hymen iô Hymen, dauncing all around,
> Whilst freshest Flora her with Yuie girlond crownd.

$$(1.1.48)^{28}$$

One of the things he cannot (yet) accept is the effeminization of his masculine heroism that a marriage with Una would represent. His one heroic act so far has been to slay the feminine monster Error. When he is tempted by a vision of feminine beauty, he is confused and filled with "feare of doing ought amis." At this point in the text, Redcrosse still equates virtue with manly heroism, so he flees Archimago's house. And in doing so, he leaves behind not only the false Una (whom he is, on one level, right to avoid), but also the true Una (whom he should never abandon under any circumstances).

Commentators have identified the "sacred fountain" of Archimago's cell with the "fons sacer" of Ovid's *Amores* 3.1. Sitting by his sacred fountain, the singer of the *Amores* is approached by two Muses—the chaste and severe Muse of Tragedy and the seductive Elegiac Muse. While the Muses are both feminine, they offer a clearly gendered choice of subject matter: Tragedy incites the poet to "sing the deeds of men" (3.1.25); while Elegy boasts she has taught the poet's beloved Corrina "to slip away from her couch in tunic ungirdled and move in the night with unstumbling foot" (3.1.51–2). Though he has praise for both, the singer chooses—at least for the moment—the elegiac over the tragic. Redcrosse, on the other hand, rejects the woman who comes to him undressed in the night and turns instead to heroic deeds:

> Long after lay he musing at her mood,
>> Much grieu'd to thinke that gentle Dame so light,
> For whose defence he was to shed his blood.

$$(1.1.55)$$

But just as the poet of the *Amores* cannot completely dismiss Tragedy and heroic deeds (he ends with an admission that the "labor aeternus" of Tragedy presses on him [3.1.68–70]), so too Redcrosse cannot free himself from visions of erotic passion:

> At last dull wearinesse of former fight
>> Hauing yrockt a sleepe his irkesome spright,
> That troublous dreame gan freshly tosse his braine,
> With bowres, and beds, and Ladies deare delight:

> But when he saw his labour all was vaine,
> With that misformed spright he backe returnd againe.

(1.1.55)

The extent to which Redcrosse has internalized the erotic vision of Una is registered by the ambiguity of the phrase "his irkesome spright," which refers at once to Redcrosse's troubled soul and Archimago's tempting spirit.

In leaving Archimago's house and deserting Una, Redcrosse hopes to escape the feminine and its erotic temptations and keep himself within a securely masculine world of martial combat as opposed to sexual passion. This decision has disastrous consequences within the poem. For one thing, Una is abandoned and placed in danger. For another, Redcrosse weakens himself. After leaving Una and the feminine behind, he fights and defeats a series of male opponents— Sans Joy, Sans Loy, and Sans Foy—all of whom seem on some level to be mirrors of his own spiritual state (cantos 1.3–5). But wearied from his exertions (as Arthur was from hunting) he stops to rest. This is the point at which disaster overtakes him.

As part of the spoils of his martial victories, Redcrosse has won a woman, Duessa, the poem's incarnation of schism and disunity—the opposite of Una. Although he fled in terror and dismay from the notion that he and Una might sexually desire each other, Redcrosse has no fear of enjoying Duessa's favors once he has won them in combat. Not only do the two of them "of solace treat, / And bathe in pleasauce of the joyous shade" (1.7.4), but Redcrosse also unknowingly drinks from the fountain they find in the shady glade, a fountain that Phoebe (that is, Diana, goddess of chastity) has transformed into an effeminating poison:

> And lying downe vpon the sandie graile,
> Drunke of the streame, as cleare as cristall glas;
> Eftsoones his manly forces gan to faile,
> And mightie strong was turnd to feeble fraile.

(1.7.6)

By this point in his quest, despite his manly rejection of Una's affections, and despite his success in battle, Redcrosse has become utterly effeminized. So alienated is he from his masculinity, that he is immediately attacked by the phallic giant Orgoglio, who, as many commentators have suggested, is an embodiment of the masculine sexual energies that Redcrosse, like any other Christian gentleman, ought to keep firmly under rational control.[29] The attack comes just as he is about to have sex with Duessa:

> Yet goodly court he made still to his Dame,
>   Pourd out in loosnesse on the grassy grownd,
>   Both carelesse of his health, and of his fame:
>   Till at the last he heard a dreadfull sownd,
>   Which through the wood loud bellowing, did rebownd,

That all the earth for terrour seemd to shake,
And trees did tremble.

(1.7.7)

Orgoglio is "An hideous Geant horrible and hye," a "monstrous masse of earthly slime, / Puft vp with emptie wind, and fild with sinfull crime." Redcrosse is powerless to oppose him; Orgoglio is utterly relentless:

> when the knight he spide, he gan aduance
> With huge force and insupportable mayne,
> And towardes him with dreadfull fury praunce;
> Who haplesse, and eke hopelesse, all in vaine
> Did to him pace, sad battaile to darrayne,
> Disarmd, disgrast, and inwardly dismayde,
> And eke so faint in euery ioynt and vaine,
> Through that fraile fountaine, which him feeble made,
> That scarsely could he weeld his bootlesse single blade.

(1.7.11)

Orgoglio's "mercilesse" stroke is like a cannon going off:

> As when that diuelish yron Engin wrought
> In deepest Hell, and framd by Furies skill,
> With windy Nitre and quick Sulphur fraught,
> And ramd with bullet round, ordaind to kill,
> Conceiueth fire, the heauens it doth fill
> With thundring noyse, and all the ayre doth choke,
> That none can breath, nor see, nor heare at will,
> Through smouldry cloud of duskish stincking smoke,
> That th'onely breath him daunts, who hath escapt the stroke.

(1.7.13)

Saved by "heavenly grace" (1.9.12) from the full force of the blow, Redcrosse is flattened by the shock alone. One could not hope for a better description of effeminate weakness succumbing to phallic strength.

In the figure of Orgoglio, one finds one of the most powerful descriptions in Elizabethan literature of the monstrous nature of unrestrained masculine aggression. Though his defeat by Orgoglio leads Redcrosse to the verge of self-annihilation in the cave of Despaire (1.9.35–54), he is revived not by restoring his masculine aggressivity but by his visit to the House of Holiness (1.10)—a place governed entirely by women: Dame Celia and her daughters Fidelia, Speranza, and Charissa. Rejuvenated by his stay in the House of Holiness, Redcrosse goes on to defeat the dragon that which had ravaged Una's land, and book 1 of the poem ends with his betrothal to her.

Thus, far from endorsing an entirely masculine and martial view of heroism, in the first book of *The Faerie Queene* Spenser presents masculinity as potentially

monstrous (Orgoglio), defines divine inspiration as an erotic dream (Arthur's encounter with Gloriana), and argues that the task of Holiness is to learn to love Truth
in body as well as in mind. Rather than see martial masculinity as positive and
effeminate weakness as negative, Spenser argues for a temperate mean between the
two—a union of Redcrosse and Una that avoids both irresponsible weakness and
brutal aggression. It is no coincidence that the establishment of this mean at the
end of book 1 leads to the Legend of Guyon, the Knight of Temperance, in book 2.

The best known attack on erotic pleasure in *The Faerie Queene* is Guyon's
destruction of the Bowre of Blisse at the end of the second book. Again, the allegory
here seems straightforward enough. Masculine and rational temperance must reject loose, feminine sexuality. But while the moral content of the episode is clear,
Spenser goes out of his way to present the Bowre as a place of beauty, whose destruction is bound to be seen as a loss, even if a painfully necessary one. One must
be careful not to reduce *The Faerie Queene*'s attitude toward sexuality and sensual
pleasure to Guyon's destruction of the Bowre. Though, as Temperance, he is right
to act as he does, immediately following his destruction of the Bowre, Guyon is
thrown from his horse by Britomart, the female knight of chastity (3.1.6–7). Britomart's chastity, as all readers of the poem are aware, is not abstinence but wedded
fidelity. She is, in fact wracked with sexual desire for Artegall, her destined husband. While the primary weddings in the Faerie Queene tend to be endlessly deferred—neither Una and Redcrosse, Britomart and Artegall, nor Gloriana and
Arthur are actually married within the space of the poem—Spenser's *Epithalamion*
and *Prothelamion*, not to mention the marriage of the Thames and the Medway in
book 4, all celebrate marriage as an ideal erotic union. While Temperance is a classical virtue that acts on the level of purely human affairs—making sensible deci-
sions between extreme behaviors—for Spenser wedded Chastity is a transcendent
virtue in which sexuality is subsumed into a spiritual union of opposites that mirrors the very bonds by which the elements of creation are held together.

The sinful sexuality of the Bowre of Blisse is replaced in book 3 by the fruitful
sexuality of the Gardens of Adonis. And in the second half of the poem—books 4,
5, and 6—all of the most complex and compelling allegorical sites are erotic ones:
Scudamor wins Amoret from Venus's Temple (canto 4.10); in 5.7 Britomart has
her own erotic dream vision of union with Artegall in Isis Church; (canto 5.7) and
Calidore learns what Courtesy ought to be in his vision of the graces dancing naked
on Mount Acidale (canto 6.10). It is not by chance, either, that the Bowre of Blisse
is described in exquisite detail, before it is destroyed, thus allowing the reader (and
Guyon) to experience its delights. In several early-seventeenth-century manuscript
poems, "bowre of blisse" is used as a synonym for the female genitals.[30] One wonders if it was so before Spenser brought Guyon there, or if *The Faerie Queene* made
a temporary addition to the erotic vocabulary of early modern England.

The Bishops' Ban and Marlowe's Ovid

The eroticism that suffuses *The Faerie Queene* did not impede the poem's circulation. While it had many critics (most famously Lord Burleigh)[31] and was not

nearly as popular with the queen herself as Spenser may have hoped, there was never any effort to suppress Spenser's text. Indeed, its status as a great English poem was secure by the time of Spenser's death, although if frequency of printing is any guide, it was not as popular as Ovidian texts such as *Venus and Adonis* or *Hero and Leander*. These texts, despite their playful approach to gender boundaries and expectations, were also allowed to circulate freely. While their depiction of gender and eroticism may have been disturbing to some readers, the authorities apparently saw no reason to limit their circulation. The amount of control the state exercised over printing in Elizabethan England is a matter of debate. Some have argued that the licensing procedures constituted an effective and often-employed instrument of control over what material was printed;[32] others contend that the Elizabethan state apparatus did not have the resources to enforce a sustained effort at censorship of the press.[33]

To what extent were cultural concerns about effeminizing poetry reflected in state policy? The works of Christopher Marlowe provide a useful example of the vagaries of Elizabethan censorship, and their treatment by the authorities demonstrates the ways in which effeminizing erotic writing was seen as a national threat. At the time of Marlowe's death he was under accusations of atheism, yet there seems to have been little effort to keep his works off the public stage. Indeed, Marlowe's *Dr. Faustus* and *Tamburlaine* were two of the three most popular plays on the Tudor-Stuart stage, from their first performances in the late sixteenth century until the closing of the theaters in 1642.[34] It was not *Tamburlaine* or *Hero and Leander*, but a much less renowned text of Marlowe that was suppressed by the authorities because of its treatment of gender identity and "unmanly" weakness.

In 1596, in an order of High Commission, John Whitgift, archbishop of Canterbury, declared his intention to personally regulate

> divers copies books or pamphletts [which] have been latelie printed and putt to sale, some conteyning matter of Ribaldrie, some of superstition and some of flat heresie. By means whereof the simpler and least advised sorts of her majesties subjects are either allured to wantonness, corrupted in doctrine or in danger to be seduced from that dutifull obedience which they owe unto her highness.[35]

Three years later, on June 1, 1599, Whitgift and Richard Bancroft, bishop of London, issued the proclamation known as the Bishops' Order, an order that represents one of the most overt efforts of the Elizabethan authorities to control the burgeoning London book trade. It specifies that both histories and plays must henceforth be licensed by the state, bans satires and epigrams altogether, and lists some dozen volumes that are to be called in and destroyed, most of which are collections of satiric verse.[36] On June 4 a book burning was held at the Stationers' Hall.

One of the books thrown on the pyre that day was a slim volume containing forty-eight epigrams by Sir John Davies and ten of Ovid's Elegies from the *Amores*, translated by Christopher Marlowe. The Bishops' Order has generally been understood as an effort to control political discourse in England, and thus it has been argued that the offensive portion of the Marlowe/Davies volume was Davies's Epigrams—which fell, after all, under the general ban on epigrams and satires.[37] And yet, as Whitgift's linkage of wantonness, corrupt doctrine, and social disobedience in the 1596 order makes clear, works thought of as ribald or licentious were not differentiated from politically subversive or heretical works but were included in a broad range of material that could seduce the innocent. Erotic writing was clearly seen as having political consequences.

Given an understanding of corruption that does not draw strong distinctions between a "private" realm of the erotic and a "public" realm of politics, it is quite possible that Marlowe's translations of Ovid may have been perceived as socially disorderly. For while Marlowe's Elegies are—generically speaking— erotic lyrics rather than overtly political satires, they raise potentially troubling issues of sexual power and masculine gender identity. The decision in the *Amores* to reject the "Muse upreared . . . of Armes" in favor of the "numbers soft" of love (Elegy 1.1.5, 22) had been strongly criticized in Augustan Rome and was still perceived as threatening to the patriarchal social structures of Elizabethan England. For to a greater extent than Ovid's originals, Marlowe's translation of the Elegies celebrates effeminacy and argues for the pleasures of subjection. It is better, the volume suggests, to be a captive of pleasure than a conqueror of men.

Marlowe's Elegies were certainly not alone in their focus on issues of male sexual dysfunction and the uncertainty of masculine gender identity. But though other poems of the 1590s that addressed similar concerns were harshly criticized for their obscenity, they were not named in the Bishops' Order. This is because they circulated not in print but in manuscript. Marlowe's translations of Ovid seem to have been disseminated primarily through the public space of the printed book market rather than through elite coterie circles. While many copies of Davies' Epigrams are found in manuscript, surviving manuscript copies of Marlowe's Elegies are extremely rare.[38] Although the *Amores* were readily available to anyone who could read Latin, their appearance in print in English could easily be a cause for concern to those, like Archbishop Whitgift, who were worried about what "the simpler and least advised sorts of her majesties subjects" were reading. Accompanying a widespread eagerness to translate canonical classical texts into the vernacular was a corresponding anxiety that such translations cheapened the material they made available. And in the case of erotic writing like the *Amores*, the need to keep such texts from circulating beyond an educated male elite was especially strongly felt. What if women read them? What if servants did? The 1590s volume is very thin and small; it could easily have been concealed on one's person—perhaps it was carried about in codpieces in the manner of similarly diminutive volumes of ballads or Petrarchan sonnets, to be produced at an opportune moment to serenade one's beloved. Master Matthew in Jonson's *Every Man In His Humour* carries Samuel Daniel's *Delia*—among other things—in his hose for just such a purpose (5.5.19–20).

Despite the book burning at the Stationer's Hall, in the long run the Bishops' Order was largely ineffective, as can be illustrated by the subsequent fate of the Marlowe/Davies volume. Not only do several copies of the book still exist from the 1590s, but by the early seventeenth century a new edition appeared, this time including not just ten Elegies but Marlowe's complete translation of the *Amores*. My interest here, however, is with the editions that appeared in the 1590s. Like the later editions, the 1590s texts were published surreptitiously and purport to have been printed at Middleburgh in the Low Countries; their compiler is unknown; it is almost certain, however, that neither Marlowe nor Davies had any hand in the publication of their poems.[39] It is generally held that the translations of Ovid are a product of Marlowe's youth at Cambridge. Why, if Marlowe had translated all the elegies, were only ten chosen for publication in the 1590s? Was it a simple matter of availability, or is there a discernible principle of inclusion?

It has been argued that the elegies chosen were simply those that are most licentious,[40] but the simplicity of this scheme is refuted by the inclusion of Elegy 1.15, which deals not with sexual frolics but with the immortality of poetry. Fredson Bowers and others who have done bibliographic work on Marlowe's Elegies have detected "no discernible order" (p. 151) in the organization of the volume, beyond the choice to open the volume with the first elegy of book 1, which serves as an introduction both to Ovid's complete collection and the selection in the 1590s translation. And yet, while there is no obvious logical principle of inclusion, the poems of the 1590s volume do combine to form a rough narrative.

Almost any selection of random texts, of course, will yield a narrative if one is sought there. But the narrative that can be discerned in the selection of Marlowe's elegies published in the 1590s is a narrative of effeminacy and masculine sexual failure that has strong resonances in late-sixteenth-century English culture as a whole.[41] After the first elegy, in which the speaker promises to write of nothing but love, comes elegy 1.3, in which the narrator devotes himself to his beloved alone, and 1.5, in which he has intercourse with her on a lazy afternoon. The next two texts included, Elegies 3.13 and 1.15, deal with the discourses of love—in the first, the speaker admonishes his beloved not to speak of her infidelities, and in the second he praises the immortality of his own poetic arts. In contrast to the imputed immortality of poetry, the next poem, Elegy 1.13, deals with the transience of time: it is a plea, like Donne's "The Sun Rising," that time might stand still for the lovers.

Thus, despite its seemingly random and jumbled selection of Ovid's poems, the collection nonetheless has a clear beginning, in which a monogamous relationship is constructed: first the speaker devotes himself to speaking of love, then to a particular woman, at which point the relationship is consummated. This construction of monogamy is undermined in the seventh and eighth poems of the collection: in Elegy 2.4 the speaker meditates on his potential desire for all women, and in Elegy 2.10 he finds himself in the dilemma of loving two at once. The ninth poem in the collection is the infamous Elegy 3.7 (here numbered 3.6), on the speaker's impotence, and the volume concludes with the second of the *Amores*,

Elegy 1.2, in which the speaker represents himself as a bound captive before love's triumphal chariot.

If one accepts the narrative I have constructed, the 1590s selection of Elegies represents the male speaker's decision to devote himself to sexual love for a woman as a fall into impotence and powerlessness, a loss of manly strength, and even of identity. The speaker of the Marlowe's elegies begins by rejecting virile martial pursuits for effeminate, sexual ones and ends by being symbolically castrated: "I lately caught will have a new made wound, / And captive like be manacled and bound" (1.2.29–30). His protestations of monogamy and fidelity in the earlier poems ("If men have faith, Ile live with thee for ever" [1.3.16]) prove impossible to fulfill:

> I cannot rule myself, but where love please,
> Am driven like a ship upon rough seas.
> No one face likes me best, all faces move.
>
> (2.4.7–9)

Desire once pursued leads not to fulfillment or satiety but rather to a proliferation of desire and loss of control: "pleasure addes fuell to [the speaker's] lustful fire" (2.10.25).

> Oft have I spent the night in wantonesse,
> And in the morne beene lively nere the lesse.
> He's happy who loves mutuall skirmish slayes,
> And to the Gods for that death Ovid prayes.
> Let souldiours chase their enemies amaine,
> And with their blood eternall honour gaine.
>
> .   .   .   .
>
> But when I dye, would I might droupe with doing,
>
> (2.10.27–32,35)

The "death" of orgasm is here contrasted with the honorable, manly death of a soldier. But the pleasurable loss of identity in climactic physical ecstasy is paralleled in the next poem by the loss of gender identity that comes with the speaker's impotence. Having lost his sexual potency, Marlowe's speaker is no longer fully a man: "Like a dull Cipher, or rude block I lay, / Or shade, or body was I who can say? . . . Neither was I man nor lived I then" (3.6.15–6, 60).

Most troubling of all to the patriarchal hierarchy of gender that seeks to found itself on quantifiable sexual difference is that the speaker's weakness—like that of Goddard's Metamorphiz'd Mick—is embodied in the very organ that should guarantee his superior status: his penis. Marlowe's speaker has lost rational control of his body, and faced with his inability to control his desires, he renounces further use of his recalcitrant member:

> like one dead it lay,
> Drouping more then a rose puld yester-day.
> Now when he should not jette, he boults upright,

> And craves his taske, and seekes to be at fight.
> Lie downe with shame, and see thou stirre no more,
> Seeing thou wouldst deceive me as before.

> (3.6.65–70)

The speaker's masculine member has changed to a vaginal rose.

Of course, despite his authorship of *Hero and Leander*, Marlowe did not consistently represent gender ambiguity in a positive light; much of *Tamburlaine*, for example, is devoted to denigration of effeminate weaklings, among them Tamburlaine's own son Calyphas.[42] Like Calyphas, who prefers "a naked lady in a net of gold" to the swords and cannons of the battlefield (*Tamburlaine* 2.4.1), in the final poem the speaker of Marlowe's Elegies succumbs to "martial justice" and is made a captive. He, like the "effeminate brat" Calyphas, has forfeited his masculine identity and the social prerogatives it carries and has been reduced to the subordinate position of a woman or a child. This is exactly the outcome Stephen Gosson had predicted.

> Whilest [poets] make Cupide triumph in heaven, and all the gods to marche bounde like miserable captives, before his charriot, they belie God, and bewitch the reader with bawdie charms.[43]

The elegies are much more ambivalent than *Tamburlaine* in their attitude toward subjection. As a group, they celebrate the surrender to erotic pleasure at least as much as they warn of its dangers. Despite his sexual failure in Elegy 3.6, the speaker never renounces his pursuit of pleasure, and in Elegy 1.2 he gives himself willingly to the bondage of Love: "Loe I confesse, I am thy captive I, / And hold my conquered hands for thee to tie" (1.2.19–20). Marlowe's Elegies may thus be interpreted as advocating seriously what *Hero and Leander* advocates laughingly: that the blurring and shifting of gender boundaries is desirable and that the loss of traditional masculine gender identity is a price worth paying for sensual delight.

I believe that the refusal of the Elegies to denounce the effeminate subjection and loss of masculine identity that they describe in such detail may have played a major role in their banning under the Bishops' Order. Although many poems published in the 1590s could be read as advocating a surrender to Love, Marlowe's Elegies go further: they link effeminacy to precisely the form of sexual activity that early modern culture was moving to validate above all others. In a period in which there seems to have been an increasing effort to regulate sexuality in the form of heterosexual, monogamous marriage,[44] the 1590s selection of Marlowe's elegies argues that, even when employed in monogamous devotion to a woman, the "numbers soft" of love will lead to promiscuity and a loss of rational control—a loss that, as its figuration as military defeat suggests, has consequences that go beyond those of personal sexuality.

While Puritan pamphleteers and others were actively promoting companionate marriage as an ideal in the period, there was a certain amount of resistance to the concept. Francis Bacon, for example, in his 1625 essay "On Marriage and the Single Life" demonstrates a marked ambivalence toward marriage. Though he does not disapprove of marriage as such, he argues that "certainly the best works and of greatest merit have proceeded from the unmarried or childless men".[45] Bacon contends that "unmarried men are best friends, best masters, best servants," though he adds that marriage often makes men better subjects, and that while generals should not marry, common soldiers may fight better if they are defending their wives and children. Bacon thus associates marriage with subjection and subordination and suggests that, ideally, the male members of the ruling class should not marry. That Bacon's ideal goes against one of the fundamental principles of a patriarchal society—the need to marry and procreate in order to produce legitimate male heirs—points to the theoretical contradictions inherent in the notion of a society in which males are considered superior, but can only reproduce their perfections through sexual union with "inferior" women.[46] Both *The Fifteen Joyes of Marriage* (an anonymous translation [c. 1507] of an antifeminist French poem by Antoine de la Sale) and a recent translation of Ercole Tasso's "booke against woemen," or *Of Marriage and Wiving*[47] were singled out for burning by the Bishops' Order, in all likelihood because they were seen as subversive in their opposition to marriage as a social institution.

While like these banned antifeminist texts, the 1590s arrangement of Marlowe's Elegies associates sexual passion for women with subjugation, and like the antitheatrical pamphlets it links erotic poetry with effeminization and loss of control, its moral vision is far removed from that of antifeminist writers or moralistic pamphleteers; the Elegies do not function as a cautionary tale. They celebrate desire as much as they warn of its dangers, and coupled as they are with the subversive wit of Davies' epigrams—many of which are quite bawdy—their own subversiveness appears in heightened relief.

By the time the Marlowe's Elegies appeared in print, Marlowe had been dead for some years. But in his lifetime, Marlowe was clearly known both as a writer of erotic works and as a (reputed) advocate of disorderly erotic practice. As such he was not atypical. In early modern England, young writers such as Marlowe, John Marston, and Thomas Nashe often flaunted eroticism as a way of establishing a career. But in doing so they entered into a cultural debate over masculinity in which their praise of eroticism could be read as a sign of effeminacy by their opponents. Despite the impressive cultural weight of Sidney's *Defense* and Spenser's *Faerie Queene*, poets remained open to the charge of being unmanly.

What is more, the erotic writing of struggling, impoverished writers like Nashe drew on models of literary practice that were often far removed from the aristocratic nationalism of Sidney and Spenser. If Sidney, writing *Astrophil and Stella*, found in Petrarch a powerful model of erotic discourse, Nashe and others turned to a figure both more contemporary and more provocative: Pietro Aretino, the Italian satirst and critic, whose erotic texts were among the most subversive of the sixteenth century. While English culture managed to appropriate Petrarch with relative ease, Aretino was another matter altogether.

It is not surprising that in the process of consolidating English national identity, erotic corruption was often seen as having a foreign origin. What is significant, however, is the extent to which concerns and anxieties about foreign corruption came to focus on Italy in general, and on Aretino in particular. Like Machiavelli, Aretino became an iconic figure in late-sixteenth-century England. Just as the Machiavel represented the ultimate amorality of power, the Aretine came to embody all manner of erotic disorder. And yet, because Aretino himself enjoyed a level of personal power and social influence almost unprecedented among sixteenth-century men of letters, he offered a compelling model for Elizabethan writers who, like Nashe and the young Ben Jonson, had difficulty negotiating the uncertainties of the patronage system and the emerging book market. The key to success, it seems, was to appropriate foreign eroticism in ways that would be acceptable to native English society. The processes by which these foreign erotic materials were assimilated into English culture are my subject hereafter.

Part Two

THE ARETINE
AND THE
ITALIANATE

Prologue

Englishmen Italianated

scholar looking for signs of incipient nationalism in late-sixteenth-century England could do worse than to begin with George Silver's *Paradoxes of Defense,* published in London in 1599. Silver's book defends the old English manner of fighting with short swords and condemns the newfangled foreign fashion of fencing with rapiers. He has been compelled to write, he says, to remind Englishmen of their forgotten martial traditions:

> we like degenerate sonnes, have forsaken our forefathers vertues with their weapons, and have lusted like men sicke of a strange ague, after the strange vices and devises of Italian, French and Spanish Fencers, litle remembering, that these Apish toyes could not free Rome from . . . sacke, nor Fraunce from King Henrie the fift his conquest. (sig. A1)

In this passage Silver acknowledges that fencing is a Continental practice, but for most of his text he sees it as specifically Italian. For Silver, Italian fencing with long elegant swords is more like effeminate dancing than fighting (sig. A1v). This mad fashion for Italian styles of fighting is a clear threat to English manhood: "This good have the Italian teachers of Offence done us, they have transformed our boyes into men, our men into boyes, our strong men into weaknesse" (sig. I1). Silver's volume climaxes with the story of how a valiant English gentleman flattens the Italian fencing master Vicentio with a box on the ear and then dumps a flagon of English beer over him for good measure (sig. K3).

In its concern about a cosmopolitan threat to English traditions and about the corrupting effects of effeminate foreign practices on English manhood, Silver's text is typical of many from late-sixteenth-century England. Although concern about English effeminacy did not always posit a foreign origin for the problem, and Italian culture and influence were decried for reasons that had little to do with gender identity, the two issues—Italianate corruption and the decline of English manhood—were often linked. This is partly due to the fact that erotic writing, perceived as being a major cause of effeminacy, was often represented as having an Italian origin. Texts like Silver's give voice to a widespread English concern that Italy was a source of specifically erotic corruption and that effeminizing

Italian practices threatened the masculinity of English men—and thus in a broader sense threatened the patriarchal structures of the English nation.

One of the most elaborate, eloquent, and influential articulations of this view came in 1570, with the publication of Roger Ascham's book *The Scholemaster*, a work that aimed to give principles for "the private brynging up of youth in Ientlemen and Noble mens houses" (13). Written between 1563 and 1568 and published posthumously, Ascham's manual of noble education proved quite popular; it was reprinted twice in 1571, once in 1579, and again in 1589. Ostensibly a treatise on learning Latin, *The Scholemaster* was, in fact, a crucial book in shaping English national identity in the late sixteenth century.[1] As Ascham reminds his readers, he had been Queen Elizabeth's tutor, and his work, far from merely giving advice on Latin, aspired to be a canonical handbook for the fashioning of proper English gentlemen.

Despite his novel insistence that pupils should not be beaten by their tutors, Ascham is a stern moralist. While the schoolroom itself must be a place of gentle fellowship between student and teacher, outside it there is desperate need for "more severe discipline" (49). England lacks the "good order" that was the source of the power of all the great states of antiquity, the Persians, the Romans, and above all the Athenians (49, 58–60). For Ascham, the failure of the nobility of England to raise properly virtuous and dutiful children poses a grave threat to the national interest. It is, after all, the aristocracy who set the standard of behavior for the populace as a whole. "For," he argues, "as you great ones use to do, so all meane men love to do. . . . All your lawes, all your authoritie, all your commaundementes, do not halfe so moch with meane men, as doth your example and maner of livinge" (68).

The noble classes that Ascham wants to see as the source of England's strength are also, unfortunately, the source of the very corruptions he castigates. At court, youthful innocence is mocked (53) and children are taught to curse before they learn to say grace (57). Rather than constituting a realm apart that may serve as a lofty example to the lower orders, the court is the very site of class mixing; "in the Courte . . . a yong Ientleman will ventur him self into the companie of Ruffians," and "their facions, maners, thoughtes, taulke, and deedes will . . . be ever like" (57).

In order to construct English purity, innocence, and virtue Ascham must locate the ultimate source of corruption not in the English court itself but elsewhere. The infection of English manners must have a foreign origin, and Ascham is not long in finding one. English corruption, he argues, comes directly from Italy; the infection is brought back daily by young noblemen who travel there. The Italian threat is so serious that Ascham devotes one-tenth of his volume on the education of a noble Englishman to a sustained attack on the customs, mores, and manners of Italy.[2] And lest anyone think he is unfamiliar with the vices he castigates, Ascham makes sure to tell the reader that he himself has made the treacherous journey:

> I was once in Italie my selfe: but I thanke God, my abode there, was
> but ix dayes: And yet I sawe in that litle tyme, in one Citie [Venice],

more libertie to sinne, than I ever hard tell of in our noble Citie of London in ix yeare. (83)

Perhaps Ascham led a more sheltered life in London than during his brief stay in Venice. At the time he was writing London was "notorious for its criminality,"[3] and there was widespread concern about the existence of a deviant counterculture within the capital, consisting of "the very filth and vermin of the common wealth . . . the very Sodomites of the land, children of Belial, without God, without minister; dissolute, disobedient, and reprobate to every good work."[4] The years following 1570 were marked by a increased effort to police the capital, as well as by a growing hostility toward aliens and all things perceived as foreign.[5] It is possible that growing concern with moral and social disorder in London led to the sort of demonizing of Italy seen in Ascham's *Scholemaster.*

The Scholemaster contained the first sustained English attack on Italian manners and culture, but Ascham is far from being the only English writer of the late sixteenth century to paint a lurid picture of the scandalous mores and liberties of Italy. In the 1590s, popular pamphlets like Nashe's *Piers Pennilesse* and *The Unfortunate Traveller* described the vices of Italy in graphic detail,[6] and by the early seventeenth century Italy provided the setting for the bloodiest and most perverse acts in the plays of Tourneur, Ford, Webster, and others. Traditional English humanist admiration for ancient Roman cultural achievement was contrasted with a growing distrust of contemporary Italian morals.[7]

Yet English responses to Italian culture were not univocal, and disgust with Italy was by no means universal. Italian books, many published in London, were widely read in educated circles, both in translation and in the original. Elizabeth and many of her courtiers spoke Italian fluently.[8] While there was some popular resentment of Italian luxury goods, trade relations with Italian states, especially Venice, were "generally excellent."[9] Of all the Italian states, Venice enjoyed the closest relations with England; in 1604 the Serenissima was the first Italian state to receive a resident English ambassador. Although many in England shared Ascham's vision of Venice as a pit of vice, there was also strong interest in the Venetian constitution and a certain admiration for Venetian justice, especially in the years after 1600 when the republic was in defiance of a Papal interdict. A text like Jonson's *Volpone* brings these two tendencies together by presenting both the disorderliness of Volpone and the elaborate apparatus of the courts that punish him.[10]

English notions about Rome were even more conflicted than those concerning Venice. On the one hand, of course, Rome was the seat of the papal Anti-Christ, a foreign domination against which Henry VIII had rebelled by establishing the English Church. On the other, Rome was perceived as the well-spring of classical culture, and Tudor propaganda took great pains to spread the notion that London, like Rome, was founded by Trojan exiles. Roman imperial history and iconography were useful in the establishment of English national identity.[11]

For Ascham, Rome's illustrious past is a dangerous lure. While acknowledging and praising the role of classical Rome in the creation of English humanist culture, Ascham warns that

now, that tyme is gone, and though the place remayne, yet the olde and
present maners, do differ as farre, as blacke and white, as virtue and
vice. Vertue once made that countrie Mistres over all the worlde. Vice
now maketh that countrie slave. . . . *Italie* now, is not that *Italie* that it
was wont to be. (72)

Ascham details at great length the perils faced by young Englishmen who
journey to Italy and return corrupted by Italian manners and religion. Once the
seat of the Roman Empire, Italy has degenerated into "Circes court," which will
turn the unsuspecting English traveler first into a swine, wallowing in physical
delight, then into a "dull ass" incapable of distinguishing vice from virtue. From
this he passes to the subtle relativism of the fox, breeder of mischief and disorder,
perversely "glad to commend the worse partie, and . . . defend the falser opinion" (76), and thus perverted will return home like a cruel wolf, ready to tear
asunder the body politic of England. In short, he will have become "italianate," an
inevitably pejorative term coined from the old proverb (cited by Ascham) that
"Englese Italianato, e un diabolo incarnato"—an italiante Englishman is the
devil incarnate.[12]

Ascham provides an admirably precise definition of just what being italianate
entails.

If some yet do not well understand, what is an English man Italianated,
I will plainlie tell him. He, that by living, and traveling in *Italie*, bringeth
home into England out of *Italie*, the Religion, the learning, the policie,
the experience, the maners of *Italie*. That is to say, for Religion, Papistrie
or worse: for learnyng, lesse commonly than they carried out with them:
for pollicie, a factious hart, a discoursing head, a mynde to meddle in
all men's matters; for experience, plentie of new mischieves never known
in England before: for maners, variety of vanities, and chaunge of filthy
lyving. (78)

As the organization of this passage implies, Ascham's primary reason for despis-
ing Italy is its Catholicism. Though anti-Catholic polemic was not of course new
to England in 1570, it is significant that Ascham was among the first English writers
to see Catholicism as a primarily Italian institution.[13] But while Catholicism may
have provided the foundation for English cultural antipathy toward Italy, the
disgust and fascination inspired by the italiante in the 1590s and after was not
primarily expressed in religious terms.

Besides false religion, an italianate Englishman will also acquire "a factious
hart, a discoursing head, a mynde to meddle in all mens matters"—he would, in
short, become a "Machiavellian." As well, he will take up "filthy lyving" and
introduce vices previously unknown to the purer climate of England. While
Ascham's claim that such activities were unknown in England is disingenuous,
it is clear that the "filthy" habits he means are those of the sodomite. Despite
anti-Catholic sentiment, the most common archetype of the italianate in early
modern England was not the corrupt prelate; far more prevalent were two fig-

ures of secular degeneracy: the scheming amoral Machiavellian and the perverse sodomite.[14]

It is important to distinguish between sodomy and effeminacy in early modern English culture. While a modern reader might tend to conflate the two, in the sixteenth and seventeenth centuries they were separate but related concepts. A man was effeminate if he acted in an unmanly fashion. One way he might become effeminate was to devote himself excessively to sexual pleasure, whatever its object. One could easily become effeminate within marriage, for example. Sodomy, on the other hand, could refer to a range of illicit sexual practices and was not restricted to anal sex between men, though that was one of its primary meanings.[15] Thus one could be effeminate without being a sodomite, and one could be a sodomite without being effeminate.

Nonetheless, the concepts were related. Italianate texts, authored or inspired by Italian sodomites like Pietro Aretino, could effeminate their readers by arousing and seducing them. If it were not enough that Englishmen were flocking to Italy to be debauched, Italian corruption was invading England itself in the form of filthy books. Ascham warns that one can buy "fonde bookes, of late translated out of *Italian* into English, sold at every shop in London," and cautions that

> [m]o Papistes be made by your mery bookes of *Italie*, than by your earnest bookes of *Louvain*. . . . Ten *Morte Arthures* do not the tenth part so much harme, as one of these bookes made in *Italie*, and translated in England. They open, not fond and common wayes to vice, but such subtle, cunnyng, new, and diverse shiftes, to cary yong willes to vanities, and yong wittes to mischief, to teach old bawdes new schole poyntes, as the simple head of an Englishman is not hable to invent, nor never was hard of in England before. . . . Suffer these bookes to be read, and they shall soone displace all bookes of godly learnyng. (79–80)

Similar polemic against the ubiquity of lewd foreign books in the bookshops of London also appeared in contemporary broadside ballads. Thomas Brice's 1562 ballad "Against filthy writing / and such like delighting" uses the phrase "Ethnickes trade" to explicitly link the lewd verse he condemns to both foreignness and the practices of the emergent book market:

> What meane the rimes that run thus large
> in every shop to sell?
> With wanton sound and filthie sense,
> Methink it goes not well.
> We are not Ethnickes [heathens—foreigners] we forsoth,
> at least profess not so.
> Why range we then to Ethnickes trade?
> come back, where will you go?
> Tell me is Christ or Cupid Lord?
> doth God or Venus reign?

(ll. 1–10)

As we have seen, erotic writing in England was a native practice. It was multivalent and multivoiced. It flourished in private coterie manuscripts, had great success in the public book market, and was a fundamental aspect of the plays presented in the public theaters. Not only was writing about sexual love pervasive in literary culture, it was also practiced and defended by those poets who did the most to establish a serious national literature. Yet at the same time, erotic writing was perceived by many readers as corrupting, disturbing, or disorderly. It was seen as an important cause of effeminacy—a moral and physical failing whose consequences were national as well as personal. One response to the concerns provoked by the circulation of erotic writing was to ban some of its more public and disorderly manifestations. Another was to ascribe a foreign origin to such writing.

Not surprisingly, the conflicting views over whether or not poetry was effeminizing came into sharpest conflict around the issue of erotic writing. Such writing risked effeminizing its writers and readers, but it could also be a potential source of notoriety and even fame for its author. As I will show, the complex of issues that grew up around erotic writing in early modern England tended to focus on the notion of "italianate" corruption. And erotic italianate corruption was frequently embodied in one emblematic figure: the powerful Venetian writer Pietro Aretino. Just as Machiavelli came to embody hypocrisy and political amorality, so Aretino served as a type of the effeminate—even sodomitical—erotic writer. The remainder of this study explores the role of "Aretine" writing in the construction of both masculinity and authorship in early modern England.

"Courtesan Politic"

The Erotic Writing and Cultural Significance of Pietro Aretino

For a cultural history of erotic writing in early modern England, Pietro Aretino is a crucial figure.[1] Not only did he serve as an ideal type of the erotic poet, he was also praised for his political stance as an independent satirist. Aretino was the primary figure through which early modern England represented erotic authorship to itself—an authorship that was, as we have seen, more native and more widely diffused than this cultural concentration on the mythic figure of a single Italian writer would suggest. Like Machiavelli, Aretino allowed the English to locate certain forms of perceived corruption in a single demonic image of the foreign. An examination of how the figure of Aretino was constructed and deployed in early modern English culture elucidates some of the crucial ways that erotic representation functioned in England prior to the rise of pornography.

For modern readers to whom the name may be unfamiliar, it is difficult to realize how prominent the figure of Aretino was in sixteenth-century European culture. Though in his lifetime he was one of the most well-known and widely read European men of letters,[2] Aretino's works have been largely ignored in the years since his death; the coarseness of his style, the lewdness of his subject matter, his bisexual promiscuity, and the extravagant scale on which he extorted income from patrons have all conspired to make him an unpleasant figure in the eyes of later critics.[3] And the fact that in 1558, two years after his death, all his writings were placed on the Index and banned throughout Catholic Europe insured that he would become a mythic figure of exotic transgression—known by rumor and innuendo, more talked about than read. Even today when issues of gender and sexuality, the construction of social identity, and the circulation of social power have come to play a central role in Renaissance literary studies, Aretino, who for the sixteenth century exemplifies all these issues, has received relatively little serious attention outside Italy—almost none in the context of English culture and society.[4] Even now there are few reliable English translations of many of Aretino's major works.[5] Similarly, there is no good English biography.[6]

Rather than being a traditional survey of Aretino's literary "influence" on the work of various English writers, this chapter examines the complex role the mythos of Aretino played in English culture in the late sixteenth and early seventeenth centuries. Although many of Aretino's works were widely available in Italian, none were translated into English in the period, and most were known only by reputation. Despite the limited circulation of his texts, however, Aretino became the principle iconographic figure of the erotic writer in early modern England, and his cultural importance extended far beyond the small group of English men and women who had actually read his works.

The early modern English image of Aretino owed much of its cultural potency to the fact that it was overdetermined. Besides being seen as the quintessential erotic writer, Aretino was also marked as a sodomite—and this notoriety served to blur the line between authorship of erotic texts and personal erotic practice. Ovid's excuse, "Lascivia est nobis pagina, vita proba" ("my writing is lascivious, but my life is virtuous"), cannot be applied to Aretino. Furthermore, Aretino was also seen as a significant political figure. Born the son of a shoemaker, through his writing Aretino rose to become phenomenally wealthy; despite his low birth, he was known as the "Scourge of Princes"; he represented himself as an independent writer who dared to speak truth to power and who profited handsomely from it (figure 3.1). If many found Aretino's social mobility both disturbing and offensive, the vast wealth and social prestige he attained neither through birth nor land nor trade but primarily through his writing fascinated a generation of Elizabethan writers who yearned both to be arbiters of social opinion and to be adequately rewarded for their work.

Although historically speaking Aretino's political power and financial success did not arise directly from his erotic writing, in early modern England the two mythic aspects of Aretino—the sodomite and the Scourge of Princes—were inseparably bound up together. This formulation of Aretino as both politically and erotically disorderly can be clearly seen in John Donne's anti-Jesuit polemic of 1611, *Ignatius His Conclave*. Appearing in the midst of a procession of evil Catholic "innovators" (including Columbus, Paracelsus, and Machiavelli), Aretino is credited both with his "licentious pictures" and "a long custome of libellous and contumelious speaking against Princes," a quality that, Donne argues, leads inevitably to atheism (64–7). The English figure of Aretino was thus fundamentally contradictory: it offered an enormously attractive precedent for authorial power, which was at the same time marked as disorderly, effeminate, and sodomitical—qualities that were, in theory, antithetical to authorial power by their very nature (figure 3.2). In the word "Aretine" the Elizabethans coined an adjective that powerfully linked troubling notions of foreignness, erotic disorder, authorial power, and social mobility.

Figure 3.1. *Aretino as the powerful Scourge of Princes. Titian: Portrait of Pietro Aretino. Copyright The Frick Collection, New York.*

Aretine's Pictures: The *Sonetti Lussuriosi*

Aretino's works, especially his erotic writings, have been widely misunderstood because they have generally been read divorced from their social context; they have been read, that is, as if they were pornography, a predictable, empty, and reductive discourse whose meanings are all too obvious. Though in some ways the *sonetti lussuriosi* may seem to prefigure later pornography, these similarities are more the result of systematic mythologizing and misreading than of anything intrinsic either to the text itself or the social context that produced it. The *sonetti* were not written as pornography—they became pornographic over a period of hundreds of years.

To understand the contemporary significance of Aretino's erotic writings, one must first consider his social position. He was born (as his name indicates)

Figure 3.2. *Aretino as sodomitical satyr. Medal of Pietro Aretino, c. 1536, bronze with phallic satyr on reverse. © Copyright The British Museum.*

in Arezzo in 1492, son of a shoemaker named Andrea or Luca del Tura and a woman named Margherita Bonci.[7] His father left the family while Aretino was quite young, and he was brought up with the children of a local nobleman, Luigi Bacci, who befriended his mother. He left home in his early teens, staying in Perugia for a time[8] and possibly wandering around Italy before arriving in Rome in 1517, at the age of twenty-five. In Rome he entered the household of the wealthy Sienese banker Agostino Chigi but soon left Chigi for the court of Pope Leo X.[9] While he probably came to Chigi as a simple domestic servant, he may have already been a writer; a book of poetry bearing his name and published in Venice bears the date January 22, 1512.[10]

Aretino first gained public notoriety after the death of Leo X in 1522, with a series of vicious *pasquinades,*[11] anonymous verses placed on the battered statue called Pasquino in Piazza Navona, which satirized the corruption of the Papal Conclave and supported the candidacy of Aretino's new patron, Cardinal Giuliano de' Medici. When Giuliano lost and the Dutch Pope Adrian VI was elected, Aretino was forced to flee Rome. He was sent by his patron to Mantua, where he soon became a favorite of the marquis, Federigo Gonzaga. But after a short time, he left Mantua for the camp of Giuliano's cousin, Giovanni delle Bande Nere, Italy's most famous soldier. The two became friends, and it was Giovanni who first gave Aretino his title "Flagello dei Principi," the Scourge of Princes, later repeated by Ariosto in *Orlando Furioso* (46.14).[12]

When Giuliano de' Medici became Pope Clement VII in 1523, Aretino returned to Rome. But he soon fell from favor. Aretino's friend Marcantonio Raimondi the engraver was imprisoned by the pope's counselor Giovanni Matteo Giberti for reproducing a series of sixteen erotic drawings by Giulio Romano (figure 3.3). Aretino petitioned the pope for Raimondi's release, and after he was free, wrote a series of sixteen erotic poems, known as the *sonetti lussuriosi,* to go with the engravings.[13] Though it seems that a volume was printed, probably after Aretino had fled to Venice, no copy of this edition, or of the earlier edition of the engravings alone, is known to survive. It may be that the sonnets circulated primarily in manuscript copies, written on the engraved sheets.[14] It seems the ear-

Figure 3.3. *A surviving engraving from* I modi. *Marcantonio Raimondi,* I modi, Position 1. *Engraving after Giulio Romano. By Permission of the Bibliotèque Nationale de France.*

liest surviving edition is one probably printed in Venice in 1527 in which the engravings are replaced by crude woodcuts.

Aretino's *sonetti* are crucial to any history of European erotic writing not merely because of their novel combination of visual image with written text but, more important, because of their sheer notoriety. Without a doubt the *sonetti* were the most infamous erotic verses in early modern England. By the end of the sixteenth century, the phrase "Aretine's pictures" was ubiquitous. As poems written to accompany and elucidate images, they are far more descriptive than narrative, and this in itself is an innovation in erotic writing. The *sonetti* appropriate the quintessential Petrarchan mode while utterly rejecting Petrarchan conceit; and their format, combining text and engravings, prefigures that of much subsequent erotic writing. But while in the long run the *sonetti* were certainly Aretino's most notorious work, they did not enjoy a wide circulation, nor—despite their reputed prefiguration of pornography[15]— were they widely imitated. The earliest editions were rapidly and effectively suppressed, and I know of no evidence that any of the various pirated editions circulated in sixteenth-century England. While the existence of the sonnets and engravings was well known in Elizabethan London, there is little proof that any English person owned or had even seen a copy. Thus the notion that Aretino was the artist as well as author of the volume circulated widely. The images were generally referred to as "Aretine's pictures"[16]—a formulation that stresses the pictorial over the literary and is also strongly proprietary: all such "pictures" are "Aretine."

The dynamics of gender and power and desire in the *sonetti* do not conform to those characteristic of pornography. Each engraving depicts a heterosexual coupling, every one devoted to a different position, thus the title *I modi* or, as they came to be known in eighteenth-century England, Aretino's "postures." Fifteen of the sixteen sonnets are in dialogue form; the couples discuss the positions they are engaged in and the pleasures they experience. (The remaining sonnet [15] describes the couple from the point of view of an outside observer.) While some of the engravings highlight the aggressive strength of the man and in some the woman wears a confused or pained expression,[17] the sonnets themselves do not stress male domination of the female or masculine control of the sexual encounter.[18] The speeches in the dialogues tend to be equally divided between the male and female speakers—in several sonnets the woman directs the man on how best to please her.[19] And while some of the sonnets describe rough sex, none of them represents a rape; in most both partners seem to derive equal pleasure. As a group, the sonnets celebrate sexual possibilities rather than elaborating a hierarchy of postures or attempting to dictate a "proper" form of heterosexual intercourse. The couples engage in both anal and vaginal intercourse, and several sonnets compare the relative merits of the two; some of the female speakers prefer to be buggered, others do not. Similarly, in sonnet 2 it is asserted that "a real man has to be a buggerer," whereas the male speaker in sonnet 10 initially refuses to bugger his partner, claiming "that kind of thing is meat for prelates."

While the *sonetti lussuriosi* might seem the ultimate apolitical text, consisting only of descriptions and articulations of pleasure, it is important to remember that these poems came into existence as a direct reaction to political repression, specifically the papal imprisonment of Raimondi, the engraver of Romano's drawings. Aretino petitioned the pope for Raimondi's release, and after he was free, wrote the sixteen erotic sonnets to accompany a new edition of the engravings. Aretino clearly wanted the *sonetti* to be read as a political protest as well as for erotic titillation.[20]

In a famous letter written to justify the poems, Aretino contrasts the official response to obscenity with its tolerance of violence and corruption:

> I reject the furtive attitude and filthy custom which forbid the eyes what delights them most. What harm is there in seeing a man mount a woman? Should the beasts be more free than us? It would seem to me that the thing nature gave us to preserve the race should be worn as a pendant around one's neck or as a medal in one's hat, since it's the spring which feeds all the rivers of humankind. . . . It has made you. . . . It has made me. . . . It has produced all the Bembos. . . . the Sansovinos, and the Titians, and the Michelangelos; and after them, the Popes, the Emperors, and the Kings; it has begotten lovely children and the loveliest of women. . . . and so we should consecrate special vigils and feast-days

in its honor, and not enclose it in a scrap of cloth or silk. One's hands should rightly be kept hidden, because they wager money, sign false testimony, lend usuriously, gesture obscenely, rend, destroy, strike blows, wound and kill. And what do you think of the mouth, which blasphemes, spits in your face, gorges, boozes, and vomits?[21]

This letter is typical of Aretino's use of the erotic—sex and bodily functions in general are used to level and erase distinctions between classes and between high and low culture: fucking produced the pope, Michelangelo, and the Sistine ceiling as well as Aretino, his reader, and the *sonetti*. Despite Aretino's marked stress on the male member in his letter, in the *sonetti* themselves female genitalia receive more or less equal praise.[22] Although Aretino's articulation and valorization of female sexual desire may not be as great as some critics have argued,[23] and his text always remains—of course—a *male* articulation of female desire, this aspect of his works is nonetheless markedly different from the treatment of female desire in most forms of pornography.

Until quite recently very little of critical significance has been written on the *sonetti lussuriosi*, for the simple reason that they were so quickly and effectively suppressed that very few people ever actually read them. The first English "translation" of the sonnets, by Samuel Putnam, was published in 1926—in a limited "collectors'" edition filled with errors and misinterpretations and obviously aimed at highbrow collectors of "exotic" erotic books. Reissued in an unlimited edition in 1933, this was, until 1988, the only version of the sonnets available in English. Here is Putnam's rendering of the second of the sonnets, to which he gives the cozy title "Of Fireside Sports":

> And now of feasts and fireside sports we'll sing,
>> And I will teach you a new game to play;
>> But you must come around the other way,
> Though not too fast,!—tap gently: that's the thing.
> Oh, it's a very merry prank to bring
>> A guest round by the rear! Then let him stay—
>> From deepest midnight till the dawn's first ray—
> Let's hurl a spear and stop this chattering!
> And now we enter a moist woodland dell,
>> Whose scenery would leave me breathless quite,
>> If I had any breath from that last kiss!
> Is this not better than the tales they tell
>> Around the fire upon a winter night?
>> My tale too has a point you cannot miss.

Not until Lynne Lawner's 1988 translation could an English reader have a more accurate idea of Aretino's *sonetti*. Compare Lawner's translation of the same poem.

> SHE: Stick your finger up my ass, old man,
>> Thrust *cazzo* in a little at a time,
>> Lift up my leg, maneuver well,

Now pound with all inhibitions gone.
I believe this is a tastier feast
Than eating garlic bread before a fire.
If you don't like the *potta*, try the back way:
A real man has got to be a buggerer.

HE: This time I'll do it in the *potta*,
But next time in the *cul*: with *cazzo* in *potta* and *cul*
I feel delight and you are happy and blessed.
Those who strive to get ahead are crazy,
They waste their time.
Fottere is the only thing to hanker after.
                                        Let Sir Courtier croak
Waiting around for his rival to die.
I seek only to satisfy my lust.[24]

It must be confessed that Lawner's translation is much closer to Aretino than Putnam's pompous, obscure, and euphemistic paraphrase, but some things have not changed: even Lawner's text, which follows the Italian quite closely—and she praises *I modi* as "the artful presentation of seemingly endless possibility" (p. 46)—suffers from a certain prudent reticence. For despite her celebration of the poem's explicitness, she refuses to translate the Italian *cazzo, potta, culo,* and *fottere* to the English "cock," "cunt," "asshole," and "fuck." She claims that the Italian terms give her translations "an 'archaic' flavor" and keep them from "being nothing more than pornographic exercises in a contemporary mode" (58). Thus while Lawner, unlike Putnam, demonstrates a sincere desire to translate the poems as accurately as she can, the underlying assumption remains: if Aretino's sonnets were translated word for word into contemporary English, they would be somehow "reduced" to the level of pornography—and this must not be allowed to happen. The dilemma is obvious: if one decides that the *sonetti* are "pornography," one is then obliged to defend twentieth-century pornography in order to discuss them seriously. Since, for various reasons, few academics are eager to take this step, the sonnets must be either ignored as worthless or presented as being somehow more legitimate than pornography; as Lawner puts it, "they speak to us in a language that is timeless and universal" (19). And yet since the language of the sonnets is—for the twentieth-century reader—uncomfortably close to the language of pornography, the "universal" language must be changed, usually in the name of making the translations "more authentic." Nothing could demonstrate more clearly the way the term "pornography" impedes serious historical investigation of early modern erotic writing. Lawner's appeal to vague and uncritical universal standards of value is all the more revealing in light of the fact that elsewhere in her introduction she writes at great length of the historical specificity of the *sonetti* (22–30). The more recent prose translation by Bette Talvacchia shows a similar discomfort with the language of the *sonetti*: she decries "the unrelieved coarseness and lack of imagination in Anglo-Saxon four-letter words" and compares Aretino's bawdry to Shakespeare's (xiii).

As a result of the publication of his sonnets, Aretino was again forced to flee Rome, but he soon returned, wrote more poems attacking the pope's counselors, and even directed the 1525 *festa* of Pasquino, a Roman festival of misrule.[25] By this time Giberti, the papal minister who bore the brunt of Aretino's abuse, had had enough, and he attempted to have Aretino assassinated. On the night of July 28, 1525, Aretino was attacked by Achille Della Volta, a Bolognese gentleman in Giberti's service. Aretino survived the attack but was seriously injured in the chest and right hand.[26] At the end of the year he left Rome for good.

He joined Giovanni delle Bande Nere, who was battling the imperial forces of Charles V in Lombardy, and was at his friend's side when Giovanni died of wounds he received in a skirmish near Governolo. Giovanni died in Mantua,[27] but Aretino could not remain there long. Despite his earlier affection for (and subsequent patronage of) Aretino, the Marquis Federigo Gonzaga offered in a letter to have him assassinated, if it would please the pope.[28] And so, in 1527, at the age of thirty-five, Aretino came to Venice, the city where he would spend the rest of his life.[29]

Courtiers and Courtesans: The *Ragionamenti*

In the 1530s Aretino wrote various satirical dialogues, the most famous of which, the *Ragionamenti* (also known as the *Sei giornate*), discusses the three states of women: nuns, wives, and whores. Like the *sonetti*, while the *Ragionamenti* clearly served as a model for later pornographic texts, they themselves differ greatly from pornography as a genre, both in their mode of representation of erotic acts and in their conception of the social role of sexuality and of the place of women. Although the *Ragionamenti* contain passages in which sexual activities are described in lascivious detail, the great bulk of the work fits comfortably into a tradition of satiric and political (and bawdy) dialogues going back to Lucian's *Dialogues of the Courtesans*.[30] While much of later pornography attempts to reduce all human activity to sexual acts, the *Ragionamenti* consistently relate sex to the broadest possible range of activity. Whereas the *sonetti* are insistent in their use of low terms—the equivalents of "cunt," "cock," and "fuck"—to describe genitalia and intercourse, in the *Ragionamenti* the relation between sexuality and other realms of social life is established not only by narrative but by the metaphoric language of the text itself. Fed up with the extravagant (and hilarious) sexual metaphors used by Nanna, the experienced whore who is the dialogue's primary interlocutor, Antonia, exclaims:

> Speak plainly and say "fuck," "prick," "cunt," and "ass" if you want anyone except the scholars at the University of Rome to understand you. You with your "rope in the ring," your "obelisk in the Coliseum," your "leek in the garden," your "key in the lock," your "bolt in the door," your "pestle in the mortar," your "nightingale in the nest," your "tree in the ditch," your "syringe in the flap-valve," your "sword in the scabbard," not to mention your "stake," your "crozier," your "parsnip," your

"little monkey," your "this," your "that," your "him" and your "her,"
your "apples," "leaves of the missal," "fact," *verbigratia*," "job," "affair,"
"big news," "handle," "arrow," "carrot," "root," and all the shit there
is—why don't you say it straight out and stop going about on tiptoes?
Why don't you say yes when you mean yes and no when you mean no—
or else keep it to yourself?[31]

Despite this exhortation, which is as much a celebration of metaphor as a request for plain speaking, Nanna refuses to change her florid style of speech. It is
as if the logic of decorum dictated that physical excess must be described with
rhetorical excess—a philosophy of language notably evident in the contemporary work of Rabelais. While pornography has a tendency to sexualize the world
by reducing everything to sex,[32] Aretino's writings do the exact opposite: his eclec-
tic use of metaphor relates sex to a world of activity, to nightingales, bolts, keys,
swords, vegetables, trees, animals, church regalia, and the ruins of Rome. Reading the *Ragionamenti*, one is struck not by a monotony that reduces all details to
aspects of endlessly repeated acts of heterosexual intercourse but by the endless
variety of objects and actions that can be eroticized. For while all Aretino's erotic
writings deal with prostitution and can thus aptly be described as "porno-graphos"
(whore-writing), their representation of female sexual agency, their questioning
of established gender categories, their awareness of class conflict, and their obvious embeddedness in political and social controversy all serve to differentiate them
from pornography as a genre.

Even more than Aretino's other erotic writings, the *Ragionamenti* are highly
politicized, and they cannot be understood without taking account of their
author's unique social position. When Aretino wrote the *sonetti lussuriosi* he was
a relatively minor figure at the papal court. By the time he came to write the
Ragionamenti, he was a feared and respected (and hated) satirist, who was both
politically influential and widely known. The political independence of Venice
offered Aretino an ideal haven from which to write personal invective and political satire. As long as he supported the Venetian republic, he was free to express
a remarkably broad range of political opinions. William Thomas, an Englishman who lived in Venice for a time, was eloquent in his description of the liberty granted those who dwelt there: "Al men, specially strangers, have so much
libertee there, that though they speake verie ill by the Venetians so they attempte
nothyng in effecte against theyr astate, no man shall control them for it. . . . He
that dwelleth in Venice, maie recken himself exempt from subiection."[33] Though
Aretino seems to have seriously considered moving to France and even to
Constantinople in the early 1530s, the advantages and comforts of life in Venice
insured that he remained.[34]

Before arriving in Venice, Aretino had written a *giudizio*, or prophecy, for
the year 1527, in which he predicted that, with Giovanni dead, Italy would be
laid waste by the imperial troops and that Rome itself would be sacked.[35] To the
immense credit of his reputation, everything occurred substantially as he said it
would. Unlike the solemn and abstract astrological *giudizii* published each year,

Aretino's was cutting, satirical, and full of specific gossip and invective. He had such success with his 1527 prophecy that his *giudizii* became an annual event, and at least until the mid-1530s each new year was greeted by a mock prophetic pamphlet from Aretino. These ephemeral productions, of which few copies survive, seem to have provided the first solid basis for Aretino's international popularity. Previously known primarily in the society of the papal court in Rome, as a result of the wide dissemination of his annual *giudizii* Aretino became an influential figure throughout Italy as well as in the French and imperial courts, both of which were deeply involved in Italian affairs.

Until 1536, when he moved definitively into the imperial camp, Aretino would come down either on the side of France or the Empire in his *giudizii*, according to the prevailing political winds. Aretino had begun courting François I as early as 1525, when following the French king's capture by imperial forces at the battle of Pavia he sent a letter to François counseling stoic resignation.[36] His first letter to Charles V came in 1527, following the sack of Rome, advocating mercy for Pope Clement VII, who—like François before him—had fallen into the emperor's hands. (Characteristically leaving all his options open, Aretino used the same occasion to write the captive pope a letter quite similar to the one he had sent François two years earlier.)[37] In 1533 François, hoping to gain Aretino's support in his struggle with the Hapsburgs, sent him a three-pound gold chain, the links shaped like tongues, engraved with the legend "lingua eius loquetur mendacium" (his tongue will speak falsehood); the measure of Aretino's political autonomy can be judged from his response: he complained in a public letter that the chain took too long to arrive.[38]

Alessandro Luzio's detailed study of Aretino's relationship with Marquis Federigo Gonzaga of Mantua between 1526 and 1531 remains an excellent account of the various tactics Aretino used to insure himself a steady income. Having failed to secure a suitable invitation to the French court from François I, Aretino turned his attentions to Mantua and promised to write Federigo a narrative poem called *Marfisa*, which would continue the never-ending story of Ariosto's *Orlando Furioso* to the undying fame of the Gonzaga. Over a period of three years the Marquis received from Aretino a flood of hopeful progress reports and a trickle of completed stanzas. Long periods of procrastination were punctuated with threats either to destroy the manuscript or to change the dedication to praise one of Federigo's rivals. Thus skillfully managing his affairs, Aretino managed to solicit gifts, favors, and large amounts of money from the marquis. The deal eventually fell through, and Federigo definitively broke with Aretino in 1531.

Aretino's literary output in the 1520s and 30s was by no means limited to inferior imitations of Ariosto. By the early 1540s he had written five comedies and one tragedy for the stage and a series of religious tracts—including a paraphrase of Genesis and a translation of the seven penitential Psalms that later served as a model for Sir Thomas Wyatt.[39] Given his licentious reputation, which was all the more widely established by the association of his name with works he did not actually write, it is easy to forget (or to dismiss the fact) that Aretino wrote devotional tracts as well as erotic sonnets, bawdy dialogues, and arrogant letters.

Aretino's biographers have traditionally seen his devotional works as the height of hypocrisy and thus, in a strange way, even worse, from an ethical point of view, than his erotic writings.[40] Hypocritical these works might have been, but to say so is to make an argument about intentions rather than results. When Aretino's *Sette Salmi di penitentia* (1534) was translated into English and published in 1635 it was erroneously attributed to Savonarola, implying that someone at some point could not tell the difference.[41]

For my purposes, Aretino's most important and resonant work from this period is the *Ragionamenti*, or *Dialogues*, which appeared in two parts, the first in 1534, the second in 1536. The first is a dialogue between two courtesans, the young (but by no means naive) Antonia and the older, more experienced Nanna. Nanna is trying to decide how to bring up her adolescent daughter Pippa, and the dialogue is a debate over which of the three possible states of adult womanhood Pippa should enter. In her time Nanna has been a nun, a wife, *and* a whore, and as she recounts her adventures to Antonia each day of the dialogue is devoted to one of these conditions in an attempt to compare the three and to decide which is best. Having weighed the alternatives, Nanna and Antonia come to the conclusion that Pippa will be best off as a whore. The second part of the *Ragionamenti* continues the discussion: on the fourth day Nanna instructs Pippa on her future vocation, on the fifth Nanna warns her daughter about the viciousness of men, and on the final day of the dialogue, Nanna and Pippa listen to a midwife who explains to a wet nurse how to be a procuress.

If Castiglione wrote the *Book of the Courtier*, in the *Ragionamenti* Aretino wrote the Book of the Courtesan. Much of the strength and humor of the *Ragionamenti* comes from its appropriation of the elevated form of the Platonic dialogue to discuss erotic service rather than ideal service—the economics of sex rather than the metaphysics of love. The bawdiest and most explicit sexual description comes on the very first day, as Nanna and Antonia discuss the life of nuns. Nanna recounts her induction into a convent as a young virgin and her immediate debauchery, beginning with a gluttonous banquet at the end of which glass dildos are distributed as a final dessert (81–4;19–22). Left alone in a room with several useful cracks in the walls, the innocent Nanna observes a veritable panopticon of sexual activity—all performed by the other nuns and the monks from a neighboring monastery: heterosexual coupling, buggery, bisexual orgies, lesbian sex with dildoes, and masturbation, a technique Nanna quickly learns for herself before her first encounter with a prelate (89–108;27–48).

Later chapters contain a fair number of erotic descriptive passages but nothing to compare with the first. The explicit and graphic description of sex that made the *Ragionamenti* infamous is thus almost entirely in the service of a savagely satiric attack on clerical corruption. The reputation of the *Ragionamenti* as an "erotic classic" can obscure the fact that the text is part of a sustained campaign by its author against the papal court, which had cast him out and tried to have him killed. Though he was reconciled with Pope Clement and Giberti in September 1530, the reconciliation was purely practical—the moment Clement died in 1534

Aretino resumed his attacks on Giberti.[42] It is significant that the same year saw both the publication of the first part of the *Ragionamenti* and the revision and first printing of Aretino's play *La Cortigiana*, which provides a highly critical vision of life as a servant at the papal court of the 1520s. Aretino's resentment is clearly visible in the extended parody of Virgil's *Aeneid* in the *Ragionamenti*'s second volume. Here Aeneas, the traditional embodiment of Roman virtue, is represented not as a pious hero exiled by the fall of Troy but as a boorish and cowardly papal courtier fleeing the sack of Rome (424;248).

Far from being a frivolous sexual fantasy, the *Ragionamenti* are a political and politicized text that critiques various social abuses and attempts to intervene—as propaganda at the very least—in actual power struggles between sixteenth-century Italian states. Far more radical, however, is their treatment of the politics of gender. The *Ragionamenti* constitute one of the most remarkable documents on the status of women produced in sixteenth-century Europe. Though they are profoundly ambivalent about women's moral status, they offer, nonetheless, a scathing indictment of the social options facing women in early modern Italy. And while they were often read as an attack on female corruption, they also sympathize with the cunning, cleverness, and energy of their female protagonists to a greater degree than almost any other text of the period.

After describing how her mother removed her from the convent because she had been beaten black and blue by her clerical lover, on the second day of the dialogue Nanna describes her experiences as a wife: if the life of nuns is utterly given over to orgiastic pleasure, the wives Nanna describes are concerned above all with duping their husbands to attain satisfying sex elsewhere. While there is still a measure of explicit erotic description, the text is far more concerned with the cunning and technique required to deceive the jealous husbands than with the sex that results. Some passages are not all that different from Boccaccio, an author of whom—unlike Petrarch—Aretino tended to speak well.

A concern with practicality comes into its own on the third day when Nanna describes the life of whores. The life of a nun may be one of polymorphous promiscuity, the life of a wife devoted to adulterous deception, but the life of a whore is business, first, last, and always: "a whore turns everything to her advantage" (239;166). Unlike nuns and wives, whores are not particularly concerned with sex, let alone affection: "It's impossible," Nanna says, "for a woman who submits to everyone to fall in love with anyone" (241;119). Clichéd as it is, this formulation points to the source of Nanna's power: she is neither sentimental about love nor awed by the pleasures of sex; and thus she is free from some of the more obvious forms of male domination—unlike many of the women whose stories she tells she will not be duped into trusting the men she has sex with. Nanna is well aware that the world (or at any rate her world) is a site of naked gender struggle, and she intends to win. "There wasn't a single man who slept with me," she boasts, "who didn't part with a piece of his hide" (248;127). If wives use their cunning to get sex, whores use theirs to get power and property. Much as Nanna appreciates sexual pleasure (and the power it brings), she—like Aretino—is well aware that the power that comes with wealth is often more useful.

At the heart of the *Ragionamenti* is an unresolved ambiguity about the status of whores, and indeed of women in general. Nanna goes so far as to argue that "all women who become infatuated with [men] are whores" (443;268), and when Antonia protests that it is hard to believe a woman capable of the cunning and deceit with which Nanna fleeces her customers, Nanna replies, "Whores are not women, they are whores" (256;135). This memorable formulation encapsulates the ambivalent attitude of the *Ragionamenti* toward the women it represents. On the one hand, Nanna and Antonia can be read as monstrous—as whores they are not even women; they are subhuman predators. On the other, as the ultimate decision to make Pippa a whore suggests, being a courtesan offers a woman a way to transcend some of the social limitations placed on her by her gender. Unlike the majority of women, for example, Nanna manages her own property, conducts her own business affairs, and commands troops of armed men (238–9;115–6). Whatever their ultimate moral status, the text clearly revels in its tales of Nanna's cunning and exults in the triumph of the whores' deceit over masculine stupidity.

While on one level the stories Nanna and Antonia tell are a form of self-criticism that lays bare the sins of women before men, Aretino more than once suggests that a similar collection could be compiled from the lives of "priests, monks, and laymen." At the beginning of the third day's conversation, Antonia says stories of men's foolishness and deceit should be written down "so that the women you mention could hear and laugh at them, in the same way these men laugh at us who, just to appear wise, provide them with so many criticisms of ourselves" (229;105). If Nanna and Antonia's attempts "to appear wise" reveal them as corrupt, the same could be said of the men they describe. As this passage suggests, in Aretino's view, rather than revealing universal truths, stories are social constructions that support or attack the interests and worldview of specific social groups.

In fact, the fifth day of the dialogue is devoted to stories of men's mistreatment of women, and it is here that Nanna is most outspoken about misogyny and male viciousness in general. She tells stories of whores robbed by men, others gang-raped, others driven to suicide. Structurally, this section merely reverses the trend of the other sections of the dialogue, in which whores trick and swindle their clients, but Aretino takes care to point out the differences between the two sorts of aggression. As Nanna says,

> [i]f you set on one side all the men ruined by whores, and on the other side all the whores shattered by men, you will see who bears the greater blame, we or they. I could tell of tens, dozens, scores of whores who ended up under carts, in hospitals, kitchens, or on the streets, or sleeping under counters in the fairs; and just as many who went back to slaving as laundresses, landladies, bawds, beggars, bread-vendors, and candle peddlers, thanks to having whored for this man or that; but nobody will ever show me a man who, due to the whores, became an innkeeper, coachman, horse-currier, lackey, quack, cop, middleman, or mendicant bum. (443;269)

Such passages of eloquent and perceptive social analysis must be set against others in the *Ragionamenti*—such as the description of the vile aging Mother of Discipline in Nanna's convent (106–8;45–7)—which dredge up every cliché of conventional sixteenth-century antifeminist discourse. Aretino's awareness of the social construction of power relations, and his willingness to lay them bare, does not translate into a coherent rejection of essentialist conceptions of gender. When on the second day of the dialogue Antonia tries to lay the blame for female sexuality on women's subordinate social position, saying, "if you take into account the poverty in which we women are born, that is reason enough that we do whatever men ask of us, not that we are bad, as people believe," Nanna sharply disagrees, asserting that women's sexual desire is natural and inescapable.

> We are born of the flesh and in the flesh we die, the genitals make us, and the genitals destroy us. . . . For every woman pleased with her husband there are thousands disgusted with theirs. . . . Feminine chastity is like a glass decanter which, no matter how carefully you handle it, finally slips out of your fingers when you least expect it and is shattered completely. If you don't keep it locked up in a chest, it is impossible to keep it whole; and the woman who does can be considered a miracle, like glass that falls and doesn't break. (197;102)[43]

This formulation of female insatiability would seem to fit neatly into the clichés of sixteenth-century antifeminism, were it not that Aretino says much the same thing of men, children, and humanity in general in the prefatory letter to the *sonetti lussuriosi*. Aretino's appreciation and valorization of sexual pleasure and the physicality of existence are genuine, and this quality of his writing, so different from the majority of sixteenth-century discourse on women, serves to undermine to some degree the misogynist social constructions of women his text is working with. Aretino's Nanna, Gargantuan as she is, is portrayed far more positively than any female character in the works of Rabelais, an author whose fabled carnevalesque celebration of the lower body is frequently accompanied by a disgust for female genitalia that is almost entirely absent in Aretino.

Aretino's dialogues (like their Platonic models) are multivalent; they do not offer a simple, clear-cut vision in which whores are bad or whores are good. Nanna is clear-sighted *and* vain, plain-speaking *and* corrupt, an experienced whore *and* a mother concerned for the well-being of her child. Writing on gender relations and homoeroticism, Eve Sedgwick has argued that only by playing essentialist notions of gender against arguments that gender is socially constructed can a space for sexual freedom be achieved.[44] Nanna's strategy is somewhat similar—she blames social forces for the lot of whores, yet is unwilling to see herself as a passive subject of external pressures: men's cruelty results in women's ruin, but for Nanna women's desires are fundamentally their own—their sexual appetite does not have its roots in their oppression.

Ambivalent about gender relations, the *Ragionamenti* are much clearer in their view of the relations between masters and servants. Strategic praise of specific princes aside, Aretino's writings as a whole tend to champion clever servants over their masters. Nanna declares that "factors, grooms, lackeys, gardeners, porters, and cooks" are better lovers than "gentlemen, nobles, and monsignors" because they are more taciturn, less arrogant, and do not force whores to engage in such aristocratic degeneracies as sodomy, oral sex, and torturously uncomfortable positions (457;320). Sex is better, she ironically suggests, if one does not learn it from books like *I modi*.

Despite its unwillingness to attribute female sexual avidity to women's subordinate social position, Aretino's text repeatedly foregrounds the power relations that structure the social world its characters inhabit. Nanna is well aware that if she has in some fashion managed to transcend the common lot of women, she is very much in the minority, and her position is precarious.

> A whore always has a thorn in her heart which makes her uneasy and troubled: and it is the fear of begging on those church steps and selling those candles ... and I must confess that for one Nanna who knows how to have her land bathed by the fructifying sun, there are thousands of whores who end their days in the poorhouse. Indeed ... whores and courtiers can be put in the same scales; in fact you see most of them looking like defaced silver coins rather than bright gold pieces. (256;135–6)

Despite their seemingly different functions, status, and gender, courtesans and courtiers are much the same;[45] their job is to pleasure the powerful, and the vast majority of both are ground under and end their lives in poverty and misery. For despite the occasional Nanna, who knows how to turn the self-interest, lust, and greed of the wealthy to her own advantage, both whores and courtiers are expendable; their talents are consumed by their patrons until they lose their luster and, like coins worn bare in circulation, they are discarded.

A passage like this one must be read with an awareness of Aretino's own situation. Having experienced for himself the condition of a low-born servant in a nobleman's household, Aretino never loses sight of the realities of class relations.[46] Son of a provincial craftsman, he got his palace on the Grand Canal in much the same way Nanna got hers in Rome, through shrewd, self-interested manipulation of the vanity of those more powerful than himself. While there is much misogyny in the *Ragionamenti*, Aretino's representation of Nanna and Antonia nonetheless offers a vision of female power and intelligence—power and intelligence that are in many ways similar to Aretino's own. Nanna's summary of her own career provides as good a description of Aretino as any written:

> I was so sweet and amiable at the start ... that whoever spoke to me for the first time went around singing my praises to the skies; but when he got to know me better, the manna turned sour. ... I ... took great delight in causing scandals, kindling feuds, breaking up friendships, rousing hatreds. ... I was always dropping the names of princes and passing judgment on the Turks, the Emperor, the King, the famine of foodstuffs, the wealth of the Duke of Milan, and the future Pope. ... I

skipped from dukes to duchesses and talked about them as if I had
trampled over them like doormats with my feet. (262;143)

Given the equivalence it posits between courtesans and courtiers and the fact that
Aretino, like Nanna, owes his success to skillful deception of the powerful, the
Ragionamenti can be read as a kind of crossgendered autobiography, an anatomy
of social manipulation not so different from that practiced by Aretino himself.[47]

Through the crossgendered identification of Nanna and Aretino—an identification strengthened by Aretino's own polyvalent sexual practices—the *Ragionamenti* use the profession of the courtesan as a metaphor for other forms of service
and employment in Renaissance Italy, such as doctors, soldiers, courtiers, and grooms
(435;261). At the end of the third day Antonia justifies the decision to make Pippa a
whore in a passage that clearly establishes the relationship not only between the three
states open to adult women but also between prostitution and other professions.

> The nun betrays her sacred vows and the married woman murders the
> holy bond of matrimony, but the whore violates neither her monastery
> nor her husband; indeed she acts like a soldier who is paid to do evil,
> and when doing it, she does not believe that she is, for her shop sells
> what it has to sell. . . . Gardeners sell vegetables, druggists sell drugs,
> and the bordellos sell curses, lies, sluttish behavior, scandals, dishon-
> esty, thievery, filth, hatred, cruelty, deaths, the French pox, betrayals, a
> bad name and poverty. (275;158)

The list of wares a courtesan has to sell does not seem at all promising, but given
that all three options given women are corrupt, whoredom is the least hypocritical, and its similarity to accepted forms of power such as commerce and the
military implies that it is no worse than many other "respected" trades.

While the *Ragionamenti* are undoubtedly misogynist in their image of whores
as merchants of filth, hatred, cruelty, and death, they are equally critical of a society
that limits women to positions that are necessarily corrupt and corrupting. And
thus the best choice for Pippa's future is not in doubt:

> Go [to the brothel] freely with Pippa and make a whore of her right
> off; and afterward, with the petition of a little penance and two drops
> of holy water, all whorishness will leave her soul. . . . Beyond all this, it
> is a fine thing to be called a lady, even by gentlemen, eating and dress-
> ing always like a lady, and continually attending banquets and wed-
> ding feasts. . . . What counts is to satisfy every whim and caprice, being
> able to be pleasant to each and all, because Rome always was and al-
> ways will be . . . the whore's plaything. (275–6;158)

If Antonia's appeal to the luxury of a courtesan's life can be read as a conventional attack on the vanity of women in general and whores in particular, one
must consider the example of Aretino's own career, which argues emphatically
that eating and dressing well and being treated with (at least superficial) respect
are fine things, whose real social value is not to be underestimated.

For although Aretino's satire relentlessly unmasks the hypocrisy of his society, bluntly revealing the naked workings of power and oppression, it refuses to offer any alternatives. Rome always was and always will be corrupt; to believe otherwise is foolish, to pretend otherwise is criminal. As the first lines of Aretino's play *Cortigiana* (1534) put it, papal Rome is "Coda Mundi"—the asshole of the world.[48] But to speak the truth about society is not to transcend it, nor even, for Aretino, to change it. Rather than attempting to change social structures (an endeavor Nanna's knowing cynicism would find hopelessly naive) Aretino sought constantly to find a comfortable place for himself within them. As Nanna tells Pippa, despite papal corruption "[w]e are still Christians, and they are still sacerdotes; and the soul must tend to its affairs" (420;245). The Catholic ritual of penance is at once a farce and (paradoxically) the only way to escape the sinfulness of the world. This dual vision of religion as both utterly necessary and utterly corrupt lies behind Aretino's ability to write both the *Ragionamenti* and the *Life of the Virgin*, the *sonetti lussuriosi* and the *Seven Penitential Psalms of David*.

Aretino was well acquainted with women like those portrayed in the *Ragionamenti*; he filled his house with female courtesans (known locally as the "Aretines") as well as his many male lovers. His published correspondence includes several letters to the famous courtesan Angela Zaffetta, whom he treats with marked respect, pointedly ignoring the ritual degradation through "trentuna" or gang rape that she received early in the 1530s (and that is the subject of a viciously misogynist poem by Aretino's follower Lorenzo Veniero). Aretino's fascination with the wiles of fictional courtesans in the *Ragionamenti* is nowhere to be found in his praise of La Zaffetta; he commends her for "employing cunning, the very soul of the courtesan's art, not with treacherous means but with such skill that whoever spends money on you swears he is the gainer" and for not wanting "to be called a mistress of wiles . . . [like] those women who study all the points made by Nanna and Pippa." He concludes by claiming that "lying, envy and slander, the quintessence of courtesans, do not keep your mind and tongue in ceaseless agitation. You embrace virtue and honor men of virtue, which is alien to those who sell themselves for the pleasure of others."[49]

Thus while in the *Ragionamenti* Aretino shows an ambivalent admiration for the cunning his text imputes to whores, when praising an actual courtesan he is at pains to separate her from her profession—a suggestion, perhaps, that Nanna is more attractive as a fictional construct, a crossdressed representation of Aretino himself, than as an actual woman. While his identification with his female protagonist mitigates the degree to which the *Ragionamenti* is *merely* a male fantasy of female sexuality, it is clear from his letter to La Zaffetta that Aretino does not endorse Nanna's sexual independence and cynical loquacity when they are detached from himself and belong to an actual woman. Nonetheless, his respect for La Zaffetta seems genuine. His later letters compare his affection for her to his fondness for his daughters and reveal that he was in the habit of inviting her to dine with himself and Titian.[50]

Eroticism and Authorial Power: Aretino's *Lettere* and Nicolò Franco

Aretino was notorious in England not only for his "pictures" or his authorship of the *Ragionamenti* but also for his political influence and authorial power. Elizabethan authors like Thomas Nashe and Ben Jonson, struggling to create authority for themselves through patronage networks, the book market, and the popular stage, found in Aretino a compelling model of authorial success. Although Aretino's prestige was not directly or simply related to his erotic writing, the combination of disorderly eroticism and social power that characterized the mythology around Aretino in England provided a powerful counter to common notions that erotic writing was debilitating and effeminizing.

Once established in Venice, Aretino's financial and social success was certainly enviable. He settled in a palatial house, rented from Domenico Bolani, a Venetian nobleman. Casa Aretina—situated on the Grand Canal overlooking the Rialto—became one of the most popular gathering places in the city;[51] the canal and street next to the house both came to be named after Aretino.[52] He was renowned for his generosity.[53] Aretino's closest friends in Venice were Sansovino (another Roman exile) and Titian, for whom he often acted as an agent, arranging sales of his paintings to the duke of Mantua and Charles V, among others. A study of Titian's relations to his patrons concludes that "no Italian Renaissance artist handled his career more astutely" and gives much of the credit to Aretino.[54] By supporting and advancing his friend's international career, Aretino helped disseminate a continental style of grand master painting that held sway in Europe for the next three hundred years and in the process played a crucial role in the commodification of works of art.

In his lifetime (if not after) Aretino was recognized as a perceptive and authoritative art critic,[55] and he may well have been trained as a painter himself in his youth.[56] In his secretary Ludovico Dolce's *Dialogue on Painting*[57] —published in 1557 just after Aretino's death—he appears as the primary interlocutor, arguing for the superiority of Raphael (whom he may have known when they were both in Chigi's household in Rome) over Michelangelo (with whom his relations were always strained, Michelangelo's contempt stemming from Aretino's unsolicited advice on how to paint "The Last Judgment").[58] While the views of Dolce's Aretino should not be confused with those of Aretino himself, it is nonetheless significant that he was taken seriously enough as a critic to be made the spokesperson in a theoretical work on art.

While other Italian writers (most famously Petrarch) had followed the classical tradition of publishing their Latin epistles, Aretino was the first major European vernacular writer to publish his letters; five volumes were printed in his lifetime and a sixth in 1557, immediately following his death. The first volume, published January 1538, was so successful it was reprinted ten times in that year alone.[59] Here too, as with his promotion of Titian's paintings, Aretino is a pioneering figure in the commodification of artistic production. Until all his works were placed on the Index of Prohibited Books in 1558, Aretino's *Lettere* were widely seen as the most influential model for published correspondence, and he had many imitators.[60]

Although Aretino's letters were published as (fairly weighty) books, their outspoken and conversational tone, often irreverent or critical of the nobility, has led them to be thought of as pamphlet literature, a misconception that has led to the notion that Aretino was "the father of modern journalism." This misconception, influentially asserted by Jacob Burckhardt (1860), originated with Philarète Chaslès (1834) and has been uncritically accepted in almost every subsequent study.[61] Whatever subsequent positive connotations the epithet "journalist" might carry, it was introduced into the discussion of Aretino primarily as a way of attacking his writings for their low style and supposed ephemeral concerns, their opportunism, their anti-intellectualism, their rejection of classical models, their support of the low-born against the aristocratic, and their insistence on specific attacks on individuals. Although the commodification of writing was a crucial element of Aretino's achievement, he had little to do with the rise of periodical literature, which developed fully only in the eighteenth century. Thus although the word "journalist" no longer carries the full weight of Chaslès's disdain, it remains an anachronistic term that serves to obscure the specific ways that Aretino made his works available to the public.

Before the publication of the first volume of the *Lettere*, Aretino's letters, like those of other major literary and political figures, had circulated fairly widely in manuscript—his letters to François I, Charles V, and Clement VII were written to be read not only by the rulers to whom they were addressed but by a wider court readership. Mass production in the form of a printed book, however, gave Aretino's letters a much larger public audience, going far beyond court circles. His published volumes of letters played much the same function as his earlier *giudizii*—they provided the public (and his patrons) with invective, panegyric, current gossip, and the author's views on topics ranging from literary theory and art criticism to politics, love, sex, and food.

Now firmly in the service of Charles V, from whom he received a annuity of two hundred scudi beginning in 1536,[62] Aretino continued to seek the favor (and gifts) of other rulers, from Henry VIII of England—to whom he dedicated the second volume of his letters (1542) (and received 75 pounds in return),[63]—to Barbarossa, king of Algiers, whom he instructed on the treatment of Christian captives and from whom he received a flattering letter.[64] As late as 1538 François I was offering him a gift of six hundred scudi in hopes of prying him away from the emperor.[65]

In his lifetime, Aretino's financial success, political power, and social notoriety were envied by many young Italian writers—some of noble birth, many whose origins were as humble as his own. Rather than attaching themselves to a prince or court, they wrote instead for the flourishing Venetian printing houses, of which there were almost five hundred, accounting for almost half the Italian printing industry in the sixteenth century. Known to Italian literary history by the term *poligrafi*, none of these writers achieved anywhere near Aretino's level of success. Though the *poligrafi* have traditionally been dismissed as hacks, in recent years Paul Grendler and others have argued convincingly that their writings constitute a serious and broad critique of sixteenth-century Italian society, attacking the abuses of Catholicism (without embracing Protestantism), bitterly condemning the political failings of the Italian princes and their inability to expel foreign powers from the peninsula, and rejecting as pedantic and irrelevant the learned classicism of the Italian humanists. Like Erasmus, the *poligrafi* represent an ultimately untenable attempt to criticize the Catholic Church and imperial hegemony without becoming Protestant.[66] Their satire and invective, like the writings of Aretino that inspired them, came into existence largely as a result of the unique conditions of the printing trade in Venice. For while censorship laws were established in the Serenissima in the late fifteenth century, before the 1560s they were rarely enforced, so until the influence of the Council of Trent made itself felt, Aretino and his imitators enjoyed an almost unprecedented freedom of the press.[67] Elizabethan satirists such as Nashe, Jonson, Greene, and Marston certainly never experienced anything similar.

Many of the *poligrafi* spent a portion of their career in Aretino's service. The wounds Aretino suffered in 1525 may have injured his hand so severely that he had difficulty writing.[68] In any case, once established in Venice, he was assisted in his work by a succession of male secretaries, most of whom were probably also his lovers. The first of Aretino's secretaries to gain a notoriety in his own right was Lorenzo Veniero, a young Venetian nobleman who in the early 1530s wrote two obscene and brutally misogynist narrative poems, *La Puttana errante* (*The Wandering Whore*) and *La Trentuna di Zaffetta* (*The Rape of Zaffetta*), both of which would later be falsely attributed to Aretino and to which I shall return shortly.

The most important of Aretino's secretaries was Nicolò Franco, a young man of humble birth from the small southern town of Benevento.[69] He came to Aretino in 1536, with a letter of introduction from Titian, and helped Aretino edit the first volume of his letters (1538), as well as assisting him with translations from Latin.[70] Aretino's relations with Franco are worth examining in detail, for they demonstrate better than any other facet of Aretino's career the social conditions that enabled his success, as well as revealing the limits of his power and influence, which were—like Nanna's—maintained only precariously. Franco aspired to be an independent literary and social authority like his master, and he possessed many characteristics in common with Aretino—including a willingness to use erotic writing as a satiric weapon and a fierce rage at the social obstacles confronting an intelligent, educated man of low birth and little means. But he lacked Aretino's access to the Venetian press and in his later life had to deal with the repressive mechanisms of the Counter-Reformation, which Aretino was spared by his timely death in 1556. Not only were these constraints responsible for Franco's failure to establish himself as an independent writer on the scale of Aretino, they led ultimately to his death.

At first, Aretino praised Franco highly; he wrote a flattering letter to Franco's older brother Vincenzo, in which he praises Nicolò's writing as being "of the same rank as my own."[71] It is clear that for a time at least Aretino saw Franco as a worthy successor, but for reasons that remain unclear, the two soon quarreled. In early 1538, soon after the publication of the first volume of letters, Aretino faced charges of blasphemy and possibly sodomy[72] and was forced to flee Venice for a time until the intervention of Francesco Maria della Rovere, duke of Urbino, made it safe for him to return.[73] Sodomy was a serious crime in Venice, and convicted sodomites were burned alive between the pillars of justice on the Piazza San Marco. Given what seems to have been a relatively high incidence of homosexual relations in Renaissance Venice, prosecutions for sodomy were fairly rare—convictions even more so—but of all sexual crimes it was by far the most zealously prosecuted and most harshly punished.[74]

It has been argued that Franco was behind these charges of blasphemy, though he protested otherwise in letters written at the time.[75] It is possible the break with Franco was precipitated by the publication of the anonymous and hostile *Vita di P. Aretino*, falsely attributed to Francesco Berni, a follower of Aretino's old enemy Giberti.[76] The *Vita* attacks Aretino as a sodomite in no uncertain terms, accusing him of buggering various young men in his household (24–9) and of engaging in orgies (36–7). The tract goes on to claim that charges of buggery were brought against Aretino by the mother of one of the women he seduced but says nothing of the outcome, noting only that they were followed by the accusations of blasphemy that caused Aretino to flee Venice temporarily (39–40). While this is the most detailed account of the charges brought against Aretino that we have, the *Vita* is both highly polemical and riddled with inaccuracies, and none of its claims can be taken as more than rumor. The *Vita* asserts that the stories of sodomy and adultery in Aretino's household were revealed by "that madman N. Franco" (3) and announces that Franco will soon publish his own letters, a volume sure to rival Aretino's (35). Perhaps as a result of these insinuations of Franco's treachery and independence, shortly after the *Vita* appeared, it seems, Franco was thrown out of Aretino's house.[77] In volumes of Aretino's letters printed after the autumn of 1538 the letters praising Franco were deleted, and the letter addressed to him was readdressed to Lodovico Dolce, marking the shift in Aretino's choice of literary heir.[78]

Whether or not Franco was involved in the writing of the *Vita*, he published his own letters two months later, in November 1538, hoping to establish himself as Aretino's literary rival. The volume was poorly received.[79] It was at this time that Franco first began to accuse Aretino publicly of being a sodomite.[80] Aretino is now known to have engaged in sex with men for much of his life, and indeed he wrote about his homosexual passions and affections in private letters. In the Florentine archives, for example, there is a letter from Aretino to Giovanni delle Bande Nere written from Reggio in 1524 that includes a poem in which Aretino writes of his chagrin and amazement at having for the first time ever been struck by lust for a woman. He adds in prose, "if I escape with my honor from this foolishness, I will b[ugger] again and again and again, as is good for me and my friends."[81] But before 1638 and the *Vita* attributed to Berni there is no indication that Aretino was accused of sodomy, despite the many vicious polemics directed at him. A famous sonnet that Berni actually *did* write in the late 1520s asserts that Aretino is arrogant, ignorant, a liar, a parasite, a whoremaster, a cripple, a traitor, hated by man and beast, God and the devil, and claims that his sisters are both whores in Arezzo but nonetheless refrains from calling him a sodomite.[82]

Realizing that Venice was no longer safe for him, Franco left in June of 1540 and settled eventually in Casale Monferrato in Piedmont, where he wrote a book of obscene sonnets, *Rime contro Aretino et la Priapea,* in which he explicitly and at great length attacked Aretino as a sodomite. This volume consists of 495 sonnets—297 in the *Rime contro Aretino* and 198 in *La Priapea.*[83] In one of the first sonnets of *La Priapea*—addressed to "the arch-divine Pietro Aretino, Scourge of Cocks"—Franco apologizes for presenting Aretino with a book filled with "so many cocks," but concludes that Aretino's "huge ass may be satisfied / finding its accustomed food here" (65). These lines set the tone for the rest of the volume.

Franco's unsuccessful career offers a useful contrast to that of Aretino. In many ways their careers are strangely parallel: both were low-born and left the provincial centers in which they were raised as soon as they could; both attached themselves to the households of powerful men (in Aretino's case Clement VII, in Franco's Aretino himself); both were outspoken and disorderly to the point where agents of their patron attempted to have them assassinated; and both were forced to flee the city that had given them scope for a successful career (Rome for Aretino, Venice for Franco). Most important for our purposes, both used erotically explicit writing as a satirical vehicle designed to crush enemies and generate authority for themselves. But their subsequent histories could not be more different. Aretino's power and prestige grew enormously after his establishment in Venice; Franco was forced for many years to wander from city to city and from patron to patron.

What allowed Aretino to succeed, and why was Franco unable to duplicate his success? Such questions do not admit of definitive answers. It is not enough to simply assert that Aretino was more gifted than Franco (though there is a measure of truth in this). Aretino was able to succeed because of his access to the Venetian press, which offered greater freedom than any other as well as a wider dissemination of texts. Cut off from Venice, Franco was forced to attach himself to noblemen rather than to printers and was consequently much less able to play one patron off against another as Aretino did. In addition, Aretino was lucky to die when he did; the full weight of the Counter-Reformation was not brought to bear on the *poligrafi* until after the establishment of the Index of Prohibited Books in 1559.

As Franco's subsequent career demonstrates, had Aretino lived on into the 1560s and 70s he might not have escaped charges of blasphemy and sodomy as easily as he did in 1538. For almost twenty years after leaving Venice, Franco wandered around Italy, serving one patron after another. In 1559 he was attached to the court of Pope Pius IV and elected to the Accademia Romana, moving for the first time in his life in the elevated social and literary circles to which he aspired. He fell from favor under Pius's successor Pius V, however, and in 1568 he was arrested by the Inquisition for his earlier antipapal writings, the sonnets of *Priapea* among them. After being tortured, he was hanged on Rome's Ponte Sisto on March 10, 1570. Elizabethan writers who envied the freedom of speech and social prestige Aretino enjoyed might have been less enthusiastic if they had followed Franco's career instead.

Whatever the content of the charges against him in 1538, Aretino's reputation and prestige were left intact. Though he did not succeed in silencing his former secretary, Franco's ranting accusations of sodomy seem to have had little effect. Aretino's most effective response came with his second volume of letters in 1542; the list of addressees was more impressive than ever.[84] In July 1543 Aretino's career reached its peak when, traveling with Guidobaldo, duke of Urbino, he met Emperor Charles V at Verona. The emperor apparently did Aretino the honor of riding alone with him for several minutes and, before leaving, may have tried to entice Aretino to come with him to the imperial court in Vienna. Whatever Charles offered, Aretino refused: if he had consented to become a courtier he would have rapidly lost the independence that was the source of his power and influence.

This refusal to place himself within the confines of a given aristocratic court should not be taken as proof that, since Aretino's writings were so popular, he survived solely by the sales of his printed books and was thus independent of the aristocracy. Although his texts were widely disseminated and purchased in large numbers, Aretino's political power and influence owes little to the common people or the popular voice. Despite his championing of servants over masters and low culture over high, his attacks on various patrons were dangerous because they would be read by courtiers and other noblemen, not because they would rouse the lower orders against their masters. Aretino's plays and dialogues sympathize most strongly with cunning servants—the underdogs at court, not the urban proletariat outside the courts, let alone the peasantry. Aretino did not use the market to escape the patronage system—such a move would scarcely have been possible in the sixteenth century. Rather he used the market to destabilize the patronage system by insuring, through the wide dissemination of his texts among the aristocracies and courts of the various competing Italian states, that he was never, after 1527, dependent on any one patron or any homogenous or allied group of patrons. At the highest level, he played the pope, the king of France, and the emperor against each other, and such a game was only possible because, living in Venice—an independent mercantile oligarchy—he was beyond the direct reach of all three and at the same time perfectly situated to take advantage of the single largest printing center in Europe. Aretino achieved his enormous and unique success because he used the Venetian press and the uncertain balance of power in Italy prior to the Council of Trent and the treaty of Cateau-Cambresis as a means to manipulate the patronage system. Despite the large sales of his many books he never lived by the press alone. After 1559, with the renunciation of French claims in Italy and the establishment of imperial hegemony—and with it the vigorous papacy of the Counter-Reformation—Aretino's position would have quickly become untenable.

The later years of Aretino's life were relatively uneventful, despite a row with the English ambassador to Venice in 1547 over money sent by Henry VIII that did not arrive.[85] Never on good terms with the Farnesi Pope Paul III, Aretino profited greatly from his successor, Julius III, who acceded to the papal throne in 1549. Like Pietro, Julius was also from Arezzo, and Aretino lost no time in sending him a flattering sonnet, which netted him a thousand gold crowns. Shortly afterward he was given the honorary post of Gonfaloniere of Arezzo, and in June 1550 Julius made Pietro a Cavaliere of San Pietro (with an annuity of eighty scudi). The great ambition of Aretino's later life—to be made a cardinal—was ultimately disappointed, however, despite a journey to Rome in 1553.

In 1555 Aretino refused a request from Anton Francesco Doni, a *poligrafo* with whom he had previously been on good terms, for a letter of introduction to the duke of Urbino. This slight provoked Doni's thundering response in his 1556 work *Terremoto* (*Earthquake*), a torrent of invective that begins by calling Aretino the Anti-Christ and prophesies that he will die before the year is out.[86] Indeed, Aretino died in Venice in 1556, ending a brilliant career as a satirist in a fit of apoplexy at age sixty-four when "one evening about the fifth hour sitting in a chair he fell backward."[87] He was buried in the Church of San Leo, and his epitaph was rumored to be:

> Qui giace l'Aretin, poeta tosco,
> Che disse mal d'ognun fuorche di Christo
> Scusandosi col dir: non lo conosco.

Or, as it appears in an English verse miscellany from the early seventeenth century:

> Heere lyes Tuscan Aretine whose pen
> Both ill of woemen spake, & ill of men
> Nay god himselfe should ne'er have scapt him so
> Had he but knowne there had beene one or no.[88]

Financially, it is difficult to measure the extent of Aretino's success.[89] He claimed in 1540 to have an income of six hundred scudi a year, a figure that would dwarf the pension of one hundred marks given Ben Jonson by James I in 1616.[90] Whatever the figures, Aretino was unquestionably, in financial terms, the most successful writer of his era—and he was all the more exceptional in that he gained his entire fortune, both his regular income from patrons and publishers and the profusion of occasional gifts, primarily through his writing. At the time of Aretino's death his books were still selling well, and the sixth and final volume of his letters was published posthumously in 1557. The next year, however, his reputation went into eclipse. All his works were placed on the Index and banned by the Catholic Church. Despite a fairly brisk clandestine trade,[91] the ban proved effective: except for some of his devotional works, published under a pseudonym in the seventeenth century, few of Aretino's writings were reprinted in Catholic Europe during the next three hundred years.

Cazzi, Puttane, Pornographos: The Myth of Aretino

In his attack on Italianate corruption in *The Scholemaster*, Roger Ascham only once mentions Machiavelli by name (83); and he does not name Aretino. But just as in England Machiavelli became emblematic of Italian political cunning and amorality, so Aretino came to embody all the moral and sexual corruption that Ascham identifies as italianate. Why and how did English culture come to focus its anxieties about foreign eroticism on Aretino?

Aretino did not assume emblematic status in England during his lifetime, despite the fact that he had dealings with the English court and dedicated the second volume of his letters to Henry VIII. The letter presenting Aretino's *Lettere* to Henry has survived, and it gives clear indication that at the English court Aretino was considered primarily as a critic of papal and political corruption rather than a writer of erotic texts. The letter was written September 4, 1542, by Edmund Harvel, an Englishman in Venice, and has been summarized as follows.

> Peter Aretin, "much famous for his wit and liberty of writing in th'Italian tongue" has asked me to send this book of his letters "lately printed and dedicate to your Majesty," whom he venerates both for the 300 cr[owns] you before gave him and for your virtues. He has long been persecuted by the Roman prelates, whose detestable vices he has scourged with his vehement and sharp style. The man is poor, and depends only on the liberality of princes. He expects some small reward from Henry, whom, in return he will glorify with his pen in spite of Roman prelates.[92]

Despite his work on behalf of the fervently Catholic Charles V, Aretino was clearly willing to allow himself to be represented to Henry VIII as an enemy of the pope— an impoverished (!) critic of papal vice. After Henry's death, William Thomas, clerk of the council to Edward VI, sent Aretino a copy of his tract *Peregrine*, a work defending Henry's break with Rome. Thomas was concerned that Aretino not turn against Henry after the king's death and with the gift of his book attempted to insure that Aretino "with [his] mountaine of . . . naturall reasons shouldest have matter sufficient accordingly to defend" Henry's cause. In his letter, Thomas is obviously flattering Aretino and even attempting to bribe him (he mentions a gift for Aretino in Henry's will although the will itself makes no mention of such a legacy). But it is interesting to note that Thomas describes Aretino in the same register of terms that would later be used over and over in praise of Shakespeare:

> Like as many tymes the wild woodes, and barraine mountayns as yeilde more delight unto the seldome travaild Citizens, then doe the pleasant Orchardes and gardens, whose beautie and fruite hee dayly injoyeth, soe hath it nowe pleased me to directe this my litle booke unto thee *whose virtue consisteth onlie in Nature without any arte*, then unto any other, whome I knowe both naturall, virtuous, & learned.[93] (italics mine)

Thomas's hopes that Aretino would be an advocate for Henry's church were frustrated, although Aretino continued to pursue opportunities for patronage offered by the English monarchy. His sixth volume of letters, published shortly after his death, was dedicated to Queen Mary (1557) and congratulated her on the reintroduction of Catholicism in England.

In the decades following the release of Ascham's *Scholemaster* in 1570, Aretino is frequently linked with Machiavelli in English representations of foreign corruption. John Eliot's *Ortho-epia Gallica* (1593), a volume written to teach Englishmen French, responds to those who believe Italians and French are too "high minded," "capricious and proud" to "fit themselves long to the nature of us English," by admitting: "There are some wicked heads, I say beasts or serpents who have empoysoned by the venime of their skill, our English nation, with the bookes of *Nicholas Machiavell*, and *Peter Aretine*, replenished with all filthinesse and vilanie (sig. D2v). If italianate Englishmen learn their villainy from Machiavelli, they get their filthiness from Aretino.

This formulation is also evident in Thomas Lodge's prose tale *A Margarite of America* (1596), which features a corrupt courtier "who had Machevil's prince in his bosome" and "mother Nana the Italian bawd in his pocket" (sig. C4v). In his *Theological Discourse of the Lamb of God* (1590) Richard Harvey accused Aretino of being "a great courtier or rather courtisan": "he, I say of all other, was the arrogantest rakehell, and rankest villen, saving your reverence, that ever set penne to paper, like cursed Sodomites, jesting and sporting at that which good men in naturall modestie are ashamed to speake of (sig. N4v). Among Aretino's "damnable book[s]" Richard Harvey includes an "Apologie of *Pedarastice*" (sigs. N4r–N4v) and concludes that Aretino is a worse atheist than Machiavelli (sig. O). Harvey's association of Aretino with sodomy is echoed in E. K.'s gloss to *Januarie* in Spenser's *Shepheardes Calender*, which claims that the "develish . . . Unico Aretino" has written "in defence of execrable and horrible sinnes of forbidden and unlawful fleshlinesse."[94]

Though several of Aretino's works deal with pederasty, the "Apologie" Richard Harvey ascribes to him is spurious. As Aretino's notoriety grew in Elizabethan England, a range of works came to be associated with him many of which he had nothing to do with and some of which probably never existed. As we have seen, the engravings that accompanied the bawdy sonnets of Aretino's *I modi* became known as "Aretine's pictures," and in time he was credited with the images as well as for the poems. Just as in the early modern period "sodomy" itself was an indefinite term, referring to a wide range of possible actions and behaviors, all seen as sexually transgressive or threatening to the natural and social order, so Aretino's name became emblematic, and almost any licentious foreign writing or painting was ascribed to him.

Despite the unavailability of Aretino's notorious *sonetti*, by the last years of the sixteenth century texts of some of his other major writings were actually being printed in London. These London editions were, in fact, the most widely available copies of Aretino's texts printed after his works were placed on the Index in 1558. In 1584, John Wolfe,[95] an English printer who had traveled to Italy and published books in Florence in 1576, published an unexpurgated Italian language edition of Aretino's *Ragionamenti*,[96] and he followed it in 1588 with an Italian edition of four of Aretino's comedies, as well as another volume of dialogues. Wolfe's 1584 *Ragionamenti* includes two shorter erotic works, the *Ragionamenti di Zoppino* (a brief survey of famous Roman courtesans, falsely ascribed to Aretino) and the *Commento di Ser Agresto* (a bawdy academic dialogue correctly ascribed to Annibale Caro).[97]

All Wolfe's volumes of Aretino were published under false imprints, and seem to have been intended for sale on the Continent, where—in Catholic countries—all of Aretino's works were on the Index.[98] Wolfe was the first English printer to involve himself heavily in the European market, and in the late 1580s he published foreign-language propaganda at the instigation of William Cecil, Lord Burghley, Elizabeth's secretary of state.[99] Despite bitter disputes with the Stationer's Company throughout the 1580s, Wolfe had one of the largest printing facilities in London: in 1583 he owned five presses, a number equaled only by Baker, the royal printer. Wolfe had better connections with European markets than any other English printer, and his editions of Aretino are known to have been sold at the Frankfurt Book Fair,[100] along with twenty other titles printed by him, including his edition of Machiavelli.[101]

Of Wolfe's volumes of Aretino, the most popular was the 1584 *Ragionamenti*, which is more salacious than the plays or dialogues he printed later. While neither of the 1588 volumes was ever reprinted, the 1584 *Ragionamenti* was reprinted line for line at least five times before 1660—once in London (c. 1597) and four times on the Continent.[102] Perhaps because of relatively poor sales of the 1588 volumes, Wolfe never carried through with his plans[103] to publish editions of Aretino's letters and poems.

Along with its wide dissemination on the Continent, Wolfe's Aretino found its way into English libraries as well as European ones. William Cecil[104] and Sir Christopher Hatton, Elizabeth's lord chancellor,[105] both owned copies of the *Ragionamenti*, as did Ben Jonson, though this volume is not included in David McPherson's catalogue of Jonson's library.[106] Jonson's friend William Drummond of Hawthornden owned Wolfe's edition of the *Quattro Comedie*,[107] and while little is known of Shakespeare's library, there is some evidence that he too was familiar with the comedies, as well as Aretino's tragedy *Orazia*.[108] John Florio's English–Italian dictionary of 1598 includes Aretino among the seventy-two authors read for vocabulary, and his expanded edition of 1611, *Queen Anna's New World of Words*, uses Aretino's *Quattro Comedie* as a source text.[109]

The fact that London was the main source of new editions of Aretino helps account for his status as a cultural archetype in England. But the volumes published by Wolfe represent only a fraction of Aretino's writings and, given the effectiveness of the Inquisition's suppression of Aretino's works on the Continent, knowledge of Aretino's career in early modern England was often inaccurate. To understand the place of Aretino in Elizabethan culture one must take into account the many works that were commonly, if falsely, ascribed to him. These works—many strikingly different from Aretino's own writings—contributed greatly to the establishment of Aretino as an emblematic figure of erotic and authorial transgression in early modern England and to subsequent legends that he was the "father of pornography."

Some idea of the range of materials ascribed to Aretino in Elizabethan England is given by Gabriel Harvey's list of works ascribed to him in *A New Letter of Notable Contents* (1593):

> [Aretino] Paraphrased the inestimable works of Moses, and discoursed the Capricious Dialogues of the rankest Bawdry. [He] penned one Apology of the divinity of Christ, and another of Pederastice, a kinde of harlatry, not to be recited: [he] published the Life of the Blessed Virgin, and the Legende of the Errant Putana: [he] recorded the history of S. Thomas of Aquin, and forged the most detestable Black-booke, *de tribus impostoribus mundi.* (sig. D; 1:289–90)

Despite the wide range of subject matter included in Harvey's list, most of these texts can be identified as works by Aretino—his paraphrase of Genesis (1538), the *Ragionamenti*, *I tre libri de la humanita di Christo* (1535), *La Vita di Maria Vergine* (1539), and *La Vita di San Tomaso Signor d'Aquino* (1543). But the three most notorious texts in the list—*De tribus impostoribus mundi*, the "Legende of the Errant Putana," and the so-called Apology of Pederasty—were not his. *De tribus impostoribus mundi* refers to a volume denying the truth of Christianity, Judaism, and Islam, which, while scandalous, was certainly not by Aretino.[110] Both Gabriel and his brother Richard attribute an apology of pederasty to Aretino, and though he never wrote anything that would fit that description, the brothers may be referring to *La Cazzaria* (*The Book of the Prick*) (c. 1530), a dialogue by Antonio Vignali, one of the Academy degli Intronati (The Academy of the Stunned) of Siena.[111]

The Intronati were one of the most prominent literary societies of sixteenth-century Italy, perhaps best known to students of Renaissance English literature as the authors of *Gl'Ingannati* (1538), the play on which Shakespeare based *Twelfth Night*. *La Cazzaria* is a dialogue between two men, Arsiccio and Sodo, both actual members of the Academia, and it is organized as a series of fifty-two questions on subjects ranging from anatomy ("Why balls don't enter into either the cunt or the asshole," "Why the asshole is behind the cunt") to psychology ("Why man does not like to be seen fucking"), linguistics ("Why the common people don't understand the beauty of the Tuscan language"), and philosophy ("Why cocks can be said to constitute matter; why cunts are called natural") (169–71). The latter half of the dialogue consists of a fable—modeled on various mythological fables of the origin of human society—explaining at great length why bodies and desires are structured as they are, in which personified cocks, cunts, balls, and assholes struggle for supremacy. That the narrative of their conflict is also an allegory of the intestine civil struggles in Siena in 1524 offers yet another indication of how intimately erotic and political discourses were linked in early modern Italy.

Mock dialogues like *La Cazzaria* represent a vernacular continuation of the humanist Latin tradition of learned—and often homoerotic—bawdry.[112] *La*

Cazzaria is openly in favor of male homoerotic activity; there are many misogynist passages, and sex with women is seen as a poor alternative to sex between men (38, 52). The dialogue itself can be read as a seduction of the passive (and suggestively named) Sodo by the active Arsiccio, and it ends with a strong hint that the Arsiccio has definite designs on the younger man (137). While *La Cazzaria* is definitely comic in tone, there is no indication at any point that its praise of sex between men is ironic. In this regard it is more outspoken than any other published text by or attributed to Aretino.

Although there is no definite proof that *La Cazzaria* circulated in early modern England, at least two sixteenth-century Londoners were familiar with the volume. John Florio's 1598 Italian-English dictionary, *A Worlde of Words* (1598) provides the first English translation of the dialogue's title: the Italian "Cazzaria" is accurately defined as "a treatise or discourse of pricks"—although Florio neglects to inform his reader that the word comes from "cazzo," an Italian slang term for "penis." In addition to the reference in Florio's dictionary, John Wolfe's preface to his 1584 London edition of Pietro Aretino's *Ragionamenti* promises the reader that the appearance of that volume will be followed by the publication of similar works, including "il comune de l'Arsiccio" (Arsiccio's commune) (sig. A2r)—a clear reference to *La Cazzaria*. However, this volume (and many others promised) was never published. Sections of *La Cazzaria* were later incorporated into the erotic classic *Il libro del perchè* or, as it was known in eighteenth-century England, *The Why and the Wherefore.*[113]

The other text from Harvey's list, "The Legende of the Errant Putana," refers to one of the two texts known as the *Puttana errante*—one a poem by Lorenzo Veniero, the other an anonymous obscene dialogue sometimes attributed to Nicolò Franco. It is difficult to determine which of these two completely different texts Gabriel Harvey was familiar with. The poem, an erotic mock epic narrative by Aretino's follower Lorenzo Veniero was from the very first thought to be by Aretino; in fact the preface to Veniero's second poem, *La Trentuna di Zaffetta*, claims that part of his reason in writing the latter poem is to prove that *La Puttana* was his.[114] Veniero's admiration for Aretino is apparent throughout his *Puttana errante.*[115] Indeed Aretino clearly put his support behind Veniero's poem, contributing a dedicatory sonnet in which he compares Veniero to Homer and Virgil, and mentioning Veniero's *Puttana* in his 1531 *Capitolo* to the Duke of Mantua, as well as in the *Ragionamenti.*[116]

Veniero's *Puttana* was published in Venice, probably in 1531.[117] A mock epic in four cantos, it chronicles the progress through Italy of an unnamed whore—a monstrous parody of epic warrior women such as Ariosto's Bradamante and Marfisa. It is believed the figure of the Puttana is based on Elena Ballarina, a Venetian courtesan against whom Veniero held a grudge, and indeed both of Veniero's poems are marked by a vicious, ugly, and outspoken hatred of women. The Puttana is a monstrous figure of female lust and excess, an animated vagina dentata "who did more with her cunt than Orlando / Did with his sword and lance" (12).

Unlike Aretino or Nicolò Franco, Veniero was a wealthy Venetian nobleman; his son Masseo (to whom the *Puttana errante* was later attributed)[118] became bishop of Corfu. Whereas Aretino's texts always side with servants against their masters, Veniero makes sure that his monstrous Puttana is low-born; she is descended from thieves, traitors, hangmen, and a renegade priest for good measure (14–20).

Having "great spirit in her cunt and ass," the poem's unnamed heroine decide[s] to become a Whore Errant (*Puttana errante*) and like a proper epic hero sets out for Rome (22). In the course of the four cantos of the poem she engages in a series of Brobdingnagian sexual feats—fucking Jews, Moors, Turks, Christians, renegades, kings, popes, and abbots; taking twenty men at once—ten in her vagina, ten in her anus; imprisoning three watchmen in her anus and a monk in her vagina; servicing the entire armies of Germany and Spain; as well as having sex with a veritable menagerie of animals, including dogs, horses, and an entire den of lions. She is granted a degree in whoring from the University of Siena and engages in an academic disputation as to which sort of cocks are the best. The poem concludes with her celebrating a triumph in the streets of Rome, "in imitation of Caesar and Marcellus" (124). Her chariot is preceded by all the men she has fucked, as well as a crowd of witches and magicians, mobs of old women, and young women who have aborted their pregnancies. Then comes a huge cart carrying all the things she has stolen, including an unnamed item robbed from Veniero. Following the chariot in which she rides is an army "as large as Xenophon's or Caesar's," made up of ten thousand whores. The procession is concluded by the Seven Deadly Sins and a huge model of a cock (124–38).

In short, the Puttana is a monstrous epitome of disorderly, chaotic female sexuality—devouring penises, overstepping all "natural" sexual bounds—mixing in the krater of her vagina Jew and Moor and Christian, prince and beggar, human and animal. In her grotesque triumph she subverts masculine martial ideal and ritual. Though constantly subjected to sexual attack, she devours her assailants. By the end of her progress she has appropriated the emblems of phallic power to her own uses, and all men are captives tied to her chariot. The world is well and truly upside down.

At first glance, some aspects of the Puttana might suggest she is a figure of feminine power and sexual autonomy—she caricatures and subverts models of phallic authority, she has strong sexual desires and is generally active rather than passive. Yet while she is figured as powerful, in no sense does she constitute an image of female *empowerment*. The powers she is given are at every turn defined as monstrous and degrading, and the poem is clearly calculated to provoke hatred toward women—specifically toward the actual courtesans Veniero is writing against. If women like Elena Ballerina had any power at all, it was socially precarious in the extreme. When one remembers that Veniero was by birth a member of the highest levels of Venetian society, his cruelty stands out in its full malevolence. The Puttana is a monstrous projection of patriarchal male fear of the feminine, and the poem's male narrator treats her with a mixture of fascinated horror and disgust.

If Veniero's *Puttana errante* gives full expression to a powerful image of monstrous female power and depravity, his other poem, *La Trentuna di Zaffetta* (*The Rape of Zaffetta*) spells out in graphic detail the actual punishment inflicted on courtesans who displeased the powerful men who employed them. A *trentuna* thirty-one was a gang rape, usually initiated by the wealthy client and his friends and continued by a group of servants or peasants—a ritual of actual and symbolic degradation that was employed against courtesans who were perceived to be acting too independently. The custom of trentuna is a vivid reminder of the social place of the whore in Venetian society; whatever wealth and prestige she has accumulated is taken from her—she is graphically and violently made aware of her status as the property of all men, from the most powerful to the most menial. Veniero's text makes the ritual nature of the trentuna shockingly clear by comparing the rape to a Good Friday Mass, in which all the town participates (48–9). *La Trentuna di Zaffetta* is based on an actual rape, which was suffered by Angela Zaffetta, the celebrated Venetian courtesan whom Aretino praised in his letters. Although Veniero's text may be the most brutal, he was far from the only writer to describe a trentuna. In fact, they became something of a staple in Italian erotic writing of the sixteenth century.[119]

As far as it is possible to determine, Veniero's *Puttana errante* had little circulation and limited impact following its original publication in the 1530s. The other text known by the title *Puttana errante* is in prose and is perhaps the single most influential piece of early modern European erotic writing. It was rewritten, updated, translated, and republished for three hundred years after its first appearance.[120] And at least as early as the seventeenth century it was invariably—and incorrectly—ascribed to Aretino. Of all early modern erotic texts, the prose *Puttana errante* bears the closest relationship to the subsequent genre of pornography and may well have played a constitutive role in that genre's formation.

The textual history of the prose *Puttana errante* is, to say the least, obscure. The attribution of the dialogue to Nicolò Franco, made by G. Legman in 1962 and adopted by subsequent writers,[121] is purely speculative. The earliest known manuscript copy (MS 677, Bibliotèque de Condé, Chantilly) is dated around 1560, and by the mid-seventeenth century the text was circulating widely in print.[122] The title *Puttana errante* bears no resemblance to the content of the dialogue. Where in Veniero's poem it has the specific meaning "whore errant" (which is lost in the English translation "Wandering Whore") the title is largely inappropriate in relation to the prose dialogue to which it is appended.

Whoever wrote it, the prose *Puttana errante* is a crucial text in the history of European erotic writing, for it provides a missing link between the satirical, politicized eroticism of Aretino's *Ragionamenti*—on which it is clearly based—and the pornotopian male fantasies promulgated in the pornography of the eighteenth and later centuries. The *Puttana* takes its form (a dialogue between two courtesans) from the *Ragionamenti*, but its content is relentlessly sexual: after a brief introduction the dialogue consists mainly of an unbroken series of descriptions of intercourse, and it concludes with a list of thirty-five possible postures, each given a suggestive title, such as "Moorish style," "Riding the donkey," "the sleeping boy," and "The playful cunt" (sigs. C6v–C8v).

Although it begins with a discussion of a courtesan who arrived from Venice as a poor girl and rose to become the mistress of Cardinal Borghese, the *Puttana errante* has none of the social and political concerns of Aretino's *Ragionamenti*. Here the art of the courtesan is the art of pleasing a man, not the art of fleecing him. Like Aretino's Pippa, Giulia is instructed by Maddalena on how to be a successful courtesan, but whereas in the *Ragionamenti* Pippa is told how to turn every situation to her own advantage and to protect herself from the malice and deceit of her clients, Giulia's instruction is mostly on proper feminine deportment: she must "speak gracefully to everyone, never tell lies or be deceitful, but always do as she promises" (A4v–A5)[123]—advice that would fill Nanna with horror.

The narrative form of the *Ragionamenti* is autobiographical and developmental—we see Nanna go from being a young innocent to a corrupt nun, from a crafty wife to a successful courtesan. The *Puttana errante* retains the developmental narrative and some motifs used in the *Ragionamenti*, most notably Nanna's sexual initiation through voyeurism, but unlike Nanna's narrative, Maddalena's autobiography is purely sexual, and her coming of age takes the form that would become canonical in later pornographic texts. She begins as an innocent, then sees her cousin Frederigo masturbating, a sight that arouses her to the point where she quickly learns to do the same for herself. Having mastered autoeroticism, she progresses to homosexuality, first seeing Frederigo engage in sex with another boy, and then being herself seduced by her aunt, who shows her that "women can have such pleasures without men" (A7v–A8). Repeating the by now common pattern of learning by looking, Maddalena observes Frederigo again, this time with his new wife Catherina, before her own initiation in heterosexual intercourse with Ruberto, Frederigo's former playmate, who now finds himself without a partner.

While Maddalena begins by dividing sexual activity into three theoretically equal forms—woman with woman, man with man, and man with woman (A6)—the latter form receives by far the most attention in the text. In a manner that prefigures the classic narratives of pornography, homosexual relations are seen largely as a prelude to heterosexual intercourse.[124] Once discovered, this final form of sexual congress is then repeated ad nauseam for the remainder of the text. At first Maddalena and Ruberto have little privacy, and they are forced to make love in the stables, either standing up or using a stool. Only when Ruberto is taken ill on a visit to his sister and Maddalena seduces her cousin Frederigo does she finally acquire a bed. Having mastered both likely and unlikely sexual positions in these various settings, Maddalena confronts the consequences of her fertility, learning how to have sex during her period and traveling to visit her Pisan aunt in order to abort an unwanted pregnancy. Later she marries, is unfaithful, and is subjected to the seemingly inevitable trentuna. Disgraced, she travels to Rome, where she becomes a courtesan, and her narrative ends with her relating her three-way encounter with a cardinal and a sixteen-year-old boy. The remainder of the text consists of an enumeration and description of the positions of heterosexual sex that have been described in the course of the dialogue.

While there are some important differences between the prose *Puttana errante* and later genres of pornography, this anonymous text is much more recognizably pornographic than any text by Aretino. While stressing elements that later pornography would almost entirely avoid, such as homosexual contact between men, abortion, and menstruation, the *Puttana errante* takes elements present in Aretino, such as an enumeration of sexual positions *(I modi)*, voyeurism, sexual initiation, and rape *(I ragionamenti)*, and reconfigures them to produce a text in which sexuality is, perhaps for the first time, represented as constituting a separate sphere—a "pornotopia" set aside for the private pleasures of the male reader.

Given the lack of information, it is impossible at this point to determine which of the two texts known as *La Puttana errante* was identified with Aretino in early modern England. Nor is it possible to ascertain the extent of knowledge of these texts. Over time Veniero's poem did not circulate nearly as widely as the prose dialogue, but Harvey's reference to "the Legende of the Errant Putana" would seem to refer more to the poem than the prose text, as would Nashe's remark in *Lenten Stuff* (1599) that "the posterior Italian and Germane cornugraphers, sticke not to applaud and cannonize unnaturall sodometrie [and] the strumpet errant" (3:177). That John Florio used a work called "P. Errante del'Aretino" as a vocabulary text for his 1598 dictionary suggests that at least one copy (of one of the two texts) reached London. But generally speaking it seems that these texts were known only by repute and that few copies of either made their way into England in the sixteenth century. Since Nanna mentions *La Puttana errante* in the *Ragionamenti*, it is possible that Harvey and Nashe are simply misreading Aretino; Florio's inclusion of the work in his vocabulary list suggests closer acquaintance.

Neither *La Cazzaria* nor either of the texts called *La Puttana errante* deal with their erotic material in the manner characteristic of Aretino. Both *La Cazzaria* and Veniero's poem are aristocratic in their outlook, disdaining the serving classes, for whom Aretino tends to demonstrate a certain amount of sympathy and respect. As a result, they have little or none of Aretino's delight in the swindle, the duping of authority. In addition, all of these texts are more antifeminist than Aretino's own writings, which tend to play with gender boundaries and to take a degree of pleasure in their constructions of female power and desire. The long association of these works and others with Aretino has only served to blur the distinctive qualities of his own writing.

In his lifetime, Aretino was seen far more as a political figure than as an erotic writer. Those—like Franco and the anonymous writer of the 1538 *Vita*—who attacked him for sexual disorderliness tended to focus on his actions rather than on his writings. His writing of the *sonetti lussuriosi* and the *Ragionamenti* certainly did not prevent him from being respected and sincerely praised by many of his contemporaries. Those who opposed him most strongly tended to be either political opponents like Giberti and Berni or literary rivals like Franco and Doni. Until the final years of his life, accusations that he was an atheist were rare, and, as we have seen, his devotional works circulated widely.

In early modern England, some writers, most notably Thomas Nashe, still saw Aretino as a figure of primarily political significance. But the most radical aspects of Aretino's social critique were soon elided. The shifts in the ways Aretino was read can be seen most vividly in successive editions of the *Ragionamenti*. In its original form, Aretino's *Ragionamenti* is a complex work that addresses a host of social issues: the place of women; corruption in the church; men's cruelty to women; the hypocrisy of marriage; the nature of service; and the way courtesans manipulate the vanity of their clients. But like that other socially complex and multivalent dialogue from Renaissance Italy, Castiglione's *Book of the Courtier*, the *Ragionamenti*'s nuanced views of social issues were radically simplified in transmission. While the complete text continued to circulate in Italian even after being placed on the Index in the 1550s, the work was not translated as a whole until modern times. Instead, translators focused their energies on one section of the work: the third book of the first volume, which describes the lives of whores. While this is not the most obviously titillating part of the text, it is the most orthodox in its depiction of gender roles. Rather than attacking monasticism, implying that all husbands will be cuckolded, or demonstrating the sexual cruelty of men, it details the ways in which whores trick their naive clients. When published on its own and no longer preceded (and balanced by) the corrupt life of Nuns and hypocritical life of Wives, the life of Whores was easily assimilated into a tradition of antifeminist writing that saw *all* women as manipulative whores, out to destroy innocent young men (figure 3.4).

A Spanish translation, entitled *Colloquio de las Damas* (*Dialogue of the Ladies*), was published in Seville in 1548, and despite the strong role of the Counter-Reformation Church in Spain, this text was republished in 1607, when all of Aretino's works—even his devotional texts—had been on the Index for fifty years. The 1548 Spanish edition seems to have provided a model for a 1580 French edition, entitled *Le Miroir des Courtisans* (*The Mirror of Courtesans*), published in Lyon. A Latin edition entitled *Pornodidascalus seu Colloquium Muliebre* (*Dialogue of Whores, or the Dialogue of the Women*) and translated from the Spanish text was published in Frankfurt in 1623, probably to capitalize on the international book market held there. Perhaps the German provenance of the Latin edition explains the lack of a German translation—the Latin volume opens with an address to the youth of Germany (["Iuventuti Germanici"] (sig. A1v).

A free English adaptation of the Third Day of Aretino's *Ragionamenti* first appeared in London in 1658 in the waning days of the commonwealth when much erotic English verse from the period 1600–40 was also coming into print for the first time. The English version was entitled *The Crafty Whore . . . or a dialogue between two subtle bawds* (figure 3.5). It maintains the general organization and structure of Aretino's work, while departing widely from it in detail. Despite its title, *The Crafty Whore* is much more bland than the *Ragionamenti*—there is no explicit description of sexual acts, for example. It is also, in places, strongly moralistic. Interpolated passages warn of the dangers of venereal disease (sig. C8v–D1r), and the dialogue ends with both whores renouncing their past sins and resolving to retire to a "remote Cell or Hermitage," where they will weep for their sins in the best fashion of penitent Magdalenes (G7v–G8r). The dialogue is followed by a sixteen-page "Dehortation from Lust." Overall, *The Crafty Whore* sends an ambivalent message about sexuality to its readers. It provides (relatively

Figure 3.4. *Young noblemen corrupted by Courtesans, music, gaming, and dalliance. Crispin de Passe, scene from Prodigal Son series, 17th century. By Permission of the Folger Shakespeare Library.*

bland) sexual titillation while condemning it at the same time, and although this stance may be typical of much of the discourse of eroticism in Protestant societies, it could not be farther from Aretino's own practice.

All of these translations of the third book of the *Ragionamenti* were presented to their readers not as texts of erotic delight or as comic tales but rather as horrifying and fascinating warnings of erotic corruption. The full title of the 1548 Spanish edition is: "A Dialogue by the famous and great demonstrator of vices and virtues, Pietro Aretino, in which are discovered the falsehoods, deceitful speeches, and tricks which women in love use to entrap the fools . . . who love them"[125] (sig. A1v). The Latin translation goes further, referring to "the nefarious and horrendous wiles of shameless women" (A1r).[126] The French edition's title is clearest of all about the text's moral function: "The Mirror of Courtesans: In which are introduced two Courtesans, by one of whom are discovered the many tricks, frauds, and betrayals which are daily committed. Serving as an example to ill-informed youth" (sig. A1r).[127] As late as the Latin edition of 1623 Aretino is presented to the reader not as a writer of deliberately titillating and corrupting erotica but as a moralist displaying naked virtue and vice. The printer's introduction that appears in slightly modified form in the Spanish, French, and Latin editions defends Aretino's writing by appealing to its august precedents: "This manner of warning youth is not new and has no little authority, for it is used in Holy Scripture."[128] Marginal glosses refer the reader to denunciations of female sexuality in Proverbs and Ecclesiastes.

Figure 3.5. *Another young man gulled: The frontispiece to* The Crafty Whore. *The engraved frontispiece to* The Crafty Whore *(1658), British Library (Shelfmark E.1927[1], Wing C6780). By Permission of the British Library.*

While interest in these texts may well have benefited from the scurrilous reputation of Aretino, the introductory passage inserted by the printer is not simply tongue-in-cheek in the manner of many latter-day pornographers' defenses of free speech. It represents a serious attempt to derive a sober moral lesson from Aretino's text. Rather than delighting in the wit and skill of Nanna the trickster, these introductions lament the loss of paternal wealth through young men's profligate spending on pleasure.[129] The printer also warns of the threat of syphilis in an earnest tone far removed from the mocking voice of Nanna.

> All flesh has corrupted its path, as a result of which the Lord God has once again sent forth a deluge upon the earth, not of water . . . but of a plague neither known or understood by the ancients and of which the doctors make no mention, and which every nation blames on foreigners. . . . For just as every day the flesh invents new ways to sin, so too divine justice finds new plagues and scourges to afflict and punish it.[130]

With the rise of pornography as a discourse and a literary genre in the late seventeenth century, the political and social content of Aretino's works was consistently downplayed, and his texts were presented to their readers *as if they were* pornographic. Just as Shakespeare's plays were modified to suit the tastes of eighteenth-century theater audiences, so too Aretino's texts were presented in a manner that brought them closer in line to prevailing canons of literary taste. A 1660 edition of the *Ragionamenti* published by the firm of Elzevier in Amsterdam offers telling insight into the reception of Aretino in the mid-seventeenth century. The text is based on the 1584 London edition of John Wolfe and includes his introduction. While Wolfe's introduction praises Aretino and contends that his work is valuable for its attack on hypocrisy, the 1660 edition demonstrates a much greater concern to position the volume for its reader. It adds another editor's introduction and also includes copious marginalia "to explain and clearly describe the most obscure passages and difficult words" (sig. A1r). These annotations are by and large serious—even pedantic—providing common synonyms for difficult dialect words, alerting the reader to the workings of irony in the text, and giving the literal referents for Aretino's prolific (and often elaborate) sexual metaphors. At one point, the editor advises the use of a good dictionary (sig. A4v).

While Wolfe's introduction praises Aretino for his love of truth (sig. A3v), the new introduction provides a much more elaborate moral justification for printing and reading Aretino's dialogues.

> So great was Aretino's talent for writing with singular eloquence about any subject he proposed himself that for this he was named "divine": but above all his other works these capricious and pleasant *Ragionamenti* are worthy of esteem. Capricious indeed, and marvelous that such a genius gave himself over to writing of such matters in this manner: but also so pleasing, and so funny that it is not possible to read them without laughter and admiration. Also, you may say to me, not without loathing and disgust, because of the many difficulties and the great filthiness that are in it. It is true, I confess it, you will find in it many things which are difficult to understand, and many things which are nauseating to read. So what? Beautiful things are often difficult, and pleasures are for the most part accompanied by disgust. It is necessary to read

this book with patience and a moderate appetite . . . to retrieve good
moral precepts from it which will stay in your head and save you from
the wickedness of this filthy world. (sig. A2r–A2v)

Here the wickedness the reader is warned against turns out not to be explicit sexual
detail as such, but rather the "wickedness of evil women": as in the earlier editions of book 3, Aretino's text is offered as a manual for recognizing and escap-
ing the maliciousness of whores (sig. A3r–A3v). The ambiguity of the representation of female power in Aretino's text is thus erased, and along with it any hint
of the extent to which Aretino's text attributes the limited options of women to
a social structure that ignores female desire and intelligence. The colloquial style
of the text, so unfashionable to the neoclassical literary tastes of the later seventeenth century, is excused on the grounds that women and other illiterates often
ignore the proper rules of grammar (sig. A4). Aretino's "divine eloquence" can
only be made an object of praise by separating it from its low content and
anticlassical style. For all its desire to provide high-minded excuses for reading
Aretino's lascivious dialogue, at no point does this preface (or Wolfe's from 1584)
suggest that the *Ragionamenti* might have any political or social significance.

If the erotic explicitness of Aretino's writing came to overshadow the social
significance of his work, so too its low style and subject matter have kept it at a
safe distance from the canons of Great Literature. In the nineteenth century
Aretino was made to fit neatly into a narrative of mannerist decline from the
pinnacle of cultural achievement represented for Burckhardt and others by the
Renaissance. While showing a grudging admiration for Aretino's "clear and spar-
kling style" and "grotesque wit," Burckhardt characterizes him as being "desti-
tute of the power of conceiving a genuine work of art" and describes his relations
with the nobility as "mere beggary and vulgar extortion" (124). It was in the nineteenth century, in response to appraisals such as Burckhardt's, that Aretino's work
came to understood primarily under two different—but related—names: "pornography" and "journalism." While these terms have largely determined the
context in which discussions of Aretino take place, neither has any precise meaning
in the early modern period. Only by laying these notions aside can one begin to
trace the compelling mix of fascination, admiration, and horror that circled
around the image of Aretino in Renaissance England.

"The English Aretine"

Thomas Nashe

In the fourth act of Thomas Middleton's play *No Wit, No Help, Like a Woman's* (1611–12), a masque is held—a pageant of the four elements: Earth, Water, Air, and Fire. The first to speak is Fire, who identifies himself as representing a specifically sexual heat: "the wicked fire of lust,"

> corrupted with the upstart fires
> Of avarice, luxury, and inconstant heats,
> Struck from the bloods of cunning, clap-fall'n daughters,
> Night-walking wives, but, most, libidinous widows.

> (4.2.70–3)

Lust here is seen as having a female source and is located most strongly in widows (the masque, in fact, is an attack on the remarriage of a wealthy widow). But English widows have not always been lustful—their looseness is a new innovation, and it has a foreign origin: it is "Aretine."

> Rich widows, that were wont to choose by gravity
> Their second husbands, not by tricks of blood,
> Are now so taken with loose Aretine flames
> Of nimble wantonness and high-fed pride,
> They marry now but the third part of husbands,
> Boys, smooth-fac'd catamites, to fulfil their bed,
> As if a woman should a woman wed.

> (4.2.87–93)

This passage may serve to indicate the extent to which the figure of Aretino became embedded in the erotic discourses of early modern England: By the early years of the seventeenth century Aretino's name has entered the language, become an adjective to describe illicit desire—"tricks of blood" and "nimble wantonness."[1] Far from retaining its original Italian meaning "from Arezzo," the adjective "Aretine" here barely even refers to Pietro Aretino the author. It refers instead to a range of disorderly sexual practices associated with Aretino and his writings in early modern England.

In many English texts of the late sixteenth century Aretino's name is associated with an undefined sexual corruption—described as "filthiness and villainy" or "that which good men in natural modesty are ashamed to speak of."[2] Middleton, however, is quite explicit here in the association he draws between "Aretine flames" and specific forms of sexual disorder: those related to gender ambiguity and homoeroticism. The rich widows who burn with "Aretine flames" come to take on characteristics that are traditionally masculine; they follow their own sexual desires rather than pursuing prudent matches, and they end by taking womanish boys instead of men to their beds. While daughters were the property of their fathers and wives the property of their husbands, widows (like Aretino's Nanna) enjoyed a measure of autonomy. They could own property and bequeath it, and they were able, unlike other women, to be the head of their household; many widows took over their deceased husband's businesses. In addition, widows had the right to choose their next husband, or to choose no husband at all, thus exercising a degree of control over their sexuality that was denied to maidens or wives.[3] These limited freedoms could serve, as here, to figure widows as mannish—enjoying privileges generally granted only to men, they could become like men themselves.

In Middleton's text, "Aretine flames" not only produce mannish women, they are also linked to effeminacy. Burning with Aretine flames, Middleton suggests, mannish women no longer desire men, but boys. The figure of the boy is doubly marked as effeminate. First, in Renaissance England young boys were not simply considered young men but were in many ways treated as figures of indeterminate gender. Boys lived with women and until the breeching age of six or seven were not distinguished in dress from girls.[4] Between the breeching age and puberty, boys' bodies were marked by "feminine" characteristics such as softness, smoothness, and beardlessness. The adolescent boy, however, was also prone to another form of effeminacy. Given the lengthy period between puberty and the average age at which young men married in early modern England, adolescent boys tended to be involved in a wide variety of illicit sexual practices—including sex with married women, with men or other boys, or with prostitutes.[5] In Middleton's text, anxiety about the uncertain place of boys in the established hierarchy of gender and their participation in disorderly sexual practices reveals itself in the equivalence suggested between boys, catamites (boys anally penetrated in homoerotic intercourse), and women.

Aretine sex is unruly sex—filthy sex, sex that transgresses or confuses proper social and gender boundaries. In Middleton's text, as was often the case in early modern English culture, the Aretine is an entirely negative quality. It constitutes a specific element within a broader range of italianate corruption. But just as attitudes toward Italy in early modern England were not uniformly negative, so too with attitudes toward the Aretine. For some English writers and readers, Aretino was an attractive figure. They saw Aretine disorder as socially empowering rather than sexually debilitating. The figure who most consistently defended and celebrated the Aretine was Thomas Nashe.

Nashe, a Cambridge-educated pamphleteer, playwright, and polemicist, became known as "the English Aretine" for his biting wit, his "filthy rhymes,"

and his railing attacks on various social abuses. Nashe himself is a disorderly figure, complex and contradictory. His social views were generally conservative—
he supported the Church in the Marprelate controversy, for example. But his
life of urban poverty and his inability to maintain steady relations with his patrons often led him to bitter criticism of the aristocracy and the status quo. He
was a disciple of Ascham,[6] yet he had nothing but praise for Aretino. His friends
included Marlowe and the young Ben Jonson, and like them he was often in
trouble with the authorities. As an impoverished writer seeking patronage, he
was constantly engaged in self-fashioning and self-promotion. His most characteristic persona was that of "Piers Penniless," a raging, impoverished scholar,
overeducated and underemployed. Nashe saw in Aretino a potent mix of polemical
freedom, exotic eroticism, fantastic wealth, and authorial power.

Nashe's celebration of Aretine energies manifested itself in two related areas.
First, it formed a central theme in Nashe's very public quarrel with Cambridge
professor Gabriel Harvey, the most famous literary feud of the 1590s. Second,
Aretino's erotic writing gave Nashe a model for his most notorious verse—the
erotic narrative poem "Nashe his Dildo," now known as "The Choice of Valentines." Neither of Nashe's attempts to appropriate Aretino can be regarded as
successful, at least as far as Nashe's own life and career are concerned. Rather
than making him an authority unto himself, Nashe's self-fashioning as the English
Aretine served in the long run to single him out for exemplary punishment. Nashe's
view of Aretino as a powerful, Juvenalian political satirist was gradually being sup-
planted by the more enduring notion—expressed by Middleton and many others—
that associated the Aretine with corrupt, effeminate, sodomitical excess.

"Whatsoever sprouteth farther would be lopped": Nashe, Harvey, and Aretino

In its effort to control some of the more disorderly products of the book trade,
the 1599 Bishops' Order not only banned satire as a genre, it also directed "[t]hat
all NASSHes bookes and Doctor HARVYes bookes be taken wheresoever they
may be found and that none of theire bookes bee ever printed hereafter."[7] It is
generally assumed that Nashe's and Harvey's books were banned in an effort to
put a forcible end their long-running literary feud. There is no space here to un-
tangle the complexities of Nashe's quarrel with Harvey, but it is important to
note the large role that Nashe's erotic writing played in the dispute. Because of
the sheer amount of polemical material it generated, the quarrel between Nashe
and Harvey offers an unparalleled example of the ways in which eroticism could
be deployed to construct and deconstruct authorial power in early modern England.
Whatever else may have been at stake in Nashe's wrangling with Harvey, both
figures used their dispute as a means of self-promotion in an attempt to carve
out a space for themselves as authors and authorities.

In an attempt to demonstrate the unruliness of Nashe's texts (and life) Harvey
frequently identified him with the monstrous and foreign figure of Aretino.[8]
Nashe—who tended to get the better of Harvey throughout the quarrel—turned

Harvey's accusations of Aretinism on their head by taking them as a compliment. The association of Aretino with gender slippage and instability provides an important subtext to Harvey's attacks on Nashe in the 1590s. Professor of rhetoric at Cambridge from 1574 to 1592, Gabriel Harvey knew Aretino's works as well as any English person of his time,[9] and his reactions to the Italian writer are recorded both in his published writings and his private marginalia. Harvey's marginalia reveals that he owned a copy of the *Quattro Comedie* printed by Wolfe[10] and that he was also familiar with Aretino's comedy *Il Filosofo*, his tragedy *Orazia*, and some of his religious writings. Harvey's judgment that Aretino's works are "the quintessence of his unique genius; and the mirror of all the arts of courtesans" suggests he may have read the *Ragionamenti* as well as the comedies.[11] He was also acquainted, it seems, with Aretino's letters.

At least initially, Harvey's attitude toward Aretino seems to have been one of respect and admiration: in a letter to Spenser published in 1580, Harvey lists Aretino among "the most delicate, and fine conceited Grecians and Italians."[12] And in his letter-book, Harvey writes that he wishes a projected volume of his poems to be "sett in as witty and fine order as may be, Aretinelyke."[13] Indeed, an admiration for Aretino may not have been uncommon among educated Englishmen in the 1580s.[14] But as Harvey's career progressed his admiration for Aretino waned, a tendency that parallels the rise of anti-italianate discourse in England throughout the 1580s and 1590s. While in 1580 Harvey was willing to praise Aretino in print, in the early 1590s he uses the infamy of Aretino's disorderly eroticism to attack the growing popularity and social authority of railing satirists like Nashe.

Though they cannot be precisely dated, Harvey's various marginalia referring to Aretino offer some insight into the ways his thinking on Aretino changed during the years between 1580 and 1592. In three separate places in his copy of Quintilian, Harvey lists Aretino as a great and indispensable writer, along with Machiavelli, Rabelais, Bembo, Paracelsus, Tacitus, Suetonius, Luther, and Quintilian himself.[15] In notes in other volumes Harvey praises Aretino for his "courting Italian Comedies" (165) and includes him with Petrarch, Ariosto, and Tasso in a list of "fowre famous heroique poets, as valorously braue, as delicately fine" (162). Harvey comes back again and again to Aretino's skill in hyperbole and amplificatio (137, 168, 196)—a facility Harvey himself seems to envy and wish to acquire.

For Harvey, Aretino's skill in hyperbole makes him unique, singular, independent. "Aretine's glory, to be himself: to speak & write like himself: to imitate none but him selfe & ever to maintaine his owne singularity, yet euer with commendation and compassion of other" (156). To a modern reader, this looks like high praise indeed. But in the early modern period, individuality was not necessarily a quality to be prized too highly. Ascham concludes his attack on italianate Englishmen in *The Scholemaster* by accusing them of being "mervelous singular in all their matters," and he links this "singularity" to social disorder. Such men become "busie searchers of most secret affairs: open flatterers of great men . . . and spitefull reporters privilie of good men" (85). Such license is a direct result of what Ascham views as the pernicious liberty of the Italian city-states, where a common man, "being brought up in *Italie*, in some free Citie . . . may freelie discourse against what he will, against whom he lust: against any Prince, agaynst any governement, yea against God him selfe and his whole Religion" (85–6).

In another note in the same volume in which he mentions Aretino's "singularity," Harvey commends Aretino for his sophisticated knowledge of "fashions"—just the sort of knowledge Ascham abhominated in young Englishmen. Harvey writes: "Machiavel, & Aretine knew fasshions, and were aquainted with ye cunning of ye world. . . . They had lernid cunning enowgh: and had seen fasshions enowgh: and cowld and woold use both, with advantage enowgh. Two curtisan politiques" (147). This passage demonstrates both admiration of the worldliness of Aretino and Machiavelli and contempt for the way their knowledge has corrupted them. The tone is one of horrified fascination. Aretino and Machiavelli slip from being knowing observers of corruption to being active manipulators and "curtisan politiques"—that is, political courtesans—a phrase that links sodomy with political disorder. Aretino appears an attractive, even fascinating figure whose good qualities, like the classical tradition of Italy itself, come to be seen as enticing temptations, luring Englishmen to their doom: he is dangerous because, like the Circe Ascham saw reborn in Italy, he is seductive. He has all the seductive energy that Sidney associates with the supposedly virtuous figure of the "right poet."

In his pamphlets printed against Nashe in the 1590s, Harvey's private ambivalence about Aretino's rhetorical prowess is replaced by public disgust at Nashe's insolent Aretine overreaching. Attacking Nashe in his *Four Letters*, Harvey writes: "had not Aretine been Aretine, when he was, undoubtably thou hadst beene Aretine, gramercy capricious, and transcendent witte, the onlie high Pole Artique and deepe Minerall of an incomparable stile" (sig. E2v;1:201). Here the ambivalence is gone: Aretino's independence and individuality are clearly represented as monstrous rather than admirable. In the *New Letter* Harvey calls Aretino a "monster of extremity," an "abomination of outrageous witt." In his private notes, Harvey says Aretino's glory is "to be himself." Here, Harvey writes, "It was his glory to be a hellhounde incarnate."

In *Pierces Supererogation*, the most elaborate of his pamphlets against Nashe, Harvey attacks Nashe for writing an "unprinted packet of bawdye, and filthy Rymes in the nastiest kind" (sig. F4; 2:91). While the only surviving example of such writing by Nashe is his erotic narrative poem "Choice of Valentines"—known in some versions as "Nashe his Dildo"—it is possible that this text may have been part of a larger body of similar work.[16] But Harvey's attack on "Choice of Valentines" is elaborated in terms that go beyond personal enmity, and that adopt the discourses of effeminacy and national weakness in ways that echo Gosson and Stubbes. That works like "Choice of Valentines" debase the purity of poetry is a given for Harvey, but Nashe and his writings pose as great a threat to the commonwealth of England as to the commonwealth of letters. Harvey fears that the importation of effeminizing poetic models from Italy will result in a weakening of English manhood, undesirable at any time but extremely dangerous in the 1590s, when England stands poised on the brink of imperial adventure. The late 1570s and 1580s saw Gilbert's voyage to Newfoundland, Drake's circumnavigation of the globe, Frobisher's search for the Northwest Passage and Raleigh's expeditions to Virginia; the defeat of the Armada in 1588 marked the beginning of fifteen years of open war with Spain, a war fought not only at sea but in the Low Countries, France, and Ireland. When one can read of all these "famous discoveryes, & adventures" in Hakluyt, there can be no more "wanton leasure for the Comedyes of Athens; nor anye bawdy howers for the songes of Priapus, or the rymes of Nashe." "The date of idle vanityes is expired," Harvey announces; England needs "Spartan invincibility" (sigs. F4v–F6r;2:92–5).

The collapse of Italian political independence over the course of the sixteenth century offers Harvey a compelling example of a once imperial power reduced to servility, and he makes an explicit connection between republican liberty and the enfeebling poison spread by "pernicious writers, depravers of common discipline."

> Ferraria could scarcely brooke Manardus, a poysonous Phisitian: Mantua hardly beare Pomponatious, a poysonous Philosopher: Florence more hardly tollerate Macchiavel, a poysonous politician: Venice most hardly endure Arretine, a poysonous ribald: had they lived in absolute Monarchies, they would have seemed utterly insupportable. (sig. F5v;2:94)

If Harvey blames the downfall of the Italian city-states on the corruption of their intellectuals, London, on the other hand, is paralleled with Rome at the onset of its imperial glory; and just as imperial Rome was forced to banish Ovid, so too must London rid itself of Greene and Nashe.

Harvey's objection to Nashe's "filthy rymes" is thus more than a matter of literary propriety and aesthetics: "better a Confuter of letters," Harvey writes, "than a counfounder of manners": "Cannot an Italian ribald [Aretino], vomit-out the infectious poyson of the world, but an English horrel-lorrel must licke it up for a restorative; and attempt to putrify gentle mindes, with the vilest impostumes of lewde corruption?" (sig. F4r;2:91).

While "Choice of Valentines" is based more on works by Ovid and Chaucer than on any specific Italian text,[17] Harvey aligns Nashe with Aretino because it is Aretino who gives Nashe a model of cultural practice to follow.

Harvey was not the only writer to make a connection between Nashe and Aretino.[18] In *Wit's Misery and the World's Madness* (1596), Thomas Lodge calls Nashe "the true English Aretine" in a list which praises Lyly for his "facility in discourse," Spenser for his knowledge of the ancients, Daniel for his invention, and Drayton for his formal skill (sig. I). Whatever its valence, the association with Aretino was one Nashe cultivated rather than avoided. Some scholars have questioned Nashe's knowledge of Italian.[19] But given his enthusiasm for Aretino, there is no reason to assume he was utterly ignorant. In his 1580 letters to Spenser, Gabriel Harvey complains that at Cambridge there are "over many acquainted with *Unico Aretino*" (sig. D2v;1:69) and if there was indeed "a kind of vogue for Aretino at Cambridge,"[20] it is hard to believe that Nashe, who attended Cambridge from 1581 to 1588, would have been unaware of it. As his prologue to *Strange*

News demonstrates, Nashe knew Aretino's *La Cortigiana* well enough to make an accurate reference to it.[21] More important, even if he did not read a word of Aretino, Nashe quite clearly wished to impress it upon his readers that he had.

The Aretino Nashe defends and praises is a very different figure than the "poysonous ribald" denounced by Harvey. For Nashe, Aretino is a figure of almost inconceivable authorial autonomy, political influence, and financial success. In his popular pamphlet *Pierce Penniless* (1592), Nashe presents Aretino as a Juvenalian figure, scourging the vices of the powerful, in particular the arrogant and foolish ingratitude of patrons: "We want an *Aretine* here among us, that might strip these golden asses out of their gaie trappings, and after he had ridden them to death with railing, leave them on the dunghill for carion" (1:242).

If subsequent writers have seen Aretino's relations with the nobility of Europe as "mere beggary and vulgar extortion,"[22] Nashe sees Aretino as a man of talent who gets a steady income and a degree of respect from his patrons. For Nashe, Aretino comes to represent the ideal satirist, set free from economic necessity, an agent of social justice who is himself above the law. Far from taking the conventional view of Aretino as a sodomite and atheist, Nashe sees him as a defender of religion against "atheism, schism, hypocrisy, and vainglory" (1:242). Nashe's portrayal of Aretino not merely as the Scourge of Princes, but as a literary Scourge of God, laying bare the abuses of both Church and State, may seem a little unlikely, until one remembers the ease with which Nashe himself self-righteously adopts the persona of Christ to attack the corruptions of London in *Christ's Tears over Jerusalem* (1593).[23] In the narrative of *The Unfortunate Traveler* (1594), Aretino intervenes personally to free the narrator and protagonist Jack Wilton from an unjust imprisonment on charges of counterfeiting, and Wilton uses this occasion to deliver a two-page panegyric of Aretino, praising his rescuer for his outspoken attacks on "all abuses." For Wilton, Aretino is a champion of free speech who speaks truth to power. "He was no timerous servile flatterer of the commonwealth wherein he lived. His tongue and his invention were foreborne; what they thought, they would confidently utter. Princes he spared not that in the least point transgrest" (2:265).

And while Aretino's *Vita della virgine Maria* might "somewhat smell of superstition," it is nonetheless as a religious writer that he is most admirable: "*Tully, Virgil, Ovid, Seneca* [all, of course, pagans] were never such ornamentes to Italy as thou hast bin. I never thought of Italie more religiously than England till I heard of thee" (2:226). Wilton even comically compares Aretino to Christ casting out demons: "No houre but hee sent a whole legion of devils into some heard of swine or other" (2:264). It is indicative of the general failure to recognize the importance of Aretino in early modern England that Charles Nicholl has argued in *The Reckoning* that this praise of Aretino must be a coded reference to Marlowe.

Nashe's identification with Aretino culminates in the preface to *Lenten Stuff* (1599) where he openly states:

> Of all stiles I most affect & strive to imitate *Aretines*, not caring for this
> demure, soft *mediocre genus*, that is like water and wine mixt togither;
> but give me pure wine of it selfe, & that begets good bloud, and heates
> the brain thorowly: I had as lieve have no sunne, as have it shine faintly,
> no fire as a smothering fire of small coales, no cloathes, rather than wear
> linsey wolsey. (3:152)

Nashe envies Aretino's social power as well as his linguistic vigor. Aretino's forceful
rhetoric is equated with political power, wealth, and status. Nashe defines powerful
language as language that is a means to power, language that carries authority,
language that must be listened to.

While Nashe never explicitly praises Aretino for writing erotic verse, choosing instead to concentrate on his political influence and rhetorical power, this separation of the erotic and the political is supported neither by Aretino's works—which
constantly employ the erotic as a satiric weapon—nor by his wider English reputation, in which the image of the powerful satirist is bound up with that of the
excessive and effeminate sodomite. Although Nashe makes a tactical decision not
to mention Aretino's erotic works, it is unlikely that he was unaware of them. To
understand Nashe's relation to Aretino one must look not only at explicit state-
ments made about Aretino throughout Nashe's work but also at his writing of
"Choice of Valentines." For while Nashe's poem is in no sense "based" on any
previous work by Aretino, as Harvey realized all too well the complex appropriation and rewriting of Aretino's legacy throughout the works of Nashe is far more
significant than any precise verbal echo of Aretino's erotic writings in "Choice of
Valentines." For rather than copying Aretino in a few particulars, Nashe founds
his very concept of what a writer can and should be on the example of Aretino.

If Nashe's prose works offer a coherent if unorthodox interpretation of Aretino's
sociopolitical significance, the writing of "Choice of Valentines" emphasizes that
Nashe, like Aretino, believed that scandalously explicit erotic writing could play
an important part in the creation of authorial power. Unlike Aretino, however,
Nashe was quickly proven wrong in this assumption. Given the sociopolitical differences between Elizabethan England and pre-Tridentine Venice, the model of
Aretino ultimately proved unworkable for Nashe. The writing of "Choice of Valentines" seems to have brought Nashe little financial success and even less prestige.

Indeed, Nashe's writing of erotic verse was read by his opponents as a sign
of unmanly weakness. Writing and selling amorous verse, Nashe faced accusations of being—at least figuratively—a male whore. In *Have With You to Saffron-
Walden* (1596), Nashe answers Gabriel Harvey's charge he has "too much acquaintance in London ever to doo any good, being like a Curtezan that can deny no
man" (3:26), by equivocating:

> As newfangled and idle, and prostituting my pen like a Curtizan, is the
> next *Item* that you taxe me with; well it may and may not be so, for
> neither will I deny it nor will I grant it; onely thus farre Ile goe with
> you, that twise or thrise in a month, when *res est angusta domi*, the

bottome of my purse is turnd downeward and my conduit of incke will no longer flowe for want of reparations, I am faine to . . . follow some of these newfangled *Galliardos* and *Senior Fantasticos*, to whose amorous *Villanellas* and *Quipassas* I prostitute my pen in hope of gaine. (3:30–1)

Although it is incorrect and misleading to conflate early modern notions of effeminacy and sodomy, these two notions come together here. For if Nashe is accused of being effeminate and selling himself like a courtesan, those to whom he sells himself are men, specifically "Galliardos" and "Fantasticos," both terms used in the 1590s to describe sodomites. The name of a "quick and lively dance," "galliard" could also refer to "a man of courage" or of "fashion" (*OED*); in practice, it often connoted a fop. Gosson includes the galliard in a list of effeminizing dances (*Schoole* sig. A8), and in *Twelfth Night* the ridiculous Sir Andrew Aguecheek is said to have a leg "formed under the star of a galliard" (1.3.130). "Fantastico" is a much rarer term, occurring most memorably in *Romeo and Juliet* when Mercutio rails against Tybalt in a passage full of sodomitical innuendo as being an "antic, lisping affecting fantastico," a "fashion-monger" skilled in "the punto reverso" who "fights as you sing prick-song"—"a very good blade! A very tall man! A very good whore!" (2.4.19–35).[24]

Despite its defense of Nashe's "normal . . . love-life" and "the huge heterosexual gusto" of his texts,[25] Charles Nicholl's biography of Nashe provides much evidence that Nashe was represented as effeminate and sodomitical in the 1590s. Nicholl stresses the effeminacy that characterizes many of the caricatures of Nashe, including the well-known woodcut from Richard Lichfield's *Trimming of Thomas Nashe* (1597), which shows Nashe in an unbuttoned doublet, beardless, and in chains, an image of bondage to passion not entirely dissimilar from that of the captive bound before Love's chariot in Marlowe's elegies (figure 4.1).

Against the figure of the poet as an Aretine courtesan selling effeminate rhymes and weakening the nobility who purchase his services, Harvey posits an earlier, virile poetic tradition, associated with what Stephen Gosson refers to as the "olde discipline of Englande" (sig. B8r). As Gosson sees it, the proper function of poetry is to encourage martial and patriarchal virtue. Poetry, properly used, is a call to arms that will instill manly discipline. This praise of martial poetry has its roots in the third book of Plato's *Republic*, where mournful and lax music is banished in favor of the warlike Dorian and Phrygian modes, and one who devotes himself too much to music of any kind is said, like the cuckold Menelaus, to melt and liquefy his spirit, till he has degenerated into a "soft spearfighter."[26]

While Gosson sees proper martial poetic traditions as largely irretrievable, a paradise from which England has fallen, Harvey is more optimistic; he believes there are still genres of poetry—even erotic poetry—that are vigorous and virtuous. Harvey is not, at heart, xenophobic; even in *Pierce's Supererogation* he makes it clear that not all Italian writing is to be shunned. Following his castigation of Nashe's "filthy rymes," he passes to a discussion of Petrarch.

The trimming of Thomas Nashe.

But fee, what art thou heere? *lupus* In *fabula*, a lop in a chaine? Nowe firra haue at you, th'art in my fwinge. But foft, fetterd? thou art out againe: I cannot come neere thee, thou haft a charme about thy legges, *no man meddle with the Queenes prifoner*, now therefore let vs talke freendlye, and as *Alexander* fayd to hys Father *Philip*, who beeing forely wounded in the thigh in fight, and hardly efcaping death, but could

E 2   not

Figure 4.1. *Nashe as a beardless, effeminate captive. Thomas Nashe in chains from Gabriel Harvey (?),* The Trimming of Thomas Nashe *(1597), STC 12906, Henry E. Huntington Library (Shelfmark: 61318).*

Petrarckes Invention is pure Love it selfe: And Petrarckes Elocution, pure Bewty it selfe: His *Laura* was . . . a nimph of Diana, not a Curtisan of Venus. Aretines muse was an egregious bawd & a haggishe witch of Thessalia: but Petrarcks verse, a fine loover. (sig. F4v;2:92)

Harvey prefers Petrarch to Aretino because in his figuration the Petrarchan lover is ultimately chaste, a follower of Diana rather than Venus. A man who pursues Diana's nymph is strong and manly precisely because he never attains his desires; he is perpetually hard; he never "spends his strength."[27] The proper, manly lover will thus, like the explorers Harvey eulogizes, spend his life seeking his desire in the rugged woods, rather than satisfying it with a courtesan in the court or the city. His desires may therefore be usefully harnessed to the nascent imperial project—his virile firmness will ultimately strengthen England in its contest with Spain. Thus, proper emulation of Petrarch will lead to a Spartan discipline epitomized for Harvey by that "Inglishe Petrarck" Philip Sidney, whose *Arcadia*, like Hakluyt's volume of travel narratives, stands opposed to the "filthy rimes" of the English Aretine Thomas Nashe. For Harvey, *Arcadia* offers proper examples not only of courtly love but also of "sage counselling" and "valourous fighting" (sig. F8r;2:100).

If Sidney's life and work offer a model of masculinity to be emulated, Nashe's "Aretinizing," reaching as it does beyond the "pleasurable witt" of an amorous Petrarchan sonneteer, deserves to be castrated: "whatsoever sprowteth farther," Harvey warns, "would be lopped" (sig. F4v;2:92)—a formulation that neatly encapsulates the effeminizing dynamic whereby excess of sexual energy results ultimately in a lack of virility. While readers of early modern poetry have long considered the sonnets of Sidney and Shakespeare to be "anti-Petrarchan" in their undermining of conventional conceits, Harvey sees another, more disruptive, form of anti-Petrarchism in Nashe and Aretino: an utter rejection of courtly love and its metaphors in favor of sexually explicit language and the erotic exchanges of the brothel.

Harvey's description of Aretino's muse as a "haggishe witch of Thessalia" is telling, for it points at the heart of Harvey's anxiety about Nashe's erotic writing. "Choice of Valentines" is not merely sexually explicit; it is explicit about male sexual inadequacy. Since antiquity the Thessalian witch has served as a type of emasculating witchcraft, the enchantments and potions which Nashe's poem refers to as "Ovid's cursed hemlock" (l. 124)—a direct reference to *Amores* 3.7, which Nashe would have known best in Marlowe's recent translation.[28] While Harvey, Gosson, and others see emasculating poetry as emblematic of general moral and social weakness, for Tomalin—the narrator and protagonist of "Choice of Valentines"—the threat of emasculation is distressingly literal.

Nashe's "Choice of Valentines" and Masculine Gender Identity

> There is a bush fitt for the nonce
> That beareth prickes and pretious stones
> This fruit in feare some Ladies pull
> Tis round and smothe & plumpe & full
> It yields deare moisture, pure and thicke
> It seldome makes a Ladye sicke
> They put it in and then they move it
> wch makes it melt and then they love it
> so what was round and plump and hard
> growes ranke and thine and poor and marde
> The sweetnes suckt they wipe and staye
> And throwe the emptye skin away.
>
> —"A Riddle of a goosberye bush" (c. 1620)[29]

Despite its comic tone and disingenuous title, this anonymous riddle offers a vision of sexuality quite different from that prescribed by the patriarchal gender hierarchy of early modern England. Here phallic power utterly expends itself in use—the penis is devoured by the woman who takes pleasure from it, and the discarded, emasculated husk is thrown away. As the poem makes graphically clear, the *use* of the penis is a deeply contradictory undertaking. For the sexual act that initiates paternity and theoretically establishes the ability of a man to master his subordinates is also debilitating and self-destructive: "what was round and plump and hard / growes ranke and thine and poor and marde."

We have seen that uncertainty or anxiety over male sexual functioning is the subject not only of printed works such as Marlowe's translations of the *Amores* but also of many bawdy comic poems found in the manuscript commonplace books kept by young men of the Inns of Court and the universities in the late sixteenth and early seventeenth centuries. Perhaps the most sophisticated of these manuscript texts is Nashe's "Choice of Valentines"—known in some versions as "Nashe his Dildo"—a poem that represents Nashe's most forceful attempt to gain for himself the notoriety as erotic writer that was crucial to the establishment of Aretino's English reputation. Set in a brothel and focusing on the use of a dildo, Nashe's poem, like the "Riddle of a goosberye bush," addresses the contradictions at the heart of early modern masculinity, contradictions that, as we have seen, were highly politicized. And while "Choice of Valentines" is often confusing and contradictory in its representation of sexuality, the poem's refusal or inability to cohere is indicative of a broader social uncertainty about masculine sexual power and gender identity.

Although Nashe's poem gives its readers a fair degree of explicit description of sexual intercourse, it does not aim at arousing its male readers in a straightforward and uncomplicated manner. In its graphic depiction of the whore Francis, who, left unsatisfied by her overexcited lover Tomalin, gets her "full sufficeance" from a dildo, "Choice of Valentines" is not merely sexually explicit; it is explicit about male sexual inadequacy and female sexual autonomy—both sensitive and disturbing topics, given the hierarchy of gender that characterizes early modern society. And in the early 1590s when poetry as a whole could be seen as effeminizing, liable to "transnature" its male reader "into a woman or worse,"[30] the emasculation of Tomalin in "Choice of Valentines" seems to have been perceived as particularly threatening, despite the obvious comedy in the poem's presentation of his plight.[31]

The narrative of "Choice of Valentines" is easily summarized: It is Valentine's Day, and Tomalin, the boastful and somewhat foolish narrator of the poem, searches for his beloved Francis. She, however, has left her rural residence for an urban brothel.[32] Tomalin goes to the brothel, where he is reunited with Francis. Overcome with the sight of her beauty, he ejaculates prematurely, but she soon revives him and they engage in intercourse. Tomalin comes, and Francis seems to, but she is still unsated, and—Tomalin being of no further use in this regard—she satisfies herself with a dildo. Tomalin rails against the dildo until he is silenced by Francis, at which point he pays the madame his bill and leaves the brothel. The tone of the poem is broadly comic, at points parodic, and in general the text mocks its hapless protagonist as much as it commiserates with him.

Although the poem's narrative is relatively straightforward, its text is somewhat vexed, even in the authoritative version published by McKerrow in 1905. As Jonathan Crewe and others have noted, the pronoun references are often vague or ambiguous, and at various points the identity of the speaker is unclear. It is, of course, impossible to tell whether or not such ambiguities are intentional. In its details, the text often seems confusing, and it makes little effort to reconcile the contradictory expectations it raises.

The genre of "Choice of Valentines" too is somewhat unclear; leaving aside accusations that it is pornographic,[33] it has been variously described as being Ovidian, Chaucerian, Spenserian, parodic, and pastoral.[34] The poem draws on many of these traditions, without fitting neatly into any generic category. Harvey is correct, however, in his perception that Nashe's work is radically anti-Petrarchan. In fact, "Choice of Valentines" opens with a dedicatory sonnet that clearly announces Nashe's intention to surpass recent Petrarchan erotic poetry, by a return to earlier (and presumably more explicit) models of erotic writing:

> Complaints and praises everie one can write,
> And passion-out their [pangs] in statlie rimes,
> But of loves pleasure's none did ever write
> That hath succeeded in theis latter times.

Nashe calls for a discourse of pleasure to replace the Petrarchan discourse of frustration. Given the frequent references to Aretino in almost all Nashe's prose works, the claim that no one has succeeded in writing of pleasure is puzzling. Since Nashe was clearly aware of Aretino's success in erotic writing, one could argue that here the omission is both considered and strategic; when Nashe himself comes to write of love's pleasures, it seems, he has no desire to invoke powerful recent precedents. Perhaps the inability to describe pleasure successfully can be seen to parallel Tomalin's lack of success in his management of pleasure—either Francis's or his own. Or, more pointedly, Tomalin's boast that he is uniquely qualified to speak about sex can be seen as a compensation for his sexual dysfunction and inability to satisfy his partner. Certainly the dedicatory sonnet's assertion that "all men act what I in speache declare" can be applied not only to sexual activity itself but also to Tomalin's sexual shortcomings, thus attesting to widespread anxiety over virility. Although in writing of explicit erotic material Nashe's *practice* owes everything to the unspoken example of Aretino, as a particular text "Choice of Valentines" is much more frank about its debts to Chaucer and Ovid. Once Tomalin arrives at the "house of venerie" (24) we are dealing not with ironic anti-Petrarchism, but with a more thoroughgoing Aretinizing rejection of Petrarchism altogether.

The poem's inability to deal effectively and coherently with material it insists on taking up is indicative of a broader social incoherence about sexual power and gender identity—specifically about the place of the urban brothel in the larger erotic economy. Is a brothel a site of illicit erotic freedom of exchange or of the degradation of sex by commerce? Is it a site of male dominance, where a man can get whatever he pays for, or (as Nashe's text would tend to suggest) a site of masculine submission—dysfunction even—in the face of dominant and (relatively) autonomous women such as Francis and the Madame?

Traditionally tolerated and sanctioned by state and ecclesiastical authority, after 1570 the London brothels became the subject of a campaign of judicial suppression.[35] Thus, although brothels had always existed in London, their place in the erotic economy of the city was changing and uncertain in the late sixteenth century. Apart from any criminal activities that occurred in their precincts, brothels violated the social order as sites of visible female sexuality, itself inevitably seen as disorderly.[36] And whether or not female brothel keepers exercised any significant economic power, the brothels' linkage of potentially uncontrolled female sexuality with female control of capital (however limited) seems to have been particularly disturbing, especially after 1546, when all efforts to regulate the stews officially had been abandoned. In terms of Nashe's poem it is significant that the space of male anxiety is defined as the criminal space of the brothel; Nashe's dildo appears in the hands of a whore, whereas in later poems by Marston and others the dildo, like the coach, is part of the paraphernalia of aristocratic women.[37] For Nashe, who always remained a social conservative, despite the bitterness of his attacks on ungrateful patrons, the sexual deviance and emasculation represented by the dildo is associated more with the criminal underworld than with the court.

"Choice of Valentines" begins by contrasting the practice of prostitution in the cities with rustic traditions of courtship in the country; searching for Francis, Tomalin learns she has been driven from her village to a brothel in London by the local authorities (l. 21). Some critics have attempted to idealize the rural world from which Francis has been banished by reading it as pastoral, "the world of pure essences and uncompromised beings"—a reading that valorizes "natural" rural sexuality at the expense of the urban commercial world of the brothel.[38] But while the urban brothel may be a disturbing site of female sexual power and dominance, "Choice of Valentines" refuses to idealize its "natural" opposite; the rustic sexuality of the beginning of the poem is described in terms both nostalgic and parodic and is at no point presented as a serious alternative to the experience of the brothel. Its genealogy is more Chaucerian than classical, and the atmosphere evoked is that of a medieval English feast-day, not of pastoral otium:[39]

> It was the merie moneth of Februarie
> When yong-men in their iollie roguerie
> Rose earelie in the morne fore breake of daie
> To seek them valentines so trimme and gaie
>
> . . . .
> And goe to som village abbordring neere
> To taste the creame, and cakes and such good cheere,
> Or see a playe of strange moralitie
> Shewen by Bachelrie of Maningtree;

Whereto the Contrie franklins flock-meale swarme,
And Ihon and Jone com marching arme in arme.

(1–4,9–14)

The erotic economy of this world is one of natural choice. The choosing of valentines is a Chaucerian motif, taken from the courtly dream-allegory *The Parliament of Fowls*. In Chaucer's poem the choice of valentines—the ritual springtime choosing of a mate—is ironically contrasted with artificial aristocratic conventions of Petrarchan service and courtly love. While the common birds, such as geese and turtledoves, simply choose a single fitting sexual partner, the noble male eagles all compete for a single female who as a result must defer her choice for a year. Idealized simplicity of choice is thus set against the delayed gratification implicit in the Petrarchan model of courtship.

While the *Parliament of Fowls* uses notions of natural choice to mock the artificiality of Petrarchism, "Choice of Valentines" presents the rustic "natural" world as itself artificial—"a playe of strange moralitie"; Nashe's rustic youths *are* Petrarchan lovers: on the hallowes of that blessed Saint, / That doeth true louers with those ioyes acquaint," Tomalin goes as a "poore pilgrim to [his] ladies shine" (15–7). In this passage Nashe plays the two traditions of erotic writing off against each other, using the obvious anachronism of his Chaucerian material to discredit the language of Petrarchism by pointing out the similarity of Petrarchan conceit to the language of medieval Catholicism generally the subject of ridicule in Elizabethan England. The parodic preciousness of "pilgrim" Tomalin seeking "Lady" Francis is largely absent from later sections of the poem, in which both Petrarchan and traditional rural sexualities are undermined by their juxtaposition with the urban commercial world of the brothel. In Nashe's poem, unlike Chaucer's, there is no natural choice of valentine.

The naive and artificial language used to describe the rustic world foregrounds the fictional nature of Nashe's representation of rural sexuality. Of course the exchanges of the brothel are not as detached from the rural traditional world as Nashe's text would suggest; there were country whores as well as city whores,[40] and the persecution of Francis by the town authorities suggests she may have been a prostitute even before entering the brothel. The contrast of urban and rural, modern and traditional sexualities is a fictional construct the poem both creates and undermines.

The text also deliberately sets up a fairly complex relationship between Tomalin and Francis. Rather than describing a casual or anonymous encounter, the poem is at pains to establish that the two lovers have been previously involved in the country. Initially Tomalin goes to the brothel specifically to find Francis, and he rejects the other women offered him by the Madame (49–54). But although Tomalin insists on seeing Francis, his stated reasons have nothing to do with their previous relationship, let alone any affection he might have for her. Both his demand to see Francis and the Madame's response are expressed entirely in the language of commodity and exchange: he must have "fresher ware" (54) or, as the Madame puts it, "a morsell of more price" (59). When the couple are reunited, Francis protests that despite her residence in the brothel she loves

Tomalin exclusively and claims she will leave the brothel with him: "now the coaste is cleare, we wilbe gonne" (91). Yet she does *not* leave the brothel with him, nor is that possibility ever mentioned again. The narrative of romantic quest and reunion, like the contrast of urban and rural sexualities, is lost in the shuffle as the poem takes up the issues that become its abiding concerns: male inability to satisfy female desire and the resulting use of the dildo by Francis. Tomalin's inability to control the physical manifestations of his lust—his premature ejaculation, his inability to fully satisfy Francis' desires—evokes anxieties that cannot be fully expressed in terms of a perverse departure from natural rural sexuality nor contained within the narrative of courtship and affective union the poem attempts to construct for Francis and Tomalin as a couple.

While the first sight of Francis provokes Tomalin's blissful exclamation "Sing lullabie my cares and fall a-sleepe" (76), the lovers' encounter proves to be something less than carefree; Tomalin has difficulty controlling the heat of his passion. At Francis's first flirtatious tossing of her head, Tomalin cries "Oh, who is able to abstaine so long? / I com, I com;" (98–9), and whether or not we are to take him at his word here it soon becomes clear that, for Tomalin, the beauty of Francis's naked body is a prospect as dangerous as it is enticing. For all the effort expended to construct an opposition between the urban and rural, the rural landscape left behind by the text's shift to the city has reappeared at the heart of the brothel in the form of Francis' body:

> A prettie rysing wombe without a weame,
> That shone as bright as anie silver streame;
> And bare out lyke the bending of an hill,
> At whose decline a fountaine dwelleth still.

> (109–12)

For Jonathan Crewe (49), this description too is pastoral and Ovidian; Francis's body here signifies a plenitude, a fertile feminine landscape like those of Donne's Elegies 18 and 19, awaiting a male conqueror to bestride it like a colossus. However, the feminized landscape in Donne is consistently described in terms more epic and global than pastoral. The various geographic metaphors of Donne's Elegies 18 and 19—most famously the image of the vulva as "America" (19.27) all suggest the epic voyages of exploration and conquest advocated by Harvey rather than pastoral otium.

In fact Francis's body bears more resemblance to the edenic gardens of Renaissance epic than to the classical pastoral pleasance of Theocritus and Virgil. The erotic landscape of Francis's body recalls such sites as the Mount of Venus in Spenser's Gardens of Adonis more clearly than any classical text:

> Right in the middest of that Paradise,
> There stood a stately Mount, on whose round top
> A gloomy grove of mirtle trees did rise,
>
> . . . .
>
> [which] like a girlond compassed the hight,

And from their fruitfull sides sweet gum did drop,
That all the ground with precious deaw bedight,
Threw forth most dainty odours, and most sweet delight.

(*Faerie Queene* 3.6.43)

The paradisal gardens of Renaissance epic are primarily sites of entrapment, to be resisted or destroyed, but not (like Donne's America) to be conquered, colonized, and inhabited.

If—like Venus's mount—Francis's body offers the fertile pleasures of a paradisal garden, it is not without its perils: the fountain "hath his mouth besett with uglie bryers / Resembling much a duskie nett of wyres" (113–4). A Spenserian analogue to the net of wires is found not amid the vital fertility of the Gardens of Adonis but in the sensual artifice of the Bowre of Blisse; it resembles the seductive veil that both adorns and conceals Acrasia's face:

a vele of silke and siluer thin,
That hid no whit her alablaster skin,
But rather shewd more white, if more might bee:
More subtile web *Arachne* cannot spin
Nor the fine nets, which oft we wouen see
Of scorched deaw, do not in th'aire more lightly flee.

(2.12.77)

As many commentators have pointed out, the "subtile web" that intensifies and epitomizes Acrasia's perilous attractiveness is both complimented and contrasted by the other "subtile net" thrown by the Palmer, which traps Acrasia and her lovers and thus permits the destruction of her Bowre (2.12.81). Though hardly subtle, Francis' "duskie nett of wyres"—her pubic hair—combines the connotations of both these Spenserian nets; it is at once an enticing aspect of the erotic landscape and an emblem of entrapment and loss of heroic virtue.

The classical image underlying the Palmer's subtle net is that of the net of Vulcan, which traps Venus and Mars in their adulterous embrace. In both Homer and Ovid[41] the net of Vulcan not only represents enslavement to the body and its desires, but is more specifically a mechanism for producing shame; it subjects an illicit sexual act (adultery) to the gaze of one's peers. Nashe's allusion to Vulcan's net hints at the social work his poem is designed to accomplish: it places Tomalin's shame before an audience of (male) readers. By thus making public Tomalin's private weaknesses, the specter of male inadequacy can safely be exorcised; the only punishment suffered by Mars, after all, is the laughter of the gods. It is no accident that many poems dealing with male weakness and inadequacy—from "Choice of Valentines" to the "Riddle of a goosberye bush"—are comic. But coterie readership of erotic verse was not exclusively male. Exposing Tomalin's failings to men, Nashe also potentially exposes them to women. Indeed, as we have seen, one of the six surviving texts of "Choice of Valentines" was owned by Margaret Bellasys. Whatever Nashe's intentions in mocking Tomalin, it did not—

as far as we can tell—succeed in provoking liberating laughter among men: according to John Davies of Hereford Nashe's poem was torn to pieces by "goodmens hate" for revealing the secrets of the dildo.[42]

In many ways, the shame of being in Vulcan's net is the shame of sex itself; for early modern men sex is at once a proof of virility and a sign of physical weakness. In early modern medical theory, male orgasm was considered physically debilitating; a "spending" of vital strength, a kind of death. While we currently speak of orgasm as an achievement or fulfillment—one "comes" (a term that *was* used in Elizabethan England)—the two most common euphemisms for orgasm in the early modern period were "to spend" and "to die," both of which imply a loss of vital energy or material.

The moral and physical weakness occasioned by yielding to lust is graphically described by Philip Stubbes in *The Anatomy of Abuses*: besides bringing everlasting damnation, sexual activity outside marriage

> dimmeth the sight, it impaireth the hearing, it infirmeth ye sinewes, it weakeneth the ioynts, it exhausteth the marrow, consumeth the moisture and supplement of the body, it riveleth the face, appalleth the countenance, it dulleth ye spirits, it hurteth the memorie, it weakeneth ye whole body, it bringeth it into a consumption, it bringeth ulcerations, scab, scurf, blain, botch, pocks, and biles, it maketh hoare haires, and bald pates: it induceth olde age, and in fine bringeth death before nature urge it, malady enforce it, or age require it. (sig. H4)

Such dire predictions are important not so much for their excessiveness, which after all is part of the rhetoric of the genre in which Stubbes writes, but for their insistence on the *physical* debility that results from moral softening. In a time when average life expectancy was only forty years—less in the cities—and plagues of various sorts a relatively common occurrence, fear of sheer physical decay is not to be underestimated. And if at first sight Stubbes's list seems comic, in the age of AIDS laughing at such prognostications is not as easy as it once might have been.

In "Choice of Valentines," then, as in the paradisal literary gardens of *The Faerie Queene*, *Orlando Furioso*, *Gerusalemme Liberata*, and elsewhere, the female body is a trap, tempting the hard erect masculine body to weaken itself.[43] But whereas in these epic texts lust represents a *metaphorical* softening, a loss of moral vigor, for Tomalin the threat of emasculation is quite literal. The sight (and touch) of Francis's naked beauty soon brings pilgrim Tomalin's lust "to dye ere it hath seene Jerusalem" (120). He ejaculates prematurely. "Lyke one with Ovids cursed hemlock charm'd," his limbs "spend their strength in thought of hir delight" (124–6).

The reference to Ovid is significant. Unlike other Ovidian lyric poems of the 1590s, such as Marlowe's *Hero and Leander* and Shakespeare's *Venus and Adonis*, "Choice of Valentines" largely rejects the mythologizing of passion in favor of the matter-of-fact sexual world of the *Amores*. Ovid's "cursed hemlock" refers to the potion that Ovid's protagonist blames for his sexual dysfunction in *Amores* (3.7), a text Nashe would have known best in Marlowe's recent translation.

Despite the fact that Marlowe's translation deals with utter impotence rather than premature ejaculation, the terms used to describe impotence in Marlowe's text are strikingly similar to those Nashe applies to Tomalin's situation in "Choice of Valentines," both conditions being aspects of a more general thematic of male incapacity. In addition to making explicit reference to Ovid's "cursed hemlock," Nashe describes Tomalin leaving the brothel "leane and lank as anie ghoste" (310), uncertain, like Ovid's speaker, whether he is shade or body. Speaking ruefully of his recalcitrant member, Marlowe's speaker laments:

> as if cold hemlocke I had drunke,
> It mocked me, hung down the head and suncke,
> Like a dull Cipher, or rude blocke I lay,
> Or shade or body was I, who can say?
> What will my age do, age I cannot shunne,
> Seeing in my prime my force is spent and done?
> I blush, that being youthfull, hot, and lustie,
> I prove neither youth nor man, but old and rustie.
>
> (13–20)

This passage associates impotence with both debilitating drugs and the inability of age, yet what makes the speaker's failure so disturbing is that he is in the prime of youthful masculine heat and should be able to do better. Eventually he ascribes his impotence to two distinct factors, enchantment and shame:

> Why might not then my sinews be inchanted,
> And I grow faint, as with some spirit haunted?
> To this ad shame, shame to perform it quailed mee,
> And was the second cause why vigor failde mee
>
> (35–8)

As Harvey's characterization of "Aretines muse" as "a haggishe witch of Thessalia" suggests, enchantment and witchcraft constitute one of the traditional explanations for impotence. But here—as in "Choice of Valentines"—this answer seems neither to satisfy the speaker nor to allay his anxiety. Though Marlowe's speaker begins by blaming his female partner, he ends by exonerating her, saying:

> Huge okes, hard Adamantes might she have moved,
> And with sweete words cause deafe rockes to have loved,
> Worthy she was to move both Gods and men,
> But neither was I man nor lived then.
>
> (57–60)

The final line of this passage gives an indication of the extent to which masculine performance is linked to identity; if the speaker cannot show himself a man, then he has no being at all.

In "Choice of Valentines" Tomalin's inability is attributed to Francis's ardent passion as well as to hemlock; his lack of control is provoked by excessive female sexual desire: "hir arme's are spread, and I am all unarm'd" (123). The armed encounter of Francis and Tomalin echoes the traditional contest of the weapons of Mars and Venus, a contest whose inevitable outcome is suggested by the anonymous early modern epigram "Upon a Soldier," found in some of the same manuscripts as Nashe's poem: "Though Mars hath given thee wounds, yet as I take it / Mars hurts not armed so much as Venus naked."[44] The notion of nakedness overcoming armor is, of course, not limited to texts of lower genres such as epigrams. In *The Faerie Queene*, as in much Renaissance epic poetry, the disarming of the hero is almost always a metaphor for a yielding of the self to lust. As we have seen, it is when Redcrosse disarms for the first time that he is attacked by the phallic giant Orgoglio.

In her discussion of impotence in the writings of Montaigne, Patricia Parker has argued that in the late-sixteenth-century impotence and other forms of male sexual failure were the subject of "an obsessive preoccupation" of "almost epidemic proportions," which was manifested in a wide variety of "distinct and interconnected contexts—legal, medical, theological, [and] literary."[45] Parker demonstrates that impotence was often represented as a loss of masculine heat, resulting in effeminization. Both Aristotle and Galen agreed that women were colder and moister in their humors than hotter, dryer men.[46] Both authorities also agreed that men (being hotter) were more perfect than women; women were less fully developed, lacking the heat necessary to force their genital organs outward.[47] An anecdote mentioned both by Montaigne and the famous surgeon Ambroise Paré—which has been the subject of much critical attention[48]—tells of a person named Marie Germain, who began life as female only to have male genitals spring from between her legs in adolescence in the heat of jumping over a ditch.[49]

In theory, since male anatomy was seen as more "perfect" than female, the principle that Nature tends toward perfection would seem to insure that the only possible change of gender would be from imperfect femininity to masculine perfection. Indeed this view is argued in vernacular medical texts such as Paré's work *On Monsters and Marvels*:

> The reason why women can degenerate into men is because women
> have as much hidden within the body as men have exposed outside;
> leaving aside, only, that women don't have so much heat, nor the ability to push out what by the coldness of their temperament is held as
> if bound to the interior. Wherefore if with time . . . the warmth is
> rendered more robust, vehement, and active, then it is not an unbelievable thing if the latter, chiefly aided by some violent movement,
> should be able to push out what was hidden within. Now since such
> a metamorphosis takes place in Nature for the alleged reasons and examples, we therefore never find in any true story that any man ever
> became a woman, because Nature always tends towards that which is
> most perfect. (32–3)

Paré's argument for natural perfection is far from convincing, however, coming as it does in the midst of a book wholly devoted to monstrous *imperfections* of nature. If for a number of reasons children can be born with two heads, no arms, four arms, two sets of genitals, or numerous other defects that are by Paré's definition against nature, why in the case of sexual transformation does Nature suddenly infallibly tend toward perfection?

In her reading of Montaigne's Essay 3.5 ("On some verses of Virgil"), Parker demonstrates that while Montaigne's text draws at times on Aristotelian notions of female passivity, the examples it cites are overwhelmingly of powerful women, and the essay is ultimately much more concerned with masculine weakness (350–9). This preoccupation with an effeminizing loss of masculine heat belies the view of Stephen Greenblatt and others that in the one-sex Galenic model of gender widely current in early modern Europe the only possible change of gender was from female to male. Indeed Thomas Laqueur has argued that Castiglione's *Book of the Courtier* is

> rampant with anxiety . . . that men . . . consorting closely with women could become like them," and he cites Hoby's 1561 translation on the debilitating effects of such effeminacy: "their members were readie to flee from one an other . . . a man woulde weene they were at that instant yielding up the ghost.[50]

While Parker's discussion is concerned primarily with France, many of the texts she discusses, such as Montaigne's *Essais* and the writings of Paré were translated or otherwise available in England in the late sixteenth and early seventeenth centuries; she argues in fact that a similar concern with effeminacy and loss of masculine vigor was manifested throughout early modern Europe and was especially evident in England, thanks to the rule of a female monarch and the transvestite practices of the popular theater.[51] Stubbes, for example, argues that wearing womanish and luxurious clothing will actually make a man's body softer (sig. C1v–C2). Although such widespread social anxiety cannot be traced solely to the fact that a female monarch was on the throne, in its focus on Tomalin's sexual disfunction, "Choice of Valentines" gives local expression to a wider concern about the fragility of masculine gender identity.[52]

"Choice of Valentines" is far from being the only English text of the period to explicitly address anxiety over male sexual performance. Certainly concern about impotence and premature ejaculation and a general male anxiety over both performance and pleasing female partners are common themes of other erotic poetry that was circulated, like "Choice of Valentines," in manuscript at the Inns of Court, the universities, and elsewhere. One example among many, is the following text from Feargod Barbon's manuscript (MS Harl. 7332, fol. 46v).

> Sweet harte lett me feele thy cunny
> Take it in good parte
> And Ile give thee some munney
> Doe not starte

For now I am stiff standing
   And Cupid with his Darte hath me at his commanding.

Heere is golde what else may content thee
   Zoundes doe not scolde
What will nothing tempt thee
   quickly holde
Tis ten to on thowt lack it
   O lett me now inioy thy love or I will teare thy placket.

This fayre mayd sadly sate a musing
   Being sore Afrayd
Of this yonge mans using her
   Thus she sayd
Good sir, I am contented
   So aftar yow will marry me that I may not repent it.

So in hast to bed they went to gether
   Hee the mayd unlast
Himselfe being nevar the unrediar
   in the wast
And with this his sudden fall
   That hee forgott his swoord by his side
   His Bootes his spurres. And all.

When the couple finally come to bed the importunate man loses his erection and is "never the unrediar" to perform as he would like. The loss of sword and of boots and spurs (the attributes of a horseman, or one privileged to ride) is a clear enough metaphor for the protagonist's "sudden fall." But the most striking thing about this short text is the elaborate preliminaries before the fall. The text goes to some lengths to demonstrate the male protagonist's use of lascivious language, his attempt to pay for his pleasure, his threat of rape if refused, as well as dwelling on the woman's fear and her (probably futile) attempt to have their union legitimized with at least the promise of marriage. And all for nothing. The man's sudden collapse renders all these considerations irrelevant. His desperation is similar to Tomalin's, and as in Tomalin's case, his aggressive posturing makes his sudden fall all the more ridiculous.

The comedy inherent in masculine inability to perform as required is marked in another text from the Feargod's collection (fol. 45):

And English lad long woed a lasse of Wales
And entertained her with such pretty tales
Although she understood not yet to trye him
She gave consent at last to underly him.
So having dallied to there full sosiety
The wench to show some womanly sobriety

> Sayd in her language shee was well apayd
> And diggon digon once or twice she sayd
> Diggon in welsh dooth signefy enough
> Which he mistaking answered thus in snuff
> Dig on that can Quoth hee for I so sore
> Have digd allready that I can digg no more.[53]

In texts as diverse as *Henry IV, part 1* and *Chaste Maid in Cheapside* Welshness is associated both seriously with the fertility of nature and comically with lasciviousness. Shakespeare's play even repeats stories about Welsh women castrating dead and wounded soldiers (1.1.43–5). Perhaps it is this somewhat daunting reputation that causes the English lad to overreact. In any case, in this text male anxiety about the inability to satisfy the demands of female lust is represented as being excessive to the situation itself; the lass of Wales is quite content, but the English lad assumes she must want more of him; and while he cannot give more, another might be able to: "Dig on that can."

Though in "Choice of Valentines" Tomalin does have two orgasms, his condition is described in terms similar to those used to describe impotence because of his inability to control his expenditure. If his ejaculation is premature and his seed wasted, his pleasure is not enough to "shewe [himself] a man" (126). While a modern reader tends to assume that conception is not a desirable result for either a prostitute or the man she has sex with, this assumption is informed by attitudes about sexual autonomy, contraception, and population control that are quite different from those of sixteenth-century Europe. In the erotic discourses of Elizabethan England, the importance, even necessity, of conception seems to have been the subject of a more pressing preoccupation than our own society places on its opposite, contraception. Laqueur points out that in early modern society with its high rate of infant mortality, premature ejaculation was not generally taken lightly: "any waste of semen was a matter of the most poignant seriousness" (101). Indeed Valerie Traub has posited that sexual anxiety in early modern England focused more on nonreproductive practices (that is, those which involved ejaculation outside the vagina) than on any other aspect of sexual activity.[54] Marriage tracts argued that impotent men should be forbidden from engaging in sex of any kind, for if they could not give their spouse "due benevolence"—which is "one of the most proper and essential acts of marriage"—"by these signes of impotencie God sheweth that he calleth them to live single."[55]

Tomalin's waste of seed, while unintentional, is nonetheless disturbing to an erotic economy that insists on proper spending to ensure conception. Similarly disturbing is his inability to satisfy Francis, for her pleasure is as indispensable to conception as his. While there were some theorists who denied it, it was still generally believed in the sixteenth century that female orgasm was necessary for a woman to conceive.[56] As well, proper rhythm—keeping "crochet-time," as "Choice of Valentines" puts it—was thought to be necessary for conception because the womb was thought to close after the woman's orgasmic ejaculation of feminine seed. While the state of popular beliefs about sex is difficult to ascertain with any precision, and one must not rely too heavily on medical treatises, often written in Latin, to explain daily practice, the concern in "Choice of Valentines" with Francis's pleasure suggests that—even in the description of an encounter in a brothel—the imperative of ensuring conception (and thus female pleasure) seems to still carry some force.

Though Tomalin is soon revived by Francis's skillful dandling of his "sillie worme" and the couple quickly engage in intercourse, the specter of male anxiety first raised by Tomalin's sudden fall remains to haunt the remainder of the poem. As his penis lies limp, Tomalin begins to describe it in the third person, as if it were somehow separate from him: "I kisse, I clap, I feele, I view at will, / Yett dead he lyes not thinking good or ill" (129–30). This third person address continues through the description of the couples' subsequent lovemaking. Increasingly, Francis is described as taking the active (male) role in their encounter. Though she is compared to that icon of proper feminine passivity "poore pacient Grisell" (152), this construction of woman as passive receptacle is immediately undermined; in the very next lines she "giue's, and take's as blythe and free as Maye, / And ere-more meete's him in the middle waye" (153–4). Francis's carefree ease here is in sharp and comic contrast to Tomalin's frenzy of activity as he

> on her breeche did thack, and foyne a-good;
> He rubd' and prickt, and pierst her to the bones,
> Digging as farre as eath he might for stones.
>
> (144–6)

At this point the description of their lovemaking is interrupted by a lengthy passage of Neoplatonic metaphysical conceit, which constitutes one of the text's more opaque moments. The mythologizing that Nashe rejects elsewhere in the poem is here in abundance. And yet these lines (155–68) also represent a serious attempt to describe the confused gender dynamics of Tomalin and Francis's intercourse.

While Jonathan Crewe has argued that this passage describes an ideal "ordered system" of "secure identities and differences" (50), the traditional hierarchies one would expect in such as system are nowhere to be found. Tomalin is compared to a star sucking in the influence of the sunbeams that come from Francis, who is identified with the sun, fairest planet of the sky—an identification that contradicts the traditional gendering of the Sun (Apollo) as masculine and the Moon (Diana) as feminine.

It is Francis, not Tomalin, who is the main source of heat:

> So fierce and feruent is hir radiance,
> Such fyrie stake's she darts at euerie glance,
> As might enflame the icie limmes of age,
> And make pale death his surquedrie aswage
> To stand and gaze upon hir Orient lamps

Where Cupid all his chiefest ioyes encamps,
And sitts, and playes with euerie atomie
That in hir Sunne-beames swarme aboundantlie.

(169–76)

The unorthodox gendering of this passage suggests that the subtextual mythic model here is not Apollo and Diana but Aurora the goddess of dawn and her lover Tithonus, an immortal swain ravaged by age and unable to satisfy her lust. In texts as diverse as the *Amores* (3.7.42), the *Aeneid* (4.585), and *The Faerie Queene* (1.2.7,3.3.20), cold Tithonus serves as an example of impotent weakness. While it was generally believed that men were (or should be) hotter than women, there was a certain amount of debate in medical circles over whether or not the hottest of women (and thus the most "masculine") were hotter than the coldest (that is the most effeminate) men. The assumption that humors and temperature, while differentiated on the basis of sex, could in fact overlap provided a way of accounting physiologically for such phenomena as dominant wives and successful queens.[57] Francis's excess of heat and Tomalin's lack of it suggest that since he has shown himself incapable of managing his desire, she is taking the masculine part in their encounter; sexual authority has passed to Francis.

Although this passage merely suggests Francis's usurpation of the superior masculine position, others go further, giving her explicitly masculine characteristics. Francis's rising skirt reveals a "mannely thigh" (103), and in passages of metaphorical description her vagina is twice referred to with the masculine pronoun: a fountain with briars at *his* mouth, and a mouth given *his* full sufficiency by the dildo (113,258). Crewe has described the ambiguity of pronoun reference in the poem as "a kind of anarchy or androgynous indifference" (48–51), which he sees as destabilizing literary form. More important, by linking the fear of male impotence and inadequacy to loss of gender identity these shifting references undermine a stable order of gender; they express a troubling emasculation rather than an indifferent androgyny.

The long metaphoric passage, confused as it is, clearly marks an attempt to escape from the frail uncertainties of the body into an ideal realm; but in this metaphorical space it is once again Francis, not Tomalin, who is dominant. Like cold Tithonus, Tomalin needs Francis's heat, but as before he proves unable to control his temperature: "Thus gazing, and thus striuing we perseuer, / But what so firme, that may continue euer? (177–8) Tomalin's metaphysical reveries are brought to an abrupt halt as Francis cries, "Oh not so fast" (179). He is, once again, overexcited, but this time Francis manages to avert a second unnecessary expenditure. At her instigation they pace themselves better, until Tomalin comes, bursting once again into metaphor and enthusiastically comparing his ejaculate to Jove's golden shower and the flooding of the Nile. But immediately after thus exulting in his potency, Tomalin more somberly characterizes his orgasm as a mixture of "blisse and sorrow" (191–2). Francis comes as well, it seems: "she ierks hir leggs, and sprauleth with hir heeles" (201). But whether she has come or not,

Tomalin is finished for the day and wants but one thing more: "Oh death rock me a-sleepe; / Sleepe—sleepe desire, entombed in the deepe" (203–4).

Though here Tomalin picks up on the conventional trope of womb as tomb, it is he rather than Francis who has become cold and clammy. While "no tongue maie tell the solace that [Tomalin presumes] she feeles" (202), Francis has no trouble articulating her dissatisfaction; and she proceeds to do so in a lament on the transience of sexual delight (205–36), which ends with an image of Tomalin (and/or his penis) as the cold winter that freezes up the stream of her pleasure. And so Francis rejects the "faint-hearted" penis which "falselie hast betrayde [their] equale trust" (235–36) and vows that from now on her "little dilldo shall suplye their kind" (239). A lengthy description of the dildo follows (240–94).

Nashe is renowned for his coinage of new words,[58] and according to the *OED* "dildo" is one of them. Since the word was also a common ballad refrain, it is possible that it existed in that capacity before and Nashe uses it here as a comic term to describe the unnamable. It is pleasant to speculate that "Hey nonny nonny," "ding a ding," or even "fa la la" might have done as well. Ballad refrains that sound innocent now often had erotic connotations in the sixteenth century: In the anonymous play *The Wit of a Woman* (1604) a young girl's father complains about immodest modern dances, saying that "in such lavoltas, [women] mount so high, that you may see their hey nony, nony, nony, no"[59]—a passage that suggests that "Hey nonny nonny" might have been common rhyming slang for "cunny." If so, the famous song from *Much Ado About Nothing* (2.3.61–76) advising maids to convert their sighs over unfaithful lovers into "hey nonny nonny," sung with wistful nostalgia in Kenneth Branagh's film, may well be much bawdier than one would have thought.

In any case, Nashe's novel use of the term "dildo" soon passed into common usage. In Donne's second Satire, plagiarizing authors are said "To outdo dildoes" (32). And in his second Elegy, Flavia, the prospective bride, is said to be so ill-favored that even her own dildo is loth to touch her (53–4). An anonymous poem in a manuscript collection (Rosenbach MS 1083/15, c. 1600–20) that also contains a garbled copy of "Choice of Valentines" refers to a woman who "made hir Dildo of a mutton bone" (p. 26). When Lovewit returns to his house in the final act of Jonson's *Alchemist* he finds evidence of the disorder wrought in his absence: "The empty walls worse than I left them, smoak'd . . . And madam with a dildo writ o' the walls" (5.5.39–42). Autolycus in *The Winter's Tale* "has the prettiest love songs for maids . . . with such delicate burdens of dildos and fadings, 'jump her and thump her,'" (4.4.190–8). And in Middleton's *Chaste Maid in Cheapside* Mr. Allwit, happy to be relieved of his marriage debt (and others) by Sir Walter Whorehound, ends his anatomy of the carefree joys of being a cuckold by singing "La dildo dildo la dildo, la dildo dildo de dildo," much to the amusement of the servants (1.2.56).

Nashe's poem gives perhaps the most detailed description of a dildo in Renaissance English literature:

He is a youth almost tuo handfulls highe,
Streight, round, and plumb, yett hauing but one eye,
Wherin the rhewme so feruentlie doeth raigne,
That Stigian gulph maie scarce his teares containe;
Attired in white veluet or in silk,
And nourisht with whott water or with milk;
Arm'd otherwhile in thick congealed glasse.

(269–75)

This description is echoed by another poem (also in Rosenbach MS 1083/15) in which young women are warned that if they suffer from green sickness, they must take proper medicine (a penis) and accept no substitutes:

But yet this Caveat lett me give though late
that in the place of that I do proscribe
You use no other balme adulterate,
which men of art most worthylye deride
Itt is a balme made artificially
filld in a slender glass all covered
with satten or such like most curiously
and by our caves form just is measured
To your disease your selves this [ ] apply
with out success of any remedy
Save that some feeling ease you gett thereby.

(p. 15–16)[60]

The object described in both this text and Nashe's conforms in most details to the dildos of Murano glass that play a prominent part in the first part of Aretino's *Ragionamenti*.[61] These are hollow and are filled with (preferably warm) liquid before use.[62] The dildo Nashe describes would seem to have a hole at the tip through which ejaculation could be simulated. Perhaps the "attire" of velvet or silk would have covered the shaft of the dildo during use to provide greater variety of sensation.

Though there is some textual confusion in this passage regarding the identity of the speaker, Francis's attitude toward her dildo is fairly clear: it will not only adequately "suplye" her demand for a penis, but is happily also free from any risk of conception: "by Saint Runnion he'le refresh me well, / And neuer make my tender bellie swell" (245–6). While women in England were not prosecuted for using dildos, as they were in other European countries, notably France,[63] Francis's outspoken preference for nonprocreative sex sets her at odds with the imperative of conception posited earlier, and her attitude serves to reveal the gap between women's understandable desire to avoid pregnancy and the general social dictum that sex should have as its end not pleasure but procreation.

While Tomalin is clearly disgusted and horrified by the dildo and what it represents, his description of it is somewhat ambivalent. Tomalin begins by characterizing the dildo as an usurping "weakeling," a rival that "Poore Priapus" must thrust to the wall (247–8). Yet in his subsequent condemnation of the dildo it seems anything but weak; indeed Tomalin asserts that the dildo offers a plenitude of pleasure and satisfaction: "He giue's yong guirls their gamesom sustenance, / And euerie gaping mouth his full sufficeance" (257–8). In attacking the dildo, Tomalin cannot help fetishizing it to some degree, and thus paradoxically increasing its power. Tomalin's anxiety, first provoked by the feminine landscape of Francis's body, comes to focus not on the vagina he cannot fill but on the image of the phallus that paradoxically can do what he cannot.

By personifying the dildo, "Choice of Valentines" represents it as monstrous—a human being that is deformed and dysfunctional: "a blind mischapen owle," "bedasht, bespurted, and beplodded foule" (288,287). It is a eunuch, a dwarf, and impotent: a "senceless, counterfet, / Who sooth maie fill, but neuer can begett" (263–4). The dildo is unnatural, something that exists when it should not and inserts itself where it should not: "he creepe's betwixt the barke and the tree, / And sucks the sap, whilst sleepe detaineth thee [the penis]" (251–2). The image of the dildo inserted in the painfully intimate space between bark and tree suggests both a disrobing (a stripping of bark from the tree)[64] and an unnatural presence (how can anything natural come between a tree and its bark?). The active sucking of the sap suggests that the dildo itself has agency; that in provoking the flow of female seed it is stealing precious fluid.[65] Paradoxically, while Tomalin's inability to show himself a man eventually provokes Francis's disdain, the dildo's inability to *procreate* is no impediment to its enjoyment of the sexual favors that Tomalin sees as his right. From Francis's perspective, what counts is not fertility but the ability to remain hard.

To attack the monstrousness of the dildo, Tomalin's speech draws on the conventions that would become commonplaces of 1590s satire and its attack on such social monsters as effeminate pages and powerful women. The dildo takes on all the attributes of perverse service: it is both "Eunuke" and "dwarf"—the monstrous servants with whom Ben Jonson would later populate the household of *Volpone*. Worse, the dildo is a *woman's* servant—"my Mistris page"—who "wayte's on Courtlie Nimphs." The court may speak of love in the refined discourse of Petrarchism, but behind the frustrating disdain of the cold lady and the impotent service of her courtly lover lies the "perverse" supplement of her "page": the dildo.[66] As in Jonson's *Epicoene*, where a group of City women use their youthful pages to fulfill their sexual desires, service here is clearly eroticized and deployed to attack the threat of female autonomy, especially sexual autonomy.[67] Marston's satires consistently accuse court women of perverse sexual practices—including bestiality, oral sex, and the use of dildos. In *The Scourge of Villanie*, he describes a Lady whose desires are satisfied with the aid of her maid, her monkey, and her glass dildo (3.30–2).

Ironically, Tomalin's attack on the dildo bears more than a passing resemblance to Harvey's attack on Nashe. Like Harvey's Nashe, the dildo is personified as a sly, disdainful Machiavellian skilled in "forraine artes" (251, 259), a "weakeling"(248) who nonetheless possesses a paradoxically strong power to corrupt and must be castrated in order to insure the masculine vigor of the realm: "Poor Priapus," Tomalin laments, "Behould how he [the dildo] usurps in bed and bowre, / And undermines's thy kingdom everie howre" (247, 249–50). Just as—according to Harvey—poisonous ribalds like Nashe and Aretino are insupportable in an absolute monarchy, so must the dildo be driven from the monarchy of Priapus.

Next to Francis's little prosthetic, Tomalin is but an empty skin; he staggers from the brothel "as leane and lank as anie ghoste" (310). The dildo is thus both the embodiment of Francis's power and Tomalin's failing; its thick congealed glass focuses all the issues of sexuality and power raised in the poem. Paradoxically "Choice of Valentines" presents the brothel as a place where male sexuality is as commodified as female; Tomalin goes to the brothel to purchase sexual pleasure, only to find himself exchanged for the dildo. While the text does not say so explicitly, by selling her own sexual favors in the brothel, Francis is able to purchase not only the velvet gowns of a lady but also the sexual autonomy represented by the possession of a dildo. In contrast to Francis's riches, Tomalin ends the poem with nothing more to spend, having paid the Madame a sum "which for a poore man is a princelie dole" (308). All that remains to him is an empty boast of virility, "What can be added more to my renowne? / She lyeth breathlesse, I am taken doune" (311–2), and an appeal to the masculine community at large for reassurance: "Iudge gentlemen if I deserue not thanks" (314), a request that, all things considered, might more appropriately—if not propitiously—be addressed to Francis.

Following the main text of the poem comes a concluding sonnet, addressed to Nashe's patron Lord Strange, which ironically casts doubts on Nashe's own masculinity: in writing the poem, Nashe admits he has indeed been effeminate, for in speaking of the dildo he has "A lyke to women, utter[ed] all [he] knowe[s]." And while he claims that he has followed Ovidian precedent, he blames not the male poet but "Ovid's wanton Muse" for the lasciviousness of his text. Sexual knowledge, it is suggested, is ultimately feminine—just as in the brothel it is Francis who has the power to make Tomalin silent and the Madame who has the power to make him pay.

In arguing that "Choice of Valentines" places sexual power and dominance in female hands I am not asserting that this formulation reflects social realities in any simple fashion. For all its undoubted benefits, the use of a dildo is not a reliable indicator of real social power. Despite her shaming of Tomalin, the social situation of Nashe's Francis is even more precarious and ambiguous than that of Aretino's Nanna. While the wealthiest whores in London rode in carriages and dressed like court ladies, Elizabethan brothels cannot be read as unambiguous sites of female power any more than Nanna's garden can. But they could be perceived as *potential* sites of female power—especially given the uncertain place of the brothel in the erotic economy of Elizabethan London. "Choice of Valentines" posits female dominance and male insufficiency in a cathartic attempt to exorcise male anxiety in laughter at poor Tomalin. As we have seen, the poem was not entirely successful in this endeavor.

Nashe's Dildo: Theme and Variations

Neither the poem's attempts at catharsis nor its failure can be attributed in any simple fashion to Nashe's intention in writing the text, for it is likely that none of the surviving versions give an accurate redaction of his text. Like most lyric poetry produced in England in the 1590s, "Choice of Valentines" was not printed but circulated privately in manuscript among a select coterie audience. Once "Choice of Valentines" began to circulate, its disturbing text was radically rewritten; three of the six extant texts eliminate the dildo altogether, drastically reconfiguring the dynamics of sexual power in the poem. While the level of individual intention underlying these excisions in the text is impossible to determine, they are nonetheless culturally significant.

"Choice of Valentines" was not published until 1899, when a limited edition, edited by John S. Farmer, was privately printed in London for subscribers only. Farmer's text is based on the Petyt version of the poem, with some readings from the Bodleian manuscript.[68] Although it was clearly intended for collectors of pornographic curiosities, this edition contains a certain amount of "scholarly" annotation, and if Farmer had not brought the text to public consciousness, it is possible McKerrow would not have felt obliged to include it in his definitive edition of the works of Nashe. The fact that "Choice of Valentines" first saw print as a piece of would-be pornography has had the unfortunate consequence of bringing the sixteenth-century text itself into the category of the pornographic—unfortunate because this assimilation of the poem to the most reductive and "obvious" of literary genres has served largely to limit discussion of the poem's significance within its own culture.

The dedicatory sonnet that accompanies the most complete versions of "Choice of Valentines" (Petyt, Folger, and Bodleian texts) is addressed to Ferdinando Stanley, Lord Strange, to whom Nashe also dedicated *Piers Penniless* (1592). It seems that Nashe came into Strange's circle "sometime before the early summer of 1592." But it does not seem that Nashe was attached to Strange for very long; in September 1592 he stayed with Archbishop Whitgift,[69] and in the spring of 1593 he dedicated *The Unfortunate Traveler* to the earl of Southampton. In any case, Strange died April 16, 1594, so "Choice of Valentines" could not have been written after that date. If one assumes that "Choice of Valentines" is among the "filthy rymes" Harvey refers to in *Pierces Supererogation* (1593), a date of 1592 for the poem's original composition seems even more likely.

Although the composition of "Choice of Valentines" can be dated with some degree of accuracy, the six known extant copies of the poem are found in poetical miscellanies from the first quarter of the seventeenth century. It is quite possible that none of the differing versions of the text represent Nashe's own poem in the form he wrote it. Three of the six manuscript versions were not known to exist when the text was edited by Ronald B. McKerrow in 1905.[70] Besides the Petyt, Bodleian, and Dyce texts that McKerrow discusses, other copies of Nashe's text have since been found in manuscripts in the Folger, the Rosenbach collection in Philadelphia, and in the manuscript in the British Library once owned

by Margaret Bellasys.[71] When dealing with "Choice of Valentines," one is dealing not with one single erotic narrative but rather a related series of them. To
discuss "Choice of Valentines" in its specific social context it is crucial to take
the various "corrupt" versions of the text into account, for they offer valuable
insight into the ways Nashe's "filthy" text was read and transformed by contemporary readers.

The textual history of "Choice of Valentines" is far from clear, and while
there is much bibliographical work still to be done on this poem, here I will be
interested more in the literary and social significance of the various versions of
the texts than in the bibliographical relation between them. The most authoritative text of "Choice of Valentines" is in the Petyt collection of the Inner Temple
Library (Petyt MS 538, vol. 43, fols. 295v–298v); it is this version that McKerrow
more or less reprinted in his edition and that subsequent editors have simply
copied from McKerrow. The Petyt text is attributed directly to Nashe; his name
appears both at the end of the poem and after the epilogue. Nothing is known of
the provenance of this manuscript, which is bound in a composite folio volume
made up mostly of legal and political prose texts. While McKerrow claims that
the section of the manuscript containing "Choice of Valentines" was "apparently
written not long before the end of the seventeenth century" (3:399), the hand in
this section is not untypical of the early seventeenth century, and the material
itself dates from 1600–07, so the Petyt manuscript of the poem could well be
contemporaneous with the other five—all from the last years of the sixteenth or
the early years of the seventeenth century.

Two of the five other texts of the poem resemble the Petyt text fairly closely.
The text closest to the Petyt version is the Folger manuscript (Folger MS Va 399,
fols. 53v–57),[72] a commonplace book of ninety-four leaves from the early seventeenth century, in which the poem is given the more pointed title "Nashes Dilldo."
While some of its readings are clearly garbled, in just as many other places it gives
readings clearer than those found in Petyt.

The other manuscript whose text closely resembles Petyt is at the Bodleian
Library, Oxford (MS Rawl. poet. 216).[73] This volume also contains an English
translation of Ovid's *Ars Amatoria* (fols. 2r–91r), an antifeminist poem entitled
"The Description of weomen" (fols. 92r–93v), a riddle on the penis (fols. 94v–
95r), a bawdy poem based on dicing (fol. 95v), and "Nashe his Dildo" (fols. 94r,
96r–106r). The original owner of the volume seems to have been Henry Price
(1566–1600), whose name appears on fol. 113v. Chaplain to Sir Henry Lea of
Oxfordshire, Price was a scholar at St. John's College, Oxford, a noted preacher,
and elegant Latin poet who published both a Latin elegy and a sermon before
dying at Woodstock at age thirty-four. The Bodleian text has both the dedicatory sonnet and the epilogue, though the epilogue appears not at the end of
Nashe's poem but as the epilogue to a translation of Ovid's *Ars Amatoria*, a striking
example of how material was transformed in manuscript transmission to suit the
needs of its transcribers. As in the Folger manuscript, this text gives the title as
"Nash his Dildo," and given its occurrence in two substantially complete texts,
perhaps this is the title by which the text should be known today. Yet the de-

scription of Francis's dildo, which made the poem notorious in its day, is absent from the other three known versions of Nashe's text.

The fourth version of the poem is in the Dyce Collection in the National Art Library of the Victoria and Albert Museum in London (Dyce MS [44] 25 F 39, fols. 2–4). This text of the poem is complete as written but shortens the poem by more than half. It is much less specific than the Petyt and Bodleian texts about the circumstances of its production—there is no mention of Nashe, the poem is not given a title, and the dedication is not directed to a specified patron.

This text is arguably the most remarkable of the six, for it is partially written in cipher. Almost every line of text has at least one or two encoded words, and some lines are entirely encrypted. This is the only poem in the volume to appear in cipher, though two other poems in the same manuscript are written with every word spelled backward. In general the Dyce manuscript's use of cipher serves to titillate and draw attention to itself rather than to conceal; it makes the poem seem bawdier than it is. For example, line 11 of the dedicatory sonnet reads "But of *dtzyc wdyxczvyc* [loves pleasures] none did ere indite." It is unlikely that the use of cipher was intended to save the text from falling into the "wrong hands," since the volume of which it is part is filled with bawdy verse from beginning to end. And while cipher is used to conceal innocent as well as obscene passages, much of the poem is "in clear" and there is enough clearly intelligible to make the poem instantly recognizable to someone familiar with the text from another source. In addition, the code is quite elementary, consisting of a simple one-for-one correspondence between letters; it could easily be decoded in an hour or so.

It seems obvious then that the cipher is a way of increasing and prolonging the pleasure of the text. Reading thus becomes an act of deferred gratification. The text, like the body of the beloved, becomes something hidden and secret, to be uncovered slowly, to be played with. The concealment of the most innocent phrases makes every phrase seem illicit. If, as Roland Barthes has suggested, textual pleasure is by definition perverse, then the Dyce manuscript of "Choice of Valentines" becomes a particularly concrete and literal example of text as fetish. The intermittence of cipher and legible text becomes a potential erotic site analogous to the flash of skin between two pieces of clothing; "it is this flash itself which seduces, or rather: the staging of an appearance as disappearance"[74] By concealing its eroticism the text increases it dramatically.

As fascinating as the cipher are the vast textual differences between the shorter Dyce text and the more complete Petyt, Folger, and Bodleian texts. In Dyce Francis is less individualized—all of her speeches are omitted. In Petyt the man's payment to the Madame is the final frustration of a humiliating experience; in Dyce no payment is mentioned. The Dyce text omits the metaphors comparing the lovers to stars and Tomalin's ejaculation to Jove's shower of gold and the flood of the Nile, omissions that insure that the Dyce version of the poem is firmly centered on the graphic description of the sex act itself.

These gaps in the Dyce text, simplifying and hardening it, would already bring it closer to a fantasy intended to arouse its (male) readers than the more complex and contradictory Petyt text. But the greatest gap in the Dyce manuscript comes with the almost complete omission of the final third of the poem. Gone is Francis's lament on the transience of sexual pleasure and gone all reference to the dildo. As a result, Dyce is not a poem about male sexual anxiety and lack of potency but rather a narrative of successful male sexual performance and conquest, which concludes simply:

> *No tongue may tell the solace that she feels.*
> What can be added *more to my renown?*
> *She lyeth breathless, I am taken down.*

(italicized passages in cipher)

The irony (even poignancy) of this question in Petyt has disappeared entirely. The "problem" of female pleasure and the "solution" of the dildo, both so disturbing to Tomalin in the Petyt text, are utterly erased.

The most "corrupt" copy of the poem is in the Rosenbach Collection, in Philadelphia (Rosenbach MS 1083/15 fols. 9v–11v).[75] Nothing certain is known of the manuscript's compilers, but on the basis of its content there is some connection with both Oxford and the Inns of Court. It seems to have been compiled around 1605–18 by three different persons. One of the hands resembles that of Sir John Harington. The Rosenbach text of Nashe's poem is the shortest extant and the most widely variant. A third of the lines are not found in any other version of the poem, and only one-fifth are identical to the corresponding lines in Petyt. Despite these drastic changes, the poem is more or less coherent—though the dildo section is missing once again, as are the dedicatory sonnet and the epilogue. Given the utterly jumbled and truncated state of the Rosenbach text, it seems likely that it was pieced together from memory rather than being copied directly from another version. As well as dropping the dildo, the Rosenbach text also lacks the valentine motif (it is set in May rather than February), and thus neither of the poem's two recorded titles could be accurately used to refer to this version. Nor is the name of Nashe anywhere in sight. While textually it seems that this text is based on Petyt or another "complete" version of the poem, in spirit the Rosenbach text is closest to Dyce; its narrative boasts of sexual conquest rather than dwelling on sexual anxiety.

If it does indeed constitute a text reconstructed from memory, the Rosenbach manuscript gives a fascinating glimpse of one reader's reception of the poem. While the Petyt text is complex and contradictory, addressing the ticklish subject of sexual inadequacy and dissatisfaction, the Rosenbach text is a simple seduction poem, combining bawdy jokes with passages of explicit sexual description to tell a narrative of male sexual success (which, as we have seen, is measured both by ability to defer and control ejaculation and by the bringing of pleasure to the female). Any meditation on the transience of sexual pleasure is absent in the Rosenbach text. Francis is almost anonymous; her only traits are her stunning physical beauty and her eagerness to have sex. The pastoral setting of the early part of the Petyt text and the issues it raises are entirely absent; rather than seeking a former lover, in Rosenbach (l. 10) the speaker really is looking for "hacknies" to hire (Petyt, l. 26), until the familiar "three chinned foggy" Madame (Rosenbach, l. 13; Petyt, l. 29) clarifies the nature of the establishment. As in Petyt the speaker is rendered temporarily impotent by the naked beauty of Francis, yet despite his awestruck hesitation, he is not overly troubled by sexual anxiety.

When seen in relation to the Petyt text, Rosenbach extends even further the radical simplification we have already seen in the Dyce text. In these shortened texts Francis is less individualized—all of her speeches are omitted, along with all hint of a previous relationship between her and Tomalin. With Francis silenced, there is no lament for the transience of sexual pleasure, nor any anxiety about excessive female desire. The woman here is no more sexually avid than the man, and in any case, there is no dildo to provide an alternative. Without the dildo to focus Tomalin's anxiety and Francis's autonomy, these elements in the text simply dissipate, pushed to the side in the narrative of assured masculine mastery. For if poor Tomalin can do nothing but rage at the prosthetic that has usurped his rightful power, the men who transmitted Nashe's text were at no such disadvantage: in the Rosenbach text, lines from Petyt describing the mighty powers of the dildo are appropriated by the speaker to describe his own penis— a bit of wish fulfillment that sums up eloquently the fundamental difference of outlook in these two texts of an ostensibly identical poem.[76] The Dyce and Rosenbach versions, despite their comparatively stark descriptions of physical sex, nonetheless fulfill many of Gabriel Harvey's conditions for the ideal imperial text, praising as they do the exploits of "mighty Conquerours" (*Supererogation,* sig. F7v; 2:98).

There is one other copy of the poem, and it is found in Margaret Bellasys's manuscript (British Library MS Add. 10309, fols. 135v–139v).[77] This text also omits all reference to the dildo, but it tells a far different story from the Dyce and Rosenbach texts. It is the only text of Nashe's poem one can reasonably assume to have been owned and read by a woman (figure 4.2). Margaret's text, entitled "Gnash his valentine," follows the Petyt version closely but ends at line 232, thus omitting all of the dildo section. In a few places, the order of couplets is reversed, but otherwise textual variations are insignificant. With the latter third of the Petyt text gone, the Bellasys text ends with Francis's complaint of the transience of sexual pleasure and her frustration with Tomalin's inadequacy:

> Staie, staie sweete ioye, and leave me not forlorne
>
> . . . .
>
> He heare's me not, hard-hearted as he is:
> A second spring must help me or I burne.
> No, no, the well is drye that should refresh me.
>
> (213,221,224–5)

The final lines describe (female) Nature, overborne by (male) winter, shutting up "hir conduit" and resolving not to "let hir Nectar over-flowe" (230–1). These lines reverse contemporary gender constructions, both by their imaging of

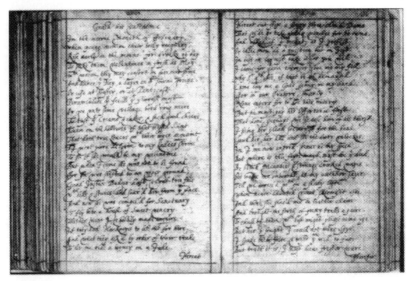

Figure 4.2. *A page from Margaret Bellasys' copy of Nashe's "Choice of Valentines." British Library MS Add 10309, folio 135 verso, which contains the beginning of a copy of Thomas Nashe's poem "The Choice of Valentines," here entitled "Gnash his valentine." By Permission of the British Library.*

Francis's sexual satisfaction as drinking from a well (hardly a phallic image) and in their insistence that it is Tomalin's coldness that provokes Francis to shut "up hir conduit." As we have seen, in Renaissance physiognomy, cold is a feminine characteristic.[78] What is interesting in this passage is not so much Tomalin's figuration as "winter" as the suggestion that it is his incapacity that provokes Nature/Francis to shut her conduit and that (in the canonical version) she turns to the dildo as a result. This too is a reverse of the traditional paradigm, in which women's desire provokes men's impotence or exhaustion; here male inability stifles female desire.[79]

These lines with their provocative reversals appear in the canonical Petyt text, but whereas in that version they serve to set the stage for the even more provocative reversal of the dildo, in the Bellasys text they constitute the conclusion of the poem and thus stand out in higher relief. The Bellasys text leaves its readers with the eloquent voicing of a woman's dissatisfaction without offering them the solution of the dildo; it thus becomes a narrative that stresses female sexual frustration more than male anxiety. The question, of course, is whether the poem was adapted to this purpose by Margaret Bellasys or whether this was the only version she was permitted to see.

In all three of the truncated versions of "Choice of Valentines" one can see the fulfillment of Gabriel Harvey's desire that when it comes to erotic writing, "whatsoever sprowteth farther would be lopped." In these texts the silence about the dildo functions in two separate but related ways: while Dyce and Rosenbach remove the emblem of male anxiety, the Bellasys text erases a source of female pleasure. When the stiff steely dildo is inscribed as a potent emblem of masculine gender anxiety, women must not read what Cupid's poet writes. The gaps in the Bellasys text suggest that for the poem's female readers, the dildo is not an option; in these truncated texts it appears in the realm of cathartic male fantasy but not in that of female practice.

Ben Jonson and the Erotics
of a Literary Career

$\mathcal{T}$he manuscript transmission of Nashe's "Choice of Valentines" gives some indication of the ways in which some male writers (and readers) worked to modify early modern discourses of the erotic, silencing the voices of women and dissociating erotic poetry from effeminacy. In this final chapter I examine the ambivalent place of Aretine eroticism in the works of Ben Jonson. While neither overtly concerned with national identity (like *The Faerie Queene*) or explicitly erotic (like "Choice of Valentines"), Jonson's plays for the public stage offer a fascinating example of the effort required to dissociate eroticism from effeminacy and to appropriate the Italianate while remaining securely English. In his early works Jonson stages various attractive figures of erotic disorder and social subversion, figures in which he himself appears to be invested to a significant degree. As his career progressed, however, Jonson became increasingly concerned to separate his own poetry (figured as classical and male) from an effeminate bawdy language he increasingly associates with women and fools.

Ben Jonson's literary career has often been seen as an extended project of authorial self-fashioning, in which a pardoned felon, the son of a bricklayer, created a place for himself as a successful court poet and an influential social arbiter (figure 5.1).[1] Though he never achieved the independence that Aretino did and his influence and income dropped off rapidly after the accession of Charles I in 1625, Jonson's rise, especially under King James, is nonetheless impressive. Such formulations, however, by seeing Jonson's career as a relatively uninterrupted progression to higher and higher levels of social respectability, tend to stress the resolution rather than the ongoing dynamic of significant conflicts and contradictions in Jonson's work: between his lower-class origins and his courtly aspirations, between his involvement in the popular theater and his avowed commitment to classicism, between his criminal activities and his insistence upon the virtue of poetry, and between his attraction to disorderly eroticism and his disgust for the feminine.

Rather than concentrating on Jonson's eventual social success, I wish to focus on these contradictions, contradictions that, however they may have been resolved

Figure 5.1. *Ben Jonson, artist unknown, after Abraham van Blyenberch. By courtesy of the National Portrait Gallery, London.*

in Jonson's life, are inscribed deeply in much of his most popular and compelling work. For all Jonson's self-fashioning as a virtuous classical Poet, he retained an ambivalent attraction to and fascination with the disorderly, the low, the criminal, the theatrical, the sodomitical. At the heart of this paradox is Jonson's relation to the discourses of the erotic and the effeminate, relations that can be elucidated to a large extent by an examination of Jonson's deployment of the figure of Aretino. Always willing to acknowledge his debt to ancient models of classical decorum such as Horace, Jonson was much more reticent and ambivalent about his relationship to contemporary literary discourses,[2] and his response to Aretine modes of erotic expression, never openly acknowledged, manifests itself in a series of conflicted, contradictory gestures rather than in conscious explicit acts of self-fashioning.

Epicoene Fury: Jonson and the Gender of Poetry

As a preface to his play *Volpone*, Ben Jonson published an epistle addressed "to the most noble and equal sisters the two famous Universities" in which he defended the morality of his plays and "the dignity of poetry." He appeals to the learned judgment of Oxford and Cambridge and notes that they have received his work with "love and acceptance." Against those who claim that "stage poetry [is] nothing but ribaldry, profanation, blasphemy," he argues that poetry is, in fact, identical with virtue. "For, if men will impartially . . . look toward the offices and function of a poet, they will easily conclude to themselves the impossibility of any man's being the good poet, without first being a good man." Rather than explore the flawed logic that equates great art with the moral goodness of its creator, I wish instead to focus on the gender of Jonson's poet. It is impossible, he says, for good poetry to be written by anyone who is not a good *man*. Despite its description of Oxford and Cambridge as two "most noble and equal sisters," the preface to *Volpone* insists that poetry is not feminine or effeminizing but fundamentally masculine. The figure of the good poet Jonson constructs here is resolutely male, and its erotic energies are directed to domination and control of the female. The preface ends with Jonson seeing Poetry as a sort of sacred whore, a woman who should be available only to a select elite (of which he himself is, of course, chief):

> I shall raise the despis'd head of *poetrie* againe, and stripping her out of these rotten and base rags, wherwith the Times have adulterated her form, restore her to her primitive habit, feature, and majesty, and render her worthy to be imbraced, and kist, of all the great and master-*spirits* of our world. (129–34)[3]

The author is constructed here as the potent male who masters the erring female text. As Wendy Wall has demonstrated, such formulations in which authorship is gendered male while text is gendered female were common in early modern England.[4] Wall links the feminization of the text to the rise of print: "The printed page is always a fallen woman because it is, by definition, highly public and common." Even the technology of printing was gendered: "pressing" was a euphemism for the press of the male body on the female in sexual intercourse. "The page is encoded as feminine while the machinery of the press, the writer, and the ink are depicted as masculine" (219–20). Such encoding helped to distance masculine authors from their effeminate (and potentially effeminizing) vocation of poetry. Through these highly gendered constructions of authorship, male writers were actually able to argue that, rather than effeminizing them, their poetry enhanced their masculinity, demonstrating as it did their mastery of the feminine text and their superiority to the feminine Muse.

Jonson returned to his decidedly erotic reading of the relation between the poet and the Muse in one of his most savage attacks on female eloquence, his "Epigram on the Court Pucell" (*Underwoods* 49). This poem, written against Cecelia Bulstrode, is a scathingly misogynist attack on Bulstrode's presumption in writing poetry and setting herself up as a literary authority. As "On the Court Pucell" makes clear, if the act of poetic creation is an erotic one, in which the Muse is mastered by the male poet, the very notion of a woman writing becomes perverse and sodomitical. "What though," Jonson asks rhetorically, "with Tribade [lesbian] lust she force a Muse?" (7) In Jonson's epigram, Mistress Bulstrode, the female poet, is figured as a lesbian and as a whore who blurs the boundaries between politics, religion, and sex, making "State, Religion, Bawdrie all a theame" (12). From such filthiness Jonson hypocritically stands aloof: "I am no States-man, and much lesse Divine, For bawdry, 'tis her language, and not mine" (25–6). Thus Jonson attacks a female poet in an effort to distinguish the work of a "good" poet (himself) from the effeminate rhetoric associated with the italianate by Ascham and others. By defining bawdry as feminine language, Jonson attempts to save his own writing from the charges of effeminacy leveled at all poetry by polemicists such as Gosson and Stubbes.

While in the Epistle to *Volpone* and elsewhere, Jonson insists on the endur-ing substance of his own work, which speaks truth to "understanders," the Pucell's feminine writing is (like feminine beauty) all on the surface; she "labor[s] with the phrase more than the sense" (14). As we have seen, Gosson attacked poets by comparing their beautiful, ornamented language to "chaste Matrons apparel on common Curtizans,"[5] and Jonson uses a similar formulation to attack the Pucell's writing, which he compares to the "tires," "velvet gowns," "spangled petticoats," "stuffs and laces" she wears to cover a body he figures as repulsive and undesir-able (17–9, 28).

While Horatian Ben Jonson shelters poor ragged poetry in the majesty of his masculine verse, the female poet is nothing but a whore who puts men's "poor instrument[s]" in her "case," an image that figures the Pucell's body itself as merely another layer of covering, which is empty when not filled by male "substance." The figuration of the Pucell's "case," or vagina, as a mere shell for the "instru-ment" of the male wit suggests that, for Jonson, all truth or significance is phallic. Lacking a penis, a woman can either remain chastely silent or become an "epicoene fury" (8) perversely transgressing gender boundaries by attempting the mascu-line act of creating meaning.

Or so Jonson would have it. Far from being the contemptible whore Jonson constructs in his epigram, Mistress Bulstrode was, in fact, a Gentlewoman of the Bedchamber to Queen Anne and a relative of Lucy Harrington, countess of Bedford, one of Jonson's more reliable patrons.[6] Unlike the countess of Bedford, however, Bulstrode seems not to have admired Jonson's writing. The exact nature of her "censure" is unknown. It seems she presided over meetings of a coterie of poets and wits—including John Donne—at whose meetings Jonson and his works may have been ridiculed.[7] In his epigram Jonson sexualizes the meetings held in Cecelia Bulstrode's rooms; "her chamber [is] the very pit / Where fight the prime cocks of the game, for wit" (3–4). Her social authority over a group of male wits is reconfigured as whorish. Bulstrode's chamber—another figure for her vagina—becomes the site of a masculine struggle for intellectual dominance. In this image Bulstrode's own significance and authority is erased. It is the male rivalry that is important; the "chamber" in which it is located is merely another empty case.

While the dynamics of this situation suggest those described by Eve Sedgwick in *Between Men*, where male rivals play out their "homosocial" relation by strug-gling to win dominance over a woman, it is reductive to see the figure of Cecelia

Bulstrode merely as a conduit for a struggle that is fundamentally one between men. Jonson's insistence that Bulstrode is no more than an empty case is necessary for his own self-fashioning; his efforts to separate true poetry from effeminate bawdry depend on his argument that a woman cannot, by reason of her gender, be a good poet. His argument for the primacy of the male "instrument" over the female "case" represents an attempt to ground poetic eloquence on physical gender difference. However, this move is a contentious one, for, as we have seen, absolute physical gender difference was by no means a universally accepted medical fact in the early modern period.[8]

The history of transmission of the "Epigram on the Court Pucell" reveals the gap between Jonson's putative superiority to Mistress Bulstrode and their actual relative social positions. Because Cecelia Bulstrode was a woman of some standing and influence at court, Jonson's "bold" denunciation of her had to be kept as private as possible. For all the text's self-righteous bravado he dared not print the poem in her lifetime. But although he kept the poem from the press, he did not keep it safe from prying fingers. Many years after Mistress Bulstrode's death in 1609, Jonson told Drummond of Hawthornden how "that piece of the Pucelle of the court was stollen out of his pocket by a Gentleman who drank him drousie, and given Mistress Bulstraid, which brought him great displeasur" (*Conversations* 646–8). No doubt.

In public, especially after Bulstrode's death, Jonson presented a very different notion of her poetic worth. For hypocritical fawning even the fulsome dedications of Aretino do not surpass the elegy Jonson wrote for Cecelia Bulstrode. The woman whom he surreptitiously attacked as a sodomitical whore he describes in his funerary verse as

> first, a Virgin; and then, one
> That durst be that in Court: a virtu' alone
> To fill an Epitaph. But she had more.
> She might have claymed t' have made the Graces foure;
> Taught Pallas language; Cynthia modesty
>
> (ungathered verse, 9:3–7)

Jonson's epitaph was sent with a covering note "To my right worthy friend Mr. Geo: Garrard," in which Jonson ascribes his writing of the epitaph to "the obedience of freindship [sic]."[9] The poem was—Jonson says—composed on the spot as a tour de force while Garrard's messenger waited. While Jonson claims he had not previously heard of Bulstrode's death and much regretted the news, he was told that "greater Witts" (among them John Donne) had already written epitaphs for Cecelia Bulstrode. Thus though "streightened with time" Jonson nonetheless gave the messenger a poem to take away to "let [Garrard] know yor power in mee." Jonson's epitaph is written not so much for the dead woman as in tribute both to the power Garrard's masculine friendship commands in him and to his own power to compose poems every bit as good as those of "greater [male] Witts."

The composition of these two completely contrary poems on Mistress

Bulstrode gives a stark example of the dilemma Jonson faced. To assert his superiority over competing wits, he had to write verse that flattered people he obviously despised. More important, the verses reveal the difficulty of drawing distinctions between masculine eloquence and effeminate bawdry. In a culture in which poetry itself is posited as effeminizing, how can one present oneself as a masculine author and authority? One strategy, embodied in the "Epigram on the Court Pucell" is to draw distinctions based primarily on biology: female poets are whorish (as Gosson said of Sappho); male poets are not. While such biological determinism would have great success in later centuries, in the early modern period, biological difference alone was not enough. Since masculine gender identity depended on performance, and merely having a penis was not enough to show oneself a man, male authors would need to prove their masculine authority in other ways. A bricklayer's son, a branded felon, an actor, and rumored to be an Aretine sodomite, Jonson had a lot to overcome if he was to let greater wits know his power successfully.

Aretine Jonson: *Every Man Out* and *Volpone*

Despite his subsequent successful self-presentation as a classicist, Jonson began his career as a railing satirist and collaborated with Thomas Nashe on the banned (and now lost) play *Isle of Dogs* (1597). Lynda Boose has described the printed satire of the 1590s as a "new and aggressively sexualized form of distinctly English literature" characterized by "a language not of lascivious delight but of sexual scatology" (192–3). Boose suggests that this strain of writing was stimulated and energized by the example of Aretino's *Ragionamenti* (194), but although English satire of the 1590s is rhetorically similar to the *Ragionamenti* in its employment of sexualized language, it differs crucially from Aretino's work both in the object of its attack and in its treatment of gender. While, as we have seen, the *Ragionamenti* are characterized by the crossgendered identification of Aretino with Nanna, the satiric works of Marston and others are resolutely masculine in their outlook. And whereas the chief targets of Aretino's satire are princes and prelates, the ruling classes in both church and state, the victims of English satires of the 1590s tend to be women and erotically disorderly men.

In 1590s England, then, a novel form of erotic discourse emerged. While it owed much to the traditions of Juvenal's satire—especially his sixth satire, against women—in the context of vernacular literature these texts were unprecedented in their linkage of explicit eroticism to discourses of misogyny and sexual disgust. Boose contends that, following the 1599 Bishops' Order, the sexualized language of satire shifted from "a poetry culture to a theater culture" (194) and notes that it is after 1600 that the lurid italianate genre of Jacobean tragedy first begins to take hold of the English stage. While Boose is right to draw attention to the spread of sexualized satiric discourse from the book market to the theater following the Bishops' Order, as we have seen, the theater was perceived as being fundamentally erotic long before 1599. The writers who wrote most vehemently against effeminizing poetry in the late sixteenth century were also those who were most outspokenly antitheatrical. Indeed, as Stephen Orgel has argued, the Elizabethan anti-theatrical polemicists all assume that "the basic form of response to the theater is erotic" (30). The public theaters presented their audiences with crossdressed boys, clothed commoners in luxurious garments, and staged scene after scene of seduction. They were frequented by apprentices and prostitutes and relatively independent city women.[10] They were the site of flirtations and assignations.[11] And they were located in the liminal spaces of the city, sharing the space with brothels and bath houses.[12]

Unlike his collaborator Nashe, Jonson does not seem to have considered Aretino a political figure worthy of praise and emulation or foster an image of himself as the "English Aretine." Yet Jonson knew Aretino's works well[13] and was clearly attracted by the various transgressive energies embodied in the mythology surrounding the Italian writer. Rejecting the explicit eroticism and the outspoken political polemic for which Aretino was notorious, in *Every Man Out of His Humor* (1599) and *Volpone* (1605) Jonson grappled with the model of authorship and authority offered by Aretino in an attempt to appropriate the social authority that Aretino's writings—both erotic and political—had created for him. By staging Aretinesque figures in these plays, Jonson was able to appropriate the transgressive erotic energy characteristic of Aretino's own writings and to distance himself from it at the same time. In *Epicoene: or the Silent Woman* (1609), Jonson reworked Aretino's play *Il marescalco* (*The Stablemaster*) in an attempt to distance his own theatrical and poetic work from the taint of sodomy and effeminacy powerfully marked by the figure of Aretino in English culture. In *Epicoene*, Jonson transforms *Il marescalco*'s critique of power and service in the all-male world of the court of Mantua into an attack on effeminacy and female eloquence in the city of London. And in the process, the erotic delight characteristic of Aretine discourse is subordinated to a misogynist antieroticism that, rather than celebrating erotic possibility and embracing gender ambivalence, rigorously attempts to distance the male author from the threat of effeminacy by condemning women's speech.

Jonson's engagement with troubling yet attractive Aretine models of eroticism arguably begins with the figure of the italianate epicure Carlo Buffone in Jonson's 1599 play *Every Man Out of his Humor*. *Every Man Out* has generally been considered one of Jonson's minor works; no performance has been staged since 1675 and many believe that, because of the play's unorthodox structure and inordinate length, it is in fact unplayable in its present form.[14] Because of this general neglect, it is often forgotten that as a published text, *Every Man Out* played a crucial role in Jonson's career. Not only was it his first authorized publication but, whatever its success as a stage play, the three quarto editions that appeared in 1600 alone suggest that it was extremely successful as a printed book—an estimated fifteen hundred copies were sold.[15] It seems possible that Jonson himself saw *Every Man Out* primarily as a printed text; the claim made on the title page of all three quartos, that the text is being published not as performed but "as it was first composed by the Author B. I.," suggests that Jonson gave priority not to the version of his text that was acted in the playhouse but to the "originary" longer version that was later published.[16]

It is likely that the popularity of *Every Man Out* can be attributed in part to the similarity between the material of the play and that of salacious printed satire, in verse and prose, of the 1590s. Like the satires of John Marston and William Goddard, *Every Man Out* violently attacks various forms of socially and erotically disorderly behavior, from affected dress to the smoking of tobacco and various forms of sodomy. As we have seen, the proliferation of similar writings in late 1590s London was a source of concern to the authorities and led ultimately to the proscriptions of the 1599 Bishops' Order. The publication of *Every Man Out* provides yet more evidence, however, of the Order's ineffectiveness. By the spring of 1600, in the guise of a play-script, described both in the Stationers' Register and on its title page as a "Comicall satire,"[17] satire was moving right back to the stalls from which it had been banished less than a year earlier.

And yet the ban seems to have left its mark on *Every Man Out*. Perhaps reflecting the recent pressure brought to bear on satirical writers, Jonson's "comical satire" betrays a certain ambivalence about the relationship between order and disorder, between high and low forms of satire, between author and text—an ambivalence reflected in a bewildering array of competing authorial figures: the "actual" author, Ben Jonson, is represented by Asper, the presenter, who disguises himself as Macilente, an envious scholar. Within the play, Macilente's authority as a satirist is challenged by Carlo Buffone, a disorderly Aretine railer who bears a strange resemblance to the "actual" author Ben Jonson.

In many ways *Every Man Out of His Humor* is more a gallery of characters than a play—there is little "plot." The first three-quarters of the play present a series of excessive, "humorous"[18] figures who transgress Jonson's ideal social norms of conduct in one way or another: a uxorious citizen, his proud and adulterous wife, a profligate student, foppish courtiers, and a miserly farmer. What all these figures have in common is an unwillingness or inability to act in a manner appropriate to their social position: masters act without dignity (the knight Puntarvolo serenading his wife) or submit to the authority of their subordinates (the citizen Delirio deferring to *his* wife); those of the lower sort take on the affectations of their superiors (the student Fungoso dressing in imitation of the courtier Briske) or blindly follow fads and fashions (the fool Sogliardo smoking tobacco). In the final scenes of the play, one by one the characters are "purged" of their humors, mostly through cruel punishments inflicted by Macilente, an envious scholar who is revealed at the conclusion to be Asper, the fictional "author" of the play.

Asper, who is described in the list of characters accompanying the text as being "of an ingenious and free spirit, eager and constant in reproof" (Character 1), seems to function as a fairly transparent agent for Jonson himself; he defines and enforces the ideal social norms of behavior that Jonson seeks to inculcate in his audience. Yet, as if Macilente/Asper's condemnation of folly were not enough, *Every Man Out* also includes an elaborate apparatus—which in the folio Jonson calls the "Grex" or chorus—whereby the actions of the play are repeatedly discussed by two actors sitting in the audience, representing Asper's friends Mitis and Cordatus. It is not clear whether this self-reflective level of the text was included in performance. Whatever its provenance, the inclusion of Cordatus and Mitis represents an awkward and somewhat unsuccessful authorial attempt to exercise a high level of control over interpretation.

Asper's efforts to instruct the audience through his disguise as Macilente are insufficient on their own because Macilente, like the characters he punishes, is himself subject to an irrational and excessive humor, in his case envious frustration at his lack of advancement. But Macilente's authority within the frame of the drama is also undermined by the figure of Carlo Buffone. Buffone, a drunken, libelous Aretine epicure, plays an ambivalent role in *Every Man Out*. On the one hand, much like Macilente, he functions as a scourge of others' follies.[19] On the other, Buffone is himself a foolish and impertinent figure, who must ultimately be punished for his excessive railing by being beaten by the outraged knight Puntarvolo and having his mouth sealed with wax.

Even before the opening of the action of *Every Man Out*, the commentary of the Grex attempts to control the audience's reaction to Buffone by explicitly representing him as a social overreacher and "atheistical" railer—an italianate "monster" who "will preferre all Countries before his native":

> He is . . . an impudent common jester, a violent rayler, and an incomprehensible *Epicure*; one, whose company is desir'd of all men, but belov'd of none; hee will sooner lose his soule then a jest, and prophane even the most holy things, to excite laughter: no honorable or reverend personage whatsoever, can come within the reach of his eye, but is turn'd into all manner of varietie, by his adult'rate *simile's*. (Third Sounding 356–69)

Similarly, in the "Character of the Persons" published with the play, Buffone is described as "A Publike, scurrilous, and prophane Jester; that (more swift than *Circe*) with absurd *simile's* will transforme any person into deformity." Buffone is a creature of excessive appetite; he is feared and hated for his outspoken criticism of his social masters and is reputed to be blasphemous, worshiping his own wit above all else. "His religion [is] rayling, and his discourse ribaldry"(Character 25–34). Unlike Macilente—whose railing is justified to a certain extent by the revelation that he is the fictional author Asper in disguise—Buffone and his attacks are unlicensed. He engages in disorderly railing rather than principled moral critique. Or so the authorial interpretation of the play would have its audience believe. In fact, the distinctions Jonson attempts to draw between licensed and unlicensed criticism are continually breaking down. Besides the intervention of the "Grex" there is little indication that Macilente's "envious apoplexie" is any better than Buffone's scurrilous profanity (Character 10, 25).

The fact that Jonson chose to name his normative free spirit Asper (bitter) suggests that, at this point in his career, Jonson still has a personal stake in the Juvenalian mode of bitter or railing satire practiced with such virtuosity by his former collaborator Thomas Nashe. In contrasting the lean, bitter Macilente (whose name means "emaciated") with the corpulent Buffone ("fat clown"),

Jonson attempts to draw a sharp distinction between two differing satirical personae. While both are Juvenalian railers, Jonson attempts to separate the figure of the slighted and ignored intellectual from that of the disorderly epicure and sodomite. These two figures are precisely those Nashe combined in his adoption of the epithet "the English Aretine"—a formulation that links Nashe's Macilente-like persona Piers Penniless to the figure of Aretino.

Every Man Out can thus be read as an attempt by Jonson to free railing, Juvenalian satire from Aretine disorderliness and to renew its moral foundation by associating it with the struggle of poor "sufficient Schollers" (such as Macilente) and "ingenious and free spirits" (such as Asper) to achieve social status and financial rewards. That the distinction is not an easy one is suggested by Macilente/Asper's final address to the audience: he refuses to beg for applause but admits that if the audience bestows its favor, "you may (in time) make leane MACILENTE as fat, as Sir JOHN FAL-STAFFE" (5.11.85–87). Popular success—unasked for, but not necessarily unwelcome—runs the risk of turning the lean man of merit into the very epitome of overblown disorderly excess. In fact, the distinction between the fat, excessive railer and the lean, hungry scourge collapses almost as soon as it is introduced. Lean Asper's boast that he will "strip the ragged follies of the time, / Naked, as at their birth" (Second Sounding 17–8) sounds very much like Nashe's longed-for English Aretino, who will "strip these golden asses out of their gay trappings" (*Pierce Penniless* 1.242). It may be that the excessive railing characteristic of Juvenalian satire cannot help but suggest further excess—intemperate rhetoric implies physical intemperance and social disorderliness.

The effects of Buffone's social disorderliness are clearly visible in *Every Man Out*. The Aretine Buffone is an expert on the arts of social climbing and manipulative pretense. In the play's second scene he advises Sogliardo, a rustic "clowne" with pretensions to gentility, on how to pass for a gentleman. He tells Sogliardo, "you must pretend alliance with Courtiers and great persons: and ever when you are to dine or suppe in any strange presence, hire a fellow with a great chaine (though it be copper it's no matter) to bring you letters, feign'd from such a Noble man, or such a Knight, or such a Ladie," (1.2.71–8). Besides demonstrating Buffone's general shrewdness and his cynicism concerning displays of authority, this passage also loosely associates Buffone with the outward emblems of Aretino's success, his letters to and from the nobility, and his famous gold chain from François I—the latter prominently displayed in many engraved portraits of Aretino, including the frontispieces of the first two volumes of his letters.

Buffone's effective substitution of a cheap chain and forged letters for an expensive chain and authentic letters is emblematic of his "adulterate similes" that indiscriminately exchange the true for the false. Like Ascham's corrupting italianate, Buffone is associated with the transformative feminine witchcraft of Circe: his irrational, illogical rhetoric "will transforme any person into deformity." The subversive power of Buffone's "absurd similes" echoes Gabriel Harvey's concerns about Aretino's unruly rhetorical skill. Buffone represents the seductive capacity of effective speaking to pervert truth and unbalance judgment. Most disturbing of all, Buffone—like Circe—is attractive: his "company is desired of all men."

204   *The Aretine and the Italianate*

Buffone's body—like the body of Falstaff, that other fat clown—is frequently represented as a leaky, open (female) body rather than a hard, defined (masculine) one.[20] Buffone's "swilling up" of sack (Character 31)—a phrasing that suggests both drinking and spewing—points to what Gail Kern Paster has termed the "leakiness" of the female body as represented in early modern England.[21] In addition, Buffone's inordinate fondness for pork (5.5.45–55) prefigures Jonson's most powerful figure of female bodily incontinence and excess: Ursula the pig-woman in *Bartholomew Fair*.[22] Like his Circean rhetoric, the feminine excessiveness of Buffone's body is an emblem both of disorderly speech and usurped authority. Seen in this light, Buffone comes to seem more and more like Aretino's own disorderly, "excessive," feminine self-portrait, the figure of Nanna—another Circean figure desired of all men but standing outside the discourses of love.

Like Aretino, effeminized Buffone can be read as a corrupting sodomite, well-acquainted with "nimble-spirited *Catso's*" (Italian for "penis") (2.1.20–1).[23] His Circean language is full of homoerotic double-entendres: asking a boy drawer to bring him wine, he says, "draw me the biggest shaft you have, out of the butt you wot of: away, you know my meaning, GEORGE, quicke" (5.4.19–21). From his first appearance in the prologue onward he is frequently accompanied by a boy page, and whether or not he engages these boys in homoerotic activity himself, he is clearly recognized as a judge of quality in such matters. The foppish courtier Fastidious Briske wastes no time in getting Buffone's opinion on his own suggestively named minion Cinedo (an Italian term translated in Florio's 1598 dictionary as "a buggring boy"): "How lik'st thou my boy, CARLO?" he asks (2.1.4). And in his instruction of Sogliardo in the ways of the court Buffone makes sure to introduce him to the advantages of having a youthful body-servant, advising him to "keepe no more but a boy, it's ynough" (1.2.142). Sogliardo later enters into a homoerotic relationship with Shift, a "thred-bare sharke" (Character 84) whom Buffone characterizes as Sogliardo's "villainous Ganimede" (4.3.83).

In the end, Buffone is punished for his socially disruptive overreaching—specifically for mocking his social superior, the "vaine-glorious Knight" Puntarvolo. Although Puntarvolo is himself a foolish figure, his punishment of Buffone represents an assertion of his proper authority and social duty that purges him of his "humor" of "vain-glory." Just as shrews were punished with scold's bridles, Buffone's excessive, disorderly body is "cured" by being sealed; the railer's mouth is stopped with wax.[24] Buffone's punishment points clearly to the dangers of "self-creating" authority. In this context, Buffone's relation to Jonson's own situation in 1600 is especially relevant.

The almost neurotic uncertainty about the proper positioning of the author in the text and the care taken to revise *Every Man Out* for printing suggest Jonson's concern—a concern that would come to be characteristic—to take as much control as possible over his texts and, by extension, over his self-representation as an author and an authority. In 1600, when *Every Man Out* was first published, Jonson very much needed to rehabilitate himself: imprisoned in 1597 for his collaboration with Nashe on the lost play *Isle of Dogs* and, more seriously, in 1598 for the murder of actor Gabriel Spencer in a quarrel, Jonson was anything but a convincing authoritative figure in a position to advocate rational, normative social behavior.

Jonson's inability to set himself above other satirists and to disassociate himself from his unruly, criminal past is one theme that emerges clearly from the tangled dispute—dignified with the name of "Poetomachia"[25] or "Poets' Quarrel"—that raged between himself and John Marston and Thomas Dekker from 1599 to 1602.[26] The origins of the quarrel are somewhat vague, but the issues involved are clear enough: attempting to distinguish himself from those theatrical satirists whose writings most resembled his own by adopting an urbane Horatian persona, Jonson found himself attacked as an insolent, disorderly—even sodomitical—upstart.

In *Every Man Out, Cynthia's Revels* (1600), and *The Poetaster* (1601) Jonson attacked Marston for being an ignorant courtly poetaster given to esoteric language, a caricature whose most vivid incarnation is the figure of Crispinus in *The Poetaster*, who is made to vomit up the outlandish words he has written as punishment for his bad verse (5.3.465–530). In response, Marston portrayed Jonson as a pedantic moralistic flatterer and upstart whose works were unpopular in court circles. The Jonsonian figure of Lampatho Doria in *What You Will* (1601) is ridiculed as "a meere Scholler, that is a mere sot" (4.1) who naively presents the worldly court with "A Commedy, intitled *Temperance*" (5.1).[27]

The most detailed attack on Jonson, however, came from Marston's ally Thomas Dekker, who in the character of Horace in *Satiromastix; or, the Untrussing of the Humorous Poet* (1601), drew explicit attention to the gap between Jonson's Horatian pretensions and the realities of his social position, pointedly referring to Jonson's killing of Gabriel Spencer (4.2.61), his subsequent escape from execution by reciting the "neck verse " (1.2.117), his past as a bricklayer (1.2.139), and his failed career as a histrionic actor (4.1.125–35). Dekker characterizes Jonson as "self-creating Horace" (5.2.138), who is punished for daring to speak harshly of his betters.

Significantly, Dekker links Jonson's social transgressions to his disorderly sexual practices. The play characterizes Jonson as an "ingle" (or catamite) who is kept for sexual favors by the illiterate nobleman Asinius Bubo. He is attacked for his "mindes Deformitie" (preface 26), called a "hermaphrodite" (1.2.290), and said to share little more with the Roman Horace than his name and his "damnable vices" (5.2.250). Throughout *Satiromastix* Jonson's attempt to ingratiate himself with the nobility is cast in homoerotic terms: he is said to "exchange curtezies, and complements with Gallants in the Lordes roomes" (5.2.304–5) and to "skrue and wriggle himselfe into great Men's famyliarity" (5.2.255–6). Dressed as a satyr for a court entertainment, "Horace" is publicly punished by being "untrussed" in a ritual that evokes Apollo's flaying of the disorderly satyr Marsyas— a locus classicus of the punishment of an overreaching, erotically charged artist by balanced, rational order. If Jonson does not reform himself, Dekker suggests, he will become indistinguishable from Buffone, his own caricature of an Aretine railer (5.2.332–3). If "Horace" wishes to rehabilitate himself, he needs to seal his mouth and learn proper manners.[28]

Rather than disentangle the genealogy of the Poet's Quarrel, let alone determine which—if any—of the participants profited from it, I wish merely to note the extent to which the dispute used Jonson's reputedly disorderly eroticism to critique his attempts at self-definition and his social aspirations. Clearly at this point in Jonson's career, despite his attempts to position himself and his writings effectively, he was still seen by his rivals (and presumably by a substantial portion of the audience at the exclusive private halls where their plays were performed) as a sodomitical railer. Attempting to set himself off as a superior poet and judge, Jonson was (at least in parody) accused of "satirisme," "arrogance," overreaching, sodomy, and atheism—a set of charges matching precisely those labeled as "Aretine" in early modern England. Given the seriousness with which Jonson approached the task of choosing an authorial precedent and persona, his flirtation with Aretine authorial figures in *Every Man Out* suggests that the railing persona used against him by his rivals was one that he himself found compelling.

In the years following the Poets' Quarrel Jonson moved away from presenting himself as an Aretine railer in what one might call his critical writings— the prefaces, epistles, and poems in which he laid forth his views on the nature of poetry and its social function. Yet, despite his assiduously cultivated air of serene classical detachment, Jonson remained firmly dependent, for both his fame and his income, on the anticlassical, erotically provocative, and morally ambiguous practices of the public theater. His dissociation from the figure of the disorderly railer in his explicit acts of self-presentation is accompanied by an increasingly central role for erotically disorderly, manipulative, theatrical characters in his plays.

In *Volpone*, a work often seen as his first truly successful theatrical production, Jonson explored the relationship between discourses of italianate eroticism and the erotic performance and display characteristic of the English stage. In *Every Man Out* the Aretinizing Buffone is an aggressively theatrical character in an ambivalently theatrical text; in *Volpone*, Aretinizing is firmly associated with the erotically disorderly space of the theater. When Corvino, his jealousy temporarily overmastered by greed, rationalizes giving his wife Celia to Volpone, he links Aretino's scandalous texts to the performance and spectatorship of erotic activity in Renaissance theaters:

> Should I offer this [i.e., Celia]
> To some yong *Frenchman*, or hot *Tuscane* bloud,
> That had read ARETINE, conn'd all his printes,
> Knew every quirke within lusts laborinth,
> And were professed critique, in lechery;
> And I would looke upon him, and applaud him,
> This were a sinne.

> (3.7.58–64)

Corvino's formulation reworks common notions of corrupting italianate literature in particularly Jonsonian terms: the young Tuscan or Frenchman reading

Aretino becomes a perverse parody of the familiar figure of the critic and censor. More than this, Corvino believes that watching the display of lechery is in itself a sin. In this formulation, the worst offense is neither participating in sexual disorder nor being expert at it: it is being an approving spectator, one who looks and applauds. This image of the aroused spectator applauding expert erotic performers is one to which the play returns repeatedly; a fascination with the erotic nature of theatrical display lies at the heart of *Volpone*.

Where Corvino goes wrong, of course, is in his estimate of Volpone's erotic knowledge. Ironically, the figure he would set against the perverse young italianate is, in fact, a perverse old italianate, and one who is in many ways reminiscent, in fact, of the author of the *sonetti lussuriosi*.[29] Throughout the play, Volpone's eroticism is coded in specifically Aretine terms. Like Aretino, Volpone is a wealthy Venetian who lives in an opulent house on the Grand Canal, surrounded by a group of monstrous servants—in his case a parasite, a dwarf, a eunuch, and a hermaphrodite. And like Aretino, Volpone increases his wealth by manipulating the greed and vanity of those around him—he lives off the gifts of the rich and powerful men and women who court him.

The Venetian setting of *Volpone*, which Jonson evokes with much detail, is crucial to the play. In early modern England Venice was widely perceived as a site of erotic disorder and racial mixing: the epitome of the modern urban environment,[30] opposed in every way to the sort of traditional aristocratic rural household Jonson idealizes in poems such as "To Penshurst."[31] Venice was a republic, with relatively few feudal traditions; its economy was mercantile, based not on ownership of land but on trade. As well as being a major commercial port, sixteenth-century Venice was also the foremost industrial center in Italy, with large workshops for printing and glass-making, and especially shipbuilding.[32] Above all, in the imagination of early modern England Venice is a liminal space, where Christian Europe comes into direct and constant contact with the Islamic world, where the familiar meets and mingles with the foreign, the alien—a mingling that is at the center of Shakespeare's *Othello*. And, as the plot of *Othello* indicates, the mingling of familiar and alien was often seen in erotic terms. The wealth, beauty, and relative independence of Venetian courtesans were renowned throughout Europe,[33] and we have seen how Ascham attempted to mitigate the sexual corruptions of London by comparing them to the unparalleled "libertie to sinne" found in Venice (83).

In early modern London, arguably the most prominent site of mixing of the familiar and the alien, a space of "ambivalent spectacle and cultural license" where traditional social hierarchies were disrupted by the values of the capitalist marketplace and where patriarchal morality was challenged by erotic display, was the space of the theater itself.[34] Situated in the heart of the mercantile metropolis of Venice, Volpone has often been read as a protocapitalist.[35] But rather than amassing wealth by trade (1.1.31–51) or through inherited property (1.1.73–5), Volpone's riches are generated theatrically through seductive and eroticized performance. This alienation both from "respectable" commerce and the traditional social structures of kinship and alliance is the condition for Volpone's performative self-fashioning (as invalid, as mountebank, as commandadore), and can be read as analogous to the uncertain space of the theater within the social economy of Elizabethan London.

Linked to traditional social networks of power, wealth, and privilege only through his performative skill, Volpone is also ambivalently related to traditional orders of eroticism and gender. It has often been remarked that Volpone's passion for gold is consistently expressed in terms not only of religious devotion but of sexual pleasure and desire.[36] Less often noticed is that the erotic dynamics of Volpone's relation to his gold are utterly fluid. In the play gold is gendered both masculine and feminine: it is both the "sonne of SOL" (1.1.10) and as bright and lovely as Celia, the female object of Volpone's lust (1.5.111–4). Volpone's own gender position is similarly mutable. Though the play begins with Volpone uncovering the body of his gold and exulting in the "glad possession" (1.1.32) of it—thus taking the (traditionally masculine) active role in relation to his treasure—moments later Volpone genders himself feminine, comparing himself to the "teeming earth" about to be made fertile by the "long'd for sunne." This confusion of gender marks both Volpone's possession of his treasure and his desire for Celia as sodomitical—that is, perverse and disorderly—as well as pointing to the innate eroticism of the relationship of Volpone to his wealth. And although his lust for Celia provides the driving force for much of the action of the play, there are hints throughout the play that Volpone has erotic relations with men as well as women. At several points in the play he passionately embraces Mosca, twice exclaiming, "let me kisse thee" (1.3.79, 1.4.137). Volpone's remark that he and Mosca "have liv'd like *Grecians*" (3.8.15) also characterizes their relationship as an erotic one.[37]

Volpone's ambivalent gender position and his erotic attractiveness are explicitly linked to his theatricality. In the very scene in which he attempts to seduce Celia, Volpone brags of his virility by recalling an occasion on which he served as an object of both male and female desire:

> I am, now, as fresh,
> As hot, as high, and in as jovial plight,
> As when (in that so celebrated *scene*,
> At recitation of our *comoedie*,
> For entertainement of the great VALOYS)
> I acted young ANTINOUS; and attracted
> The eyes, and eares of all the ladies, present,
> T'admire each gracefull gesture, note, and footing.

(3.7.157–64)

While Volpone stresses for Celia the desire of "all the ladies," the part he played was that of Antinous, the famous minion of Emperor Hadrian. "Great Valoys," the spectator for whom Volpone performs, is the future Henri III of France,[38] a ruler whose homoerotic passions were as well known in the sixteenth century as those of the emperor Hadrian or Jonson's own King James.

As a large body of critical work has made clear in the past decade, the eroticism of early modern English theater was strongly associated with both the display of gender ambiguity and the practice of social mobility.[39] Jean Howard has argued that the "theatrical preoccupation with crossdressing in the period from roughly 1580 to 1620 signaled a gender system under pressure" (94) and has pointed out that the erotic dynamics of the Elizabethan theater included the empowerment of female spectators and other socially marginal groups, who, having paid a minimal price of admission, were licensed to look as well as to be looked at (78–80). The spectacle of Volpone as Antinous would tend to suggest that the desires aroused by theatrical display are polyvalent: if men delight in Volpone's graceful display as Hadrian's minion, women are no less affected.

In *The Anatomie of Abuses* Philip Stubbes saw the theater as "Venus pallace"—a site of erotic danger for both men and women: plays were "plaine devourers of maydenly virginite and chastity" that would teach women to be immodest and men to be whoremasters. According to Stubbes, "wanton gestures" and "bawdie speaches" are not confined to the stage; the audience too displays "such laughing and fleering: such kissing and bussing: such clipping and culling: such winkinge and glancinge of wanton eyes . . . as is wonderfull to behold." And if the spectators are aroused by the lewdness of the actors, the actor himself is also aroused, both by his own display and that of the spectators: as the male monarch and the female courtiers are won over by Volpone's graceful performance, he himself is "hot, high," and "jovial." Indeed, Stubbes suggests that the polyvalent sexuality that characterizes the playhouse is carried over into the off-stage lives of the performers: actors, he asserts, hold "secret conclaves" in which "they play the Sodomits, or worse" (sigs. L7v–L8v).[40]

Whether or not Stubbes was accurate in his description of secret gatherings of Elizabethan players, the multivalent eroticism of Volpone's public display is clearly reflected in his household, which is a very catalogue of gender confusion. Both master and servants delight in performance: Volpone's impersonation of the mountebank Scoto of Mantua—a figure of public popular entertainment—is paralleled by the servants' private and aristocratic pageant on the transmigration of the soul of Pythagoras, the "juggler divine" (1.2.7). Volpone's servants (who are rumored to also be his children) constitute a gallery of freaks of nature not unlike that in Ambroise Paré's *Monsters and Marvells*: a dwarf (neither adult nor child), a eunuch (neither man nor woman) and a hermaphrodite (both man and woman). Volpone characterizes the clients who come to visit him as "Women, and men, of every sexe, and age" (1.1.77), a formulation that suggests a fairly wide range of gender positions. And while Corvino, Corbaccio, and Voltore are relatively clearly inscribed within "proper" gender order, one must not forget that Lady Politic, whose very name suggests her identity as a mannish woman, is also among Volpone's suitors. Lady Politic is conversant with Aretino's *sonetti lussuriosi* and their accompanying illustrations, and in a manner oddly reminiscent of Gabriel Harvey she equates Aretino with Petrarch, Tasso, Dante, Guarini, and Ariosto (3.4.79–80, 95–6).

The ambivalent relation between Volpone and his author is evident both in the epilogue of the play, where Volpone addresses the audience directly, and in the epistle dedicating the play to the universities, in which Jonson directly addresses the reader. The play ends, of course, with Volpone and Mosca exposed and their crimes harshly punished by the Venetian senate. Volpone, who as actor and orator has been both inciter of vice and object of desire, must now be transformed into a public example of the rigors of justice—an object of pity and terror, not of pleasure. The Avocatoro announces:

> Let all, that see these vices thus rewarded,
> Take heart, and love to study 'hem. Mischiefes feed
> Like beasts, till they be fat, and then they bleed.

> (5.12.149–51)

Rather than studying lechery, like Corvino's Frenchman or Tuscan, the spectator can now take a different pleasure from the spectacle of blood shed. And rather than inciting the hot blood of sexual desire, the sight of fat Volpone's punishment will function as a social purgative, a cure for vice.

But in the space of Jonson's theater, the salutary spectacle of bleeding mischief is no sooner invoked than banished. The immediately following lines, spoken by Volpone, turn the image of the sacrificial beast of tragedy to the ritual feast of comedy. Where the Avocatoro sees a fattened beast being slaughtered, Volpone the epicure sees a banquet:

> The seasoning of a play is the applause.
> Now, though the FOX be punish'd by the lawes,
> He, yet, doth hope there is no suffring due,
> For any fact, which he hath done 'gainst you;
> If there be, censure him: here he, doubtfull, stands.
> If not, fare jovially, and clap your hands.

> (epilogue 1–6)

While within the frame of the play, Volpone's vice has been "punished by the laws," the actual spectators at a performance are suspended between the position of the Avocatoro, who would censure Volpone, and great Valois and the ladies, who "admire each graceful gesture, note, and footing." Ultimately, of course, they are asked to judge, like Valois and the ladies, on erotics and aesthetics rather than morals—or to put it another way, on whether or not they have been pleased, rather than whether their pleasures were licit or illicit. The audience, like Volpone, ends the play in "jovial plight."

The epicureanism of the epilogue, its tendency to side with pleasure over moral justice is in sharp contrast to the stern moralism of Jonson's prefatory epistle, which opens both the quarto and folio editions of the play. Significant for the introduction to a play that so delights in mischief, the epistle to *Volpone* insists—as we have seen—on "the impossibility of any mans being the good Poet, without first being a good man" (21–2). Jonson, echoing Gabriel Harvey and sixteenth-century humanism in general, insists on the virtue of rhetoric: since truth is more convincing than falsehood, the most effective rhetoric will be that which expresses the truth; therefore the most eloquent poetry will necessarily be virtuous. But as Harvey's outrage at Aretino's rhetorical prowess reminds us, this idealistic defense of poetry is easily contradicted in practice. For, as Jonson's own case suggests, a good poet need *not* be a particularly good man—he could be an ingle or a murderer. Realizing that such objections were bound to be made, Jonson attempts to preempt them, and he attacks the view that contemporary writers' "manners [and] natures are inverted . . . [and] that now, especially in *dramatick* . . . or stage-poetrie, nothing but ribaldry, profanation, blasphemy, all licence of offense to god, and man, is practis'd" (32–8).

Despite Jonson's disapproving epistle and the punishments nominally meted out at the end of the play, *Volpone* is in many ways a celebration of ribaldry, profanation, blasphemy, and all license of offense to god and man. While the play morally condemns Volpone, the staging of his vices cannot help but make them seem attractive. If the moralism of Jonson's preface reveals an ambivalence about Volpone, his reluctance to punish such similar figures as Face in *The Alchemist* and the various rogues of *Bartholomew Fair* offers some indication of how much he felt the attraction.

The Aretine Englished: *Epicoene* and *Il Marescalco*

In his "Epigram on the Court Pucell" Jonson attacked Cecelia Bulstrode for her "epicoene fury" (8), a term denoting both effeminacy and androgynous indeterminacy. The word reappears as the title of his most thoroughgoing attack on feminine eloquence, erotic autonomy, and social power, his play *Epicoene, or the Silent Woman*, written in 1609, the year of Mistress Bulstrode's death. In *Epicoene,* rather than appropriating Aretine erotic energies by staging italianate characters, Jonson rewrote and appropriated an Aretine text, the play *Il marescalco* (*The Stablemaster*).[41]

Jonson's rewriting of *Il marescalco* is indicative of the ways in which the polyvalent eroticism and the sensual delight of Aretino's texts were assimilated to a native English satiric mode that, while characterized by sexualized invective, firmly rejected sexual pleasure as effeminizing. Where Aretino celebrates male homoeroticism, Jonson condemns "epicoene" women. Where Aretino condemns court society, Jonson celebrates an aristocratic coterie of male wits. Aretine writing uses disorderly eroticism to critique social power structures; *Epicoene* uses sexualized invective to critique disorderly eroticism. Jonson's appropriation of Aretine material in *Epicoene* thus constitutes an important step in the shift of erotic writing from its status as a sign of disorderly effeminacy to its pornographic future as an expression of masterful masculinity. In this it is analogous to the various editions of book 3 of the *Ragionamenti* and the preface of the 1660 Amsterdam edition, which present Aretino's celebratory fantasy of female cunning as a tract against the evils of women.

Il marescalco was the second of Aretino's plays to be written and the first to be published. In it, he continues the critique of court life that characterizes his first play, *La cortigiana*. These two plays, written in the middle 1520s and revised and published in the early 1530s, after Aretino settled in Venice, constitute a sustained critique of life at the courts of the Italian princes. As such, they are in constant dialogue with Castiglione's idealizing *Book of the Courtier* (published 1528), whose lofty formulation of the life and duty of courtiers they contradict at every turn. In *La cortigiana*, Maco, newly arrived in Rome, sends his servant running after a peddler who is selling "the book that will make [him] a courtier." Asking for this volume, the servant is warned about syphilis and given a volume on "*The Life of the Turks*" (1.2).[42] Taken together, *La cortigiana* and *Il marescalco* anatomize the world of the courtier in the same cynical, critical, bitter fashion as the *Ragionamenti* does the world of the courtesan.[43]

The plot of *Il marescalco* is a simple one: the Marescalco (or Stablemaster) is told that the Duke of Mantua, his master, has decided to honor him by giving him a wife. The marriage is to take place the very same day. The match is a good one; no one has anything but praise for the bride, who is educated, talented, well-born, and wealthy. But the Marescalco is not interested in marriage; his desires are exclusively homoerotic, and in general he dislikes women. The action of the play consists almost entirely of a series of conversations between the increasingly distraught Marescalco and various members of the community—his ingle, the boy Giannico; his elderly Nurse; his friends Ambrogio and Messer Jacopo; and his social superiors the Count and the Knight; as well as the court Pedant and a Jewish peddler. All play on his fears of marriage and argue he should accept the match, thus exacerbating his anger and frustration. At the conclusion of the play, the Marescalco is dragged to the altar, loudly complaining that he has a hernia and is unable to consummate the marriage, only to find that his intended "bride" is in fact a transvestite boy, Carlo da Fano, one of the Duke's pages. The Marescalco and the other courtiers all realize they have been tricked by the Duke, and the scene collapses in laughter all round. The Marescalco is very pleased with his new "bride," and the play ends with everyone going off to dine at the Duke's expense.

The play's sympathies are almost entirely with the put-upon Marescalco. If his frustration at his predicament is a source of rough amusement to the other characters in the play as well as (presumably) the play's audience, he is nonetheless a figure with a certain dignity, and much of the play's narrative tension comes from the fact that he is not simply a scapegoat or pariah but rather a useful and honorable member of the court who is clearly being treated unfairly. Such arbitrary treatment is (accurately) presented as being a constant feature of court life, and in all likelihood it is one with which most of the original court audience of the play would have had personal experience.

Although his impotent rage is a source of comedy, the Marescalco articulates his grievances passionately and eloquently, with a critical directness unthinkable in a Stuart masque, declaring simply, "I want to live in my own way, sleep with whomever I please, and eat whatever I enjoy." A loyal courtier, he initially responds to the news of the proposed marriage by resolving to bear with the situation and to trust in the Duke's affection for him. "It seems to me that everyone in the world takes pleasure in my affairs . . . patience: as long as the Duke is pleased with me, I'll love him; because it's a sign of affection [amore] when a master jokes with his servant" (1.6).

The erotic language used here to describe the relation of master and servant suggests the extent to which the Marescalco's homoerotic preferences, far from being particularly aberrant, are seen as something of a norm in the court society of the play. While the joke played on the Marescalco revolves around his homoerotic preferences and desires, he is far from the only character in the play to have such desires. If the humble Marescalco has his boy Giannico, the high-born Knight also keeps a page as a "consort" (2.11). The Pedant—who is portrayed as a pompous ass with far less dignity than the Marescalco—clearly engages in sexual activities with his male students, who take revenge on him both by taunting him unmercifully and by exploding a firecracker in the back of his breeches. If these exchanges did not make the point clearly enough, the Pedant's speech is marked by the constant use of the diminutive "culo"—which is also the Italian for "asshole."[44]

Thus, rather than simply punishing the Marescalco for his homoerotic desires, the play presents a range of male homoerotic relationships, some "ridiculous"— like that of the Pedant and his students, others "normal"—like that of the Knight and his page. The boys too have a wide range of responses to their erotic relationships with their elders. While Giannico teases his master almost without a break, he is nonetheless fond of the Marescalco and plans to stay with him after his marriage (5.7). The court world of *Il marescalco* is an almost exclusively homosocial one. The revelation that the "bride" is in fact male removes from the play the only female character represented as an object of sexual desire. As far as the play itself is concerned, there *are* no young women in Mantua to marry—all the sexual relations represented on stage are between men. It is noteworthy that the only character who speaks out against these homoerotic relations is the sole woman with a significant role in the play: the Marescalco's old Nurse. Her objections are not taken seriously, however, and largely serve to point up her ignorant piety. Unaware of the network of homoerotic relations among male courtiers, the Nurse naively sees marriage and procreation as the road to favor at court (1.6), and her blind faith in the naturalness of marriage is paralleled by her pious muddling of various Latin prayers and her faith in dreams and witchcraft. The Marescalco, on the other hand, believes that (for him at least) sex with *women* is unnatural: "I would as soon have thought of marrying a woman," he says, "as of flying" (1.9). Besides the Nurse, the character who most often repeats homilies about the virtue and necessity of marriage is the Pedant, who—it seems—has sex only with the boys he instructs. That this "feeble-minded" hypocrite is the one who administers the wedding vows provides eloquent comment on the supposed sanctity of marriage.

But although the "wedding" at the conclusion of *Il marescalco* is an outrageous parody of the rites of compulsory heterosexuality, there is no implication that Carlo the Page will be taken away from the Marescalco; indeed, given the ardor with which the cross-dressed Carlo kisses his "husband" ("the tongue!" exclaims the Marescalco), one has every reason to believe the relationship will be consummated.

Not only is the Marescalco rewarded for his pains by getting what he wants, he is far from being the only butt of the joke: the senior courtiers, such as the

Count, the Knight, and Ambrogio, have been taken in too (5.10). The jest of marrying the Marescalco to Carlo rather than to the woman he had been promised thus serves as a leveling device, employed by the Duke of Mantua to erase, for a time, the distinctions among his servants and to remind them all of their subordination to him. The tension that has built up between servants and master during the course of the play is likewise temporarily relaxed by the feast that the duke offers to all as a reward for the tricks that have been played on them.

But while the play ends with a banquet of social reconciliation and finds much to praise about the Duke of Mantua, it nonetheless stands behind the Marescalco in his observation that "our masters are evil beasts!" (5.2). A particular prince might be good and just at a particular time, but in general rulers are cruel and capricious with their servants. While Duke Federigo is often praised as being a good master, there is a constant awareness throughout the play of the anger and frustration experienced by various courtiers, most of all, of course, the Marescalco, who is torn between his desire to serve his master well and his rage at what he sees as an unwarranted and unbearable intrusion into his sexual life. Although the plot of *Il marescalco* tends to stress the orderly working out of social tensions between princes and courtiers, masters and servants, what resonates most strongly in the play is the anger and frustration of servants at the absolute and arbitrary power of masters. The Marescalco's scathing condemnations of the Duke's power are neither punished nor convincingly refuted.

Whereas the plot of *Il marescalco* turns entirely on the Duke's practical joke, which functions both to erase distinctions between courtiers and to stress their subordination to the Duke's authority, *Epicoene*, like most of Jonson's writing, is concerned more with the *creation* of distinctions. In *Epicoene* a coterie of witty young men led by Dauphine conspire to gull Dauphine's selfish and eccentric uncle Morose out of his house and income. Dauphine disinherits Morose by tricking him into marrying Epicoene, a woman reputed to be so reticent as to be practically mute. Since Morose cannot bear to hear "noise" and hates any speech but his own, he finds a mute wife an attractive proposition.

As Karen Newman has noted, "noise" in the play is repeatedly and increasingly gendered feminine (185–6), and in many ways Morose's hatred of noise signifies his deep disgust for women, his ambivalence about marriage, and his inability, once married, to master his wife. Sure enough, as soon as Morose and Epicoene are married, she shows herself to be loud and loquacious, and he is driven nearly mad by her incessant and assertive speech and the accompanying din of the wedding celebrations. Morose's inability to bear his wife's new-found volubility brings him to the point of rejecting his social position altogether; he even offers to be his nephew's ward if only Dauphine will arrange to invalidate the marriage (5.4.161).[45] As soon as Dauphine has obtained the concessions he has been seeking, he publicly disgraces his uncle by revealing that "Epicoene" is a crossdressed boy. This final humiliation reduces Morose to silence once and for all.

The downfall of the Patriarch in *Epicoene* is not an attack on patriarchy as such—Morose is punished by the wits not because he is a master but because his inability or unwillingness to marry and to maintain a household mark him as eccentric and disorderly. Like the "humorous" fools and knaves of *Every Man Out* he does not live up to the station he has been placed in and thus must be scourged by those who, while his social subordinates, are his intellectual superiors and understand his social role better than he does. Morose's fall clearly demonstrates what is at stake in debates about effeminacy. Once unmanned by his admission of impotence, Morose can be replaced by Dauphine, whose shrewd manipulation of the situation has revealed his innate (masculine) ability to rule.

Even more than *Every Man Out*, *Epicoene* is a cruel play, informed at every level by the ruthless struggle of the young male wits to establish and defend their putative social, intellectual, and moral superiority over those around them. What ultimately distinguishes Dauphine and his friends from the other characters in the play are questions of gender position and erotic practice. Like the courtiers in *Il marescalco*, the young male wits in *Epicoene* are represented as engaging in homoerotic activities. Clerimont keeps his "ingle at home" as well as his "mistress abroad" (1.1.23–4). Yet in the world of *Epicoene* homoeroticism is not the "matter-of-fact" norm it is in Aretino's staged court of Mantua: the mere suggestion of pederasty is enough to destroy the authority of a figure such as Morose, who cannot—as the wits can—forcefully assert his patriarchal rights by demonstrating his sexual mastery of women. Like the Marescalco, Morose publicly feigns sexual incapacity in order to annul his marriage. But Morose is a master and thus his public protestation of impotence implies a renunciation of patriarchal prerogative. Morose's marriage to a boy comes to be an emblem of his unfitness to hold social authority, a failing already suggested in his obsessive hatred of noise, his rage at the prospect of entertaining guests, and his efforts to rob Dauphine of his inheritance. Thus, as Mario DiGangi has argued, although Morose has not actually had sex with the boy Epicoene—and Dauphine may well have—it is he and not Dauphine who is marked in the play as a disorderly sodomite.[46] The association of sodomy with Morose helps distance Dauphine and the other wits from a similar taint.

Dauphine, in fact, has more in common with his uncle than it might seem at first glance: he is antisocial, keeping almost entirely to his room (4.1.51–6), and like Morose, he refuses to marry, thereby robbing the play of the traditional marital ending of comedy.[47] Like both "impotent" Morose and the crossdressed boy he marries, Dauphine is associated with epicene effeminacy.[48] His name—taken from "Dauphin," the name for the French royal heir apparent—is given in feminine form, with a final "e," this in a play that repeatedly links Frenchness with sexual perversity (4.6.27).

In *Epicoene* the homosocial (and homoerotic) community of wits is under constant pressure, and to maintain their social position Dauphine and his friends must continually work to distance themselves from the stigma of effeminacy. In Jonson's play the threat of effeminization is represented in three different but related forms: first Morose, powerless before feminine "noise" and unable to master his wife; second the foppish La Foole and the cowardly Daw, both of whom pretend to be gallants but lack the manly courage to back up their empty boasts; and third and most important, the Collegiates, a group of erotically and socially independent city women who ride in coaches (4.6.15–20), discuss politics, philosophy, and literature (1.1.70–77) and—like the "Aretine" widows of Middleton's *No Wit, No Help, Like a Woman's* (4.2.87–93)—take boys and womanish catamites to their beds (1.1.11–7).

Epicoene is driven by misogyny. For the bulk of act 2, scene 1, Truewit duns Morose with a lengthy harangue against women in general and marriage in particular that encapsulates the standard litany of antifeminist polemic of the period: women are unruly, disobedient, and manipulative; they talk too much, they are unchaste, they spend too much money. Here and elsewhere (1.1.81–127) Jonson inveighs at length and in detail against the use of cosmetics. The play opens with a denunciation of the Collegiates and their "masculine . . . hermaphroditical authority" (1.1.76–7). The masculine, epicene, quality of the Collegiates constitutes a threat to both the gender system and erotic practices that underpin the homosocial society of the wits. The very title of the play, with its connotations of gender ambiguity, refers as much to them as to Dauphine's crossdressed boy. While this speech is closely parallel to Ambrogio's taunting of the Marescalco (*Il marescalco* 2.5), in Aretino's play Ambrogio's speech is only one of three different set-piece speeches on the subject of marriage, none of which is straightforwardly endorsed by the play as a whole. Ambrogio's excessive attack on marriage is preceded by the Nurse's equally excessive praise of it (1.6). While there is a certain amount of misogyny in *Il marescalco*, it is presented as one view among many and is in any case subordinated to the question of the Duke's control of the Marescalco's body.

Jonson's attack on the independence of city women is echoed in other contemporary satirical texts. William Goddard, for example, makes the same connections between independence, coaches, and mannishness that Jonson does:

> To lee [see] Morilla in hir Coatch to ride,
> With hir long locke of haire uppon one side,
> With hatt & feather worne ith' swaggring'st guise,
> With butt'ned bodies skirted dublett-wise
> Unmask't and sitt ith'boote without a fann,
> Speake: could you Iudge her lesse then bee some man?
>   If lesse? then this I'me sure you'd Iudge at leaste,
>   Shee was part man, parte woman; part a beaste.[49]

On a theoretical level, the Collegiates' assumption of masculine characteristics threatens their male associates with effeminacy; in the early modern economy of gender there is room for only one master: when women are mannish, men are bound to be womanly. This dynamic is most clearly evident in the play in the case of Master and Mistress Otter. Otter, a sea captain, is utterly ruled by his dominant wife, who retains control of the money she has brought to the marriage and whom he meekly addresses as "Princess" (3.1). The reciprocal relationship between mannish women and effeminate men, implicit in *Epicoene*, is made explicit in the pamphlet controversy over gender slippage that flared in the early 1620s.[50] The *Haec Vir* tract of 1620 concludes by blaming the mannishness of women on male effeminacy:

Since . . . by the Lawes of Nature, by the rules of Religion, and the Customes of all Civill Nations, it is necessary there be a distinct and special difference betweene Man and Woman, both in their habit and behaviours: what could we poore weake women doe lesse (being farre too weake by force to fetch backe those spoiles you have unjustly taken from us), than to gather up those garments you have proudly cast away and therewith to clothe both our bodies and our minds? (sig. C2v)

While the rhetoric of this passage is designed to downplay women's power by claiming that women assume authority only when men relinquish it, in *Epicoene* clearly the Collegiates pose a more active threat. If effeminate men can produce mannish women, mannish women can produce effeminate men.

Indeed the threat represented by the Collegiates goes beyond the merely erotic. Jean Howard has characterized the Collegiates as "women who have moved or might move from their proper place of subordination" (106). Their money and the mobility it buys them (they all have coaches) allow them to escape the authority of their husbands and create a community of female taste that threatens the brotherhood of wits formed by Clerimont, Dauphine, and Truewit. Their intellectual discourse, which criticizes and censures male wits, represents a staging of the "epicoene fury" for which Jonson attacked Mistress Bulstrode.[51] In the terms of Jonson's play, their speech is feminine noise, a grotesque parody of masculine eloquence.

In his "Epigram on the Court Pucell" Jonson saw Mistress Bulstrode's poetry not only as perverse unlicensed speech but also as a commodity to be bought and sold. He compares her verse to clothes ("stuffs and laces") whose circulation was associated not with the court (to which Bulstrode actually belonged) but with the commercial practices of the city. The epicene Collegiates are also city women. Karen Newman has pointed to the protocapitalist roots of the Collegiates' independence: they are consumers par excellence: "In *Epicoene*," Newman argues, "the talking woman represents the city *and* what in large part motivated the growth of the city—mercantilism and colonial expansion" (187). Thus, as a phenomenon, the Collegiates represent the same troubling set of issues represented by the figure of Volpone, chief among them the disturbing ability of "freely" circulating capital to blur gender categories. If the trade of Venice produces Volpone (Aretino) and his monstrous household, the commerce of London produces such "monstrous" creatures as Lady Centaure (Cecelia Bulstrode) and Mistress Otter, whose names suggest an unnatural mixing of kinds (the otter was traditionally unclassifiable, neither beast nor fish).[52]

In *Epicoene* Jonson reduces autonomous and independent women to the commodities they buy. Lady Haughty, the leader of the Collegiates, is condemned for her "pieced beauty" (1.1.81). Mistress Otter is reduced to nothing more than a collection of cosmetic devices pieced together "like a great German clock" (4.2.90). An early exchange between Clerimont and Truewit demonstrates how easily this disgusted antierotic objectification of women can shift to an eroticized objectification similar to that characteristic of later genres of pornography. After hearing Clerimont's song "Still to be neat," which argues that beneath a cosmetic exterior "All is not sweet, all is not sound," Truewit replies:

> I love a good dressing before any beauty o' the world. . . . If she have good ears, show 'em; good hair, lay it out; good legs, wear short clothes; a good hand, discover it often; practise any art to mend breath, cleanse teeth, repair eyebrows, paint, and profess it. . . . Many things that seem foul i' the doing, do please, done. (1.1.88–109)

Such advice on feminine display is reminiscent of the training Giulia receives from Madalena in the protopornographic prose *Puttana errante* (sigs. A4v–A5; see chapter 3). In Truewit's view, women ought to do "foul" things if it makes them more attractive to men. He does not praise cosmetics; he condones their repulsiveness if the end result is pleasing to him. As in Marston's "Pigmalion," true feminine beauty must be constructed according to men's instruction and for men's benefit. The notion that a woman is no more than a collection of parts is epitomized in Dauphine's creation of "Epicoene"—dressing his page in woman's clothes, Dauphine can produce a woman.

Il marescalco shows a more provocative construction of femininity—the dressing of Carlo the page for the wedding. Just as Nanna in the *Ragionamenti* instructs Pippa on how to comport herself in order to be a successful whore, here Carlo is given lessons by a Matron and a Lady on how to be a successful bride. The instruction he receives concerns deportment more than dress—in order to "pass" as a bride, he must know precisely how to hold his head, how to glance, how to whisper his answer to the priest. As boys go, Carlo is a "natural" at being a girl; his cheeks are so rosy he needs no makeup, and he proves himself feminine not by his clothes so much as through his "air, speech, manner, and walk." The Lady's remark that she has "never seen a bride play her part so well" calls attention to the fact that Carlo is receiving the same training as a female bride would; to be a bride, as Nanna well knows, is to play a part. Here gender display is explicitly constructed. Although Carlo's crossgender performative skills are highly praised in the staged world of the Mantuan court, in Jonson's play Dauphine is kept at as great a distance as possible from the crossdressed Epicoene. Indeed, the suddenness of Epicoene's last-minute unmasking serves to foreclose questions about the nature of Dauphine's relations with his crossdressed servant.

If Volpone represents the subversive potential of effeminate Aretine rhetoric, Dauphine represents a dream of masculine authorial autonomy in which the feminine is utterly rejected—a dream that for Jonson can be fully realized only by an aristocratic homoerotic male in a homosocial male society. Unlike Jonson, Dauphine is tied neither to the performative practices of the theater nor to female patrons such as the countess of Bedford. When Dauphine is censured by Court Pucells he can publicly humiliate them by playing on their sexual desires for him.[53] Rather than being threatened by powerful women, he knows the secret of their construction—he can manipulate them because he knows how they are put together, how they work. He is universally admired yet answers to no one. And by successfully transferring the taint of sodomy to his uncle, he is free to reject marriage without being considered erotically disorderly.

In Dauphine then, Jonson definitively attempts to separate authorship from theatricality, masculine eloquence from effeminate noise, homoeroticism from sodomy, order from disorder. But these distinctions, while more successful than those by which Macilente is putatively set apart from the other humorous figures of *Every Man Out*, are maintained only through a massive labor of cultural construction, and they are ultimately untenable. Just as Jonson was never able to escape entirely the commercial, disorderly, anticlassical practices of the theater, so too he was never able convincingly to distinguish male poetry from effeminate whorishness. Dauphine, the ultimate figure of the autonomous male author, has a feminine name and keeps a crossdressed boy without whose feminine "stuffs and laces" his master plan could not succeed. But just as Dauphine's epicene strategem transfers his own effeminacy onto his uncle, so too Jonson's condemnation of disorderly characters like Morose and Volpone allows him to write about eroticism without appearing to be effeminate himself. Erotic material, however salacious or transgressive, is acceptable as long as it is accompanied by moral condemnation.

Some Conclusions

> You ladies all of Merry England
> Who have been to kiss the Duchess's hand,
> Say did you lately observe in the show
> A noble Italian called Signior Dildo?

> —"Signor Dildo"
> (John Wilmot, earl of Rochester)

In the later years of his life Jonson was a bedridden invalid, relatively impoverished and neglected by the court he had spent much of his life trying to please.[54] But as a cultural model, Jonson was powerful indeed. Not only did the Cavalier "Sons of Ben"—poets like Thomas Randolph and Robert Herrick—model themselves openly on Jonson, but in the Restoration and eighteenth century, the classicizing couplets and diction championed by Jonson became the norm for English poetry. When the theaters reopened in London in 1660, the first play to be performed was *Epicoene*, and it continued to be phenomenally popular well into the eighteenth century. Pepys thought it "the best comedy . . . that ever was wrote," and Dryden claimed it was his favorite play in any language.[55] But though Jonson's plays and poetics remained popular, the specificity of his appropriation of italianate cultural models was muted and eventually forgotten.

In Rochester's poem "Signior Dildo," circulated in the 1660s and published in 1703, dildos are still Italian, but they are no longer italianate. The term "italianate" was, in fact, dropping out of general usage. While English fascination with Italy—a fascination often mixed with horror—would last into the eighteenth and nineteenth centuries, by the time Rochester wrote, Italy was no longer the primary focus of national anxieties about foreign erotic corruption. That role had been taken over by France.[56] France happily fulfills that function in English culture to this day, and colloquial English is the richer for it. As early as the sixteenth century syphilis was known in England as the "French disease," and in later periods such phrases as "French kisses" (deep kisses with the tongue), "French letters" (condoms), "French ticklers" (condoms with appendages), and "Frenching" (having oral sex) all attest to the depth and persistence of the cultural shift. When the pornographic novel did arise, it arose primarily in France, and many pornographic texts in eighteenth-century England (like Pepys's *L'école des filles*) were written in French.

The reasons for the shift of cultural focus from Italy to France are too complex to explicate here, though it seems clear that they are related to Italy's general decline both as a political power and a cultural model during the seventeenth century. Other changes in erotic culture, equally difficult to pin down, can also be observed during the period from the English Restoration to the French Revolution. Broadly speaking, while sex became more and more a private concern, it also became the subject of increased cultural control. Beginning in the early eighteenth century, England saw a campaign against masturbation unprecedented in recorded history,[57] whose effects are still everywhere evident. Sex became the object of medical study and analysis to an unprecedented extent,[58] with important consequences for people's perceptions of their bodies, and for notions of sexual normality and pathology. Homosexuality began to emerge as a distinct and often exclusive sexual identity.[59] In the same years, men, rather than women, came to be credited with having the greater and more urgent sexual desires.[60] In terms of popular ideas about such wide-ranging issues as gender identity, rape, the proper raising of children, crime prevention, and family structure, the significance of this last shift has been incalculable.

These historical developments are not merely academic. They have had a profound effect, for better and worse, on how everyone in the Western world, and many people in the non-Western world, experience that most personal and private and "natural" of activities—sex. And their effects are not limited to the sexual sphere. If study of early modern eroticism teaches us anything, it is that sexuality is not, in fact, separate from politics, or law, or education, or religion. Although it seems obvious that vast shifts have occurred in cultural perceptions of sexuality, saying precisely when or how or why they occurred is much more difficult. Cultural movements and changes of this kind are not linear or progressive in any simple sense. While one may generalize broadly about cultural values or norms, such values are inflected differently in different social settings. They vary by class, region, caste, education, profession, nationality, ethnicity, and any number of other variables.

By examining at some length the role of Aretine eroticism in late-sixteenth- and early-seventeenth-century England, I have attempted to elucidate the complexity of erotic representation in a particular time and place, exploring the ways in that early modern erotic writing was engaged in discourses not only of gender but also of national identity. I have also endeavored to raise broader questions about the history of erotic writing and of erotic representation more generally—

a history that remains largely unwritten and which I am convinced is more complex and multivalent than traditional certainties about the nature of pornography and its social role would suggest. In arguing against pornography as a term of analysis in the study of the early modern period I do not wish to sanction a simplistic view of later discourses. The discourses of eroticism are every bit as complex today as they were four hundred years ago. The notion that erotic representation is transparent in significance, clear in intent, and has an obvious moral valence serves only to foreclose discussion on the cultural meanings of those representations. I want, instead, to open it up.

Notes

Introduction

1. David O. Frantz, *Festum Voluptatis: A Study of Renaissance Erotica* (Columbus: Ohio University Press, 1989); Lynn Hunt, ed., *The Invention of Pornography: Obscenity and the Origins of Modernity, 1500–1800* (New York: Zone Books, 1993).

2. Hunt, *Invention*; and Amy Richlin, ed., *Pornography and Representation in Greece and Rome* (New York: Oxford University Press, 1992); Linda Williams, *Hard Core: Power, Pleasure, and the "Frenzy of the Visible"* (Berkeley: University of California Press, 1989).

3. Walter Kendrick, *The Secret Museum: Pornography in Modern Culture*, 1987 (Berkeley: University of California Press, 1996), 1–32.

4. Kendrick, *Secret Museum*, 243.

5. Stephen Marcus, *The Other Victorians: A Study of Sexuality and Pornography in Mid-Nineteenth Century England* (New York: Basic Books, 1964); Kendrick, *Secret Museum* (1987, 1996); Williams, *Hard Core* (1989), and Hunt, *Invention* (1993).

6. Gloria Steinem, "Erotica and Pornography: A Clear and Present Difference," MS, November 1978. See also Peter Cryle, *Geometry in the Boudoir: Configurations of French Erotic Narrative* (Ithaca, N.Y.: Cornell University Press, 1994), 1–3.

7. Margaret W. Ferguson et al., eds., *Rewriting the Renaissance: The Discourses of Sexual Difference in Early Modern Europe* (Chicago: University of Chicago Press, 1986); Karen Newman, *Fashioning Femininity and English Renaissance Drama* (Chicago: University of Chicago Press, 1991); Linda Woodbridge, *Women and the English Renaissance: Literature and the Nature of Womankind, 1540–1620* (Urbana: University of Illinois Press, 1984).

8. Alan Bray, *Homosexuality in Renaissance England* (London: Gay Men's Press, 1982); Eve Kosofsky Sedgwick, *The Epistemology of the Closet* (Berkeley: University of California Press, 1990); Bruce R. Smith, *Homosexual Desire in Shakespeare's England* (Chicago: University of Chicago Press, 1991); Gregory W. Bredbeck, *Sodomy and Interpretation: Marlowe to Milton* (Ithaca, N.Y.: Cornell University Press, 1991); Jonathan Goldberg, *Sodometries: Renaissance Texts, Modern Sexualities* (Stanford: Stanford University Press, 1992); Alan Stewart, *Close Readers: Humanism and Sodomy in Early Modern England* (Princeton: Princeton University Press, 1997).

9. See Jean Marie Goulemot, *Ces livres qu'on ne lit que d'une main: lecture et lecteurs de livres pornographiques au XVIII siecle* (Aix-en-Provence, France: Alinea, 1991), as well as the essays collected in Hunt, *Invention*.

10. Catherine Belsey, *The Subject of Tragedy: Identity and Difference in Renaissance Drama* (New York: Methuen, 1985), chapters 5–8; and Newman, *Fashioning Femininity*.

11. Richard Helgerson, *Forms of Nationhood: The Elizabethan Writing of England*, (Chicago: University of Chicago Press, 1994), and Andrew Hadfield, *Literature, Politics, and National Identity: Reformation to Renaissance* (New York: Cambridge University Press, 1994).

12. Pausanias, *Description of Greece* 2.27.1.

13. B. Ruby Rich, "Anti-Porn: Soft Issue, Hard World" in *Issues in Feminist Film Criticism.*, ed. Patricia Erens (Bloomington: Indiana University Press, 1990), 405–17. For a notion of the magnitude of the debate over pornography see Franklin Mark Osanka and Sara Lee Johann, eds., *Sourcebook on Pornography* (New York: Lexington Books, 1989). In its lingering focus on tales of sexual horror this massive volume suggests that disgust for pornography can be just as obsessive as pornography itself.

14. Richlin, *Pornography.*

15. Marcus, *Other Victorians*, 278; and Susan Sontag, "The Pornographic Imagination," in *Styles of Radical Will* (New York: Delta, 1969), 35–73.

16. Marcus, *Other Victorians*, 274–7; Frantz, *Festum*, 92.

17. Williams, *Hard Core*, 126–8, lists the generically possible sexual acts in hard core films; see Marcus, *Other Victorians*, 252–65, on the conventions of flagellant fiction.

18. However, see Williams, *Hard Core*, 248–64, on hard core films made by and for women.

19. Marcus, *Other Victorians*, 277; Richlin, *Pornography*, xv.

20. Quoted in "Theory and Practice," in Laura Lederer, ed., *Take Back the Night: Women on Pornography* (New York: Bantam, 1980), 139; and picked up verbatim in the 1986 Attorney General's Commission on Pornography, *Final Report*, 2 vols. (Washington, D.C., 1986), 1:78. See also Andrea Dworkin, *Pornography: Men Possessing Women* (New York: Putnam, 1979), and Suzanne Kappeler, *The Pornography of Representation* (Minneapolis: University of Minnesota Press, 1986).

21. Marcus, *Other Victorians*, 286.

22. See, for example, Lonnie Barbach, ed., *Pleasures: Women Write Erotica* (New York: Harper, 1984), and *Erotic Interludes: Tales Told by Women* (New York: Harper, 1986); Susie Bright and Joani Blank, eds., *Herotica 2: A Collection of Women's Erotic Fiction* (New York: Plume, 1992); and Michele Slung, ed., *Slow Hand: Women Writing Erotica* (New York: Harper, 1992). In recent years the number of similar texts has grown considerably.

23. Jane Gaines, "Women and Representation: Can We Enjoy Alternative Pleasure?" in Erens, *Issues*, 75–92.

24. These views are effectively challenged by Pat Califia, *Public Sex: The Culture of Radical Sex* (San Francisco: Cleis Press, 1994).

25. See, for example, the list of safety rules provided Lady Green and Jaymes Easton, eds., *Kinky Crafts: 99 Do-It-Yourself S/M Toys for the Kinky Handyperson*, 2nd ed. (San Francisco: Greenery Press, 1998).

26. "Smut Purveyors Find Profits Online," *New York Times*, April 2, 1997. Ms. Mansfield makes over $80,000 a month in advertising revenue. According to Forrester Research, a telecommunications consulting firm, "in 1996 erotic content accounted for an estimated $52 million in sales on the Internet . . . fully one-tenth of retail business on the Web."

27. Certainly there has been a major increase in women's purchases of sex toys. The English company Ann Summers, founded by Michael Caborn-Waterfield in 1972, began as a "male-dominated" business with an all-male board. The firm is now headed by Jacqueline Gold, is "run by women, largely sells to women, and employs 7000 women

to run its Tupperware-style parties—always women-only events." In 1996, two million women attended Ann Summers "parties" and bought approximately "400,000 vibrators, 450,000 naughty knickers, and 650,000 bras." The company is one of Britain's top 250 most profitable and is worth $64 million. In 1972, 10 percent of its customers were female—now 60 percent are (Glenda Cooper, *The Independent*, June 21, 1997).

28. Kendrick, *Secret* Museum, 243. Williams, Hard Core, 268–9, notes that in the late 1980s porn videos accounted for approximately 10 percent of all video rentals in the United States.

29. Wendy McElroy, XXX: *A Woman's Right to Pornography* (New York: St. Martin's Press, 1995), especially 146–229.

30. Kendrick, *Secret Museum*, 248–9; Brian McNair, *Mediated Sex: Pornography and Postmodern Culture* (New York: Arnold, 1996).

31. See Jonathan Sawday, *The Body Emblazoned: Dissection and the Human Body in Renaissance Culture* (New York: Routledge, 1995).

32. Marcus, *Other Victorians*, 278; Sontag, "Pornographic Imagination," 39.

33. Michel Foucault, *The History of Sexuality*, vol. 1, An Introduction, trans. Robert Hurley (New York: Vintage, 1980), especially 17–49; Norbert Elias, *The Civilizing Process*, 1978, 1982, trans. Edmund Jephcott (Cambridge, Mass.: Blackwell, 1994), especially 175–6. On homoeroticism and male friendship see Alan Bray, "Homosexuality and the Signs of Male Friendship in Elizabethan England," in *Queering the Renaissance*, ed. Jonathan Goldberg (Durham, N.C.: Duke University Press, 1994), 40–61. On the relation of female homoeroticism to discourses of gynecology and the law see Valerie Traub, "The (In)significance of Lesbian Desire in Early Modern England," *Erotic Politics: Desire on the Renaissance Stage*, ed. Susan Zimmerman (New York: Routledge, 1992), 150–69. For the relation of sexuality to commerce and the state see both Ruth Mazo Karras, "The Regulation of Brothels in Later Medieval England," Signs 14 (1989): 399–433, and Steven Mullaney, *The Place of the Stage: License, Play, and Power in Renaissance England* (Chicago: University of Chicago Press, 1988), 143–7.

34. Dominique Simonnet, *L'Express*, Paris, June 12–18, 1997.

35. Dworkin, *Pornography*; Maurice Yaffe and Edward C. Nelson, eds., *The Influence of Pornography on Behavior* (London: Academic Press, 1982); Dolf Zillman and Jennings Bryant, eds., *Pornography: Research Advances and Policy Considerations*, (Hillsdale, N.J.: Erlbaum, 1989); and Catherine Itzin, ed., *Pornography: Women, Violence, and Civil Liberties* (Oxford: Oxford University Press, 1992). The transcripts of various court hearings in which Catherine MacKinnon and Dworkin attempted unsuccessfully to have pornography legally defined as discrimination, have been published in Andrea Dworkin and Catherine MacKinnon, *In Harm's Way: The Pornography Civil Rights Hearings* (Cambridge: Harvard University Press, 1998). The report of the Reagan administration's commission on pornography is available as Attorney General's Commission on Pornography, *Final Report*. Tom Minnery, ed., *Pornography: A Human Tragedy* (Wheaton, Ill: Tyndale House, 1986) is a representative collection of conservative Christian views on the subject. For a recent feminist defense of the antipornography position, see Susan G. Cole, *Power Surge: Sex, Violence, and Pornography* (Toronto: Second Story Press, 1995).

36. See Califia, *Public Sex*; McElroy, XXX; Nadine Strossen, *Defending Pornography: Free Speech, Sex, and the Fight for Women's Rights* (New York: Scribner, 1995); Avedon Carol, *Nudes, Prudes, and Attitudes: Pornography and Censorship* (Cheltenham, U.K.: New Clarion, 1994); Pamela Church Gibson and Roma Gibson, eds., *Dirty Looks: Women, Pornography, Power* (London: British Film Institute, 1993); Alison Assiter and Avedon Carol, eds. *Bad Girls and Dirty Pictures: The Challenge to Reclaim Feminism* (Boulder,

Colo.: Pluto Press, 1993); Lynne Segal and Mary McIntosh, eds., *Sex Exposed: Sexuality and the Pornography Debate* (London: Virago, 1992); and Gillian Rodgerson and Elizabeth Wilson, eds., *Pornography and Feminism: The Case against Censorship* (London: Lawrence and Wishart, 1991). In addition, Nancy Friday's popular collections of women's sexual fantasies, *My Secret Garden* (New York: Simon and Schuster, 1973) and *Women on Top* (New York: Random House, 1991), take a very positive view of the relation between female sexuality and erotic representation.

37. Tony Horwitz, "Balkan Death Trip: Scenes from a Futile War," *Harper's*, March 1993, 35–5.

38. Roger Chartier, introduction to *A History of Private Life*, Vol. 3, *Passions of the Renaissance*, ed. Philippe Ariès and Georges Duby, trans. Arthur Goldhammer (Cambridge: Harvard University Press, 1989); and Elias, *Civilizing Process*.

39. Francis Barker, *The Tremulous Private Body: Essays on Subjection* (New York: Methuen, 1984), 34.

40. Roy Porter and Lesley Hall, *The Facts of Life: The Creation of Sexual Knowledge in Britain, 1650–1950* (New Haven: Yale University Press, 1995); Tim Hitchcock, *English Sexualities, 1700–1800* (New York: St. Martin's Press, 1997), 100.

41. British Library Printed Book C. 39. a. 37 (see chapter 1, note 42).

42. Thomas Laqueur, *Making Sex: Body and Gender from the Greeks to Freud* (Cambridge: Harvard University Press, 1990); Gail Kern Paster, *The Body Embarrassed: Drama and the Disciplines of Shame in Early Modern England* (Ithaca, N.Y.: Cornell University Press, 1993).

43. Ian Maclean, *The Renaissance Notion of a Woman: A Study of the Fortunes of Scholasticism and Medical Science in European Intellectual Life* (New York: Cambridge University Press, 1980), 28–46.

44. The poem is found in Bodleian MSS Douce f. 5, fols. 29v–30v); Eng. Poet. c. 50, fol. 36v; and Rawl. poet 212, fol. 154v. I quote from the Douce f. 5 version.

45. British Library MS Add. 22603, fols. 29v–30v.

46. Thomas Tusser, *Five Hundreth Points of Good Husbandry* (London, 1573): "For twinlings be twiggers, encrease for to bring / Though some for their twigging Peccantem may sing."

47. Manuscripts associated with the Inns of Court include Bodleian MSS Add. B. 97, Don. c. 54, and Eng. Poet. e. 14 and British Library MSS Add. 21433 and 25303 and MS Sloane 1446. See Arthur F. Marotti, *Manuscript, Print, and the English Renaissance Lyric* (Ithaca, N.Y.: Cornell University Press, 1995), 35–7.

48. Lynda E. Boose, "The Bishop's Ban, Elizabethan Pornography, and the Sexualization of the Jacobean Stage," in *Enclosure Acts in Early Modern England*, ed. Richard Burt and Robert Archer (Ithaca, N.Y.: Cornell University Press, 1994), 185–200.

49. Peter W. M. Blayney, *The Bookshops in Paul's Cross Churchyard* (London: Bibliographic Society of Great Britain, 1990).

50. The best known of these is *Tottel's Miscellany* (1557). Others include *A Handful of Pleasant Delights* (1566), *The Paradise of Dainty Devices* (1576), *The Phoenix Nest* (1593), *England's Helicon* (1600), *England's Parnassus* (1600), and *A Poetical Rhapsody* (1602). Most of these texts were frequently reprinted. Many texts featuring lyric poetry from the period 1620–40 were published around the time of Charles II's restoration: *Sportive Wit* (1656), *Parnassus Biceps* (1656), *Wit Restored* (1658), *Wit and Drollery* (1661).

51. See Jonathan Bate, *Shakespeare and Ovid* (Oxford: Clarendon Press, 1993); Clark Hulse, *Metamorphic Verse: The Elizabethan Minor Epic* (Princeton: Princeton University Press, 1981); William Keach, *Elizabethan Erotic Narratives: Irony and Pathos in the Ovidian*

Poetry of Shakespeare, Marlowe, and Their Contemporaries (New Brunswick: Rutgers University Press, 1977).

52. Attempts to find unity in the volume include John Scott Colley, "'Opinion' and the Reader in John Marston's *The Metamorphosis of Pigmalions Image*," *English Literary Renaissance* 3 (1973): 221–31; Steven R. Shelburne, "Principled Satire: Decorum in John Marston's *The Metamorphosis of Pigmalions Image and Certain Satyres*," *Studies in Philology* 86 (1989): 198–218; and Frantz, *Festum*, 211–5.

53. Arnold Davenport, introduction to *The Poems of John Marston* (Liverpool: Liverpool University Press, 1960),10. All references to Marston's poems are to this edition.

54. Lawrence Stone, *The Family, Sex, and Marriage in Early Modern England: 1500–1800* (New York: Harper, 1977); Newman, *Fashioning Femininity*; Elias, *Civilizing Process*.

55. Gabriel Harvey, *Pierces Supererogation* (London: 1593), sigs. F4r–F6r; Philip Stubbes, *The Anatomy of Abuses* (London: 1583), sig. O5r; Stephen Gosson, *The School of Abuse* (London, 1579), sigs. A2r–A7v, B7r.

56. Wendy Wall, *The Imprint of Gender: Authorship and Publication in the English Renaissance* (Ithaca, N.Y.: Cornell University Press, 1993), 1. The phrase "man in print" is quoted by Wall from the 1604 introduction to *Diaphantus* by Anthony Scoloker (STC 21853, sig. A2v).

57. Helgerson, *Forms of Nationhood*, 28–34.

Chapter 1

1. Heather Dubrow, *Echoes of Desire: English Petrarchism and its Counterdiscourses* (Ithaca, N.Y.: Cornell University Press, 1995); Arthur F. Marotti, *John Donne, Coterie Poet* (Madison: University of Wisconsin Press, 1986); George Klawitter, *The Enigmatic Narrator : The Voicing of Same-sex Love in the Poetry of John Donne* (New York : P. Lang, 1994).

2. *L'école des filles* consists of a dialogue between two young women about their sexual experiences with men. See Joan DeJean, "The Politics of Pornography," in Hunt, *Invention*, 109–24.

3. Samuel Pepys, *The Diary of Samuel Pepys*, vol. 9, 1668–69, ed. Robert Latham, William Matthews, et al. (Berkeley: University of California Press, 1976), 59.

4. Ian Hunter et al., eds., *On Pornography: Literature, Sexuality, and Obscenity Law* (New York: Saint Martin's Press, 1993), 1–10.

5. Hunt, *Invention*, 20–1.

6. See Elias, *Civilizing Process*, especially 475–98. See also the essays in Ariès and Duby, *A History of Private Life, vol. 3*, especially Roger Chartier, "The Practical Impact of Writing," 111–59, and Madeleine Foisil, "The Literature of Intimacy," 327–61. On the construction of modern subjectivity see Foucault, *History of Sexuality*, Barker, *Tremulous Private Body*, and Belsey, *Subject of Tragedy*.

7. J. W. Saunders, "From Manuscript to Print: A Note on the Circulation of Poetic MSS. in the Sixteenth Century," *Proceedings of the Leeds Philosophical and Literary Society* 6 (1951): 507–28; Marotti, *Manuscript*, 1–74; H. R. Woudhuysen, *Sir Philip Sidney and the Circulation of Manuscripts 1558–1640* (Oxford: Clarendon Press, 1996), 163–73; Wall, *Imprint of Gender*, 31–34.

8. For a rare exception see *The Diaries of Lady Anne Clifford*, ed. D. J. H. Clifford (Wolfeboro Falls, N.H.: Alan Sutton, 1990), 22; and Barbara Kieffer Lewalski, *Writing Women in Jacobean England* (Cambridge: Harvard University Press, 1993), 125–52.

9. Chartier, "Practical Impact," especially 124–30.

10. Jean Marie Goulemot, "Literary Practices: Publicizing the Private," in Ariès and Duby, *History of Private Life*, vol. 3, 363–95.

11. Foisil, "Literature of Intimacy," 330.

12. Harold Love, *Scribal Publication in Seventeenth Century England* (Oxford: Clarendon Press, 1993), 229–30, etc.; see also Marotti, *Manuscript*, 75–133.

13. MS Folger V. a. 275.

14. British Library MS Add. 22601.

15. Foucault, *History of Sexuality*, 17–22, 36–46, 115–7.

16. Michael Rocke, *Forbidden Friendships: Homosexuality and Male Culture in Renaissance Florence* (New York: Oxford University Press, 1996).

17. Love, *Scribal Publication*, 177–230; Marotti, *Manuscript*, 135–208.

18. British Library MS Add. 44963, fol. 93v. See Herbert John Davies, "Dr. Anthony Scattergood's Commonplace Book," *Cornhill Magazine* NS liv (January-June 1923): 679–91.

19. Volumes that categorize texts by genre include MS Folger V. a. 103 (A), c. 1620–30; and Bodleian MS Don. d. 58. British Library MS Harl. 1836 consists entirely of epigrams (c. 1631).

20. Manuscripts that mingle explicitly erotic texts with political, devotional, and satirical poems include: Bodleian Library: MSS Ashmole 36/37, 38, 47; MSS Eng. poet. f. 25, f. 27; MSS Rawl. poet. 85, 142, 172, 199, 214; British Library: MSS Egerton 923, 2421, MSS Add. 10309, 22118, 30982; Corpus Christi College, Oxford MSS CCC 327, 328; MSS Folger V. a. 275; V. a. 319; V. a. 399; Huntington Library MSS HM 116, 198; Rosenbach Collection MSS 239/27, 1083/15, 1083/16, 1083/17.

21. Petyt MS 538, vol. 43.

22. Huntington Library MS HM 46323.

23. See Woudhuysen, *Philip Sidney*, 157—this figure is approximate and does not include single-author collections. Only twenty-five to thirty of the over two hundred extant miscellanies date from before 1600.

24. See Marotti, *Manuscript*, 1–73; Woudhuysen, *Philip Sidney*, 153–73; Mary Hobbs, *Early Seventeenth Century Verse Miscellany Manuscripts* (Brookfield, Vt.: Scolar Press, 1992),13–38; and Love, *Scribal Publication*, 35–89.

25. Marotti, *Manuscript*, 37–40.

26. See Peter Beal, ed., *Index of English Literary Manuscripts* (New York: Bowker, 1980–93), 1:2:233, 256, 274, 488. Huntington Library MS EL 8729 is one of the rare surviving examples of manuscript poetry copied on loose sheets—a copy in Ben Jonson's hand of three of his poems against Inigo Jones. For other examples see Woudhuysen, *Philip Sidney*, 155.

27. Bodleian MS Tanner 386.

28. See Woudhuysen, *Philip Sidney*, 154–55. British Library MS Add. 23229 and MS Rawl. Poet. 152 are both "composite" manuscripts.

29. Ann Moss, *Printed Commonplace-Books and the Structuring of Renaissance Thought* (Oxford: Clarendon Press, 1996), v.

30. Marotti, *Manuscript*, 4–5; Love, *Scribal Publication*, 79–83; Woudhuysen, *Philip Sidney*, 162.

31. See Marotti, *Manuscript*, 12–3.

32. Beal, *Index*, 1:1:245.

33. Marotti, *Manuscript*, 16–7n, 16, 37.

34. Jeniijoy La Belle, "The Huntington Aston Manuscript," *Book Collector* 29 (1980): 542–67, and "A True Love's Knot: The Letters of Constance Fowler and the Poems of

Herbert Aston," *The Journal of English and Germanic Philology* 79 (1980), 13–31; also Marotti, *Manuscript*, 45–46, 50, 51, 165; and Woudhuysen, *Philip Sidney*, 172.

35. Examples include Bodleian MS Eng. poet. e. 99; MS Tanner 307; and MS Add. B. 97; British Library MSS Harl. 4064 and 4955 and MS Add. 18647, and Cambridge University Library MS Add. 5778. See Beal, *Index*, 1:1:250–4.

36. British Library MS Add. 33998. See Beal, *Index*, 2:1:259; Hobbs, *Early Seventeenth Century*, 15–6; Marotti, *Manuscript*, 29, 37; Woudhuysen, *Philip Sidney*, 143.

37. Huntington Library MS EL 6893. See Beal, *Index*, 1:1:253; Marotti, *Manuscript* 24, 169.

38. British Library MSS Harl. 6917 and 6918. See Hobbs, *Early Seventeenth Century*, 67–71; Marotti, *Manuscript* 13, 43, 69–70,84, 123–5, 167–8, 204–6, 330.

39. Beal, *Index*, 1:2:589; Marotti, *Manuscript*, 22, 25–6, 62, 137–8; Woudhuysen, *Philip Sidney*, 105.

40. Bodleian MSS Eng. poet. f. 10; Rawl. poet. 148.

41. The phrase comes from J. W. Saunders's classic article "The Stigma of Print: A Note on the Social Bases of Tudor Poetry," *Essays in Criticism* 1 (1951): 139–64.

42. The precise contents of C. 39. a. 37 are: STC 18936; 22351; 969; 4276; 18975; and sixteen leaves containing thirty-three manuscript poems. See Marotti, *Manuscript*, 328.

43. Bodleian MS Rawl. poet. 216; MS Dyce (44) 25 F 39 in the Victoria and Albert Museum; and Rosenbach MS 1083/15 at the Rosenbach collection in Philadelphia all contain predominately bawdy or satiric verse.

44. Rosenbach MS 1083/15. This manuscript was edited and annotated in James Lee Sanderson, "An Edition of an Early Seventeenth-Century Manuscript Collection of Poems (Rosenbach MS. 186)" (Ph.D. diss., University of Pennsylvania, 1960).

45. Bodleian MS Rawl. poet. 153(a).

46. Corpus Christi College MS CCC 327. See Beal, *Index*, 1:1:254.

47. See Love, *Scribal Publication*, 101–7; Woudhuysen, *Philip Sidney*, 20.

48. Marotti, *Manuscript*, 130. The poem also occurs in Harvard MS Eng. poet. 686 (twice: fols. 34v and 66r); Bodleian MS Rawl. poet. 172 (fol. 15v); and Rosenbach MS 1083/17 (fol. 57v), among others. It was finally printed in *Wit's Recreations* (London: 1640), 227.

49. The two final lines appear alone are on fol. 76v of the same manuscript, where they are entitled "on a whore."

50. A shorter version of this epigram is found in Rosenbach MS 1083/17.

51. Other copies are found in Bodleian MSS Ashmole 38 (p. 149); Eng. Poet. f. 27 (p. 120); British Library MS Egerton 923 (fol. 46v); and elsewhere.

52. Laqueur, *Making Sex*, 63–147.

53. I quote Rosenbach MS 1083/15, fol. 37v.

54. Rosenbach MS 1083/15, fol. 38r.

55. Michel de Montaigne, *The Complete Works of Montaigne: Essays, Travel Journal, Letters*. ed. and trans. Donald M. Frame (Stanford: Stanford University Press, 1948), 654.

56. See Wall, *Imprint of Gender*.

57. This version, MS CCC 328, fol. 48. See also MS CCC 327, fol. 16v.

58. British Library MS Harl. 6057, fols. 55r–55v.

59. Rosenbach MS 1083/15, fol. 15r.

60. Maclean, *Renaissance Notion*, 28–46; and Paster, *Body Embarrassed*, 6–22.

61. Found in many manuscripts. British Library MS Egerton 2230, fol. 8r, has a less bawdy version.

62. Found in British Library MS Egerton 923, fols. 53r–54r, and in many other manuscripts.

63. Wall, *Imprint of Gender*, especially 279–340, on the difficulties faced by female writers.

64. Love, *Scribal Publication*, 54–8.

65. Love, *Scribal Publication*, 54–5; Woudhuysen, *Philip Sidney*, 13; and Mary Ellen Lamb, *Gender and Authorship in the Sidney Circle* (Madison: University of Wisconsin Press, 1990), 150–4.

66. See Marotti, *Manuscript*, 48–61. While some of the volumes he lists were inherited by women rather than compiled by them, others (British Library MSS Add. 10037, 10309 and 17492; Bodleian MS Firth e. 4 and MS Rawl. Poet. 108; and MSS Folger V. a. 89, V. a. 104, and V. b. 198) seem to have been compiled by or for women readers: MS Rosenbach 240/7 opens with a poem entitled "To the beautious Reader whomsoever." See also Love, *Scribal Publication*, 54–8; and Woudhuysen, *Philip Sidney*, 13.

67. A. H. Scott-Elliot and Elspeth Yeo, "Calligraphic Manuscripts of Esther Inglis (1571–1624)," *Papers of the Bibliographic Society of America* 84 (1990): 11–86; Jonathan Goldberg, *Writing Matter :From the Hands of the English Renaissance* (Stanford: Stanford University Press, 1990), 146–53; Woudhuysen, *Philip Sidney*, 38, 98–9.

68. Dyce MS (44) 25 F 39, fol. 60v. Also Rosenbach MS 1083/16, p. 35.

69. MS Folger V. b. 198.

70. Adam Fox, "Popular Verses and their Readership in the Early Seventeenth Century," in *The Practice and Representation of Reading in England*, ed. James Raven, Helen Small, and Naomi Tadmore (New York: Cambridge University Press, 1996), 125–37.

71. Sasha Roberts, "Women Reading Shakespeare in the Seventeenth Century," unpublished article. Beal, *Index*, 1:2:452, and Gary Taylor, "Some Manuscripts of Shakespeare's Sonnets," *Bulletin of the John Rylands Library* 68 (1985–86): 210–46; both follow the British Library Catalogue in its assumption that the Margaret Bellasys who signed the volume was the daughter of Thomas Bellasis, first Lord Fauconberg, and not Selby's daughter. But Lord Fauconberg's daughter Margaret died in 1624, which means that the most of volume she could have read was the "Characterismes of vices." Taylor believes that the poetry in the rest of the volume was the work of another compiler, but the volume is all in one scribal hand, and, as Sasha Roberts points out, there is no textual division between the "Charactersimes" and the poetry. In addition, as Roberts notes, Lord Fauconberg's daughter was married in 1610, and thus if we wish to assign the signature to her we would have to assume she was still using her maiden name after more than ten years of marriage.

72. Examples of scribally produced collections of poetry include Bodleian MS Rawl. poet. 160; British Library MS Add. 33998; and MS Harl. 4955.

73. Examples of presentation volumes include British Library MS Harl. 3357 and MS Add. 12049.

74. In MS CCC 327, fols. 21v–22, Donne's "The Flea" is followed by an inept re-working. See also Marotti, *Manuscript*, 147–59.

75. Hobbs, *Early Seventeenth Century*, 28.

76. On the mingling of erotic texts with other material in verse miscellanies, see Marotti, *Manuscript*, 75–134; Love, *Scribal Publication*, 214.

77. The poems are Henry Fitzsimon's poem "Of Oaths"; a popular verse beginning "A Rusticke Swaine was cleaving of a blocke"; and a short epitaph beginning "Within this Marble Cusquet lies / A Jewell rich of pretious prize."

78. Bodleian MS Rawl. poet. 147 is copied from MS Rawl. poet. 210 (B); British Library MS Add. 21433 was completely transcribed from MS Add. 25303.

79. See Marotti, *Manuscript,* 113–5. See Jonson, *The Alchemist* 2.2.62–63.

80. In Bodleian MS Rawl. poet. 153, fols. 8r–8v, a poem on women's inconstancy is immediately followed by a funeral verse on Queen Elizabeth.

81. Another example can be found in Rosenbach MS 1083/16, p. 15.

82. Marotti, *Manuscript,* 54–5.

83. MS Folger V. a. 399, fols. 53v–57r; MS Rawl. poet. 216, fols. 94r, 96r–106r. See chapter 4, 187–193.

84. There are at least two different early-seventeenth-century hands in the Feargod Barbon manuscript, though this need not be evidence of multiple compilers, given that Barbon states he is writing the manuscript to practice his handwriting.

85. The DNB entry on "Praisegod Barbon" cites Strype, *Annals* III i, 691; ii 479; and *Whitgift* ii 7.

86. I discuss these two poems, "Sweet harte lett me feele thy cunny" (fol. 46v) and "An English lad long woed a lasse of Wales" (fol. 45), in chapter 4, 178–180.

87. Jeffrey Masten, *Textual Intercourse: Collaboration, Authorship, and Sexualities in Renaissance Drama* (New York: Cambridge University Press, 1997), especially 32–40; Bray, "Homosexuality and Male Friendship."

88. The poem continues for another four lines that are now largely illegible. Each line of the text has been crossed out.

Chapter 2

1. An introductory poem in a verse miscellany associated with Christ Church, Oxford (c. 1630), suggests that by writing lewd epigrams its author will show himself "to bee a very man" (MS Folger V. a. 345, p. v).

2. MS Folger V. b. 93—a folio volume of nine hundred pages. See also Beal, *Index,* 1:2:450.

3. This passage and the others cited from Evan's collection are all attributed to a certain "H. C."

4. Quoted in *The London Stage 1660–1800, part 1, 1660–1700,* ed. William Van Lennep (Carbondale: Southern Illinois University Press, 1965), 100.

5. John Dryden, *Fables Ancient and Modern,* in *The Poems of John Dryden,* vol. 4., ed. James Kinsley (Oxford: Clarendon Press, 1958), 1462–3.

6. See Newman, *Fashioning Femininity,* 129–45.

7. Stephen Orgel, *Impersonations: The Performance of Gender in Shakespeare's England* (New York: Cambridge University Press, 1996), 29.

8. Eric Partridge, *Shakespeare's Bawdy,* 1947 (New York: Routledge, 1990); Frankie Rubinstein, *A Dictionary of Shakespeare's Sexual Puns and their Significance,* 2nd ed. (New York: St. Martin's Press, 1989); Gordon Williams, *A Glossary of Shakespeare's Sexual Language* (New Jersey: Athalone Press, 1997).

9. Lisa Jardine, *Still Harping on Daughters: Women and Drama in the Age of Shakespeare,* 1983, 2nd ed. (New York: Columbia University Press, 1989); Louis Adrian Montrose, "*A Midsummer Night's Dream* and the Shaping Fantasies of Elizabethan Culture: Gender, Power, Form," in Ferguson, *Rewriting the Renaissance,* 65–87; Mullaney, *Place of the Stage* (1988); Valerie Traub, *Desire and Anxiety: Circulations of Desire in Shakespearean Drama* (New York: Routledge, 1992); Jean E. Howard, *The Stage and Social*

Struggle in Early Modern England (New York: Routledge, 1994); Laura Levine, *Men in Women's Clothing: Anti-Theatricality and Effeminization, 1579–1642* (New York: Cambridge University Press, 1994); Zimmerman, *Erotic Politics.*

10. Polemical works attacking the theater in the period 1575–1640 include: John Northbrooke, *A Treatise against Dicing, Dancing, Plays, and Interludes, with other Idle Pastimes* (1577) London: Shakespeare Society Reprint, 1843; Stephen Gosson, *The Schoole of Abuse* and *The Ephemerides of Phialo . . . And a short Apologie of the Schoole of Abuse* (1579), STC 12093; Anthony Munday (?), *A second and third blast of retreat from plays and theatres* (1580); Stephen Gosson, *Plays confuted in five actions* (1582); Philip Stubbes, *The Anatomy of Abuses* (1584); John Rainoldes, *The overthrow of stage-plays* (1599); and William Prynne, *Histriomastix* (1633).

11. Russel Fraser, *The War against Poetry* (Princeton: Princeton University Press, 1970), 28, gives a list of texts attacking Sabbath playing that includes Thomas Brasbridge, *The poore mans jewel . . . a treatise of the pestilence* (1578); John Stockwood, *A sermon preached at Paules Crosse* (1578); Munday, *Second and third blast* (1580); John Field, *Godly Exhortation* (1583); Stubbes, *Anatomie of Abuses* (1583); George Whetstone, *A Touchstone for the Time* (1584); William Rankins, *A Mirror of Monsters* (1587); Nicholas Bownd, *The Doctrine of the Sabbath* (1595); John Norden, *The Progress of Piety* (1596); Lewis Bayly, *The Practice of Piety* (1613); and Francis Quarles, *Divine Fancies* (1632).

12. Northbrooke, 55.

13. See also British Library MS Harl. 7392, fol. 5v.

14. All references to *The Faerie Queene* are to the edition by A. C. Hamilton (New York: Longman, 1977). References to other works by Spenser are to *The Yale Edition of the Shorter Poems of Edmund Spenser*, ed. William A. Orem et al. (New Haven: Yale University Press, 1989).

15. Helgerson, *Forms of Nationhood*, 21–62.

16. Others responded publicly: Thomas Lodge, *A Reply to Stephen Gosson's Schoole of Abuse, in Defense of Poetry, Musick, and Stage Plays* (1579–80), STC 16663.

17. See Margaret Ferguson, *Trials of Desire: Renaissance Defenses of Poetry* (New Haven, CT: Yale University Press, 1983), 146; she quotes Plato's *Republic* 10.607e as a source for Sidney's notion that poetry is essentially seductive.

18. Compare *Ludovico Ariosto's Orlando Furioso. Translated into English Heroical Verse by Sir John Harington (1591)* , ed. Robert McNulty (Oxford: Clarendon Press, 1972), 1–2.

19. Louis Adrian Montrose, "'Eliza, Queene of shepheardes,' and the Pastoral of Power," *English Literary Renaissance* 10 (1980): 153–82.

20. Harington's translation (1591).

21. See also Donne's "Batter my heart."

22. Northbrooke, 39.

23. British Library MS Harl. 7312 (c. 1660–70) has a poem describing a man's wet dream (p. 106).

24. See also William Goddard, *A Satyricall Dialogue . . . between Allexander the great, and that . . . woman hater Diogynes* (Dort, 1616?), an antifeminist satire that "relates . . . three wanton sisters wanton dreames" (sigs. C1v-D1v).

25. Compare *Faerie Queene* 3.2.27–35.

26. Jonson, *The Alchemist* 1.2.105–6.

27. Judith Anderson, "'A Gentle Knight was pricking on the plaine': The Chaucerian Connection," *ELR* 15:2 (1985): 166–74.

28. Compare *Epithalamion* 145–7.

29. S. K. Heninger, Jr., "The Orgoglio Episode in *The Faerie Queene*," *English Literary History* 26 (1959): 171–87; John W. Shroeder, "Spenser's Erotic Drama: The Orgoglio Episode," *English Literary History* 29 (1962): 140–59.

30. "A Courting discourse," Rosenbach MS 1083/17, fols. 150v–152v:

> Now shee noe longer will delay these Joyes
> but with his thighes doth ioyne her naked thighes
> her wanton leggs shee opens wide and stayes
> his with her belly wch she underlayes
> Into the place of Joy, the bowre of blisse
> wch is far sweeter then Arabia is [.]

31. See *Faerie Queene* 4. proem.1.

32. Annabel Patterson, *Censorship and Interpretation: The Conditions of Writing and Reading in Early Modern England* (Madison: University of Wisconsin Press, 1984).

33. Sheila Lambert, "State Control of the Press in Theory and Practice: The Role of the Stationers' Company before 1640," in *Censorship and the Control of Print in England and France 1600–1910*, ed. Robin Myers and Michael Harris (Winchester U.K.: St. Paul's Bibliographies, 1992), 1–32.

34. Andrew Gurr, *Playgoing in Shakespeare's London.* (New York: Cambridge University Press, 1987), 136–41.

35. Lambert, "State Control," 15. She cites 20 March 1595/6 Liber A fo 67v.

36. For the text of the Privy Council order see Edward Arber, *A Transcript of the Registers of the Company of Stationers of London*, 3 vols. (London: 1876), 3:677–8; Boose, "Bishop's Ban," 188–9.

37. Roma Gill, ed., *The Complete Works of Christopher Marlowe, vol. 1,: Translations* (Oxford: Clarendon Press, 1987), 7.

38. No manuscripts of anything like Marlowe's entire sequence are extant. None of the manuscript copies definitively predates the first publication of the *Elegies*. See Beal, *Index*, 1:2:326, 631.

39. There are two significantly different 1590s editions of the volume, but both include the same ten translated elegies, in the same order. See Fredson Bowers's comments in his edition, *The Complete Works of Christopher Marlowe*, 2nd ed., 2 vols. (New York: Cambridge University Press, 1981), and Roma Gill's introduction to *The Complete Works*, vol. 1.

40. Gill, introduction to Marlowe, *Complete Works*, vol. 1, 7.

41. Patricia Parker, "Gender Ideology, Gender Change: The Case of Marie Germain," *Critical Inquiry* 19 (1993): 337–64; Pierre Darmon, *Trial by Impotence: Virility and Marriage in Pre-Revolutionary France* (London: Chatto and Windus, 1985); Laqueur, *Making Sex*, 125–32; Elias, *Civilizing Process*, especially 258–70.

42. 2 *Tamburlaine* 1.4.20–34, 4.1–2.

43. Gosson, *An Apologie*, sig. L4r.

44. Stone, *Family*, 382–4; Belsey, *Subject of Tragedy*, 138–9.

45. *Francis Bacon: A Critical Edition of the Major Works,* ed. Brain Vickers (New York: Oxford, 1996), 62.

46. Phyllis Rackin, *Stages of History: Shakespeare's English Chronicles* (Ithaca, N.Y.: Cornell University Press, 1990), 158–61.

47. The futility of the Bishops' Order may be gauged by the appearance in 1603 of a prose translation of *The Fifteen Joyes of Marriage* (STC 15257.5 sq.), this time entitled *The Batchelar's Banquet* and falsely attributed to Thomas Dekker (STC 6476).

Part II: Prologue

1. Helgerson, *Forms of Nationhood*, 28–34.
2. Roger Ascham, *The Scholemaster* (1570), ed. Edward Arber (London: 1870), 71–86. See George B. Parks, "The First Italianate Englishmen," *Studies in the Renaissance* 8 (1961): 197–216.
3. Ian Archer, *The Pursuit of Stability: Social Relations in Elizabethan London* (New York: Cambridge University Press, 1991), 204.
4. Quoted from an early-seventeenth-century sermon in Paul Slack, *Policy and Poverty in Tudor and Stuart England* (New York: Longman, 1988), 25.
5. R. Finlay, *Population and Metropolis: The Demography of London 1580–1650* (New York: Cambridge University Press, 1981), 67–8, demonstrates that foreigners formed a larger percentage of the population of London in the last third of the sixteenth century than in either the period before 1560 or after 1640. In 1567 4.7 percent of the population were aliens; by 1573 that number had risen to 5.3 percent. In 1593 it had dropped to 3.6 percent and by 1635 to only 1 percent.
6. Thomas Nashe, *The Works of Thomas Nashe*, ed. Ronald B. McKerrow, 5 vols., 1904–10, revised ed. (Oxford: Basil Blackwell, 1958): *Pierce Penniless* 1:186; *Unfortunate Traveller* 2:301; and elsewhere. All references to Nashe are to this edition.
7. David C. McPherson, "Aretino and the Harvey-Nashe Quarrel," *Publications of the Modern Language Association* 84 (1969): 1551–8; Parks, "Italianate."
8. J. R. Hale, *England and the Italian Renaissance: The Growth of Interest in its History and Art* (London: Faber, 1954), 19.
9. Hale, *England*, 20; Parks, "Italianate," 198.
10. Hale, *England*, 30–1; Myron Gilmore, "Myth and Reality in Venetian Political Theory," *Renaissance Venice*, ed. J. R. Hale (Totowa, N.J.: Rowman, 1973), 431–4; William J. Bouwsma, "Venice and the Political Education of Europe," in *A Usable Past: Essays in European Cultural History* (Berkeley: University of California Press, 1990), 266–91.
11. Frances A.Yates, *Astrea: The Imperial Theme in the Sixteenth Century* (Boston: Routledge, 1975), especially 29–87; and Helgerson, *Forms of Nationhood*, 21–104.
12. Parks, "Italianate"; Fritz Gaupp, "The Condottiere John Hawkwood," *History* (March 1939): 305–21, suggests the proverb originally referred to the fourteenth-century condottiere Sir John Hawkwood (308).
13. Parks, "Italianate," 205.
14. See Smith, *Homosexual Desire*, 43–5, on the secularization of the traditionally clerical sin of sodomy in the sixteenth century.
15. On definitions of sodomy see Bray, *Homosexuality*, 14–6; Bredbeck, *Sodomy*, 9–23, 89–96; Goldberg, *Sodometries*, xv-xvi, 19, 120–4. On sodomy laws see Smith, *Homosexual Desire*, 41–53; and Guido Ruggiero, *The Boundaries of Eros: Sex Crime and Sexuality in Renaissance Venice* (New York: Oxford University Press, 1985), 109–45.

Chapter 3

1. As early as 1897 Edward Meyer, *Machiavelli and the Elizabethan Drama* (Weimar: 1897), xi, claimed to have found over five hundred references to Aretino in Elizabethan literature.

2. Raymond Waddington, "A Satirists' Impresa: The Medals of Pietro Aretino," *Renaissance Quarterly* 42(4) (1989): 655–81.

3. Major nineteenth-century works on Aretino include Philarète Chaslès, "L'Aretin" (1834), in *Etudes sur William Shakespeare, Marie Stuarde et l'Aretin* (Paris: Aymot, 1855); Francesco De Sanctis, *Storia della Letteratura Italiana*, 1870–71, in *Opere*, vols. 8 and 9, ed. N. Gallo (Torino: Einaudi, 1958); Giorgio Sinigaglia, *Pietro Aretino* (Rome, 1882); Alessandro Luzio, "La Famiglia di Pietro Aretino," *Giornale Storico della Letteratura Italiana* 4 (1884): 361–84; *Pietro Aretino nei primi suoi anni a Venezia e la corte dei Gonzaga*, 1888 (Bologna: Arnoldo Forni, 1981); and "Pietro Aretino e Nicolò Franco," *Giornale Storico della Letteratura Italiana* 29 (1897): 229–76. For surveys of more recent criticism see Carlo Bertani, *Pietro Aretino e le sue opere* (Sondrio: Emilio Quadrio, 1901); Giuliano Innamorati, *Pietro Aretino: Studie e note critiche* (Firenze: G. D'Anna, 1957); Giovanni Casalegno, "Rassegna aretiniana (1972–1989)," *Lettere italiane* 41 (1989): 425–54. The most extensive recent study of Aretino is Paul Larivaille, *Pietro Aretino fra Rinascimento e Manierismo* (Roma: Bulzoni, 1980). In English see Christopher Cairns, *Pietro Aretino and the Republic of Venice: Researches on Aretino and his circle in Venice 1527–1556*, Biblioteca dell' "Archivum Romanicum," vol. 194 (Firenze: Olschki, 1985), and Luba Freedman, *Titian's Portraits through Aretino's Lens* (University Park: Penn State University Press, 1995). The proceedings of a series of international conferences on Aretino held in Rome, Toronto, and Los Angeles in 1992 are collected in *Pietro Aretino nel cinquecentenario della nascita* (Rome: Salerno, 1995).

4. See, however, Donald A. Beecher, "Aretino's Minimalist Art Goes to England" (2:775–85); Maria Palermo Concolato, "Aretino nella letteratura inglese del Cinquecento" (1:471–8); and Augusto Mastri, "Aretino's Presence in North American Scholarship" (2:897–910), in *Pietro Aretino nel cinquecentenario della nascita* (Rome: Salerno 1995).

5. See, however, *Il Marescalco*, translated by George Bull (in *The Stablemaster: Five Italian Renaissance Comedies* [New York: Penguin, 1978]) and by Leonard G. Sbrocchi and Douglas J. Campbell (Ottawa: Dovehouse Editions, 1986). The sonnets of *I modi* can be found in Bette Talvacchia, *Taking Positions: On the Erotic in Renaissance Culture* (Princeton: Princeton University Press, 1999), as well as in Lynne Lawner, *I Modi: The Sixteen Pleasures* (Evanston, Ill.: Northwestern University Press, 1988). The *Ragionamenti* are available in a 1970 translation by Raymond Rosenthal: *Aretino's Dialogues* (New York: Marsilio, 1994).

6. The earliest biography of Aretino, Gian Maria Mazzuchelli's *Vita di Pietro Aretino* (Padova, 1741), in *Lettere sull'arte di Pietro Aretino*, vol. 3, ed. Fidenzio Pertile and Ettore Camesasca (Milan: Edizioni del milione, 1959), was written two hundred years after his death. Most recently see Cesare Marchi, *L'Aretino* (1980); and Marga Cottino Jones, *Introduzione a Pietro Aretino* (Rome: Laterza, 1993). In English, see Edward Hutton, *Pietro Aretino: The Scourge of Princes* (1922); Thomas Caldecot Chubb, *Aretino: Scourge of Princes* (New York: Reynal and Hitchcock, 1940); and James Cleugh, *The Divine Aretino* (New York: Stein and Day, 1965).

7. See Mazzuchelli, *Vita*, 21–2, 116–24, and Luzio, "Famiglia."

8. *Lettere* 1:62 (fols. 48–49v;152–4;–). See also Mazzuchelli, *Vita*, 22–4, 129–32. No complete edition of Aretino's letters has been published since the six-volume Paris edition of 1609. Francesco Flora's edition, *Tutte le opere di Pietro Aretino: Lettere: il primo e il secondo libro* (Verona: Mondadori, 1960), consists of only the first two volumes. Paolo Procaccioli's edition, *Lettere* (scelte), 2 vols. (Milan: Rizzoli, 1990), provides a selection of letters from all six volumes. Selected letters have been translated into English by George Bull, *Selected Letters* (New York: Penguin, 1976), and by Thomas Caldecot Chubb, *The Letters of Pietro Aretino* (New York: Shoe String Press, 1967). See Flora, 975–82, and Bull,

46–7, for textual information on the letters. Flora numbers all the letters in volumes 1 and 2. All my references to Aretino's letters give the volume number, along with Flora's number (if the citation is from the first two volumes), the folio numbers for the 1609 Paris edition, and the page numbers for Procaccioli's selection and Bull's translation (where applicable)—in that order. Letters written to Aretino are collected in Francesco Marcolini's *Lettere scritte a Pietro Aretino,* Venice, 1551, (Bologna, reprint 1875).

9. Mazzuchelli, *Vita,* 24–5, 132–5; Hutton, *Pietro Aretino,* 19–25.

10. *Cortigiana e altre opere,* ed. Angelo Romano and Giovanni Aquilecchia (Milan: Rizzoli, 1989), 199–269; Mazzuchelli, *Vita,* 131; Bertani, *Pietro Aretino,* 13–4; Hutton, *Pietro Aretino,* 19–20.

11. For a selection of pasquinades see Valerio Marucci and Antonio Marzo, eds., *Pasquinate Romane del cinquecento,* 2 vols. (Rome: Salerno, 1983). See also Vittorio Rossi, ed., *Pasquinate di Pietro Aretino ed anonime per il conclave e l'elezione di Adriano VI* (Palermo: Carlo Clausen, 1891).

12. G. G. Rossi ,*Vita di Giovanni de'Medici* (Milan: 1833), 56.

13. Talvacchia, *Taking Positions,* 3–19; Lawner, *I modi,* 6–19. For Aretino's account of the affair see *Lettere* 1:315 (fols. 258–9;–;156). On the subsequent circulation of the text and engravings see David Foxon, *Libertine Literature in England, 1660–1745* (Hyde Park, N.Y.: University Books, 1965), 19–25.

14. Fiorenzo Bernasconi, "Appunti per l'edizione critica dei 'Sonetti lussuriosi' dell'Aretino," *Italica* 59(4) (1982): 271–83.

15. Paula Findlen, "Humanism, Politics, and Pornography in Renaissance Italy," in Hunt, *Invention,* 49–108; Kendrick, *Secret Museum.*

16. Donne, Satire 4.70. Marston, *Certaine Satyres* 2.139–146. Jonson, *Volpone* 3.4.97–8, 3.7.59–61; *The Alchemist* 2.2.44. Middleton, *A Game at Chess* 2.2.255–6.

17. See especially the engravings accompanying sonnets 3, 8, 11, and 15.

18. Lawner, *I modi,* 39–42; Findlen, "Humanism," 65–73.

19. See sonnets 2, 4, 7, 9, 10, 12, and 16.

20. Talvacchia, *Taking Positions,* 85–100.

21. *Lettere* 1:315 (fols. 258–9;–;156).

22. See especially sonnets 6, 9, 11, and 16.

23. Lawner, *I modi,* 36–9.

24. Lawner, *I modi,* 62, 124.

25. Mazzuchelli, *Vita,* 138; Hutton, *Pietro Aretino,* 73.

26. Talvacchia, *Taking Positions,* 13–9; Luzio, *Primi,* 32–3; Lawner, *I modi,* 6–10.

27. *Lettere* 1:3 (fols. 5v–9v; 111–116;53–9), 1:4 (fols. 9v–10v;117–9;–).

28. The letter is reproduced in Luzio, *Primi,* 62–3.

29. Cairns, *Pietro Aretino,* 13–31.

30. For eighteenth-century developments see Cryle, *Geometry.*

31. Aretino, *Ragionamenti* , 105;43–44. All references to the *Ragionamenti* give the page numbers first for *Ragionamento Dialogo,* ed. Giorgio Barberi Squarotti and Carla Forno (Milan: Rizzoli, 1988), and then for Rosenthal's translation (1994).

32. See Marcus, *Other Victorians,* 275–81.

33. William Thomas, *The Historie of Italie* (London, 1549), fol. 85.

34. *Lettere* 1:20 (fols.2v–4;129–31;65–7. See also Luzio, *Primi,* 19–20; and Mazzuchelli, *Vita,* 36–7.

35. Unfortunately only a fragment of this document has survived: see Hutton, *Pietro Aretino,* 103, and Luzio, *Primi,* 8.

36. *Lettere* 1:2 (fols. 4–5v;108–10;51–3).

37. Charles V: *Lettere* 1:6 (fols. 11–2;119–21;59–61). Clement VII: *Lettere* 1:7 (fols. 12–3v;121–3;61–3).

38. *Lettere* 1:36 (fols. 28–9;138–9;71–2).

39. *Complete Poems*, ed. R. A. Rebholtz (New York: Penguin, 1978), 452–5.

40. Hutton, *Pietro Aretino*, 250. Chubb, *Aretino*, 290.

41. See Pietro Aretino, Sette Salmi della penitentia di David. [in English] Dovai: G. Pinchon, 1635.

42. See Luzio, *Primi*, 47–51, on Aretino's reconciliation with the pope.

43. Rosenthal translates "coda" (tail) here as "prick," but since the term is not similarly gendered in the original I translate as "genitals."

44. Sedgwick, *Epistemology*, 40–4.

45. See also *Ragionamenti*, 431–2;256–7.

46. See Aretino's play *La Cortigiana* (1534) Act 5 Scene 15.

47. See Margaret Rosenthal's epilogue to Rosenthal's translation, *Aretino's Dialogues*, especially 394–9.

48. See also *Ragionamenti*, 419;243.

49. *Lettere* 1:291 (fols. 243–4;323–5;149–51).

50. *Lettere* 4 (fols. 131r–133v;779–80;–), 5 (fols. 731r–73v;881–2;–).

51. Luzio, *Primi*, 41–4; Hutton, *Pietro Aretino*, 131–7.

52. *Lettere* 3 (fols. 144v–145;587–8;–); Marcolini, *Lettere*, 2:347.

53. See *Lettere* 1:258 (fols. 205v–206v;291–3;–) and Marcolini, *Lettere*, 2:347–9, 4:352–8.

54. Charles Hope, "Titian and his Patrons," in *Titian: Prince of Painters* (Venice: Marsilio, 1990), 77–84, especially 77–80.

55. Oliver Logan, *Culture and Society in Venice 1470–1790: The Renaissance and its Heritage* (London: Batsford, 1972), 132–5; Freedman, *Titian's Portraits*.

56. Luzio, *Primi*, 109–11.

57. Mark W. Roskill, *Dolce's "Aretino" and Venetian Art Theory of the Cinquecento* (New York: New York University Press, 1968) includes a bilingual text of this dialogue.

58. *Lettere*, 1:191 (fols. 153v–155;244–7;109) and Marcolini, *Lettere*, 2:334–5. See also Bull, *Selected Letters*, 237–8.

59. Bull, *Selected Letters*, 38. See also Luzio, "Franco," 238.

60. See Procaccioli's introduction to Aretino's *Lettere*, 12–9.

61. Jacob Burckhardt, *The Civilization of the Renaissance in Italy*, 1860, trans. S. G. C. Middlemore (New York: Random House, 1954), 124.

62. *Lettere*, 1:76 (fols. 62v–63;–;–). Luzio, *Primi*, 54.

63. *Lettere*, 2:1 (sigs A2–A3v;335–7;163–5); for Henry's reply, see James Gardener and R. H. Brodie, eds., *Letters and Papers, Foreign and Domestic of the Reign of Henry VIII*, vol. 21, part 2 (London, 1910), no. 399, p. 192; and McPherson, "Aretino," 1552.

64. *Lettere*, 2:240 (fols. 200v–201v;458–60;203–5) and Marcolini, *Lettere*, 3:269–70. See also Bull, *Selected Letters*, 249.

65. Marcolini, *Lettere*, 2.1.40.

66. Paul F. Grendler, *Critics of the Italian World 1530–1560: Anton Francesco Doni, Nicolò Franco, and Ortensio Lando* (Madison: University of Wisconsin Press, 1969), 25–6, 151, 169.

67. Grendler, *Critics*, 4–5.

68. Luzio, "Franco," 231–5.

69. See Giuseppe De Michele, *Nicolò Franco: Biografia con Documenti Inediti. Studia di Letteratura Italiana* II (1915): 61–154; Carlo Simiani, *La Vita e le opere di N. Franco* (Rome, 1894); Grendler, *Critics*, 38–49; Luzio, "Franco," and Hutton, *Pietro Aretino*, 185–93.

70. *Lettere*, 3 (fols. 189r–189v;615–6;-). Luzio, "Franco," 238–43.

71. *Lettere*, 1:338 and 1:337.

72. See Mazzuchelli, *Vita*, 82–3.

73. Luzio, "Franco," 243–5.

74. Ruggiero, *Boundaries*, 109–45.

75. Luzio, "Franco," 246.

76. Fidenzio Pertile, in his annotation of Mazzuchelli's *Vita* (146 n.61), notes that the 1538 *Vita* is now thought to be by Fortunio Spira of Viterbo. This text exists only in one manuscript, which claims that it was printed in Perugia by Bianchino dal Leon on August 17, 1538. (See also Mazzuchelli, *Vita*, 145–7 nn.59, 62). The edition I refer to is in the New York Public Library and claims to be published in Perugia in 1538 but is obviously much later, possibly in London in 1821.

77. Luzio, "Franco," 247–48.

78. See Flora, *Lettere*, 1045–6.

79. Luzio, "Franco," 249–51.

80. Luzio, "Franco," 244.

81. The letter is in the Florentine archives, Cart. med. av. Princ. VI, 824; see Luzio, "Franco," 252; *Primi*, 76–9.

82. The sonnet is reproduced in Mazzuchelli, *Vita*, 30–1.

83. See Luzio, "Franco," 234–5. These figures are for the 1548 edition. I have examined a copy of the *Rime* reprinted privately in London in 1887 (British Library Cup. 402 ks). *Priapea* was supposedly originally published in an octavo edition by Gioan Antonio Guidone in June 1541 (probably in Casale Monferrato); there seem to have been other editions issued in 1546 and 1548 (possibly in Basel). These are all extremely rare. I refer to a 1790 Paris edition of *La Priapea* (British Library 1079 i9) that claims to be based on a copy of the original 1541 edition. This edition consists of 195 sonnets and six letters.

84. Luzio, "Franco," 269–71.

85. See Mazzuchelli, *Vita*, 48–9; Hutton, *Pietro Aretino*, 219–21.

86. *Il terremoto di M. Anton Francesco Doni Contro M. Pietro Aretino* (Lucca: 1861), p. 15. See Grendler, *Critics*, 62.

87. Letter to the Duke of Mantua from Ludovico Nelli, Mantuan ambassador at Venice, dated October 29, 1556, translated and quoted in Hutton, *Pietro Aretino*, 230.

88. J. A. Symonds, *The Renaissance in Italy: Italian Literature*, part 2 (New York: Scribners, 1898), 372. Marchi, *L'Aretino*, 278, attributes the verses to Paolo Giovio. Several slightly different versions of the rhyme exist, including one in Latin. It was not actually used as Aretino's epitaph. The English version is quoted from MS Dyce (44) 25 F 39, fol. 68r. See also Bodleian MSS Rawl. Poet. 160, fol. 182v, and Rawl. D. 1110, fol. 81v, as well as MSS Folger V. a. 180 (in Italian, p. 51) and V. a. 381 (p. 14).

89. A pamphlet by Gabriel Peignot, *De Pierre Aretin. Notice sur sa fortune, sur les moyens qui la lui ont procurée, et sur l'emploi qu'il en fait* (Paris, 1836—a limited edition of one hundred copies) claims Aretino had a lifetime income of 70,000 scudi/écus (3) and gives the following estimate of Aretino's annual income in the 1530s (p. 3).

200 écus	Charles V
100	marquis de Guant
100	duc d'Urbin (later doubled)
100	de Louis Gritti
100	Prince de Salerne
120	Baldovino del Monte

in 1541 he claimed to have 800 écus annual pension.

in 1542—1800 écus (my translation)

90. On Aretino's income see Hutton, *Pietro Aretino*, 228. On Jonson's pension see David Riggs, *Ben Jonson: A Life* (Cambridge: Harvard University Press, 1989), 220.

91. See Findlen, "Humanism," 55–6.

92. Summarized in Gardener and Brodie, *Letters and Papers*, vol. 17, no. 841, 462.

93. Italics added. A copy of Thomas's letter, with the text of *Peregrine*, survives in British Library MS Harl. 353, fol. 36r. See also Concolato, "Aretino," 474–5.

94. Spenser, *Yale Shorter Poems*, 34. The gloss may have been written by Richard's brother Gabriel.

95. Harry R. Hoppe, "John Wolfe, Printer and Publisher, 1579–1601," *Library*, 4th series, 14 (1933): 241–87. See also, Joseph Loewenstein, "For a History of Literary Property: John Wolfe's Reformation," *English Literary Renaissance* 18 (1988): 389–412. Clifford Chalmers Huffman, *Elizabethan Impressions: John Wolfe and his Press*, AMS Studies in the Renaissance 21 (New York: AMS Press, 1988). On Wolfe and Machiavelli see Peter S. Donaldson, *Machiavelli and the Mystery of State* (New York: Cambridge University Press, 1988), 86–110. A complete list of books known to have been printed or published by Wolfe appears in Huffman, 133–61.

96. This text contains the two volumes of dialogues that comprise the *Sei giornate*. Wolfe's *La terza et ultima parte de Ragionamenti* (1588) is a collection of other works by Aretino—*Ragionamenti de le corti* and *Le Carte parlanti*—written in dialogue form. See Denis B. Woodfield, *Surreptitious Printing in England 1550–1640* (New York: Bibliographical Society of America, 1973), 109–13, for a detailed description of all Wolfe's volumes of Aretino.

97. On *Ser Agresto* see Frantz, *Festum*, 34–8. The dialogue makes many bawdy plays on the word "fico" (fig), and while Wolfe's edition clearly ascribes it to Caro, John Marston, for one, took it to be a text of Aretino, complaining in *The Scourge of Villanie* 3.79–80 that "greasie *Aretine* / For his ranke *Fico*, is surnam'd diuine."

98. Peter Blayney has suggested to me that, while Wolfe's editions of Aretino were published under false imprints, they may not have circulated surreptitiously *in England*; the false imprints may have been designed to fool not the English authorities but the Continental ones. See also Woodfield, *Surreptitious Printing*, 9.

99. Woodfield, *Surreptitious Printing*, 24–33.

100. Woodfield, *Surreptitious Printing*, 187–8.

101. Hoppe, "John Wolfe," 244.

102. Woodfield, *Surreptitious Printing*, 113–7, 153–8.

103. *Ragionamenti* (1584), sig. A2v.

104. Woodfield, *Surreptitious Printing*, 25.

105. J. L. Lievsay, *The Englishman's Italian Books: 1550–1700* (Philadelphia: University of Pennsylvania Press, 1969), 50.

106. Neil Rhodes, *Elizabethan Grotesque* (London: Routledge and Kegan Paul, 1980), 185 n. 9. This copy is presently in the Bodleian, shelfmark Douce A. 642. Jonson's signature and his motto "Tamquam explorator" appear on sig. A1r. Both have been crossed out but are still legible. There are no other marginalia in the volume.

107. Lievsay, *Italian Books*, 38.

108. John M. Lothian, "Shakespeare's Knowledge of Aretino's Plays," *MLR* 25 (1930): 415–24.

109. Lievsay, *Italian Books*, 34, 58. See also Findlen, "Humanism," 56–7, and Roger

Thompson, *Unfit for Modest Ears: A Study of Pornographic, Obscene and Bawdy Works Written or Published in England in the Second Half of the Seventeenth Century* (London: Macmillan, 1979), chapter 12.

110. See McKerrow's edition of Nashe, 4:279.

111. For a more detailed discussion of *La Cazzaria*, see Ian Frederick Moulton, "Bawdy Politic: Renaissance Republicanism and the Discourse of Pricks," in *Opening the Borders: Early Modern Studies and the New Inclusivity*, ed. Peter Herman (Newark: University of Delaware Press, 1999) 225–42. On the Academic movement in sixteenth-century Italy see Michele Maylender, *Storie delle accademie d'Italia*, 5 vols.(Bologna: Lincino Capelli, 1926), and also Richard Samuels, "Benedetto Varchi, the *Accademia degli Infiammati*, and the Origins of the Italian Academic Movement," *Renaissance Quarterly* 29 (1976): 599–633. See also Antonio Vignali, *La Cazzaria: Dialogue Priapique de L'Arsiccio Intronato* (Paris: Liseux, 1882), viii–xii; as well as Frantz, *Festum*, 9–42; and Findlen, "Humanism," 86–94. All references to *La Cazzaria* are to the edition of Nino Borsellino and Pasquale Stoppelli (Rome: Edizioni dell'Elefante, 1984).

112. See Frantz, *Festum*, 39.

113. See Vignali, *Cazzaria*, (1882), xi–xii, on the relation of *La Cazzaria* to *Il libro del perchè*. A copy of *The Why and The Wherefore* (London, 1765) is in the British Library, PC 27 b10.

114. Lorenzo Veniero, *Le Trente et un de la Zaffetta* (Paris: Liseux, 1883), 6–7. This volume contains the Italian text and a facing-page French translation. All my references to Veniero's poems are to page numbers.

115. Lorenzo Veniero, *La Puttana errante* (Paris: Liseux, 1883), 2.

116. Veniero, *Puttana*, xx–xxi; Aretino, *Ragionamenti* , 82;20.

117. On Veniero's poem, see Gabriele Erasmi, "*La Puttana errante*: Parodia epica ispirata all'Aretino," *Pietro Aretino nel cinquecentenario della nascita*, 2:875–95.

118. Veniero, *Puttana*, xi.

119. *Ragionamenti* (183,440–2;86–7, 265–7); *Puttana errante, overo dialogo di Madalena e Giulia* (Amersterdam: Elzevier, 1660. sig. C4v).

120. Foxon, *Libertine Literature*, 30.

121. Foxon, *Libertine Literature*, 28.

122. The earliest copy of the prose *Puttana errante* I have examined dates from 1660: the dialogue, entitled *La Puttana errante, overo dialogo di Madalena e Giulia* (*The Wandering Whore, or the Dialogue of Madalena and Julia*) is published with the 1660 Elzevier edition of Aretino's *Ragionamenti* (an edition loosely based on Wolfe's 1584 London edition). The dialogue is fifty-four pages long and is appended to the end of the volume, following the *Ragionamenti di Zoppino* and the *Commento di Ser Agresto*. A recent edition of a manuscript copy of the text (MS 677, Bibliotèque de Condé, Chantilly), entitled *Il piacevol ragionamento de l'Aretino: Dialogo di Giulia e di Maddalena*, ed. Claudio Galderisi (Rome: Salerno, 1987), attributes the dialogue to Aretino and gives the date as 1531, but the attribution is so tenuous that even Giovanni Aquilecchia, who writes the volume's introduction, does not give it his full support (7–15). The Chantilly manuscript itself is dated around 1550–72. The prose *Puttana errante* may be closely based on the *Dialoghi doi di Ginevra, e Rosana* (also falsely attributed to Aretino), said to have been originally published in 1584 but not known to exist in any copies printed before 1649—see Foxon, *Libertine Literature*, 28–29. All references are to the Claudio Galderisi edition.

123. Compare *Ragionamenti*, 309–15;165–72.

124. Williams, *Hard Core*, 120–52.

125. British Library, shelfmark C. 108. a. 28.
126. British Library, shelfmark 1213 k. 21 (2).
127. British Library, shelfmark 1080. h. 21.
128. From the French edition, sig. A3r.
129. From the French edition, sig. A2v.
130. From the French edition, sig. A2r.

Chapter 4

1. Aretino's name also gave rise to a verb: "to Aretinize." Gabriel Harvey, for example, accused Nashe of "Aretinizing" (*Pierce's Supererogation,* sig. F4v;2.92). All references to Harvey's published texts give both signature references and the corresponding page numbers from Grosart's 1884 edition. If no other text is indicated, the reference is to *Pierces Supererogation.* See also Boose, "Bishop's Ban," 195.

2. John Eliot, *Ortho-epia Gallica* (London, 1593), sig. D2v; Richard Harvey, *A Theological Discourse of the Lamb of God* (London, 1590), sig. N4v.

3. Katherine Usher Henderson and Barbara F. McManus, eds., *Half Humankind: Contexts and Texts of the Controversy about Women in England, 1540–1640* (Chicago: University of Illinois Press, 1985), 75–6; and Belsey, *Subject of Tragedy,* 149–60; Stone, *Family,* 136–7; Peter Laslett, *The World We Have Lost,* 2nd ed., (London: Methuen, 1971), 8, 20, 78; Newman, *Fashioning Femininity,* 129–44.

4. Stone, *Family,* 258. Stephen Orgel, "Nobody's Perfect: Or, Why Did the English Stage Take Boys for Men?" *South Atlantic Quarterly* 88 (1989): 7–29; *Impersonations,* 10–30.

5. Stone, *Family,* 318. Laslett, *World,* gives the average age of marriage as twenty-two for women and twenty-five for men (84–6). Orgel, "Nobody's Perfect," 18, gives the corresponding ages of consent as twelve and fourteen, respectively. See also Ilana Krausman Ben-Amos, *Adolescence and Youth in Early Modern England* (New Haven: Yale University Press, 1994), 200–5. See also Guido Ruggiero, "Marriage, Love, Sex, and Renaissance Civic Morality," in *Sexuality and Gender in Early Modern Europe: Institutions, Texts, Images,* ed. James Grantham Turner (New York: Cambridge University Press, 1993), 10–30.

6. *The Anatomy of Absurdity* (1:48). See also Hibbard, *Thomas Nashe,* 16. For Nashe's own attacks on the "italianate," see *Preface to Menaphon,* 3:322; *Pierce Penniless,* 1:186; *The Unfortunate Traveller,* 2:301.

7. On the Bishops' Order, see chapter 2. n. 36.

8. McKerrow's edition of Nashe, 5:65–110; McPherson, "Aretino."

9. G. R. Hibbard, *Thomas Nashe: A Critical Introduction* (Cambridge: Harvard University Press, 1962), 186.

10. Virginia F. Stern, *Gabriel Harvey: His Life, Marginalia, and Library* (New York: Oxford University Press, 1979), 200.

11. Stern, *Gabriel Harvey,* 174. Anne Prescott has brought to my attention a reference by Harvey to "Nanna dell'Aretino" in the margin of his copy of Thomas, *Historie of Italie,* sig. V1r.

12. Harvey, *Three Proper Wittie Familiar Letters,* sig. F1v;1:93. McPherson, "Aretino," 1552–3.

13. Stephen S. Hilliard, *The Singularity of Thomas Nashe* (Lincoln: University of Nebraska Press, 1986), 182. Stern, *Gabriel Harvey,* 46.

14. McPherson, "Aretino," 1553.

15. Stern, 119, 121, 122. See also *Gabriel Harvey's Marginalia*, ed. C. G. Moore Smith (Stratford, 1913), 156.

16. Hibbard, *Thomas Nashe*, 51–5, argues that Nashe may have anonymously written a large amount of verse for patrons, who then claimed it as their own. Given Nashe's comments in *Have With you to Saffron-Walden* about prostituting his pen in "amorous Villanellas" (3:30–1), these poems might have included erotic works.

17. See Hibbard, *Thomas Nashe*, 57–9.

18. Frantz, *Festum*, and McPherson, "Aretino." Rhodes, *Elizabethan Grotesque*, 70–1, argues that the Nashian character of Ingenioso in the Parnassus Plays is clearly described in terms reminiscent of Aretino.

19. See McKerrow, 5:129–33.

20. McPherson, "Aretino," 1553.

21. Nashe, *Strange Newes*, "Letter to the Gentlemen Readers," 1:259–60; for the passage alluded to see Aretino, *Tutte le commedie*, 118.

22. Burckhardt, *Civilization*, 124.

23. Deborah Kuller Shuger, *The Renaissance Bible: Scholarship, Sacrifice, and Subjectivity* (Berkeley: University of California Press, 1994), 117–127.

24. The word "fantasticoes" (Q1) is often emended by editors. The Folio reads "phantacies."

25. *A Cup of News: The Life of Thomas Nashe* (Boston: Routledge, 1984), 7–9.

26. Gosson, *Schoole*, sig. A7v. See chapter 2. Plato, *Republic*, 398–9, 410–1. "Soft spearfighter" is quoted by Plato from the *Iliad* 17.588.

27. Nashe, "Choice of Valentines," line 126. All my references to "Choice of Valentines" give line numbers from Mckerrow's edition of the Petyt text of the poem (3:397–416).

28. See Patricia Parker, "Gender Ideology, Gender Change," 344–5.

29. Bodleian MS Ashmole 38, p. 145. The manuscript is dated to the early seventeenth century. Other copies of the poem are found in MS Folger V. a. 275, p. 124 (c. 1626–36) and Rosenbach MS 1083/15, fol. 130v (c. 1630). This poem was eventually printed in *Wit and Drollery* (1661), p. 235.

30. Stubbes, *Anatomy*, sig. O5r. See also Gosson, *Schoole*, especially sigs. A2r–A3r.

31. See Harvey, Pierce's *Supererogation*, sigs. F4r;F6r;2:91–5, and John Davies of Hereford, "Paper's Complaint" in *The Scourge of Folly* (London, 1611).

32. In the text of "Choice of Valentines" in *The Unfortunate Traveler and Other Works* (New York, 1972), editor J. B. Steane takes line 20 ("she was shifted to an upper-ground") as evidence that the brothel may be located in Upper Ground Street, " a street of low repute in Southwark."

33. "Valueless": Hibbard, *Thomas Nashe*, 57. "Pornographic": Frantz, *Festum*, 191.

34. On the poem's resemblance to the works of Ovid, Chaucer, and Spenser, see Hibbard, *Thomas Nashe*, 57–9, and Bruce Thomas Boehrer, "Behn's 'Disappointment' and Nashe's 'Choise of Valentines': Pornographic Poetry and the Influence of Anxiety," *Essays in Literature* 16 (1989):172–87, especially 174–7. On "Choice of Valentines" as parody see M. L. Srapleton, "Nashe and the Poetics of Obscenity: *The Choise of Valentines*," *Classical and Modern Literature* 12 (1991): 29–48, especially 35–7; on the poem as pastoral, see Jonathan V. Crewe, *Unredeemed Rhetoric: Thomas Nashe and Scandal of Authorship* (Baltimore: Johns Hopkins University Press, 1982,), 48–51.

35. See Karras, "Regulation," and Archer, *Pursuit*, 211–5, 231–2, 249–51.

36. Karras, "Regulation," 423.

37. Donne, Elegy 2, line 53. Marston, *Scourge of Villanie*, 3.30–2, 8.128–9, 131–2.

38. Crewe, *Unredeemed Rhetoric*, 49.

39. On the pastoral, see Thomas G. Rosenmeyer, *The Green Cabinet: Theocritus and the European Pastoral Lyric* (Berkeley: University of California Press, 1969).

40. Archer, *Pursuit*, 211–5; John L. McMullan, *The Canting Crew: London's Criminal Underworld 1500–1700* (New Brunswick: Rutgers University Press, 1984), 117–42.

41. *Odyssey* 8.266–343; *Metamorphoses* 4.167–89.

42. Davies, "Papers's Complaint," lines 65, 69–70: Paper laments that "Pierse-Pennilesse . . . made [me] *Dildo* (dampned *Dildo*) beare, / Till good-mens hate did me in pieces teare."

43. *The Faerie Queene* 2.12; *Orlando Furioso, cantos* 6–7; *Gerusalemme Liberata, cantos* 14–5.

44. MS Dyce (44) 25 F 39, fol. 82v.

45. Parker, "Gender Ideology," 345. She cites Pierre Darmon's *Trial by Impotence: Virility and Marriage in Pre-Revolutionary France* (London: Chatto and Windus, 1985).

46. Maclean, *Renaissanace Notion*, 30.

47. Ambroise Paré, *Of Monsters and Marvels*, ed. and trans. Janis L. Pallister (Chicago: University of Chicago Press, 1982), 32; Maclean, *Renaissance Notion*, 31.

48. Besides Parker, "Gender Ideology," see Maclean, *Renaissance Notion*, 39; Stephen Greenblatt, *Shakespearean Negotiations: The Circulation of Social Energy in Renaissance England* (Berkeley: University of California Press, 1988), 81; and Laqueur, *Making Sex*, 128–30.

49. Paré, *Monsters*, 31–3; Montaigne, *Works*, 69, 869–70; *Oeuvres completes*, ed. Albert Thibaudet and Maurice Rat (Paris: 1948), 96, 1118–9.

50. Laqueur, *Making Sex*, 125. He quotes from Castiglione's *Book of the Courtier*, trans. Sir Thomas Hoby, 1561 (London: Dent, 1966), 39.

51. Parker, "Gender Ideology," 363; Montrose, "Shaping Fantasies."

52. Stapleton, "Nashe"; Boehrer, "Behn's 'Disappointment'."

53. Beal, *Index*, 1:2:144, ascribes this poem to Sir John Harington, although it is not included in Norman Egbert McClure's edition of *The Letters and Epigrams of Sir John Harington, 1930* (Philadelphia 1977).

54. Traub, *Desire*, 139–41.

55. William Gouge, *Of Domestical Duties* (London, 1622), sigs. P6v, N3r.

56. Laqueur, *Making Sex*, 49–52.

57. See Maclean, *Renaissance Notion*, 38.

58. Crewe, *Unredeemed Rhetoric*, 65–6.

59. *A Pleasant Comodie, Wherein is merrily shewen: The Wit of a Woman* (London, 1604), STC 25868, sig. C1v.

60. Rosenbach MS 1083/15 (pp. 15–6). The poem is entitled "A medecine for the greene sicknes."

61. Aretino's *Ragionamenti* (84;22) describes dildos as "the glass fruits made in Murano in the shape of cocks." In Florio's 1598 Italian-English dictionary *A World of Wordes, pastinaca muranese* (a murano parsnip) is translated as "a dildoe of glass" and *pinco* as "a prick, a pillicock, a pintle, a dildoe."

62. Nanna, not having a ready source of warm water, urinates in her dildo to warm it up: *Ragionamenti*, 92;30.

63. Louis Crompton, "The Myth of Lesbian Impunity: Capital Laws from 1270 to 1791," in *The Gay Past*, ed. Salvatore Licata and Robert Peterson (Binghampton, N.Y.: Harrington Park, 1986), 11; Traub, *Desire*, 109, and "Lesbian Desire."

64. For a similar metaphor see Catullus 58.

65. Maclean, *Renaissance Notion*, 36.

66. See also Marston's *Antonio and Mellida* (c. 1601) in which the two boy pages are named Dildo and Cazzo.

67. *Epicoene* 1.1.12–17, 2.2.94–110.

68. *"The Choise of Valentines, or the Merrie Ballad of Nashe his Dildo* (London, 1899), vii.

69. Nicholl, *Life of Thomas Nashe*, 87, 135.

70. Beal, *Index*, 1:356. H. R. Woudhuysen's edition of the poem in *The Penguin Book of Renaissance Verse, 1509–1659* (New York: Penguin 1992) does not collate the Folger or Rosenbach manuscripts.

71. On this manuscript see chapter 1, 57–64.

72. Robert C. Evans, "The Folger Text of Thomas Nashe's 'Choise of Valentines,'" *Papers of the Bibliographical Society of America* 87(3) (1993): 363–74.

73. British Biographical Archive: fiche 896, plate 366.

74. Roland Barthes, *The Pleasure of the Text*, Trans. Richard Miller (New York: Hillard Wang, 1975), 10.

75. The manuscript was edited and annotated in Sanderson, "Manuscript Collection."

76. The relevant lines are Rosenbach, 120–31; Petyt 269–74, 279, 280–5.

77. On this manuscript, see chapter 1, 57–64.

78. Maclean, *Renaissance Notion*, 28–46. Laqueur, *Making Sex*, 27–8.

79. Laqueur, *Making Sex*, 129–30; Parker, "Gender Ideology," 348.

Chapter 5

1. Richard Helgerson, *Self-Crowned Laureates: Spenser, Jonson, Milton, and the Literary System* (Berkeley: University of California Press, 1983); George E. Rowe, *Distinguishing Jonson: Imitation, Rivalry, and the Direction of a Dramatic Career* (Lincoln: University of Nebraska Press, 1988); James Shapiro, *Rival Playwrights: Marlowe, Jonson, Shakespeare* (New York: Columbia University Press, 1991); also Riggs's biography *Ben Jonson* (1989).

2. Shapiro, *Rival Playwrights*, 39–73, 133–62; Jonas Barish, *The Antitheatrical Prejudice* (Berkeley: University of California Press, 1981), 132–54.

3. All references to the works of Ben Jonson are to the edition of C. H. Herford and Percy and Evelyn Simpson, 11 vols. (Oxford: Clarendon Press, 1925–52), unless otherwise indicated.

4. Wall, *Imprint of Gender*, 182–5.

5. Gosson, *School*, sigs. A2v–A3r.

6. Lewalski, *Writing Women*, 108–10; Riggs, *Ben Jonson*, 125, 152, 162.

7. Riggs, *Ben Jonson*, 152.

8. Laqueur, *Making Sex*, 63–113; Orgel, *Impersonations*, 10–30.

9. Herford and Simpson, 8:372.

10. Orgel, *Impersonations*, 17. 30. Gurr, *Playgoing*, 49–69; Howard, *Stage*, 73–92.

11. Gurr, *Playgoing*, app. 2, items 1, 3, 6, 8, 15, 17, 19, etc. (205–51).

12. Mullaney, *Place of the Stage*.

13. William Drummond's assertion that Jonson "doth understand neither French nor Italian" (Conversations 1.134) has long been judged erroneous, or at best an overstatement—see Oscar James Campbell, "The Relation of *Epieoene* to Aretinos *Il Marescaleo*," *Publications of the Modern Language Association* 46 (1931): 752–62. 762 n.39, and Herford and Simpson, 1.156.

14. Anne Barton, *Ben Jonson, Dramatist* (New York: Cambridge University Press, 1984), 68; Shapiro, *Rival Playwrights*, 56–7.

15. Riggs, *Ben Jonson*, 67.

16. Herford and Simpson, 3:419–21; Barish, *Antitheatrical*, 136–7.

17. Arber, *Transcript*, 3:159.

18. Paster, *Body Embarrassed*, 1–22.

19. Barton *Ben Jonson*, 69–71.

20. Traub, *Desire*, 55–9; Stallybrass, "Patriarchal," 123–7, and Paster, *Body Embarrassed*, 23–63.

21. Paster, *Body Embarrassed*, 23–63.

22. Ibid., 34–9; Peter Stallybrass and Allon White, *The Politics and Poetics of Transgression* (Ithaca, N.Y.: Cornell University Press, 1986), 44–59.

23. Mario DiGangi, *The Homoerotics of Early Modern Drama* (New York: Cambridge University Press, 1997), 67–72.

24. Peter Stallybrass, "Patriarchal Territories: *The Body Enclosed*," in Ferguson, *Rewriting*, 123–42.

25. Dekker, *Satiromastix*, "To the World," line 7. All references to the works of Dekker are to *The Dramatic Works of Thomas Dekker*, ed. Fredson Bowers (Cambridge: Cambridge University Press, 1953).

26. Barton, *Ben Jonson*, 58–91; Riggs, *Ben Jonson*, 72–85.

27. John Marston, *The Plays of John Marston*, ed., H. Harvey Wood (London: Oliver and Boyd, 1938), 2.290.

28. Elias, *Civilizing Process*, 68–104.

29. Mario Praz, *The Flaming Heart: Essays on Crawshaw, Machiavelli, and Other Studies in the Relations between Italian and English Literature from Chaucer to T. S. Eliot* (New York: Doubleday, 1958), 181–5.

30. David C. McPherson, *Shakespeare, Jonson, and the Myth of Venice* (Newark: University of Delaware Press, 1990).

31. Don E. Wayne, *Penshurst: The Semiotics of Place and the Poetics of History* (Madison: University of Wisconsin Press, 1984), 172.

32. Fernand Braudel, *The Mediterranean and the Mediterranean World in the Age of Philip II*, 2 vols., trans. Sian Reynolds (New York: Harper and Row, 1972), 387–94, 450; Frederic C. Lane, *Venice: A Maritime Republic* (Baltimore: Johns Hopkins University Press, 1973), 309–18, 361–4; Robert C. Davis, *Shipbuilders of the Venetian Arsenal: Workers and Workplace in the Preindustrial City* (Baltimore: Johns Hopkins University Press, 1991), 80–81.

33. Margaret F. Rosenthal, *The Honest Courtesan : Veronica Franco, Citizen and Writer in Sixteenth-century Venice* (Chicago : University of Chicago Press, 1992); Paul Larivaille, *La Vie quotidienne des courtisanes en Italie au temps de la Renaissance* (Paris: Hachette, 1975).

34. Mullaney, *Place of the Stage*, 23; Gurr, *Playgoing*, 49–79; and Howard, *Stage*, 73–92.

35. L. C. Knights, *Drama and Society in the Age of Jonson*, 1937 (New York: Norton, 1968), 200.

36. Peggy Knapp, "Ben Jonson and the Publike Riot," in *Staging the Renaissance: Reinterpretations of Elizabethan and Jacobean Drama*, ed. David Scott and Peter Stallybrass (New York: Routledge, 1991), 164–80.

37. Mario DiGangi, "Asses and Wits: The Homoerotics of Mastery in Satiric Comedy," *English Literary Renaissance* 25 (1995), 188–92.

38. John Julius Norwich, *A History of Venice* (New York: Vintage, 1989), 492–4.

39. Zimmerman, *Erotic Politics.*

40. Goldberg, *Sodometries*, 118–21; Orgel, *Impersonations*, 29–30.

41. See Campbell, "Relation."

42. All references to Aretino's plays are to *Tutti le comedie*, ed. G. B. De Sanctis (Milan: GUM, 1968), and cite act and scene numbers. All English translations of passages quoted from the plays are my own.

43. *La cortigiana* (1534) 2.6, 5.15.

44. Sbrocchi and Campbell, *The Marescalco*, 21–22.

45. All references to *Epicoene* are to the New Mermaid edition edited by R. V. Holdsworth (New York: Norton, 1979).

46. DiGangi, "Asses," 184–6.

47. Holdsworth, *Epicoene*, xxviii–xxix.

48. Holdsworth, *Epicoene*, 4 n.2.

49. Goddard, *Mastif Whelpe*, Satire 5, sigs. G4v–H1r.

50. Howard, *Stage*, 101–5.

51. It is not surprising that Jonson used some of the same antifeminist rhetoric to refer to both. Both the Collegiate Mavis in *Epicoene* (5.2.34–5) and Mistress Bulstrode in "Court Pucell" (32) are said to have faces "none can like by candle-light."

52. Holdsworth's edition of *Epicoene* 4 n.8. See also *1 Henry I V*, 3.3.123–8.

53. Dauphine's declaration to Truewit that he is earnestly in love "with all the Collegiates" (4.1.129) is clearly part of his plot to humiliate and manipulate the Collegiates rather than an expression of deep passion.

54. Riggs, *Ben Jonson*, 321–53.

55. Holdsworth, *Epicoene*, xxi.

56. Michèle Cohen, *Fashioning Masculinity: National Identity and Language in the Eighteenth Century* (New York: Routledge, 1996).

57. Porter and Hall, *Facts of Life*, 91–105; Hitchcock, *English Sexualities*, 54–7.

58. Porter and Hall, *Facts of Life*, 65–90; Hitchcock, *English Sexualities*, 42–57.

59. Bray, *Homosexuality*, 81–118; Hitchcock, *English Sexualities*, 58–75.

60. Laqueur, *Making Sex*, 149–92 ; Hitchcock, *English Sexualities*, 48–9.

Bibliography

Anderson, Judith. "'A Gentle Knight was pricking on the plaine': The Chaucerian Connection." *English Literary Renaissance* 15:2 (1985): 166–74.

Arber, Edward. *A Transcript of the Registers of the Company of Stationers of London.* 3 vols. London, 1876.

Archer, Ian. *The Pursuit of Stability: Social Relations in Elizabethan London.* New York: Cambridge University Press, 1991.

Aretino, Pietro. *Aretino's Dialogues.* 1971. Trans. Raymond Rosenthal. New York: Marsilio, 1994.

———. *Cappriciosi & Piacevoli Ragionamenti.* Cosmopoli (Amsterdam?): Elzevier, 1660.

———. *Colloquio de las Damas.* Seville, 1548.

———. *Cortigiana e altre opere.* Ed. Angelo Romano and Giovanni Aquilecchia. Milan: Rizzoli, 1989.

———. (?) *Dialoghi doi di Ginevra, e Rosana.* Bengodi (?) 1584 (?) 1649 (?)

———. *The Crafty Whore . . . or a dialogue between two subtle bawds.* London, 1658. Wing C6780.

———. *Lettere* (scelte). 2 vols. Ed. Paolo Procaccioli. Milan: Rizzoli, 1990.

———. *Lettere di M. Pietro Aretino.* 6 vols. Paris, 1608–09.

———. *The Letters of Pietro Aretino.* Ed. Thomas Caldecot Chubb. New York: Shoe String Press, 1967.

———. *The Marescalco (Il Marescalco).* Trans. and ed. Leonard G. Sbrocchi and Douglas J. Campbell. Carleton Renaissance Plays in Translation. Ottawa: Dovehouse Editions, 1986.

———. *Le Miroir des Courtisans.* Lyon, 1580.

———. *Pornodidascalus seu Colloquium Muliebre.* Frankfurt, 1623.

———. *Il piacevol ragionamento de l'Aretino: Dialogo di Giuliae di Maddalena* Ed. Claudio Golderisi. Rome: Salerno, 1987.

———. *La prima (seconda) parte de Ragionamenti.* London, 1584. STC 19911.5

———. *Quatro commedie del divino Pietro Aretino.* London, 1588. STC 19911.

———. *Ragionamento Dialogo.* Ed. Giorgio Barberi Squarotti and Carla Forno. Milan: Rizzoli, 1988.

———. *The Ragionamenti or Dialogues of the Divine Pietro Aretino.* Paris: Lisieux, 1889.

———. *Selected Letters.* Trans. and ed. George Bull. Harmondsworth: Penguin, 1976.

———. *Sette Salme della penitentia di David* [in English]. Douai: G. Pinchon, 1635. STC 19910.5

———. *The Stablemaster*. In *Five Italian Renaissance Comedies*. Ed. Bruce Penman. Trans. George Bull. New York: Penguin, 1978. 113–91.

———. *La terza et ultima parte de Ragionamenti*. London: 1589. STC 19913.

———. *Tutte le comedie*. Ed. G. B. DeSanctis. Milan: GUM, 1968.

———. *Tutte le opere di Pietro Aretino: Lettere: il primo e il secondo libro*. Ed. Francesco Flora. Verona: Mondadori, 1960.

———. *The Works of Aretino*. 1926. 2 vols. Trans. and ed. Samuel Putnam. New York: Covici-Friede, 1931.

Ariès, Philippe, and Georges Duby, eds. *A History of Private Life. Vol. 3. Passions of the Renaissance*. Ed. Roger Chartier. Trans. Arthur Goldhammer. Cambridge: Harvard University Press, 1989.

Ariosto, Ludovico. *Ludovico Ariosto's Orlando Furioso. Translated into English Heroical Verse by Sir John Harington (1591)*. Ed. Robert McNulty. Oxford: Clarendon Press, 1972.

Ascham, Roger. *The Scholemaster*. 1570. Ed. Edward Arber. London: 1870.

Assiter, Alison, and Carol Avedon, eds. *Bad Girls and Dirty Pictures: The Challenge to Reclaim Feminism*. Boulder, Colo.: Pluto Press, 1993.

Athenaeus. *The Deipnosophists*. 7 vols. Loeb Classics. Trans. and ed. Charles Burton Gulick. Cambridge: Harvard University Press, 1980.

Attorney General's Commission on Pornography. *Final Report*. 2 vols. Washington, D.C.: 1986.

Bacon, Francis. *Francis Bacon: A Critical Edition of the Major Works*. Ed. Brian Vickers. New York: Oxford University Press, 1996.

Bakhtin, Mikhail. *Rabelais and His World*. 1968. Trans. Hélène Iswolsky. Bloomington: Indiana University Press, 1984.

Barbach, Lonnie, ed. *Erotic Interludes: Tales Told by Women*. New York: Harper, 1986.

———. *Pleasures: Women Write Erotica*. New York: Harper, 1984.

Barish, Jonas. *The Antitheatrical Prejudice*. Berkeley: University of California Press, 1981.

Barker, Francis. *The Tremulous Private Body: Essays on Subjection*. New York: Methuen, 1984.

Barnfield, Richard. *Cynthia*. London, 1595. STC 1483.

Barthes, Roland. *The Pleasure of the Text*. Trans. Richard Miller. New York: Hill and Wang, 1975.

Barton, Anne. *Ben Jonson, Dramatist*. New York: Cambridge University Press, 1984.

The Batchelars Banquet. London, 1603. STC 6476.

Bate, Jonathan. *Shakespeare and Ovid*. Oxford: Clarendon Press, 1993.

Bayly, Lewis. *The Practice of Piety*. London, 1613. STC 1601.5 sq.

Beal, Peter, ed. *Index of English Literary Manuscripts. Vol. 1, 1450–1625. Vol. 2, 1625–1700*. New York: Bowker, 1980–93.

Beecher, Donald A. "Aretino's Minimalist Art Goes to England." In *Pietro Aretino nel cinquecentenario della nascita*, 2 vols. (Rome: Salerno, 1995), 2:775–85.

Belsey, Catherine. *The Subject of Tragedy: Identity and DiVerence in Renaissance Drama*. New York: Methuen, 1985.

Ben-Amos, Ilana Krausman. *Adolescence and Youth in Early Modern England*. New Haven: Yale University Press, 1994.

Bernasconi, Fiorenzo. "Appunti per l'edizione critica dei 'Sonetti lussuriosi' dell' Aretino." *Italica* 59(4) (1982): 271–83.

Berni, Francesco (?). *Vita di: Pietro Aretino.* Perugia, 1538 (?), London, 1821. (?)

Bertani, Carlo. *Pietro Aretino e le sue opere.* Sondrio: Emilio Quadrio, 1901.

Blayney, Peter W. M. *The Bookshops in Paul's Cross Churchyard.* London: Bibliographic Society of Great Britain, 1990.

Boehrer, Bruce Thomas. "Behn's 'Disappointment' and Nashe's 'Choise of Valentines': Pornographic Poetry and the InXuence of Anxiety." *Essays in Literature* 16 (1989): 172–87.

Boose, Lynda E. "The Bishop's Ban, Elizabethan Pornography, and the Sexualization of the Jacobean Stage." In *Enclosure Acts in Early Modern England,* ed. Richard Burt and Robert Archer (Ithaca, N.Y.: Cornell University Press, 1994), 185–200.

Bouwsma, William J. "Venice and the Political Education of Europe." In *A Usable Past: Essays in European Cultural History* (Berkeley: University of California Press, 1990), 266–91.

Bownd, Nicholas. *The Doctrine of the Sabbath.* London, 1595. STC 3436.

Brasbridge, Thomas. *The poore mans jewel . . . a treatise of the pestilence.* London, 1578. STC 3548.5.

Braudel, Fernand. *The Mediterranean and the Mediterranean World in the Age of Philip II.* Trans. Sian Reynolds. 2 vols. New York: Harper and Row, 1972.

Bray, Alan. *Homosexuality in Renaissance England.* London: Gay Men's Press, 1982.

———. "Homosexuality and the Signs of Male Friendship in Elizabethan England." In *Queering the Renaissance,* ed. Jonathan Goldberg (Durham, N.C.: Duke University Press), 40–61.

Bredbeck, Gregory W. *Sodomy and Interpretation: Marlowe to Milton.* Ithaca, N.Y.: Cornell University Press, 1991.

Brice, Thomas. "Against Filthy Writing / And Such Like Delighting." London, 1562. STC 3725.

Bright, Susie, and Joani Blank, eds. *Herotica 2: A Collection of Women's Erotic Fiction.* New York: Plume, 1992.

Brown, Horatio. *The Venetian Printing Press.* London, 1891.

Burckhardt, Jacob. *The Civilization of the Renaissance in Italy.* 1860. Trans. S. G. C. Middlemore. New York: Random House, 1954.

Cairns, Christopher. *Pietro Aretino and the Republic of Venice: Researches on Aretino and his Circle in Venice: 1527–1556.* Biblioteca dell' "Archivum Romanicum." Vol. 194. Firenze: Olschki, 1985.

Califia, Pat. *Public Sex: The Culture of Radical Sex.* San Francisco: Cleis Press, 1994.

Campbell, Oscar James. "The Relation of *Epicoene* to Aretino's *Il Marescalco.*" *Publications of the Modern Language Association* 46 (1931): 752–62.

Carol, Avedon. *Nudes, Prudes, and Attitudes: Pornography and Censorship.* Cheltenham, U.K.: New Clarion, 1994.

Casalegno, Giovanni. "Rassegna aretiniana (1972–1989)." *Lettere italiane* 41 (1989): 425–54.

Castiglione, Baldassar. *The Book of the Courtier.* 1561. Trans. Thomas Hoby. Everyman's Library. London: Dent, 1966.

Catullus. *The Poems of Gaius Valerius Catullus.* Ed. and trans. Francis Ware Cornish. 2nd ed. Revised by G. P. Goold. Loeb Classics. Cambridge: Harvard University Press, 1988.

Chartier, Roger. "The Practical Impact of Writing." In *A History of Private Life,* ed. Phillipe Ariès and George Duby, vol. 3, *Passions of the Renaissance,* ed. Roger Charter and trans. Arthur Goldhammer (Cambridge:Harvard University Press, 1989), 111–59.

Chaslès, Philarète. *Etudes sur William Shakespeare, Marie Stuarde et l'Aretin*. Paris: Aymot, 1855.

Chaucer, Geoffrey. *The Complete Poetry and Prose of Geo Vrey Chaucer*. Ed. John H. Fisher. New York: Holt, Rinehart and Winston, 1977.

Chubb, Thomas Caldecot. *Aretino: Scourge of Princes*. New York: Reynal and Hitchcock, 1940.

Cleugh, James. *The Divine Aretino*. New York: Stein and Day, 1965.

Clifford, Lady Anne. *The Diaries of Lady Anne Clifford*. Ed. D. J. H. Clifford. Wolfeboro Falls, N.H.: Alan Sutton, 1990.

Cohen, Michèle. *Fashioning Masculinity: National Identity and Language in the Eighteenth Century*. New York: Routledge, 1996.

Cole, Susan G. *Power Surge: Sex, Violence, and Pornography*. Toronto: Second Story Press, 1995.

Colley, John Scott. "'Opinion' and the Reader in John Marston's *The Metamorphosis of Pigmalions Image*." *English Literary Renaissance* 3 (1973): 221–231.

Concolato, Maria Palermo. "Aretino nella letteratura inglese del Cinquecento." In *Pietro Aretino nel cinquecentenario della nascita*, 2 vols. (Rome: Salerno, 1995), 1:471–78.

Cooper, Glenda. Article in *The Independent*, June 21, 1997.

Coryate, Thomas. *Coryats Crudities*. London, 1611. STC 5808.

Crewe, Jonathan V. *Unredeemed Rhetoric: Thomas Nashe and the Scandal of Authorship*. Baltimore: Johns Hopkins University Press, 1982.

Crompton, Louis. "The Myth of Lesbian Impunity: Capital Laws from 1270 to 1791." In *The Gay Past*, ed. Salvatore Licata and Robert Peterson (Binghampton, N.Y.: Harrington Park, 1986).

Crum, Margaret, ed. *First-Line Index of Manuscript Poetry in the Bodleian Library Oxford*. 2 vols. New York: Oxford University Press, 1969.

Cryle, Peter. *Geometry in the Boudoir: Configurations of French Erotic Narrative*. Ithaca, N.Y.: Cornell University Press, 1994.

Darmon, Pierre. *Trial by Impotence: Virility and Marriage in Pre-Revolutionary France*. London: Chatto and Windus, 1985.

Davies, Herbert John. "Dr. Anthony Scattergood's Commonplace Book." *Cornhill Magazine*, NS liv (January–June 1923): 679–91.

Davies, John, of Hereford. *The Scourge of Folly*. London, 1611.

Davies, Sir John, and Christopher Marlowe. *Epigrammes and Elegies*. London(?), 1599. STC 6350, 6350.5.

Davis, Robert C. *Shipbuilders of the Venetian Arsenal: Workers and Workplace in the Preindustrial City*. Baltimore: Johns Hopkins University Press, 1991.

DeJean, Joan. "The Politics of Pornography: *L'Ecole des Filles*." In *The Invention of Pornography: Obscenity and the Origins of Modernity*, ed. Lynn Hunt (New York: Zone Books, 1993), 109–24.

Dekker, Thomas. *The Dramatic Works of Thomas Dekker*. Ed. Fredson Bowers. Cambridge, U.K.: Cambridge University Press, 1953.

De Michele, Giuseppe. "Nicolò Franco: BiograWa con Documenti Inediti." *Studia di Letteratura Italiana* 11 (1915): 61–154.

De Sanctis, Francesco. *La Storia della Letteratura Italiana*. 1870–71. *Opere*. Vols. 8 and 9. Ed. N. Gallo. Torino: Einaudi, 1958.

DiGangi, Mario. "Asses and Wits: The Homoerotics of Mastery in Satiric Comedy," *English Literary Renaissance* 25 (1995): 179–208.

————. *The Homoerotics of Early Modern Drama.* New York: Cambridge University Press, 1997.

Donaldson, Peter S. *Machiavelli and the Mystery of State.* New York: Cambridge University Press, 1988.

Doni, Anton Francesco. *Il terremoto di M. Anton Francesco Doni contro M. Pietro Aretino.* Lucca: 1861.

Donne, John. *The Complete English Poems.* Ed. A. J. Smith. New York: Penguin, 1971.

————. *Ignatius His Conclave.* Ed. T. S. Healy. Oxford: Clarendon Press, 1969.

————. *Poems of John Donne.* 2 vols. Ed. J. C. Grierson. London: Oxford University Press, 1912.

Dryden, John. *Fables Ancient and Modern. The Poems of John Dryden.* Vol. 4. Ed. James Kinsley. Oxford: Clarendon Press, 1958.

Dubrow, Heather. *Echoes of Desire: English Petrarchism and its Counterdiscourses.* Ithaca, N.Y.: Cornell University Press, 1995.

Dworkin, Andrea. *Pornography: Men Possessing Women.* New York: Putnam, 1979.

————. Dworkin, Andrea, and Catherine MacKinnon. *In Harm's Way: The Pornography Civil Rights Hearings.* Cambridge: Harvard University Press, 1998.

Elias, Norbert. *The Civilizing Process.* 1978, 1982. Trans. Edmund Jephcott. Cambridge, Mass.: Blackwell, 1994.

Eliot, John. *Ortho-epia Gallica.* London, 1593. STC 7574.

England's Helicon. London: 1600. STC 3191.

England's Parnassus. London: 1600. STC 379.

Erasmi, Gabriele. "*La Puttana errante*: Parodia epica ispirata all'Aretino." In *Pietro Aretino nel cinquecentenario della nascita*, 2 vols. (Rome: Salerno, 1995), 2:875–95.

Erens, Patricia, ed. *Issues in Feminist Film Criticism.* Bloomington: Indiana University Press, 1990.

Evans, Robert C. "The Folger Text of Thomas Nashe's 'Choise of Valentines.'" *Papers of the Bibliographical Society of America* 87(3) (1993): 363–74.

Ferguson, Margaret W., et al., eds. *Rewriting the Renaissance: The Discourses of Sexual Difference in Early Modern Europe.* Chicago: University of Chicago Press, 1986.

————. *Trials of Desire: Renaissance Defenses of Poetry.* New Haven: Yale University Press, 1983.

Field, John. *Godly Exhortation.* London, 1583.

Finlay, R. *Population and Metropolis: The Demography of London 1580–1650.* New York: Cambridge University Press, 1981.

Findlen, Paula. "Humanism, Politics, and Pornography in Renaissance Italy." In *The Invention of Pornography: Obscenity and the Origins of Modernity*, ed. Lynn Hunt (New York: Zone Books, (1993), 49–108.

Finkelpearl, Philip J. *John Marston of the Middle Temple: An Elizabethan Dramatist in His Social Setting.* Cambridge: Harvard University Press, 1969.

Fletcher, John, and Philip Massinger. *The Custom of the Country.* In *The Dramatic Works in the Beaumont and Fletcher Canon*, ed. Fredson Bowers, vol. 8 (New York: Cambridge University Press, 1992), 633–737.

Florio, John. *Queen Anna's New World of Words.* London, 1611. STC 11099.

————. *A Worlde of Wordes.* London, 1598. STC 11098.

Foisil, Madeleine. "The Literature of Intimacy." In *A History of Private Life*, ed. Phillipe Ariès and George Duby, vol. 3, *Passions of the Renaissance*, ed. Roger Charter and trans. Arthur Golhammer (Cambridge: Harvard University Press, 1989), 327–61.

Foucault, Michel. *The History of Sexuality. Vol. 1. An Introduction.* Trans. Robert Hurley. New York: Vintage, 1980.

Fox, Adam. "Popular Verses and their Readership in the Early Seventeenth Century." In *The Practice and Representation of Reading in England,* ed. James Raven, Helen Small, and Naomi Tadmore (New York: Cambridge University Press), 125–37.

Foxon, David. *Libertine Literature in England, 1660–1745.* Hyde Park, N.Y.: University Books, 1965.

Franco, Nicolò. *Della rime di M. Nicolò France contro Pietro Aretino et de la Priapea.* London: Privately printed, 1887.

———. *Il Vendemmiatore poemetto in ottava rima di Luigi Tansillo; e la Priapia, sonnetti lussoriosi-satirici di Niccolo Franco.* Peking (Paris), 1790?

Frantz, David O. *Festum Voluptatis: A Study of Renaissance Erotica.* Columbus: Ohio University Press, 1989.

Fraser, Russel. *The War against Poetry.* Princeton: Princeton University Press, 1970.

Freedman, Luba. *Titian's Portraits through Aretino's Lens.* University Park: Penn State University Press, 1995.

Friday, Nancy. *My Secret Garden.* New York: Simon and Schuster, 1973.

———. *Women on Top.* New York: Random House, 1991.

Gaines, Jane. "Women and Representation: Can We Enjoy Alternative Pleasure?" In *Issues in Feminist Film Criticism,* ed. Patricia Erens (Bloomington: Indiana University Press), 75–92.

Galdarsi, Claudio, ed. *Il piacevol ragionamento de l'Aretino: Dialogo di Giulia e di Maddalena.* Rome: Salerno, 1987.

Gardener, James, and R. H. Brodie, eds. *Letters and Papers, Foreign and Domestic of the Reign of Henry VIII.* London, 1910.

Gaupp, Fritz. "The Condottiere John Hawkwood." *History* (March 1939): 305–21.

Gibson, Pamela Church, and Roma Gibson, eds. *Dirty Looks: Women, Pornography, Power.* London: British Film Institute, 1993.

Gilmore, Myron. "Myth and Reality in Venetian Political Theory." *In Renaissance Venice,* ed. J. R. Hale (Totowa, N.J.: Rowman, 1973), 431–44.

Goddard, William. *A Mastiff Whelp.* Dort(?) Netherlands 1598(?). STC 11928.

———. *A Neaste of Waspes.* Dort, Netherlands 1615. STC 11929.

———. *A Satirycall Dialogue . . . between Allexander the great, and that . . . woman hater Diogynes.* Dort(?), Netherlands 1616(?). STC 11930.

Goldberg, Jonathan, ed. *Queering the Renaissance.* Durham, N.C.: Duke University Press, 1994.

———. *Sodometries: Renaissance Texts, Modern Sexualities.* Stanford: Stanford University Press, 1992.

———. *Writing Matter: From the Hands of the English Renaissance.* Stanford: Stanford University Press, 1990.

Gosson, Stephen. *The Ephemerides of Phialo . . . And a short Apologie of the Schoole of Abuse.* London, 1579. STC 12093.

———. *Plays confuted in five actions.* London, 1582. STC 12095.

———. *The Schoole of Abuse.* London, 1579. STC 12097 sq.

Gouge, William. *Of Domestical Duties.* London, 1622. STC 12119.

Goulemot, Jean Marie. *Ces livres qu'on ne lit que d'une main: lecture et lecteurs de livres pornographiques au XVIII siecle.* Aix-en-Provence, France: Alinea, 1991.

———. "Literary Practices: Publicizing the Private." In *A History of Private Life,* ed. Phillipe Ariès and Georges Duby, vol. 3, *Passions of the Renaissance,* ed. Roger

Charter and trans. Arthur Goldhammer (Cambridge: Harvard University Press, 1989), 363–95.

Green, Lady, and Jaymes Easton, eds. *Kinky Crafts: 99 Do-It-Yourself S/M Toys for the Kinky Handyperson.* 2nd ed. San Francisco: Greenery Press, 1998.

Greenblatt, Stephen. *Shakespearian Negotiations: The Circulation of Social Energy in Renaissance England.* Berkeley: University of California Press, 1988.

Greene, Thomas M. "Ben Jonson and the Centered Self." *Studies in English Literature* 10 (1970): 325–48.

Grendler, Paul F. *Critics of the Italian World 1530–1560: Anton Francesco Doni, Nicolò Franco, and Ortensio Lando.* Madison: University of Wisconsin Press, 1969.

Gubar, Susan, and Joan Hoff, eds. *For Adult Users Only: The Dilemma of Violent Pornography.* Bloomington: Indiana University Press, 1989.

Gurr, Andrew. *Playgoing in Shakespeare's London.* New York: Cambridge University Press, 1987.

Hadfield, Andrew. *Literature, Politics, and National Identity: Reformation to Renaissance.* New York: Cambridge University Press, 1994.

Haec Vir: or the Womanish Man. London, 1620. STC 12599

Hale, J. R. *England and the Italian Renaissance: The Growth of Interest in its History and Art.* London: Faber, 1954.

A Handful of Pleasant Delights. London: 1566. STC 21105.5.

Harington, Sir John. *The Letters and Epigrams of Sir John Harington.* Ed. Norman Egbert McClure. 1930 Philadelphia: University of Pennsylvania Press, 1977.

Harvey, Gabriel. *Gabriel Harvey's Marginalia.* Ed. C. G. Moore Smith. Stratford, 1913.

———. *Gratulationum Valdinensium.* London, 1578. STC 12901.

———. *A New Letter of Notable Contents.* London, 1593. STC 12902.

———. *Pierces Supererogation.* London, 1593. STC 12903.

———. *Three Proper Wittie and Familiar Letters.* London, 1580. STC 23095.

———. *The Works of Gabriel Harvey.* Ed. Alexander B. Grosart. 3 vols. London, 1884.

Harvey, Richard. *A Theological Discourse of the Lamb of God.* London, 1590. STC 12915.

Helgerson, Richard. *Forms of Nationhood: The Elizabethan Writing of England.* Chicago: University of Chicago Press, 1994.

———. *Self-Crowned Laureates: Spenser, Jonson, Milton, and the Literary System.* Berkeley: University of California Press, 1983.

Henderson, Katherine Usher, and Barbara F. McManus, eds. *Half Humankind: Contexts and Texts of the Controversy about Women in England, 1540–1640.* Chicago: University of Illinois Press, 1985.

Heninger, S. K., Jr. "The Orgoglio Episode in *The Faerie Queene.*" *English Literary History* 26 (1959): 171–87.

Hibbard, G. R. *Thomas Nashe: A Critical Introduction.* Cambridge: Harvard University Press, 1962.

Hilliard, Stephen S. *The Singularity of Thomas Nashe.* Lincoln: University of Nebraska Press, 1986.

Hitchcock, Tim. *English Sexualities, 1700–1800.* New York: St. Martin's Press, 1997.

Hobbs, Mary. *Early Seventeenth Century Verse Miscellany Manuscripts.* Brookfield, Vt.: Scolar Press, 1992.

Homer. *The Iliad of Homer.* Trans. Richmond Lattimore. Chicago: University of Chicago Press, 1974.

————. *The Odyssey of Homer*. Trans. Richmond Lattimore. New York: Harper and Row, 1967

Hope, Charles. "Titian and His Patrons." In *Titian: Prince of Painters* (Venice: Marsilio, 1990), 77–84.

Hoppe, Harry R. "John Wolfe, Printer and Publisher, 1579–1601." *Library*, 4th series 14 (1933): 241–87.

Horwitz, Tony. "Balkan Death Trip: Scenes from a Futile War." *Harper's*, March 1993. 35–45.

Howard, Jean E. *The Stage and Social Struggle in Early Modern England*. New York: Routledge, 1994.

Huffman, Clifford Chalmers. *Elizabethan Impressions: John Wolfe and his Press*. AMS Studies in the Renaissance 21. New York: AMS Press, 1988.

Hulse, Clark. *Metamorphic Verse: The Elizabethan Minor Epic*. Princeton: Princeton University Press, 1981.

Hunt, Lynn, ed. *The Invention of Pornography: Obscenity and the Origins of Modernity, 1500–1800*. New York: Zone Books, 1993.

Hunter, Ian, et al., ed. *On Pornography: Literature, Sexuality, and Obscenity Law*. New York: St. Martin's Press, 1993.

Hutton, Edward. *Pietro Aretino: The Scourge of Princes*. London: Constable, 1922.

Innamorati, Giuliano. *Pietro Aretino: Studi e noti critiche*. Firenze: G. D'Anna, 1957.

Itzin, Catherine, ed. *Pornography: Women, Violence, and Civil Liberties*. New York: Oxford University Press, 1992.

Jardine, Lisa. *Still Harping on Daughters: Women and Drama in the Age of Shakespeare*. 1983. 2nd ed. New York: Columbia University Press, 1989.

Jones, Marga Cottino. *Introduzione a Pietro Aretino*. Rome: Laterza, 1993.

Jonson, Ben. *Ben Jonson*. Eds. C. H. Herford and Percy and Evelyn Simpson. 11 vols. Oxford: Clarendon Press, 1925–52.

————. *The Complete Masques*. Ed. Stephen Orgel. New Haven: Yale University Press, 1969.

————. *Epicoene, or the Silent Woman*. Ed. R. V. Holdsworth. New Mermaids. New York: Norton, 1979.

Kappeler, Suzanne. *The Pornography of Representation*. Minneapolis: University of Minnesota Press, 1986.

Karras, Ruth Mazo. "The Regulation of Brothels in Later Medieval England." *Signs* 14 (1989): 399–433.

Kastan, David Scott, and Peter Stallybrass, eds. *Staging the Renaissance: Reinterpretations of Elizabethan and Jacobean Drama*. New York: Routledge, 1991.

Keach, William. *Elizabethan Erotic Narratives: Irony and Pathos in the Ovidian Poetry of Shakespeare, Marlowe, and Their Contemporaries*. New Brunswick: Rutgers University Press, 1977.

Kendrick, Walter. *The Secret Museum: Pornography in Modern Culture*. 1987. Berkeley: University of California Press, 1996.

Kernan, Alvin. *The Cankered Muse: Satire of the English Renaissance*. New Haven: Yale University Press, 1959.

Klawitter, George. *The Enigmatic Narrator: The Voicing of Same-sex Love in the Poetry of John Donne*. New York: P. Lang, 1994.

Knapp, Peggy. "Ben Jonson and the Publike Riot." In *Staging the Renaissance: Reinterpretations of Elizabethan and Jacobean Drama*, ed. David Scott Kastan and Peter Stallybrass (New York: Routledge), 164–80.

Knights, L. C. *Drama and Society in the Age of Jonson*. 1937. New York: Norton, 1968.

La Belle, Jeniijoy. "A True Love's Knot: The Letters of Constance Fowler and the Poems of Herbert Aston." *Journal of English and German Philology*. 79 (1980): 13–31.

———. "The Huntington Aston Manuscript." *Book Collector* 29 (1980): 542–67.

Lamb, Mary Ellen. *Gender and Authorship in the Sidney Circle*. Madison: University of Wisconsin Press, 1990.

Lambert, Sheila. "State Control of the Press in Theory and Practice: The Role of the Stationers' Company before 1640." In *Censorship and the Control of Print in England and France 1600–1910*, ed. Robin Myers and Michael Harris (Winchester: U.K. St. Paul's Bibliographies, 1992), 1–32.

Lane, Frederic C. *Venice: A Maritime Republic*. Baltimore: Johns Hopkins University Press, 1973.

Laqueur, Thomas. *Making Sex: Body and Gender from the Greeks to Freud*. Cambridge: Harvard University Press, 1990.

Larivaille, Paul. *Pietro Aretino fra Rinascimento e Manierismo*. Rome: Bulzoni, 1980.

———. *La Vie quotidienne des courtisanes en Italie au temps de la Renaissance*. Paris: Hachette, 1975.

Laslett, Peter. *The World We Have Lost*. 2nd ed. London: Methuen, 1971.

Lawner, Lynne ed. *I Modi: The Sixteen Pleasures: An Erotic Album of the Italian Renaissance*. Trans. Lynne Lawner. Evanson, Ill.: Northwestern University Press, 1988.

Levine, Laura. *Men in Women's Clothing: Anti-Theatricality and EVeminization, 1579–1642*. New York: Cambridge University Press, 1986.

Lewalski, Barbara KieVer. *Writing Women in Jacobean England*. Cambridge: Harvard University Press, 1993.

Il Libro del perchè, La pastorella del Marino, La novella del'Angelo Gabriello, e la puttana errante di Pietro Aretino. Peking (Paris), 1872(?).

Lichfield, Richard(?). *The Trimming of Thomas Nashe*. London, 1597. STC 12906.

Lievsay, J. L. *The Englishman's Italian Books: 1550–1700*. Philadelphia: University of Pennsylvania Press, 1969.

Lodge, Thomas. *A Margarite of America*. London, 1596. STC 16660.

———. *A Reply to Stephen Gosson's Schoole of Abuse, in Defense of Poetry, Musick, and Stage Plays*. London, 1579–80. STC 16663.

———. *Wit's Misery and the World's Madness*. London, 1596. STC 16677.

Loewenstein, Joseph. "For a History of Literary Property: John Wolfe's Reformation." *English Literary Renaissance* 18 (1988): 389–412.

Logan, Oliver. *Culture and Society in Venice 1470–1790: The Renaissance and Its Heritage*. London: Batsford, 1972.

Lothian, John M. "Shakespeare's Knowledge of Aretino's Plays." *Modern Language Review* 25 (1930): 415–24.

Love, Harold. *Scribal Publication in Seventeenth Century England*. Oxford: Clarendon Press, 1993.

Lucian. "Dialogues of the Courtesans." In *Lucian*, vol. 8, trans. M. D. Macleod, Loeb Classics, (Cambridge: Harvard University Press, 1929), 355–467.

Luzio, Alessandro. "La Famiglia di Pietro Aretino." *Giornale Storico della Letteratura Italiana*, 4 (1884): 361–84.

———. "Pietro Aretino e Nicolò Franco." *Giornale Storico della Letteratura Italiana* 29 (1897): 229–76.

———. *Pietro Aretino nei primi suoi anni a Venezia e la corte dei Gonzaga*. 1888. Bologna: Arnoldo Forni, 1981.

Maclean, Ian. *The Renaissance Notion of a Woman: A Study of the Fortunes of Scholasticism and Medical Science in European Intellectual Life*. New York: Cambridge University Press, 1980.

Marchi, Cesare. *L'Aretino*. Milan: Rizzoli, 1980.

Marcolini, Francesco ed. *Lettere scritte a Pietro Aretino*. Venice, 1551. Scelta di curiosita letterare 132. 4 vols. Bologna, 1875.

Marcus, Stephen. *The Other Victorians: A Study of Sexuality and Pornography in Mid–Nineteenth Century England*. New York: Basic Books, 1964.

Marlowe, Christopher. *The Complete Works of Christopher Marlowe*. Ed. Fredson Bowers. 2nd ed. 2 vols New York: Cambridge University Press, 1981.

——. *The Complete Works of Christopher Marlowe. Vol. 1. Translations*. Ed. Roma Gill. Oxford: Clarendon Press, 1987.

Marotti, Arthur F. *John Donne, Coterie Poet*. Madison: University of Wisconsin Press, 1986.

——. *Manuscript, Print, and the English Renaissance Lyric*. Ithaca, N.Y.: Cornell University Press, 1995.

Marston, John. *Antonio and Mellida*. Ed. G. K. Hunter. Lincoln NB: University of Nebraska Press, 1965.

——. *The Metamorphosis of Pigmalions Image. And Certaine Satyres*. London, 1598. STC 17482.

——. *The Plays of John Marston*. Ed. H. Harvey Wood. 3 vols. London: Oliver and Boyd, 1938.

——. *The Poems of John Marston*. Ed. Arnold Davenport. Liverpool: Liverpool University Press, 1960.

Marucchi, Valerio, and Antonio Marzo, eds. *Pasquinate Romane del cinquecento*. 2 vols. Rome: Salerno, 1983.

Masten, Jeffrey. *Textual Intercourse: Collaboration, Authorship, and Sexualities in Renaissance Drama*. New York: Cambridge University Press, 1997.

Mastri, Augusto. "Aretino's Presence in North American Scholarship." In *Pietro Aretino nel cinquecentenario della nascita*, 2 vols. (Rome: Salerno, 1995), 2:897–910.

Maylander, Michele. *Storie delle accademie d'Italia*. 5 vols. Bologna: Lincino Capelli, 1926.

Mazzucchelli, Gian Maria. *La vita di Pietro Aretino*. Padova: 1741. In *Lettere sull'arte di Pietro Aretino*, vol. 3, ed. Fidenzio Pertile and Ettore Camesasca (Milan: Edizioni del milione, 1959).

McElroy, Wendy. *XXX: A Woman's Right to Pornography*. New York: St. Martin's, Press, 1995.

McMullan, John L. *The Canting Crew: London's Criminal Underworld 1500–1700*. New Brunswick: Rutgers University Press, 1984.

McNair, Brian. *Mediated Sex: Pornography and Postmodern Culture*. New York: Arnold, 1996.

McPherson, David C. "Aretino and the Harvey-Nashe Quarrel." *PMLA* 84 (1969): 1551–8.

——. "Ben Jonson's Library and Marginalia: An Annotated Catalogue." *Studies in Philolgy* 71 (1974): X 1–106.

——. *Shakespeare, Jonson, and the Myth of Venice*. Newark: University of Delaware Press, 1990.

Meyer, Edward. *Machiavelli and the Elizabethan Drama*. Weimar, 1897.

Middleton, Thomas. *Five Plays*. Ed. Bryan Loughrey and Neil Taylor. New York: Penguin, 1988.

———. *The Works of Thomas Middleton*. Ed. A. H. Bullen. 8 vols. London: John C. Nimmo, 1885.

Minnery, Tom, ed. *Pornography: A Human Tragedy*. Wheaton, Ill.: Tyndale House, 1986.

Montaigne, Michel de. *The Complete Works of Montaigne: Essays, Travel Journal, Letters*. Ed. and trans. Donald M. Frame. Stanford: Stanford University Press, 1948.

———. *Oeuvres complètes*. Ed. Albert Thibaudet and Maurice Rat. Paris, Gallimard, 1948.

Montrose, Louis Adrian. "*A Midsummer Night's Dream* and the Shaping Fantasies of Elizabethan Culture: Gender, Power, Form." *In Rewriting the Renaissance: The Discourses of Sexual Difference in Early Modern Europe*, ed. Margaret W. Ferguson et al. (Chicago: University of Chicago Press, 1986), 65–87.

———. "'Eliza, Queene of shepheardes,' and the Pastoral of Power." *English Literary Renaissance* 10 (1980): 153–82.

Morgan, Robin. "Theory and Practice." In *Take Back the Night: Women on Pornography*, ed. Laura Lederer (New York: Bantam, 1980), 134–40.

Moss, Ann. *Printed Commonplace-Books and the Structuring of Renaissance Thought*. Oxford: Clarendon Press, 1996

Moulton, Ian Frederick. "Bawdy Politic: Renaissance Republicanism and the Discourse of Pricks." In *Opening the Borders: Inclusivity and Early Modern Studies, Essays in Honor of James V. Mirollo*, ed. Peter C. Herman (Newark: University of Delaware Press, 1999), 225–42.

Mullaney, Steven. *The Place of the Stage: License, Play, and Power in Renaissance England*. Chicago: University of Chicago Press, 1988.

Munday, Anthony (?). *A second and third blast of retreat from plays and theatres*. London, 1580. STC 21677.

Nashe, Thomas. *The Choise of Valentines, or the Merrie Ballad of Nashe his Dildo*. Ed. John S. Farmer. London, 1899.

———. *The Unfortunate Traveller and Other Works*. 1971. Ed. J. B. Steane. New York: Penguin, 1987.

———. *The Works of Thomas Nashe*. 1904–10. Ed. Ronald B. McKerrow. 5 vols. Revised ed. Oxford: Basil Blackwell, 1958.

Newman, Karen. *Fashioning Femininity and English Renaissance Drama*. Chicago: University of Chicago Press, 1991.

Nicholl, Charles. *A Cup of News: The Life of Thomas Nashe*. Boston: Routledge, 1984.

———. *The Reckoning: The Murder of Chrstopher Marlowe*. London: J. Cape, 1992.

Norden, John. *The Progress of Piety*. London, 1596. STC 18633.

Northbrooke, John. *A Treatise against Dicing, Dancing, Plays, and Interludes, with other Idle Pastimes* 1577. London, Shakespearce Society Reprint, 1843 STC 18670.

Norwich, John Julius. *A History of Venice*. New York: Vintage, 1989.

Orgel, Stephen. *Impersonations: The Performance of Gender in Shakespeare's England*. New York: Cambridge University Press, 1996.

———. "Nobody's Perfect: Or, Why Did the English Stage Take Boys for Men?" *South Atlantic Quarterly* 88 (1989): 7–29.

Osanka, Franklin Mark, and Sara Lee Johann, eds. *Sourcebook on Pornography*. New York: Lexington Books, 1989.

Ovid. *Heroides and Amores.* Ed. and trans. Grant Showeman. Loeb Classics. Cambridge: Harvard University Press, 1977.

————. *Metamorphoses.* 2 vols. Ed. and trans. Frank Justus Miller. Loeb Classics. Cambridge: Harvard University Press, 1984.

The Paradise of Dainty Devices. London: 1576. STC 7516.

Paré, Ambroise. *Of Monsters and Marvels.* Ed. and trans. Janis L. Pallister. Chicago: University of Chicago Press, 1982.

Parker, Patricia. "Gender Ideology, Gender Change: The Case of Marie Germain." *Critical Inquiry* 19 (1993): 337–64.

Parks, George B. "The First Italianate Englishmen." *Studies in the Renaissance* 8 (1961): 197–216.

Parnassus Biceps. Ed. Abraham Wright. London, 1656. Wing W3686.

Partridge, Eric. *Shakespeare's Bawdy.* 1947. New York: Routledge, 1990.

Paster, Gail Kern. *The Body Embarrassed: Drama and the Disciplines of Shame in Early Modern England.* Ithaca, N.Y.: Cornell University Press, 1993.

Patterson, Annabel. *Censorship and Interpretation: The Conditions of Writing and Reading in Early Modern England.* Madison: University of Wisconsin Press, 1984.

Pausanias. *Description of Greece, with an English translation by W. H. S. Jones.* 5 vols. Cambridge: Harvard University Press, 1959–61.

Peignot, Gabriel. *De Pierre Aretin. Notice sur sa fortune, sur les moyens qui la lui ont procurée, et sur l'emploi qu'il en fait.* Paris, 1836.

Pepys, Samuel. *The Diary of Samuel Pepys.* Vol. 9. 1668–69. Ed. Robert Latham et al. Berkeley: University of California Press, 1976.

Pietro Aretino nel cinquecentenario della nascita. 2 vols. Rome: Salerno, 1995.

The Phoenix Nest. London: 1593. STC 21516.

Plato. *Republic.* Trans. Paul Shorey. In *The Collected Dialogues of Plato,* ed. Edith Hamilton and Huntington Cairns (Princeton: Princeton University Press, 1985), 575–844.

A Pleasant Comodie, Wherein is merrily shewen: The Wit of a Woman. London, 1604. STC 25868.

A Poetical Rhapsody. London: 1602. STC 6373.

Porter, Roy, and Lesley Hall. *The Facts of Life: The Creation of Sexual Knowledge in Britain, 1650–1950.* New Haven: Yale University Press, 1995.

Praz, Mario. *The Flaming Heart: Essays on Crawshaw, Machiavelli, and Other Studies in the Relations between Italian and English Literature from Chaucer to T. S. Eliot.* New York: Doubleday, 1958.

Prynne, William. *Histriomastix.* London, 1633. STC 20464.

La Puttana errante, overo dialogo di Madalena e Giulia Cosmopoli (Amsterdam?): Elzevier, 1660.

Quarles, Francis. *Divine Fancies.* London, 1632. STC 20529.

Rackin, Phyllis. *Stages of History: Shakespeare's English Chronicles.* Ithaca, N.Y.: Cornell University Press, 1990.

Rainoldes, John. *The overthrow of stage-plays.* London, 1599. STC 20616.

Rankins, William. *A Mirror of Monsters.* London, 1587. STC 20699.

Raven, James, Helen Small, and Naomi Tadmore, eds. *The Practice and Representation of Reading in England.* New York: Cambridge University Press, 1996.

Rhodes, Neil. *Elizabethan Grotesque.* London: Routledge and Kegan Paul, 1980.

Rich, B. Ruby. "Anti-Porn: Soft Issue, Hard World." In *Issues in Feminist Film Criticism,* ed. Patricia Erens (Bloomington: Indiana University Press, 1990), 405–17.

Richlin, Amy, ed. *Pornography and Representation in Greece and Rome.* New York: Oxford University Press, 1992.

Riggs, David. *Ben Jonson: A Life.* Cambridge: Harvard University Press, 1989.

Roberts, Sasha. "Women Reading Shakespeare in the Seventeenth Century," unpublished article.

Rochester, John Wilmot, Second Earl of. *Rochester: Complete Poems and Plays.* Ed. Paddy Lyons. Everyman's Library. Rutland, Vt.: Charles E. Tuttle, 1993.

Rocke, Michael. *Forbidden Friendships: Homosexuality and Male Culture in Renaissance Florence.* New York: Oxford University Press, 1996.

Rodgerson, Gillian, and Elizabeth Wilson, eds. *Pornography and Feminism: The Case against Censorship.* London: Lawrence and Wishart, 1991.

Rosenmeyer, Thomas G. *The Green Cabinet: Theocritus and the European Pastoral Lyric.* Berkeley: University of California Press, 1969.

Rosenthal, Margaret F. *The Honest Courtesan : Veronica Franco, Citizen and Writer in Sixteenth-century Venice.* Chicago : University of Chicago Press, 1992.

Roskill, Mark W. *Dolce's "Aretino" and Venetian Art Theory of the Cinquecento.* New York: New York University Press, 1968.

Rossi, G. G. *Vita di Giovanni de'Medici.* Milan, 1833.

Rossi, Vittorio, ed. *Pasquinate di Pietro Aretino ed anonime per il conclave e l'elezione di Adriano VI.* Palermo: Carlo Clausen, 1891.

Rowe, George E. *Distinguishing Jonson: Imitation, Rivalry, and the Direction of a Dramatic Career.* Lincoln: University of Nebraska Press, 1988.

Rubinstein, Frankie. *A Dictionary of Shakespeare's Sexual Puns and their SigniWcance.* 2nd ed. New York: St. Martin's Press, 1989.

Ruggiero, Guido. *The Boundaries of Eros: Sex Crime and Sexuality in Renaissance Venice.* New York: Oxford University Press, 1985.

———. "Marriage, Love, Sex, and Renaissance Civic Morality." In *Sexuality and Gender in Early Modern Europe: Institutions, Texts, Images,* ed. James Grantham Turner (New York: Cambridge University Press, 1993), 10–30.

Sale, Antoine de la. *The Fifteen Joys of Marriage.* London, c. 1507. STC 15257.5 sq.

Samuels, Richard. "Benedetto Varchi, the *Accademia degli InWammati,* and the Origins of the Italian Academic Movement." *Renaissance Quarterly* 29 (1976): 599–633.

Sanderson, James Lee. "An Edition of an Early Seventeenth-Century Manuscript Collection of Poems (Rosenbach MS. 186)." Ph. D. dissertation, University of Pennsylvania, 1960.

Saunders, J. W. "From Manuscript to Print: A Note on the Circulation of Poetic MSS. in the Sixteenth Century." *Proceedings of the Leeds Philosophical and Literary Society* 6 (1951): 507–28.

———. "The Stigma of Print: A Note on the Social Bases of Tudor Poetry," *Essays in Criticism* 1 (1951): 139–64.

Sawday, Jonathan. *The Body Emblazoned: Dissection and the Human Body in Renaissance Culture.* New York: Routledge, 1995.

Scoloker, Anthony. *Diaphantus.* London, 1604. STC 21853.

Scott-Elliot, A. H., and Elspeth Yeo. "Calligraphic Manuscripts of Esther Inglis (1571–1624)." *Papers of the Bibliographic Society of America* 84 (1990): 11–86.

Sedgwick, Eve Kosofsky. *Between Men: English Literature and Male Homosocial Desire.* New York: Columbia University Press, 1985.

———. *The Epistemology of the Closet.* Berkeley: University of California Press, 1990.

Segal, Lynne, and Mary McIntosh, eds. *Sex Exposed: Sexuality and the Pornography Debate* London: Virago, 1992.

Sellers, Harry. "Italian Books Printed in England Before 1640." *Library,* 4th series 5 (1924): 105–28.

Shakespeare, William. *The Complete Works of Shakespeare.* 3rd. ed. Ed. David Bevington. Glenview, Ill.: Scott, Foresman, 1980.

Shapiro, James. *Rival Playwrights: Marlowe, Jonson, Shakespeare.* New York: Columbia University Press, 1991.

Shelburne, Steven R. "Principled Satire: Decorum in John Marston's *The Metamorphosis of Pigmalions Image and Certain Satyres.*" *Studies in Philology* 86 (1989): 198–218.

Shroeder, John W. "Spenser's Erotic Drama: The Orgoglio Episode." *English Literary History* 29 (1962): 140–59.

Shuger, Deborah Kuller. *The Renaissance Bible: Scholarship, SacriWce, and Subjectivity.* Berkeley: University of California Press, 1994.

Sidney, Sir Philip. *A Defense of Poetry.* In *Miscellaneous Prose of Sir Philip Sidney,* ed. Katherine Duncan-Jones and Jan Van Dorsten (New York: Oxford University Press, 1973), 212–51.

———. *The Poems of Sir Philip Sidney.* Ed. W. A. Ringler. New York: Oxford University Press, 1962.

Silver, George. *The Paradoxes of Defense.* London, 1599. STC 22554.

Simiani, Carlo. *La Vita e le opere di N. Franco.* Rome, 1894.

Simonnet, Dominique. *L'Express.* Paris. June 16–18. 1997.

Sinigaglia, Giorgio. *Pietro Aretino.* Rome, 1882.

Slack, Paul. *Policy and Poverty in Tudor and Stuart England.* New York: Longman, 1988.

Slung, Michele, ed. *Slow Hand: Women Writing Erotica.* New York: Harper, 1992.

Smith, Bruce R. *Homosexual Desire in Shakespeare's England.* Chicago: University of Chicago Press, 1991.

"Smut Purveyors Find Profits Online." *New York Times,* April 2, 1997.

Sontag, Susan. "The Pornographic Imagination." In *Styles of Radical Will* (New York: Delta, 1969), 35–73.

Spenser, Edmund. *The Faerie Queene.* Ed. A. C. Hamilton. New York: Longman, 1977.

———. *The Yale Edition of the Shorter Poems of Edmund Spenser.* Ed. William A. Orem et. al. New Haven: Yale University Press, 1989.

Sportive Wit. London: 1656. Wing P2113.

Stallybrass, Peter. "Patriarchal Territories: The Body Enclosed." In *Rewriting the Renaissance: The Discourses of Sexual Difference in Early Modern Europe,* ed. Margaret W. Ferguson et al. (Chicago:University of Chicago Press, 1986), 123–42.

Stallybrass, Peter, and Allon White. *The Politics and Poetics of Transgression.* Ithaca, N.Y.: Cornell University Press, 1986.

Stapleton, M. L. "Nashe and the Poetics of Obscenity: *The Choise of Valentines.*" *Classical and Modern Literature* 12 (1991): 29–48.

Steinem, Gloria. "Erotica and Pornography: A Clear and Present Difference." *MS.* November 1978.

Stern, Virginia F. *Gabriel Harvey: His Life, Marginalia, and Library.* New York: Oxford University Press, 1979.

Stewart, Alan. *Close Readers: Humanism and Sodomy in Early Modern England.* Princeton: Princeton University Press, 1997.

Stockwood, John. *A sermon preached at Paules Crosse.* London, 1578. STC 23284.

Stone, Lawrence. *The Family, Sex, and Marriage in Early Modern England: 1500–1800*. Abridged ed. New York: Harper, 1979.

Strossen, Nadine. *Defending Pornography: Free Speech, Sex, and the Fight for Women's Rights*. New York: Scribner, 1995.

Stubbes, Philip. *The Anatomy of Abuses*. London, 1583. STC 23376 sq.

Surrey, Henry Howard, Earl of. *Songes and Sonnettes*. (*Tottel's Miscellany*). London, 1557. STC 13860 sq.

Symonds, J. A. *The Renaissance in Italy: Italian Literature*. Part 2. New York: Scribners, 1898.

Talvacchia, Bette. *Taking Positions: On the Erotic in Renaissance Culture*. Princeton University Press, 1999.

Tasso, Ercole. *Of Marriage and Wiving*. London, 1599. STC 23690.

Tasso, Torquato. *Jerusalem Delivered*. Ed. and trans. Ralph Nash. Detroit: Wayne State University Press, 1987.

Taylor, Gary. "Some Manuscripts of Shakespeare's Sonnets." *Bulletin of the John Rylands Library* 68 (1985–86): 210–46.

Thomas, William. *The Historie of Italie*. London, 1549. STC 24018.

Thompson, Roger. *Unfit for Modest Ears: A Study of Pornographic, Obscene and Bawdy Works Written or Published in England in the Second Half of the Seventeenth Century*. London: Macmillan, 1979.

Traub, Valerie. *Desire and Anxiety: Circulations of Desire in Shakespearean Drama*. New York: Routledge, 1992.

———. "The (In)significance of Lesbian Desire in Early Modern England." In *Erotic Politics: Desire on the Renaissance Stage*, ed. Susan Zimmerman (New York: Routledge, 1992), 150–69.

Tusser, Thomas. *Five Hundreth Points of Good Husbandry*. London, 1573.

Van Lennep, William, ed. *The London Stage 1660–1800. Part 1 1660–1700*. Carbondale: Southern Illinois University Press, 1965.

Veniero, Lorenzo. *La Puttana errante*. Paris, Liseux, 1883.

———. *Le Trente et un de la ZaVetta*. Paris, Liseux, 1883.

Vignali, Antonio. *La Cazzaria*. Ed. Nino Borsellino and Pasquale Stoppelli. Rome: Edizioni dell'Elefante, 1984.

———. *La Cazzaria: Dialogue Priapique de L'Arsiccio Intronato*. Paris: Liseux, 1882.

Virgil. *Aeneid*. Ed. and trans. H. Rushton Fairclough. 2 vols. Loeb Classics. Cambridge: Harvard University Press, 1978.

Vita di Pietro Aretino del Berni. 1538(?). London, 1821(?).

Waddington, Raymond. "A Satirists' Impresa: The Medals of Pietro Aretino." *Renaissance Quarterly* 42.(4) (1989): 655–81.

Wall, Wendy. *The Imprint of Gender: Authorship and Publication in the English Renaissance*. Ithaca, N.Y.: Cornell University Press, 1993.

Wayne, Don E. *Penshurst: The Semiotics of Place and the Poetics of History*. Madison: University of Wisconsin Press, 1984.

The Why and the Wherefore: Or, the Lady's Two Questions Resolved. London, 1765.

Whetstone, George. *A Touchstone for the Time*. London, 1584. STC 25341.

Wit and Drollery. London, 1661. Wing W3131.

The Wits, or Sport upon Sport. London, 1662. Wing W3218.

Wit's Recreations. London, 1640. STC 25870.

Wit Restored. London, 1658. Wing M1719.

Williams, Gordon. *A Glossary of Shakespeare's Sexual Language*. Atlantic Highlands, N.J.: Athalone Press, 1997.

Williams, Linda. *Hard Core: Power, Pleasure, and the Frenzy of the Visible*. Berkeley: University of California Press, 1989.

Woodbridge, Linda. *Women and the English Renaissance: Literature and the Nature of Womankind, 1540–1620*. Urbana: University of Illinois Press, 1984.

Woodfield, Denis B. *Surreptitious Printing in England 1550–1640*. New York: Bibliographical Society of America, 1973.

Woudhuysen, H. R. ed. *The Penguin Book of Renaissance Verse 1509–1659*. New York: Penguin, 1992.

Woudhuysen, H. R. *Sir Philip Sidney and the Circulation of Manuscripts 1558–1640*. Oxford: Clarendon Press, 1996.

Wyatt, Sir Thomas. *The Complete Poems*. Ed. R. A. Rebholz. New York: Penguin, 1978.

Yaffe, Maurice, and Edward C. Nelson, eds. *The Influence of Pornography on Behaviour*. London: Academic Press, 1982.

Yates, Frances A. *Astrea: The Imperial Theme in the Sixteenth Century*. Boston: Routledge, 1975.

Zillman, Dolf, and Jennings Bryant, eds. *Pornography: Research Advances and Policy Considerations*. Hillsdale, N.J.: Erlbaum, 1989.

Zimmerman, Susan, ed. *Erotic Politics: Desire on the Renaissance Stage*. New York: Routledge, 1992.

Manuscripts Cited

Bodleian Library, Oxford

MS Add. B. 97
MS Ashmole 36/37
MS Ashmole 38
MS Ashmole 47
MS Don. c. 54
MS Don. d. 58
MS Douce f. 5
MS Eng. poet. c. 50
MS Eng. poet. e. 14
MS Eng. poet. e. 99
MS Eng. poet. f. 10
MS Eng. poet. f. 25
MS Eng. poet. f. 27
MS Firth e. 4
MS Rawl D. 1110
MS Rawl. poet. 85
MS Rawl. poet. 108
MS Rawl. poet. 142
MS Rawl. poet. 147
MS Rawl. poet. 148
MS Rawl. poet. 152
MS Rawl. poet. 153

MS Rawl. poet. 160
MS Rawl. poet. 166
MS Rawl. poet. 172
MS Rawl. poet. 185
MS Rawl. poet. 199
MS Rawl. poet. 206
MS Rawl. poet. 210
MS Rawl. poet. 212
MS Rawl. poet. 214
MS Rawl. poet. 216
MS Tanner 168
MS Tanner 169
MS Tanner 307
MS Tanner 386
Bibliotèque de Cordé, Chartilly, France. MSS 677

British Library, London

MS Add. 10037
MS Add. 10309
MS Add. 12049
MS Add. 17492
MS Add. 18647
MS Add. 21433
MS Add. 22118
MS Add. 22601
MS Add. 22603
MS Add. 23229
MS Add. 25303
MS Add. 30982
MS Add. 33998
MS Add. 44963
MS Egerton 923
MS Egerton 2230
MS Egerton 2421
MS Egerton 2711
MS Harl. 353
MS Harl. 1836
MS Harl. 3357
MS Harl. 4064
MS Harl. 4955
MS Harl. 6057
MS Harl. 6917
MS Harl. 6918
MS Harl. 7312
MS Harl. 7332
MS Harl. 7392
MS Sloane 1446
Printed book: C. 39. a. 37

Cambridge University Library

Cambridge MS Add. 5778

Corpus Christi College, Oxford

MS CCC 327
MS CCC 328

Folger Shakespeare Library, Washington, D.C.

MS Folger V. a. 89
MS Folger V. a. 103
MS Folger V. a. 104
MS Folger V. a. 180
MS Folger V. a. 275
MS Folger V. a. 319
MS Folger V. a. 345
MS Folger V. a. 381
MS Folger V. a. 399
MS Folger V. b. 93
MS Folger V. b. 198
MS Folger X. d. 177

Harvard University, Cambridge, Mass.

Harvard MS Eng. poet. 686

Huntington Library, San Marino, Calif.

Huntington MS EL 6893
Huntington MS EL 8729
Huntington MS HM 8
Huntington MS HM 116
Huntington MS HM 198
Huntington MS HM 904
Huntington MS HM 46323

Inner Temple Library, London

Petyt MS 538 vol. 43, (fol. 284–303)

National Art Library, Victoria and Albert Museum, London

MS Dyce (44) 25 F 39

Rosenbach Library, Philadelphia, Pa.

MS Rosenbach 239/27
MS Rosenbach 240/7
MS Rosenbach 1083/15
MS Rosenbach 1083/16
MS Rosenbach 1083/17

Index

268   *Index*

sexual intercourse, 6, 10, 16, 28, 47, 63,
96, 105, 124, 127–128, 150–151,
159, 169, 181, 196
Shakespeare, William, 6, 22–23, 26–29,
35, 42, 44, 51, 61, 69, 72–73, 80,
95, 126, 144, 146–147, 156, 168,
175, 180, 207
Sidney, Sir Philip, 6–7, 22, 29–31, 35, 46,
72, 86–92, 108, 162, 168
Defense of Poetry, The, 30, 86–91,
108
social mobility, 29, 31, 62, 120, 209
sodomy, 7, 31–32, 91, 115–118, 120, 134,
140–142, 145, 152, 160, 162, 164–
166, 195–209, 215, 219 (*see also*
homoeroticism)
soldiers, 13, 57, 62, 71, 73, 77–79, 85–86,
89, 92, 95, 106–108, 122, 135, 149,
177 (*see also* martial ideals)
Spenser, Edmund, 6, 7, 22, 29–31, 42,
86–88, 91–103, 108, 145, 161, 163,
170, 173–174
Faerie Queene, The, 6, 29–30, 86–102,
108, 175, 177, 182, 194
Stubbes, Philip, 29–30, 79–86, 94, 162,
175, 178, 197, 209

theater, the, 29–30, 35, 69–82, 103, 118,
139, 178, 194–219 (*see also* drama)
Titian, 124, 136–137, 139

universities, the, 17, 30, 37, 41–42, 54–55, 61–
62, 64, 81, 169, 178, 195–196, 210
Cambridge, 39, 54, 105, 159–161, 163
Oxford, 17, 40–41, 44–46, 52, 188, 190

Venice, 114–115, 122–123, 127–128, 137–144,
148–150, 163, 165, 207, 210, 212, 217
Veniero, Lorenzo, 136, 139, 148–152
Virgil, 30, 50, 57, 87, 91–93, 97, 131, 148,
164, 173, 178

Wolfe, John, 145–146, 148, 156–157, 161
women, as sexually active, 15–16, 46, 49–
53, 55, 60–64, 66–67, 74–79, 97–
100, 125–126, 130–135, 148–149,
158–159, 168–170, 179–182, 186,
215–217
as sexually passive, 18–27, 49, 70, 74,
133, 150, 173–174, 181, 191–193,
195–197, 220

Zaffetta, Angela, 136, 139, 148–150

Lightning Source UK Ltd.
Milton Keynes UK
UKOW04f1705310114

225660UK00001B/75/A